MW01177997

HOW MUSIC CAME

to the Ainchan People

Timothy Callender

Order this book online at www.trafford.com
or email orders@trafford.com

Most Trafford titles are also available at major online book retailers.

Printed in the United States of America.

ISBN: 978-1-4669-6362-7 (sc)
ISBN: 978-1-4669-6363-4 (e)

Trafford rev. 11/14/2012

 www.trafford.com

North America & international
toll-free: 1 888 232 4444 (USA & Canada)
phone: 250 383 6864 ✦ fax: 812 355 4082

Acknowledgements

The following individuals, groups or firms of Barbados have contributed to the cost of printing the first edition of this book:

Mr Tony Lynch
Mr Gladstone Holder
Mr David Sealy
Mr Hutson Linton (attorney-at-law)
Mrs Ann Musgrave
Mr K. R. Broodhagen
Mr John Wickham

Mr Art Tappin
Mr Alfred Pragnell
Harold Bowen Ltd. (auctioneer)
International Book Centre Ltd.
Cloister Bookstore Ltd.
A & B Music Supplies Ltd.
Barbados Rediffusion Service Ltd.
Barclay's Bank International Ltd.

I am sincerely grateful.
Timothy Callender.

Contents

GODNOR'S
OVERTURE

Godnor's Overture

NOWADAYS THE HISTORIANS OF Ainchan are vague about, or reluctant to speak of, the history of our nation during the dynasty of the Dominauts, and earlier. They dwell mainly on what they call the Enlightened Age, or Age of Harmony; and while it is of the utmost importance to trace the origin of our present system of government and of our academic and spiritual views, we cannot neglect to tell the story of the time before Music came to the people. Our present educational policy, which entails teaching the Principles of Life as the foundation of our knowledge, would gain many examples and citations from our very ancient history, which can be employed as a medium for understanding those Principles better.

The generations of the last few centuries, who live in an age of comfort, social happiness and wisdom, an age which surpasses any of Ainchan's Great Ages of thousands of years ago, cannot appreciate the full meaning of the despair, poverty and carnage that was a way of life among the people during the rule of the Dominauts.

Neither can they appreciate the tremendous spiritual powers of our earliest ancestors, and their contributions to the health and teachings of our very old forebears. We would do well to study the numerous records and legends handed down to us, and regenerate some of the ancient traditions and principles. I trust that this history will awaken interest in the very early culture of our people.

In searching the ancient chronicles of the Ainchan people, I, Godnor, Keeper of the National Archives, have come across many startling events, many unbelievable facts, many important principles; facets of human reasoning and behavior that throw much light on our human situation, and on the composition of both our inner and outer selves. Such information will of necessity be related as I set about my primary task—which is to trace the history of the legendary Shangodoon, the ancient ancestral figure now called the Messenger of Creation and the Bringer of Harmony.

I have undertaken this historical task of my own volition, since I feel that I can make no better contribution to the history of our nation than to enlighten as many as possible about the mighty achievements of Shangodoon, and his elemental influence upon our present good government, social happiness and spiritual fulfillment—for, impossible as it seems today, all this was brought about through the heroism, integrity and inspiration of one man.

Historians usually compartmentalize our history into three very broad areas. One, the Early Age; two, the Age of the Dominants, and, three, the Golden Age of Harmony.

The Early Ages stretch from the dawn of our consciousness of time and therefore of history (how far away that is I cannot say) until the conquest of the First People of Ainchan by the race of the Dominants.

Our archaeologists are now in the process of unraveling the meanings behind the fantastic artifacts of our past. The several cities which once dotted the vast plain on which our city stands, which are now abandoned and covered or absorbed into the present enormous expanse of modern Ainchan, bear witness to the ingenuity and education of our forebears. Inventions we had thought to be our own, such the electromagnetic tools we use, have been found in these strange, forgotten cities; maps of the world and of the sun-system in which we live and beyond; maps of the human body, documents outlining organs, nerve and cell functions and techniques for mental stimulation only now being rediscovered; knowledge that is ageless, eternal, which we may employ in the present time.

The people of the Early Ages, as far back as we can trace, knew that the earth was a complete living whole, and gave it the respect accorded to a person. There were groups which worshipped the Elements of Earth, Water, Air and Fire. And those who worshipped the Supreme Creator, even as we do now; but I risk saying that our religion is much less prone to distortion and error than was the religion of our ancestors.

Our ancestors lived close to the earth, their occupations being farming, which seems to have carried very high religious significance, fishing, which called for many regular propitiations to the Spirit of the water, and hunting, the most dangerous and taboo-ridden activity of all. Men who hunted were viewed as more "outside" than "inside" the society, mainly because of the strange natural environments and forces to which they were subject. They had queer ways, and very strange beliefs and rumors of incredible things living in far distant cliffs, swamps and plateaus which only they, the hunters, had traversed.

Nowadays many of the beasts that the very old people would have hunted are no longer with us: changing weather-patterns affected the plain over the long eons of its support of human life. The farming crops, as well as the methods, have changed and in places the rivers have altered their courses, so that areas which were once fishing villages and towns have had to re-organize their way of life in order to survive.

The baked clay pots with their patterned sides and vignettes of history which were a common feature in the houses of the people, have been reproduced and are currently being used in the dwellings of our more historically-inclined people; also, the patterns of the copper bracelets found at Pragos, to the northwest of Old Ainchan, are more than decorations; they contain ciphers of important scientific and psychic knowledge.

Most of the ancient towns have buildings made of limestone or brick; many are now badly crumbled and ruined, and overgrown with thick vegetation where not buried by the earth itself.

In Ainchan there were once tall spired temples set in spacious courts with copper statues of gods and high rainbow-hued fountains placed along tree-lined canals, and there were large brick buildings with tiled roofs. The later high domed, high-arched cities that were built after the capital city, and which were existing when the Dominants arrived, were a refinement of the earlier Ainchan styles; many of our artists, in depicting the life of the earlier city-people, depict only the second type of building while telling and painting legends and histories that existed before the time of this architecture. We cannot afford such anachronisms in the depiction of our history.

As the archaeologists dig down into the heavy fertile soil laid by the two rivers that formed this mighty plain, stratum after stratum, history is uncovered, each new discovery taking them further into the past until the soil itself is the crumbled evidence of former life. Indeed, history can be traced, but the origin of all things can never be empirically known, for it is too old for memory or for preservation by the earth. History crumbles into the earth itself.

Yet, witness the evidence. As we dig into the past of our people, we travel a smooth uninterrupted journey until we come to the stratum where we see evidence of the abrupt end of the Early-Age way of life—or at the place where the former culture was destroyed and another built on its ruins.

At the time of their subjugation, the peoples of Ainchan did not dwell in one large city-state, protected by our defence-forces and confident in our fighting skills and methods of repelling invaders. The people dwelt in seven different cities,

cities which had absorbed many smaller villages and clusters of population in their rapid development. These cities, joined by roads and waterways, were separated for hundreds of miles over the awesomely broad plain, from Kenmare in the north to Dibra, farthest south; Ainchan, the largest, on the River Ruba, was the seat of government.

The wars between the Dominauts and the peoples of the plain lasted for four months. One by one the cities fell to the savage marauders that swept in from the north through the secret valleys; dread were the rumours of their hateful work in lands beyond the Great Plain. Kenmare felt the full force of their attack. The city was raped and pillaged, and its huge population disappeared northward, it is rumoured, to the goldmines of the Dominauts' vast foreign dominions. Physhon surrendered after two days' fighting, during which the public brutal execution of their people by the wild soldiers left a lasting impression on their minds, so that today no one mentions the Dominauts before a man known to have been descended from the people of that unlucky city, without bearing his fierce glances and muttered imprecations.

From the north the Dominauts travelled by horsemen, coaches and chariots; in the south, around the mouths of the Ruba and Blentha deltas, huge ships appeared, mighty sailors of the deep with vast holds which seemed specially prepared for use in these nefarious tasks. The ancient documents describe large war- and cargo-ships driven by wind with several voluminous sails on which curious black figures and unknown symbols were emblazoned.

Whether they came by sea or land, the Dominauts were fierce, implacable, intent on perpetuating themselves through war and conquest, content to live on the results of other peoples' work.

The population of Dibra, which lay closest to the sea, was decimated after the capture of the city. It is said that most of the young people were herded aboard those sinister cargo-ships and taken away; others say that the citizens were executed for their stubborn refusal to reveal where they had hidden the fabulous golden statue of Kadash, protector of their city. Both stories may be true; I, for one, having travelled in my youth with an archaeological expedition to the site of the ancient city, was surprised at the long columns stretching down the single main street, all deeply embedded with wrist and ankle chains.

Then Noosh and Pragos, two inland cities, were taken; Gnoit on the Blentha was next, and finally after twelve weeks of siege, the great city of Ainchan fell.

The coming of the Dominauts was an apocalyptic event in the lives of the Ainchan people. Some of their very travelled men had spoken darkly of other people not quite like themselves, who lived in fabulous far-off lands not quite like ours, but no one wanted to believe such outrageous tales. Such travelers were looked upon with great suspicion, and sometimes chased from taverns when they tried to say that the rumours of strange distant people could have some foundation.

Mystical seers and a few high priests of secret temples, learned in the primal ways of mankind, perhaps were certain that someday the cities would fall, for there was a very old tradition which prophesied of this; but few ordinary people

9

came into contact with these men, who by the very nature of their work, living weird ascetic lives in inaccessible places, had not the same concern as would the common man about the immediate fate of the people.

The vast populations of the cities had no idea that such beings as the Dominauts existed. Was not the Great Plain the centre of the world, the Garden of the Gods, where man had always lived? Outside that there was nothing. To the north, the terrible misty mountains, full of strange animals, rumbles, lightnings and smoke, rose recklessly, piled row after row like the teeth of some sea-creatures. Of the many curious men who had dared to go north and enter the fantastic valleys and grim lava mountains, or sail the fearsome torments that chased huge stones down to the sea, only five were known ever to have returned; only one of them was completely sane, according to the oil records. Morose, regretful and taciturn, he spoke nothing of what he had seen in those Northern Mountains, or what he had done; but the people noticed his horrible scars and the look in his eyes, and reinforced the tales of horror with the example of that man.

Southward, past the mouths of the Ruba and Blentha deltas, the great ocean roared; its turbulence kept the fishermen of the delta-mouths hugging the coastline in their fragile boats, and even the very large canoes that supplied the coastal towns with the products of Dibra were lost forever if they ventured out of the sight of land.

Westward, a huge plateau reared up, its surface splotched with broken rock and cleft and cracked into hard flat-topped hills which dropped sharply into narrow valleys with dark, swift streams—no place at all for the people of Ainchan to frequent, especially since it was definitely known that savage, rarely-seen beasts lurked in the fastnesses of this wild are. And eastward, where the land was flat, the country stretched from lush vegetation to hesitant, worn shrubs, finally thinning out to one vast desert, with frightful scorpions, poisonous centipedes and spiders, and huge birds of prey of unknown origin which hovered for days over the empty landscape, confident in the power of the desert to yield them food.

And so the people of Ainchan, self-contained and independent, were awakened by the horrors of war to the fact that they were a weak, defenseless and ordinary people, subject to the rule of others, ignorant as to the people of the world. The ancient native artists have given us paintings of their conquerors; in viewing these works of art, one is struck again and again by the sense of amazement on the part of the artists, who depicted their faces, hair, eyes, skin colour and garments with clarity, and who took especial care to represent correctly the proportions of their ships, chariots, their "smoking pillars which shot hot flame or metal through the crowds", their fortifications, and other aspects of their culture as were unusual to the Ainchan people.

The tale of bloodshed, iconoclasm, enslavement, exile and other bitter woes is well recorded, if not well known. Numbers of people died as the conquerors tortured them for information; some died in the gold and copper mines; and some in the fields, where they were forced to grow unknown crops to feed their conquerors, and for their conquerors' transshipment back to the mysterious place from which they

11

had come. Many were the seizures and banishments of people, and it is said that huge numbers were taken away in the busy, obnoxious carracks with their grim sailors which year after year sailed into the huge port of Dibra. It was from Dibra, which the Dominauts had completely taken over, banning all native folk except a select few, on pain of death, that these ships sailed; and there are records and paintings of long lines of slaves, chained by the neck, walking cavernous ships. So notorious did Dibra become, after some years that the saying arose that Dibra was a city of suction, where people drawn in and never appeared again.

But the worst sin of the Dominauts was their systematic attempt to wipe out all traces of our history and tradition, and replace them with the spurious tale that they were the Gods, and the Messengers of the Gods, that we had worshipped in the past.

They destroyed the Ainchan religious buildings and libraries; the schools, the medical centres. The high domed temples, centuries of work of diligent men, were demolished, the artifacts of the holiest places seized, the priests hanged, burned or banished to the Outer Regions of Ainchan to die in the cruel natural environment.

The legendary King Chrazius I was ruler of the Dominauts at the time of their invasion. The name Chrazius has descended to us today as a name of dire insult and curses, over which many men have fought and died to defend their honour. It is a name of blasphemy, spoken only by the lowest types of those enflamed by alcohol, carrying as it does the sound of war, rape and evil; it is the name by which our bad magicians still spread their curses.

It is an interesting and appropriate coincidence that kings by the name of Chrazius presided over both the imposition of the Dominaut dynasty and its final collapse; and while Chrazius II was a singularly weak and moronic type who died while quite a young man, the other two of that name were so exactly alike in temperament and in looks that it was whispered by those who know of such matters that Chrazius III was a reincarnation of the first Dominaut ruler of the Ainchan people, and that his rule portended some grave changes as far-reaching and radical as those that took place when his ancestor captured Ainchan.

It was Chrazius I who demanded to be worshipped as a God, and who established a spurious history to replace the antiquarian truths he was trying vainly to make disappear. Yet, by burning all the records he could lay his hands on, and by dint of intensive propaganda fed to the young children, over the course of the years the worship of those with the Royal blood of the Dominauts became the unnatural habit of the Ainchan people; for the people had become so downtrodden by their oppressors, so distrustful of their own religion, and so fearful of authority, that they feared even to think against the system under which they existed. And so Chrazius and his descendents became the Agents of God in the world, divine personages in the flesh, who were to be approached on hands and knees and addressed in the correct formula, and who had absolute divine authority over the lives and destinies of all who dwelt within their vast domains.

The chief advantage the Dominauts had over the Ainchan people was, of course, the fireweapon. Our people had no answer for this, no shields to withstand their flames or their balls of metal. In fact, few people of the Ruba plain, save the hunters and the Guards of the cities, had weapons of any significance. The weapons used by Ainchan people were various slings, spears with single, double and triple barbs; long and short swords, though the shortsword was preferred; clubs, knitted around with ropes, which were swung or thrown; axes, and spikes which were worn on the front edge of heavy leather boots, and on the elbows and knees for close infighting. For defence, they wore helmets of metal, of plaited, hardened rushes, and of hard, light wood from the byotta trees. They carried shields of plaited rushes, leather and byotta wood and wore armour about the upper body, the thighs and the shins. Some soldiers used shirts of interlocking copper rings; the use of these was becoming general around the time of the Dominaut invasion.

In the past, the invaders of our land were chiefly small unknown tribes, desperately driven by the needs of survival, who came out from the regions beyond the Great Plain **where no life** could properly exist; from the hard volcanic mountains and ravines to the north, or perhaps from the hungry desert, for harsh winters killed the mountain sheep and their shepherds alike, and the creeping, blowing sands covered and uncovered desert water-holes and oases as well, leaving men mourning before and uncertain fate.

Such invaders usually took a village or two, and then realized their predicament as the countryside for miles around mobilized; making terms, they would gradually be absorbed into the society and fuse the differing cultures.

With the Dominauts it was different. Every effort was made to separate the two races, so that they hardly came into contact with each other. The Dominauts had not come because of desperation; they came because they had heard that the land was fruitful and pleasant, with fine animals, birds and fish, and peaceful people, and much gold, while their own land and general environment were harsh and inhospitable. Ainchan and the other cities of the Great Plain, and all the peoples known collectively as the Ainchan peoples, were to be theirs perpetually, as their laws and public proclamations declared.

In those days it was dangerous to be born a common man of Ainchan. The Dominaut soldiers killed for sport, especially when away from the eyes of the general populace, and the people of the Ainchan cities had no rights. Some of the people felt sure that eventually they would all be wiped out; the Dominauts only needed them as slaves for a certain length of time. When the population of Dominauts had become large enough, the Ainchan people would be driven out of existence. Had not the decimation of the population begun, ever since the war? With the young men dead, the women were prey for the Dominaut soldiers, whom the laws against racial intermixture ignored, and soon many half-Ainchan, half-Dominaut children were being born. Most of these children would be raised by the Dominauts to become soldiers and overseers and many of them were to become spies among the Ainchans. It was a horde of these Halvers, as they were called who helped to guard the entrances and interior of the king's grim palace, which towered high into the air on the site where the most noble of the Ainchan temple-complexes once stood. But the steps leading to the palace were guarded by the fiercest and most efficient of the Dominaut soldiers, armed with their terrible fireweapons which silently spat their death of smoke and flame.

Nowadays the fireweapons build and still used by the more backward peoples of this planet, are noisy, and are not at all similar in mechanism to the ones the Dominauts employed. With those, usually there was just a puff of smoke and a flash of fire, sometimes a long thin beam that was gone in an instant. Countless people have died because of this accursed invention.

That the Dominaut fireweapons made no noise may be an amazing fact to some; but readers will see that this connects to the fact that the Dominauts passed strict laws about the level of noise to be heard in the cities. In fact, for cities of so many multitudes, the cities of the Ainchan Plain were exceedingly quiet. There was no shouting in the streets, not even in the markets or on the busy quays. Rapid hand and arm signals were used for distant communication and the Ainchan peoples became particularly adept at talking with their hands, an ability which is still noticeable today when our people speak to each other.

It is known that the priests of the First Religion used to practice shouting in unison for hours at a time, though no one knew exactly the reason for this exercise. This practice was a heinous insult to the Dominauts; for many years after the conquest of Ainchan they waged a war against the priests, outlawing them, exterminating them by execution and banishment, and desecrating their monuments.

The most permanent change the Dominauts made on the capital city and on the landscape was the huge wall they erected around the city. It has defined the city clearly since that time, and it seems that it will stand as long as Ainchan exists, for it was built to last forever as an eternal monument to the power of the Dominauts. This wall, nine feet thick, and very high, is built of great granite blocks, floated down the river on huge barges from the mountainous northern area. The people of Ainchan were enslaved to build this wall; it stands as a monument to the labour of the Ainchan people, and is their pride and not their shame.

Many people died that this structure could exist. They built the square wall, with its three huge gates on each side, and the wide roads running to these gates. They built the three stone bridges over the Ruba, before the city, and paved the mighty flight of steps that lead down to the wharves. They built the wharves of great piles of greenheart wood, for the large Dominaut sailing vessels; by this time the Dominauts had abandoned their overland route, which they had used mainly for the surprise invasion, and were arriving in ships only.

The towers over the gates and at intervals along the wall were manned, day and night, by marksmen with their fireweapons. Soldiers stood guard at all twelve gates, inside and outside; it was difficult for an Ainchan man or woman to leave the city. The three bridges were also constantly under guard.

The Ainchan people were forced, with their lives as forfeit if they refused, to wear medallions stamped with their identity and registration number at all times. The best known saying of Chrazius I is "An Ainchan neck must wear an Ainchan medal"—words that were taken very seriously.

The art of the Dominauts consisted mainly of depicting their victories in war. Many cities have houses in which there are scenes painted and etched of Dominauts conquering Ainchan as well as people of other races. At the Ainchan capital itself, the Dominauts forced the native artisans to make panels of carved stone, strips of rock-carving hundreds of yards long and twelve feet high, depicting, larger than life, the Dominauts' career of slaughter and conquest. At Noosh, where the high temple of the city once stood, there still stands the Dominaut castle; on each of its four walls, facing the four points of the compass, Dominaut faces are carved, each ten feet high; they were placed to symbolize the mastery of the Dominauts of north, south, east and west.

Today at Ainchan, those huge relief sculptures, etched deeply out of the stone, are mortared over; this was done soon after the fall of the Dominaut dynasty. The walls have many more, smaller gates now, and the city does not look, as it used to, as if it is always on the defensive. The monuments of the Dominauts are gone; they were pulled down, packed in barges and towed down the river and out to sea, so that today those monuments are at the bottom of the sea far beyond our coasts.

The Dominauts were constantly harassed by the patriots of Ainchan, men who dedicated their lives to freeing their people from the misery the conquerors had put upon them. These rebels, "men of the waste", as the Dominauts called them, ambushed caravans of the foreigners regularly, sometimes using only bows and arrows. They seized many fireweapons through these sudden attacks, and once or twice they wiped out companies of Dominaut soldiers.

The Dominauts had fierce dogs which they employed to hunt down runaway Ainchan slaves. Today many of the descendants of these dogs roam wild across the Great Plain. The wild swine, too, were brought by the rulers as a source of food; they have multiplied over the centuries.

A year after the conquest of the Ainchan peoples by the Dominauts, the women of the capital city, noticing that their menfolk were being killed openly or just disappearing, formed a delegation and went before King Chrazius I. "Why keep on killing?" they asked him. "We are in your hands. Our men do not fight your soldiers any more. They are willing to do what you say. We need our men."

King Chrazius laughed. "And our men need women," he said. "Did you not notice that there are not many women among the Dominauts—and few children? I have decreed that the Dominaut men may take wives from among you—and we do not need your men as wives!"

It became clear then that the aim of King Chrazius I was to remove the Ainchan people from the earth; and when this was rumoured among the huts, wharves, mines and fields where the Ainchan people worked, a change came on the people, and it seemed that hope had died.

The man we praise now, mighty Shangodoon, our folk hero was a lad of eighteen when he escaped from Ainchan, and King Chrazius III had been on the throne for twenty-four years. In this last king's reign corruption had spread like a pestilence through all levels of Ainchan society. From the time that Shangodoon recognized what oppression was, and how the system he had grown up under was one of distortions, which has been fabricated and thrust on the Ainchan people, he dedicated himself to freeing himself, his land and his people.

This is the authentic story of the mighty Messenger, and as I, a humble recorder, bring his history to life to the best of my ability, I acknowledge the constant inspiration of the Creator. May my pen always be Melodious; may Harmony direct the structure of my expression, and may Rhythm speak its truth to my readers, in the name of the Creator of all, whom we the Ainchan people know as **Music.**

2
THE
DOWNFALL
OF KING
CHRAZIUS III

The Downfall of King Chrazius III

I F THERE IS A single event that marks the end of Dominaut rule and the beginning of the Age of Harmony, that event is the return of Shangodoon to Ainchan after eighteen years of exile.

It is an event that has been depicted in drama, song, painting and poetry by countless Ainchan artists; each Ainchan person still feels the awe of that arrival, the majesty and power of the Messenger, his woman and his child; the historical momentousness of the occasion. The writings of our historians take on a note of wonder as they describe this beginning of freedom, this dramatic release of a long-bottled up people, a long-stifled emotion, and a long-derided culture. They love to write of the silent march of the mystified, expectant people behind the mighty figure as he strode up the wide south street of Ainchan towards the Royal Capital.

No guards at the southern main gate had tried to stop the family as they entered; no one had asked them for their identity. Something about them repelled such inane questions; one saw that these were beings of the deepest meditation, the highest principles. Their eyes seemed larger than ordinary people's and seemed to glow darkly with all the secrets of the Universe. Their bodies were beautiful, seemingly the ultimate of perfection; their heads were well shaped, their necks straight and firm, their tread rhythmic and sure, so that the people of Ainchan sensed some dreadful purpose, some aim of tremendous daring and righteousness in the strong hearts of this mystical trio, and seemed to know that all this was connected to their spiritual and political freedom.

It was against the law, of course, to congregate in numbers larger than three; but workmen dropped their picks and shovels, their bags and their lunchboxes, and edged along beside and behind the strange couple, eyeing their faces, sensing their thoughts although no word was spoken. A feeling of imminent delivery came upon the people in the market where he passed; by the shoemaker's building, by the stables. People began to hurry to join the growing procession; they fell in behind the three figures as at a given signal.

Dominaut soldiers on their mounted horses retreated before the advancing multitude, got out of the way, pretended they didn't see. But they knew something was wrong. Already the guards at the gate, and many soldiers Shangodoon had passed on the way, were fleeing the city, catapulted by the terror in their hearts. Shangodoon had glanced at each Dominaut guard he encountered, and his look had erupted in their souls the utter hopelessness of men who faced their unexpected death; so that they scampered into the desert, mindless of how death came, as long as they did not feel again that blank condemnation and bleak horror that had engulfed them as his eyes penetrated their minds.

By the time that Shangodoon and his family stood in the vast square before the Royal Capital, the centre of which contained the Palace where the King resided, a great throng of people lined the southern main highway. There was utter silence; the purpose that held them there needed no expression. This crowd was a single welded unit, one living thing that pulsed like an inspired animal with the knowledge that here was a bid for freedom.

The silence overwhelmed; so weighty it was that it crushed down upon the Dominauts with a ponderous force, so that they quailed and slunk away with their loads of guilt. They did not dare to take their fireweapons from the sheaths at their sides. They retreated up the steps of the Royal Capital, prepared to defend it only up to a point, afraid to antagonize the people too deeply, knowing that they were destined to lose the struggle. Two terrified officers had gone in to see the King or his closest ministers; there was little doubt that in the next few minutes a terrible confrontation would take place. And while the people felt the surge of freedom and knew that there was no turning back, they saw that very much blood was likely to be shed that day on both sides, and their hearts pained them yet.

Shangodoon and his family each dropped the packs they carried and opened them. The boy took a long tube of polished wood, lined with little rounds holes, out of his bag, and went and stood a little way before the people, facing the Royal Capital, his legs spread apart so that he stood very firm; he held his tube ritually in front of him, forearms parallel to the ground, palms upward, and the tube lying across them.

The woman stood behind him next, having taken from her pack a strange bowl-shaped thing of shell, with long grooves and convolutions on its curved outside, and having a flat projecting surface at one point; it had twelve strings set across little horizontal bits of wood, and small pegs to hold the strings in place and it glistened and seemed to emanate a deadly power as the woman held it cradled across her breasts with both hands.

The man now reached into his own mysterious bundle and pulled another curious object out. This was a hollow tree trunk, obviously, but over one end of it, stretched tightly, was the skin of some animal, and tightly knotted ropes and pegs ran all the way down the outside of the hollow trunk to terminate in a deep groove running around its circumference near the open end. With this weird object, the purpose of which the people could only guess, Shangodoon stood behind his wife, his hands resting on the taut skin of the upright column, his eyes focused on the door of the Royal Capital where he knew the King would come out.

Wondering at the strange instruments or weapons that these people had produced, the crowd waited tensely. They were aware that here was an act of rebellion, but mightier than that; they realized that here, now, forever, would it be decided whether they were slaves or free. Should these unusual, determined people fail in whatever stupendous plan they had in mind, all would be lost; retribution and punishment by the Dominauts would be brutal beyond anything they had experienced during the last decades.

Now the main gate of the Royal Capital was made of one huge boulder that had been tunneled through and carved upon. The hard rock had been deeply incised and there was a huge depiction of the Gnarl-bird, with the main gate incorporated into the design, so that when the gate opened, up and down, it seemed that the Gnarl-bird opened its huge carnivorous jaws. In years before, when the Dominauts had demanded as tribute each year one young Ainchan maiden, for the King, it was said, she had had to enter that disgustingly-carved mouth, all decked in her finery, to an unknown destiny, for such girls were never seen again. And yet the king had no child, neither from the Ainchan maids nor from his several Dominaut queens.

The people, gazing upward at the awesome features of the mighty God of the Dominauts, knew that terrible mouth well. When it spoke, Ainchan men had died; and it was arbitrary and spiteful. Some people said that the carving was Great Gnarl himself, and that the voice heard coming from the mouth was his; others said that it was just a huge mask, and that somewhere, high up in a hole near the nostrils, officials of the Dominaut religion made announcements through loud-talkers, and claimed that it was Gnarl himself who spoke. Some said that no real Gnarl existed, and other argued that he must for did not something make the Dominauts mightier than other people? The rapid spread of the invaders had been noted; their God had power that was easily demonstrable. That carved face had frightened the people of Ainchan for many centuries, so that some indigenous people firmly believed in Gnarl even more than the people who had brought the religion. Yet in many instances they had never reconciled themselves to the ways and principles that Gnarl-worship demanded. Even then many were thinking that Gnarl was nonsense, a hoax; and yet . . . .

Then the hateful beak opened, and down the steps that led from the interior of that huge basaltic rock, King Chrazius III, Almighty God, Father and Guide of the Universe, appeared in his brilliant robes. Upon his head there glittered the weighty gold crown that his first ancestor had made; ancient precious crystals encrusted in the gold threw their diamond-sapphire-sardonyx sparkles into the eyes of the multitude below, and in his hands the mighty fireweapon rumoured to be the father of them all yawned its many threatening mouths at Shangodoon and his family.

Halvers, their huge spears and shields upraised, spread out in formation down the steps forming a thick V of protection for the mighty monarch. Along the landing at the top of the flight of steps the crack Dominaut marksmen stood with their weapons raised and ready, and high up over the gate the eyes of the great Gnarl-bird snapped open, and two mighty fireweapons looked down from the fiercely frowning embrasures that were revealed.

At the time of Shangodoon's return to Ainchan, King Chrazius III was an aging, terrible tyrant, sixty six years of age, but seeming older, and full of gross, intemperate diseases. His eyes were discoloured and bleary from the constant ravages of painkilling, mind-altering drugs, and his fingers with their jewel-laden rings were huge, swollen and knotted in some rare, incurable ailment. Now, disturbed from the Palace rooms where he spent all his time morosely considering his place in history, this bitter despot had come prepared to execute the rebels himself. Over the years he had transferred his petulant, vindictive angers against himself into a hate for the people he ruled over; so that anyone going before him for any petty offence was a person already condemned; and each year more extortionate laws and restrictions continued to rain down upon the Ainchan people.

So far there had been no sound in the great square nor from the steps of the Royal Capital. The activity from the Palace had been a silent flurry; now all stood still, tensed in the atmosphere of confrontation, while King Chrazius raised a glass lens to his right eye to see clearly the three distant figures who stood out before the massed Ainchan people.

In the expectation that came upon the people when the King gazed upon Shangodoon; in that one long moment the world seemed to hold its breath, so grave was the silence.

Then King Chrazius shouted, pointing with a crooked finger, forcing his tattered lungs to scream the sound into the air among the vultures flying over the city.

"I know you, Shangodoon!"

"Down in the square, the twelve year old boy, son of Shangodoon, his eyes riveted on the monstrous figure of the King, said softly, "He has spoken, father. I know his vibration".

"Then, my son, strike in the name and for the glory of the Creator!" the people heard Shangodoon say, as he raised his hardened hands over the mighty column and its smooth oiled membrane. Then his palms came down, slapping in swift sudden motion, so that something jumped from between his hands and the stretched taut skin and hit and bounced mightily through the ears and heads of the assembled people.

The sound was of the earth, of life, or primal drive and phallic power. It stunned the Dominaut people and deeply startled the Ainchans. It rose and pounded at their bodies until a strange desire rocked at their hearts and made their lips quiver with its empassioned pleas and hints of pleasure. Something in them pounded a reciprocal heart-beat throb, and they groaned and shivered.

The air came alive with visions of huge pounding hoofs, flying giant beasts shaking the earth in their steady rhythmic stampede. The visions were rolling hills and smooth valleys, high pounding breakers on huge cliffs, tall-rearing mountains and patterned formations of great blocks and crystals of the inner earth. All Ainchan trembled at the unique and powerful sound.

The woman had swung her weapon forward so that her left hand had gripped the long board with its transverse frets and strings; now her left-hand fingers moved like the patterned legs of the star-spider, her right-hand fingers plucked and swept at the strings, and another tremendous force, being, god or devil, whatever the listeners thought, leaped into the air.

This one expanded and contracted, tracing broad concentric bands of sound that spiraled out among the people in waves of intense feeling. Something soothed their nerves and calmed the fears that they had felt, nullified the swift adrenalin-flow that had clenched their fists and gritted their teeth when King Chrazius had appeared. A brotherhood love made people weep and cling close, and some started stamping their feet and clapping their hands together—a capital crime.

The instrument the woman held had joined its amazing voice to the deep boom of the man's fierce, echoing device. Its tremors, slides and sudden single points and statements, its tensions and releases as it flowed out of, into and through the units of force as they pulsed from Shangodoon's hands and vibrating column, fascinated the Ainchan people. Some fell on their knees and clasped their hands; others shut their eyes tight and cocked their heads, abandoned to the ecstasy of hearing the wonderful, eternal principles that were being expressed; they tried to find the source within themselves from which this unstable, unsettling, sweet rush of feeling seemed to be flowing.

The instrument's tones ebbed and flowed, and it seemed as if bright flowers, butterflies and stars leaped and danced upon the sonorous stepping-stones of the steady beat of Shangodoon.

Then the boy raised his long tube to his lips and belted out a sound.

The sound stiffened the Ainchan people into immobility for a moment, so peculiarly did it worm its way into their experience. It lifted and sustained them on a plateau of humming joy. It took their spirits along on keen, insightful, penetrating journeys, sounding out their resonances and plumbing their depths with a bold ravishing charm. It tightened their throats and their chests and forced them into a frenzy of rhythmically stamping and clapping feet and hands, jerking elbows and knees, nodding heads; and then Dance came among the Ainchan people and the square exploded into a riot of colour and symphonic movement.

The Dominaut soldiers stood still as statues. At the first sound of Shangodoon's mighty rhythm, some of them had lowered their spears and fireweapons and stepped forward threateningly; but the strains of the woman's strings had made them falter and glare about uncertainly. Now the high penetrating fluting of the boy affected then keenly; they stood transfixed in muscular contortions, fighting to recover something of normalcy.

But King Chrazius III was tottering. He had dropped his terrible weapon, which smashed and clattered down the high stone steps, now he raised his hands to his head and a look so incredibly vicious that women bit their lips in horror, spread over his malign countenance. His lips blubbered soundlessly, and blood dribbled from a corner of his mouth down his scraggly beard.

Then, the legends say, King Chrazius burst apart and spilled himself open on the steps of the Royal Capital. Thousands saw his magnificent robes bulge outward, larger even than his incredible paunch, and then blood and guts cascaded at his feet; next his body tumbled, flumped and thumped to the bottom of the terraced steps where it lay in a huge pool of disgusting purplish ichor.

A shout went up from Ainchans and Dominauts alike. Then the Dominaut soldiers, determined to sell their lives as dearly as possible, charged down the steps loosing their fireweapons and leveling their spears.

The drum and stringed instrument, and Shangodoon and his woman, paused on a sudden pulsing high that breathlessly stopped the advancing Dominaut soliders. But the flute played on. Now it rose to a higher pitch, and the Ainchan people saw the Dominaut soldiers break and flee as their metal fireweapons suddenly crumbled into little sharded pieces. Small explosions and little flares rent and spangled the air as metal balls and thin rays of fire, flying and lancing towards the Ainchan people, exploded, and now the grim turrets high up in the eyes the Gnarl-bird crumbled under a sudden gust of ominous sound, so that the great bolts that firmed the fire-weapons loosed from the wall and thundered down among the Dominaut marksmen.

The weird ululation rose higher until, above the doubtful pandemonium that broke out, there was one penetrating note, so fierce in its intensity that men left off fighting and groveled to the ground, holding their ears, and startled birds squawked and flapped away from over the city as the pitch battered at the clouds themselves. It rose and crescendoed so that at last the most bloodthirsty soldier, the most revengeful Ainchan rebel, dropped his weapon and stood aghast at the sound.

Shangodoon and his family were the only ones moving as they crossed the wide square and mounted the long flight of steps that led up, past the spot where the repellent, deflated carcass of King Chrazius lay, to the high landing before the image of the blinded Gnarl-bird. The boy piped on, his uncanny melody winding interminable mazes in the minds of the people, questioning their souls and searching out their intentions, cancelling the butcheries and hatred that they had intended to pursue.

The steps were steep and long, but the Messenger and his family went up swiftly, until at last Shangodoon stood facing the people before the loathsome open beak of the great Gnarl-bird.

"Peace!" he bellowed, as the boy's high piping ceased; and the people jostled forward to fill the square, as Dominaut soldiers hustled the ruined body of King Chrazius out of sight.

"The King is not divine!" Shangodoon bawled forth.

The older people of the city knew the cry, knew from the very tone of its utterance that this indeed was Shangodoon, hero of the people, who, years ago, had sounded out that challenge on the walls and in the streets of Ainchan. Now the last remaining son of the Dominaut line had proved his saying true in his undignified tumble out of the world of living men; Chrazius had manifested his mortality in a most bizarre and humiliated way.

"Shangodoon!" the people roared as one.

The Dominaut soldiers were, in the main, edging away in abject terror, but still a few, unaware of the great change, were advancing with their clubs and spears. Shangodoon raised his hand.

"Put your weapons away," he said. "It is over. You are no longer employed by the king to butcher our Ainchan people. Do you know what you are defending? Your King is dead, and your God has fallen. Get out of this city!"

The aghast foreign soldiers and their lackeys melted away, clumsily footing down the steep stone steps. Their eyes were wide with a maddening terror that they themselves could not understand; later, rather than face the Ainchan people, they were to take to the hills and surrounding wildernesses, where, even today, their descendants can be seen eking out their meager existence—a fit situation for the oppressive aliens who once committed the most inhuman of crimes against our people—as the reader will see.

Throughout the city people came running, jostling and bumping each other in their haste to see the tremendous spectacle that was being rumoured about through the living quarters. Outside the walls, Dominaut soldiers and civilians streamed away from the city in hastily arranged caravans that were doomed to destruction in the outlying badlands where rebels and bandits held sway. Already rumours were racing southward to Dibra, northward and westward to the cities of the rolling savannah, and eastward to Gnoit, spreading the noise of the fall of the Dominaut dynasty at Ainchan; and scurrying horses were bearing grim tidings to the aloof lords in their luxurious fortresses and their huge bedecked sailing vessels.

Clusters of Dominauts fought at the west gate of Ainchan, striving to get on board the inadequate ships that swayed at the lengthy quays, and the large coaches and chariots, drawn by terrified horses, added danger to the pedestrians as they rushed madly about in the sudden violent exodus.

In the square, the people were craning forward, silent, unmindful of the mad scrambling of the doomed Dominauts, and Shangodoon was speaking.

"Look not upon my strange robes! I am of Ainchan, a son of this city!"

"We know you, Shangodoon!" an old man bawled. "We knew your father, the clever carver of stone and wood! For years your name has stood engraved in our hearts, for we have heard of your mighty exploits!"

"Is he the son of Aldraf?" another asked.

"The son of Aldraf, the Recorder!"

"But did not Shangodoon, son of Aldraf, die in the King's Palace many years ago?" another old man querulously murmured.

"It never was ascertained! I for one never believed the report of the Dominauts that the young man had died!"

"People of Ainchan!" Shangodoon shouted. "Do you condemn me as a murderer? Have I slain your King?"

"You have slain our enemy, oh Shangodoon!" the young men bawled at once. "You are our leader!"

"What leader? All leadership is ended!" a bearded warrior, and outlawed rebel of the ghetto, quarreled bitterly.

"Let Shangodoon speak!" a woman cried. "Let us hear the words of Shangodoon."

"Yes! Tell us your tale! How come you to be here, and what are those strange instruments of power that you, your woman and your son have used?"

Mighty Shangodoon raised his arms and nodded in acquiescence.

"So be it!" he said. "Listen to the history I have to relate, the wonders I have seen, the truths experienced, which have led me to this moment of fulfillment."

And Shangodoon began his history.

3
THE
QUEST AND
THE ESCAPE
FROM AINCHAN

The Quest and the Escape
from Ainchan

I WAS BORN IN the quarter near the most western gate of the North Wall (Shangodoon narrated) thirty-nine years ago, to Aldraf and Lilaktia, of the clan of recorders and carvers. My great-grandfather, the tenth male descendant in our family to fashion wood and stone, moved from the north side to that spot because of the many hardwood trees that could be found in that area. He was a very respected artisan and had many apprentices, but his life was marred by the constant pressure of work the Dominaut overlords laid upon him.

For generations our family has labored at the task of depicting the victories of the Dominauts over our own and other people. My great-grandfather himself carved several yards of the low-relief panels that run in the spaces between the gates; much of the work on the north side of the city is his own. He was made overseer of the Ainchan artisans who carved the scenes the Dominauts wanted on their walls.

My grandfather and father added their permanent contributions to the walls that surround this city, even as I myself was destined to do; for, when I was eighteen and decided to leave this city, I had been designated to spend my life hacking at those walls, utilizing my art in the service of these oppressors of our people.

My education was as complete as my father could afford, for tutors were expensive; but I am happy to say that many of the things I now know I taught myself, and that if one is observant there is no need of a teacher, though I am grateful for all of mine. Long after I had become a recognized artisan of the higher caliber, I continued in my practicing, endeavouring to find as many secrets of expression as I could, for I fully intended to make my country's indigenous history come to life in stone.

This urge to depict the traditional way of life of our people came upon me when I was young, and was to cause me great difficulty among my peers. I was trained in the depiction of machines, of weapons of war, of Dominaut faces and ways of life; but I wanted to paint the glories of the people that even then I was beginning to read about in the forbidden books which spoke of a past before Gnarl or the Dominauts existed, and which were branded as lies.

Yes, I have studied many of the ancient books which were thought to have been utterly destroyed many centuries ago. However long it is distorted. Truth cannot be hidden; and the forbidden books told truths that shocked me with a devastating sense of loss, for I saw how our people had wandered from the true, original culture and religion that our forefathers had known and taken up a foreign belief that operated to their detriment.

I know you are astonished that I should be so sure that the ancient books, long thought to be the imaginative work of fairytale writers, contain immortal truths that should be our guiding lights; but I have studied these books and put their principles into use with much effect, and therefore I am prepared to say that we lost much, immeasurably, when the Dominauts took our land and bathed our offspring in the propaganda of ignorance and slavery.

Even as a youth I found myself enquiring into the oldest questions mankind has ever asked himself. I wondered about my function here in this existence; I wanted to be sure of my purpose, so that I could use all my time and energy in the fulfillment of that purpose. And I did not feel satisfied with the circumstances in which I found myself, for such questionings were suspect, as you know, and forbidden to the people of Ainchan.

Yet I continued to probe into these mysteries, and to find out what the wise ones of old thought about these things. I had discovered that they felt that the body and its material environment were not all to be considered; that they groped to find the reality behind appearance, and that they accepted the invisible reality as older and more important than the visible. Gradually I concluded that the world was a symbol of something else; that the force behind living objects was the only real thing or being that existed. I wanted to be consciously a part of that force, to share its intelligence. So curious was I to know that experience—an experience which I later discovered certain men have claimed to know—that I determined that this would be my major quest, whatever the physical cost.

I read guiltily from the forbidden books of the past—guiltily, because the laws of the Dominauts carried heavy penalties for such an activity. This information was very important to me, and to us, the people of Ainchan; and so I made copious notes, and memorized much of our history too, so as to be sure of the things I said when the time came to speak—as it has now.

When I realized that our history and the history of the Dominauts were not the same, I was greatly surprised; it took much soul-searching to make me understand the difference between ourselves and to draw the line between what was our own way of life and what was imposed upon us by the alien rulers.

I discovered that the Dominauts were ignorant of, or lying about, the matters of the body and soul; and I realized that our old ancestors had a much better idea as to the real nature of human life. Since the Dominauts were wrong about such fundamental matters, and since I had grown up believing them to be right, how many inaccuracies had I accepted in my trust and ignorance of these people? I did not know. But since the Dominauts had misled my thinking, I knew that I had to be on my own and find out originally about the two peoples and their historical achievements.

It was during this process that I realized that the carvings being done on the walls were symbolic—they represented efforts by the Dominauts to propagandize further our people—and would be so for generations to come. Why should I carve these scenes, I felt, all showing Ainchans in positions of inferiority and defeat, and Dominauts in superiority and victory? I would either carve the truth, or cease in my artisanship. I felt I must find my people's history and depict exactly what happened in the past.

The burning questions that filled my mind left little room for anything else; so that from my youth my social life was affected by my need to find out. As a boy, I tired of games before my friends, and walked away; as a young lad, I spent much time by the river, when not restrained in the city, and in the forest of the North Wall; I chose solitary places for my walking and thinking; I sat for hours staring at the landscape, or lay looking at the sky. I had little concern about my appearance, and scarcely ate; and I know that people were whispering that my head was not right, that perhaps I had studied too much.

"Why do you want to think?" an old man asked me once. "What are those strange books you read, and why do you read? Do you enjoy thinking? Is not your future more secure than that of many young men of Ainchan? Why do you not learn to live in a society that you cannot change?"

It was this old man who warned my father that he was running a grave risk to allow me to keep and study those forbidden books. And my father was fearful, even although he knew the righteous nature of my enquiry. He was answerable to the Dominauts; but I am sure now that he knew that truth about them and did not believe the religious teachings they thrust upon us. He paid lip-service to the Dominauts, but once or twice he hinted some very important things to me, things that led to my discovery of profound truths the Ainchan people had always known. But he loved me, and he was trying to protect me when he told me to forget my researches, stop dreaming, and leave out the political ideas I was developing.

I think that he placed too much emphasis on the political aspect of my thinking—though, of course, that was important. What I was interested in most was my own freedom to develop the way I wanted to, without hindrance; I wanted to think for myself and be free to carry out the experiments I wanted to do without harassment. To me, knowledge was, and is, the most important of acquisitions, and seeking it, the most glorious of occupations. What was lacking was the correct sort of environment for my ideas to grow, and since the laws of the Dominauts forbade research into any of the old books which had escaped their burning, I had to find a way to change or circumvent those laws, so that I and any of my people who chose to do so could follow the traditional religious, mystical and cultural ways, without interference. So my political ideas came about as a result of my search for spiritual fulfillment. Man must be free to worship, research and believe however he desires; **that is the true freedom.**

In my readings, I came across many facts about the world that seemed incredible to me at the beginning. There were many ancient practices before the time of the Dominauts; it is hard for us to imagine now, after so many centuries of Dominaut control, exactly how advanced in the higher truths our ancestors were, especially since we have been educated to feel the opposite way.

Our ancestors believed that there was a way to conquer every enemy or any problem; that was, to find a weak spot. I took this philosophy to heart, and it was my aim to study the Dominaut culture so well that I would find the weak spot from whence to begin my operations to free myself, my land and my people.

There is a spot within this city which I believe no one besides myself knows about at this time. It was through legend, rumour and chance—which have followed me throughout my journeys—that I came across an old temple of the Ainchan priests, a strange place where rituals were held, and where the tenets of a very old religion were practised.

The priests of our land had preserved many artifacts and documents of former priests and religions, down through the Early Ages. There were large scrolls of leather with the characters burned on, in a language which I knew to be Old Ainchan; there were candle-holders, clay tablets with pictures and ancient letters engraved thereupon, old vessels and incense-burners, and various other objects, some of which were made of precious metal.

All these things that I describe will soon be revealed to you, for now we can, for the first time in many centuries, explore our past without fear of retribution. The hidden temple and the proof of the wondrous things I say are still there, but that is only one of many sights that you will see shortly.

In that old Ainchan language, so long banned from the lips of our people that few of us even believed it ever existed in written form, I found ancient maps and charts depicting places where gold, silver, copper, iron and other metals could be found; and where some of the old temples were situated. I have never had time to study many of them, and there is much to learn from them when we bring them to the light of day.

The scrolls written in very old forms of Ainchan were difficult for me to decipher, but the later forms of the language, the forms adopted in the last centuries before the Dominaut era, were understandable enough. The later scrolls explained many things. They were written by the priests of the old religion, and they told of the Dominaut invasions.

Some documents also showed that this invasion had been predicted by the wise priests who existed centuries before the time of these preservers of our culture. The secret place where all these treasures were hidden was selected by the war-conscious priests of Ainchan to store their most valuable possessions; they were hidden to save them from falling into the hands of the conquerors.

It seems that, through these old documents, much was preserved; but much was destroyed, too, when the Dominauts arrived. The old temples, the signs of which are almost non-existent, were pillaged and their objects of precious metal taken away on the invaders' ships. The priests were tortured for information on the ritual and spiritual mysteries of their religion, and for the precious treasures they were known to possess. Ainchan people did not dare to wear gold or silver because they would be tortured that they might confess the source of their wealth; and many of them gave their precious things into the hands of the priests when they realized that they were destined for slavery.

All this is history, written down and hidden for centuries by our forebears. It shows most clearly that our people have existed for many centuries, in a high state of civilization, before the coming of the conquerors, the last of whom you have seen wilt and fall before the mighty power of Music.

King Chrazius III and his ancestors were but mortal men, as you all have seen this day; I have certainly know this fact, and was forced to live with it in silence, since I was fifteen years of age. And, in fact, my life was sought and I took the lonely path of exile chiefly because I dared to state that fact at a time when it was death of the most heinous sort for a person to speak a word of blasphemy against the Dominauts or their oppressive rule. *The King is not divine.* I wrote that on the walls of Ainchan, and, I know, in the hearts of some of our people, eighteen years ago, when I returned from the mountains of the north; let us remember its significance.

I discovered the cave of the old priests, in Ainchan, when I was fifteen years old. I was excited by my find, and longed for someone to share the secret with; but for years I was forced to keep it locked within my breast. I yearned deeply for the power to read that ancient written language, and decipher the little pictures and symbols the scrolls contained.

Of course, from the time I could understand the speech of adults, I had heard stories of the Exiles, those priests of the old religion who had voluntarily left the conquered cities or had been driven out when the Dominauts arrived. In the past, these exiles roamed the countryside speaking to the people of the small, unwalled towns and villages, urging them to defy the Dominaut rulers, and even blessing the bands of warriors who regularly attacked the caravans, patrols and even the ships of the Dominauts. There were many bands of fighters who needed priests with them, and the band led by Zioga, the boldest of them all, had many knowledgeable practitioners of the old religion. I admired Zioga greatly for his courage and ingenuity; it was he who attacked the eastern and northern gates several times during my youth. This renegade, a descendant of the high priest of the former Ainchan temple, roamed the Great Plain in elusive secrecy, and every now and then young men of Ainchan escaped out of the city and joined the forces of such patriotic fighters. Strict vigilance was maintained by the Dominaut guards to see that no one left the city unless he had official authority; many people died in trying to elude the guards, who did not hesitate to use their fireweapons at the slightest excuse.

Now, I knew that to be in contact with these outlaws was a definite cause for execution; but my curiosity was far stronger than my sense of self-preservation, and I determined to enquire from these descendants of the refugees whether there was any knowledge about the old ways that they would have had from their forebears.

Few of these nomadic people had any information that I could find useful. Many of them simply would have liked me to join their cause, for they were more concerned with killing Dominauts than in living in the traditions of truth which our people had known. Many of them may be re-educated into the Ainchan ways now that their long battle for liberation is over as we all need to be re-educated into our past; and the opportunity has come.

Some of the rebels assumed that I was a spy of the Dominauts, so strange were my questions, and once I had to fight for my life against one of my accusers, who was sure that I could not be genuinely seeking after the old religion, which he felt had failed the Ainchan people.

Eventually I came across one incredibly old man, a patriarch of rebels, who was versed in so many dark sinister deeds and strange beliefs that I shuddered as I listened to some of the tales he told. He mentioned legends of the old Ainchan priests, asserting that they were masters of healing and highly knowledgeable about the human body. He spoke of the strange powers they had developed through fasting and other ascetic practices, and he described some of their mystic rites.

He said—as I knew—that there were maps made and collected by his forefathers, and that these maps, which had been left in Ainchan at the time the priests had fled, contained much information as to the location of secret religious places where priests carried on the old religion in spite of the vigilance of Dominaut patrols. He even showed me the site of one such hiding place, now abandoned and its treasures removed; and this one was so well hidden that though an outpost of the Dominauts was less than a mile away, the priests were never detected.

I learnt much from this old teller of weird tales. Between morbid comments on the scenes of destruction that he had witnessed, he chatted garrulously about demons, and flying serpents, and strange invisible things, denizens of the desert, which attacked you on the nights of the full moon. He spoke of the terrible deeds which had been done in the cities of the plain, especially at Physhon and Dibra; and he shook with anger and regretted his age, for he wished that he could kill Dominauts as he had done since he was sixteen years old.

When I asked him if it was possible that there were some hidden temples where ancient rites were still practised, he fell silent and did not speak for a long while, as if he pondered the wisdom of something he wanted to say, or did not know where to begin.

Then he spoke of a traveler who had been to the north of the country, and returned with a rumour that no one had ever confirmed. This traveler had heard, from the hill-people with whom he had dwelt, that there was an old cavern-temple high up in the mountains near the source of the Ruba river, where an elderly priest, a descendant of a long line, still lived and carried out traditional duties.

My informant said this half-jestingly, for he had heard of no man going as far north as the traveler said he had been, and besides which he had always been told that the Ruba had no beginning. Doubtfully he stated what that bold traveller had told him—that this place was perhaps the only one which had maintained the Ainchan religion in as pure a form as possible, and that there were many documents kept and translated by the priest.

The old man thought that the scrolls I wanted deciphered might be of interest to that reclusive priest, if indeed such a one and such a cavern really existed. He could not see why I was so excited about the old scrolls, he admitted; but if I dared to continue my search for clues that could throw light on those chronicles of etched leather, it was probable that, given that the traveller's story was accurate. I would find the oldest forms of the Ainchan religion, and get a primary idea of the attitudes that had guided our people long before.

His words caused me to pay very careful attention to the old geographical maps that I possessed; and after much study I found two of them which indicated where such a place might be. Excited at the discovery, and feeling certain that I was on a fruitful line of enquiry, I determined to search those northern hills until I found that ancient cavern-temple.

It was a bold decision, for it involved defying the laws of the Dominauts and risking execution. I thought carefully about the possibilities of its success, you may be sure, and considered the consequences of failure even more carefully; and, while thinking daily about my methods of possible escape from Ainchan, I started collecting money, ropes, tools and weapons that I might need on a journey.

The decision to leave came about finally, spurred on by a change in the political situation. Zioga and his band, as well as other persistent groups of rebels, had been taking recruits from the population of young Ainchan workers; large numbers of young men and women were taking to the open country to join the revolutionary bands. King Chrazius decreed therefore that all persons between the age of fourteen and fifty be kept within the city; and thus no one who, because of their age, qualified to be guarded could leave the city unless they showed papers authorizing them to do so; sometimes an armed guard accompanied such persons.

More dangerous still, and more calculated to terrorize, was the declaration that all Ainchan houses would be searched for evidence of revolutionary thought—weapons, forbidden books, or remnants of the old culture which a few knowledgeable Ainchans still held dear. In fact, in the first two weeks of the curfew and general search, a larger percentage of unlawful material was found than had been expected, and the wrath of King Chrazius increased. You will remember the public executions that took place here in this very square where we stand today, or perhaps you have heard of them; that was during the time of the Execution Curfew, as it was to be called later. The people were subdued; the purpose of the terrorism was achieved.

During this time I lived in the fear of discovery, until it reached the point where I felt I should no longer, could no longer, entertain the strain. I would have to leave; and it was better to do so, not through discovery and the necessity to flee, but of a freer will, and with more time at my disposal. Freedom beckoned, and the alternative was such as to hasten my decision to leave. I prepared myself more hastily each day and there was no place to hide the many forbidden things that I had collected in my home.

The later North Wall carvings were composed at that time, and the basic figures had been blocked-in and defined; but there was much rounding and polishing to be done, as well as details put in. My grandfather was still alive then, and he had designed some of these murals; at the end of every week he came to view the work that was done. At dawn the old man would take his four-wheeled, horse-drawn wagon about a half-mile from the city, and there, when the early morning light slanted across the walls and made the figures stand out clearly, he would view the advances that had been made in that colossal work.

His wagon was always loaded with the materials and tools of his trade-pickaxes, mallets, chisels of varying sizes, wooden poles, gravel mortar, spades and trowels; ropes and slings of canvas for workmen to sit in as they carved high up on the walls; cans of oil for fuel and lighting, and many more things. So loaded was that wagon and so jumbled were its contents, that the addition of my blankets, tools, weapons and those important scrolls, made little difference to the over-all bulk. I hid these things under the general material in the wagon one night before the old man's day of viewing the walls, and the next morning he passed safely through the gates of the north, the sentries scarcely bothering to search a wagon they had searched scores of times already.

He was about a quarter of a mile away from the city when I approached the guards at the gate, mounted on one of my father's horses. I told them that I needed to take some plans of the mural design after my grandfather, and that he had misplaced them; and after much hesitation, doubt and warning, they let me through.

It had been simpler than I had thought it would be; they had not even searched my saddlebags, which I had re-designed. In those bags, hidden compartments carried the two maps which would enable me to find the cavern-temple of the north, as well as some of the many precious stones I had found in the temple of the scrolls.

And so, congratulating myself, I galloped after my grandfather, and overtook his big double-horsed wagon just as he reached the spot where he would dismount to view the distant walls of Ainchan.

"What are you doing here?" the old man asked as I rode up.

"I am taking your wagon and horses, and I am escaping Ainchan."

"Creator of our fathers. I knew you would try this foolishness. I have been watching you, especially since the curfew began. You're endangering your family."

"I'm not going back, grandfather! I'm taking your wagon!"

"Did I tell you to go back? Do I expect you to? Take the wagon and go! And, boy, I hope you know your own goals very well. I hope you know how to stay alive."

"What will you tell the guards?"

"Oh, at least you have contemplated my situation. Well, forget me, and your family too, boy. The path that you have chosen is a lonely one. Start by forgetting that you have given me a political problem, and at my age. No, I will tell them the truth. I will say that you took my wagon and horses away from me." The old man dismounted and stepped away from the wagon, slowly shaking his head from side to side. "I expected it of you," he pointed out again.

I came down from my horse and took the saddlebags off.

"Goodbye, grandfather," I said. "Tell my father and mother that I hope to see them both again in the future; tell my sister that I wish her happiness in her future marriage. Tell them that I couldn't stay anymore, that I had to continue my search. They must understand."

"They do. We have discussed it, and they have feared for you."

"Tell them I will be safe".

"Will you stand talking? Go quickly, before the sentries realize that you are not returning! And throw the heavy things out of the wagon as you go along, or their horses will catch up with you."

I climbed onto the wagon.

"The Creator of our fathers go with you!" he shouted, as I started the horses off with a command and a shaking of the reins. Then I left my grandfather standing with my former mount; and I knew that as soon as the sentries saw that the wagon had turned north, away from the city, they would raise the alarm that another young rebel had escaped.

As the wagon rolled away I was beginning to throw things out, and rapidly I kicked and tossed away until eventually mainly the things that I had hidden in the wagon were left.

When I left Aichan, then, I took along several of the leather scrolls I had discovered. These scrolls were coated in some kind of tough resin, to protect them; and even today they are in perfect condition; though their great age can be noticed at once. There are many more I left behind that perhaps we will recover in the very near future; I believe they are still as I left them as many years ago.

Now, with these precious relics of our past, and with the chance of their decipherment and translation possible if I found this fabled cavern-temple of the north, I urged my horses exultantly, and expectant happiness filled my breast as I considered the prospects of my new-found freedom.

4
THE
JOURNEY
TO THE
NORTH

The Journey to the North

THE SUN WAS CLIMBING into the morning sky as I travelled rapidly away from Ainchan. I kept away from the river for I knew well that there would be dwellings and people along the banks for a long way upriver, and I did not care to be seen. I headed straight north, across rolling savannah country, and the horses seemed pleased by the easy terrain, the environment of tall grass, shady trees, pleasant wind and occasional wild goats and deer.

Now and then I passed clustered houses, ploughed land, and fields of corn and vegetables, and once that day, late in the afternoon, I waved to a group of farmers on their way home to some remote village, but most of the time there was no one to be seen and only few signs of human habitation.

I drove the horses hard, for I wanted to take advantage of whatever lead I had over possible pursuers, and the wagon rolled swiftly along.

Late in the afternoon, after a day of steady travel with only one break for feeding the horses, I climbed a tall tree and looked back over the miles I had come. Far away down the landscape, so greyed with distance that I hardly believed I had travelled from thence that morning, the city of Ainchan lay; and I saw five moving spots spread out along the plain, coming north, and knew that the pursuit was on. The Dominaut manhunters, cunning and fierce as predators, were after another Ainchan rebel; and I had the queerest sensation when I realized that that rebel was me, and that the question of survival was in my hands totally.

The evening closed in swiftly. It was the fifth night of the rising moon, and I determined to travel some hours after sunset for I felt confident that the pursuing soldiers would stop at the fall of darkness and make camp for the night; they could not be in so much of a hurry to get me, I assumed, for sometimes they played with any one of their hunted victims for days before they brought his body back to the city. The luxurious confidence with which these manhunters rounded up their desperate prey was well known among Ainchan men; many rebels had told me of this trait of theirs.

My horses were tired, but after only a short rest and feed we started again.

So far we had been going over trackless country; now I turned slightly toward the river, and fell upon a trail that led up into the country, running parallel to the riverbank. I knew that I was still south of Kunaree, and that this was one of the rough roads which had been hacked out of the thick brushwood of the riverbank through the forced labour of the plainspeople, for the benefit of the Dominaut soldiers. Now that nigh had fallen, I felt safe in venturing onto this way, for there was hardly a chance of meeting any of the large patrols during the night. I calculated for speed, and took the tiredness of the animals into account; and I was very sure besides that sooner or later some, if not all, of my pursuers would hit on the idea of travelling along this road.

And so, for the next five hours after the sun had gone down I was urging the horses along this pebbly-smooth road, and I was less perturbed by the fact that I was being hunted than you may imagine. I shouted loudly sometimes, enjoying my freedom and highly stimulated by recent events; indeed, I almost forgot the danger which was following.

This was a mistake on my part, to be so lax, and I was to regret my miscalculation. For, rising early in the morning and hitching up my animals, I left the sheltered grove I had found during the night, and headed for a high hill almost within the way I was going, to spy out the land behind. Then I was greatly surprised and affrighted at what I saw, for the hunters behind were much closer that I ever could have expected. They evidently had travelled all night; and yet they sat straight and energetically in their saddles. They came on as surely as if they had seen me already.

The nearest horseman was about a mile away, travelling on the road; another was behind him only a short distance, and the other three were fanned out at various intervals along the plain.

Bitterly I regretted my mistakes. I should have left the big, conspicuous, slow wagon a long time ago. You know, my people, that I had depended on the wagon longer than had been necessary; I had only really needed it to smuggle a few possessions out of the city, and as an excuse to leave. Now my sense of security had overplayed itself, and the wagon was cumbersome and a positive danger.

Here then is an important lesson for you, my people. A belief, a religion, is like a method of transport. You let it go, leave it behind, when you do not need it any longer; and you need it no longer if it does not perform a positive function in the continuance of your spiritual and physical survival, if it does not answer all the questions that you can possibly ask.

I knew now that I should have taken the horses alone from the start. I should have remembered that, all along the road and the river, there were traveller's stations which I could not use, and where the Dominaut soldiers could easily get a change of horses. Above all, I had under-estimated my own importance to them; or, if not that, the precise quality of their determination to bring back, dead, any who dared to escape from Ainchan.

Vividly I remembered the brutally broken, bloody bodies that were left for hours in the square; bodies of those caught attempting to flee the city, and of the chronic troublemakers who kept banned material in their homes. The thought of the traumatic horrors I had experienced during the current Execution Curfew gave the greatest impetus to my actions, and

I hastened to free one of my horses from the wagon, knowing that I had to travel as lightly as possible.

I left the wagon and its contents, taking my saddlebags with the maps, the scrolls of leather, my arrows and free bow, my shortsword and sheath, and some flat cakes of cornbread.

Now, as I have mentioned before, I also had a collection of rare and beautiful stones with me, many very fine specimens of various gems, some uncut, others cut and polished, many rounded and faceted in ways that showed the consummate art of the earlier gem-crafters of our nation.

These gems—sparkling diamonds, delicate mauve-grey amethysts, carved jades, not only of green, but brown and black; blue, green, orange and yellow transparent sapphires that glinted brightly even in faint light; red rubies, daintily banded agates and several specimens of white, black, brown, pink and purple coral with intricate decorations—these gems were to save my life, for I struck upon the plan of dropping them, singly and in twos and threes, over a wide circular area at first, then along the way I was travelling, knowing well that the men pursuing me would stop to search and gather them up.

For the pursuit of wealth, especially in easily portable forms, is always the important occupation of our just defeated rulers, and perhaps of all conquerors of peaceful peoples, whenever and wherever the scourge of oppression has occurred. Had not these soldiers delayed their pursuit to search for gems, and then fallen into dissembling, dissension and violence, their greed and cunning coming to the forefront at once I would have died that second day of my escape from Ainchan.

As it was, I rode as fast as my tired animal would allow me up the slope of the savannah, and slight though the gradient was, the exertion of the previous evening and night was telling on my horse, so that I was glad when three of my pursuers delayed a while at the spot where they finally caught the wagon. Down the plain I could see them moving around my former transport; and I smiled for I knew that they knew I was now much more difficult to find. I watched as two of the, dismounted and cautiously entered the covered vehicle; they examined it for a while. Then, from the thin wood through which I was now riding, I could see them turn to come after me again. The foremost one evidently was depending upon his own experience at tracking hunted victims, and for this I was glad, for it ensured that the dropped gems would be seen almost at once. Even as I was rejoicing at this fact—for they could have used their hunting dogs—I saw him bend very low in the saddle, then dismount and kneel on the earth; he examined the ground, then beckoned to his comrades, and the three of them clustered together. Then one pointed at the ground a little distance way, and they separated hurriedly and began searching among the stones and grasses.

Now the sun had risen some distance above the horizon and its light threw shadows that were longer than their objects across the rolling, slanted northern area of the mighty Ainchan plain. I imagined how its light would glint upon the exquisite gems as they lay in the dust, stones and grass, and how the men must be shouting in avarice and amazement as they hustled to claim as many of the jewels as they could. In the distance they depicted a minute pantomime, standing distinctly out against the yellow-green grass in the bright sunshine.

As I watched, I saw two puffs of smoke, grey as the men's uniforms, seemingly rising from the hands of one man, the tracker; the other two jerked this way and that, stumbled around and then fell, while the horses kept their distance, sidestepping and jittery at the sight of sudden murder.

I myself recoiled with shock, pulling my horse up, my mouth half-open, eyes wide. At this obvious, clearly witnessed act of homicide, in this sudden sharp proof of the spirit of my pursuers, my heart throbbed with a fierce muscular ache, like the pain of a tortured ligament. So quickly had the men died that I kept on viewing the scene, staring at their bodies, remembering how they were living only moments before, absorbing the reality of it all. Indeed I had always imagined that it took more decision, more energy, somehow, more *effort,* to take the life of men. What then, I thought, was the final goal of the Dominauts, what was the final situation of the Ainchan people? I shuddered, though the sunlight was warm.

Now I saw the killer stoop over one of the dead men, and knew that he was searching for the gems the dead man had succeeded in finding; soon he went over to his second victim, while the horses moved uncertainly around, avoiding both the dead and the living. Then he went after the dead men's horses, hoping to tie them, I thought; but the horses bolted, one heading back down the plain where it had come, the other heading westward towards the far-distant river.

Now the killer turned to his own horse and led it, his eyes on the ground, along the path I had taken; every now and then he stopped and picked another find from the earth.

As I urged my horse forward, I was sorry that I could not get one of the dead men's fresher horses. My own mount, I knew would have been glad too. But both the horses kept in the direction in which they had started, so that eventually one disappeared in the tall trees, plainsgrass and bamboos towards the river area, and the other was caught by one of the horsemen of the two that were left farther down the plain.

This horseman now waited for the other, and after a brief consultation they came on again leading the runaway horse. Ahead, the tracker was still tracking, but darting hither and thither every now and then to pick up a precious stone. I realized that he was more determined than ever to catch me now, for he would have guessed that I knew of some large source where many more such stones could be found. Certainly he considered my capture and killing secondary to his own accumulations of wealth, but he would need information from me; and so I had created an added determination on his part to overtake me.

But he was busy searching the ground, and now the soldiers behind were close enough and, I calculated, so visible that he must have recognized that he had been seen.

As I rode I kept glancing back, observing their movements when the sparse trees and high grass gave me the opportunity to see them.

Soon the two who travelled to the rear came into the area where my wagon was abandoned and where the slayings had taken place; and my fore-ward pursuer, now mounted, but bending low in the saddle, and moving in a zig-zag line, was searching the ground still.

I had strewn the ground with all the jewels I had carried with the exception of one large uncut diamond which I kept for a memento, and still carry today. They had been many indeed, and the tracker had missed some of them in his hasty search. Now he was out of the area where I had strewn the last of the gems, but still he observed the ground closely, not yet being convinced that there were none ahead. It seemed that he knew he could be seen by the two riders behind, for occasionally he turned in the saddle; and it was thus that he saw when they came upon the bodies he had left.

I watched him as he watched them examine the dead men; then they too began to search along the ground, leaving their horses free; and the murderer, realizing that he had missed gems that his comrades were now discovering, turned and started down the slope towards them.

At this, I became sure that I stood no immediate danger from the Dominaut manhunters; so I reined in my animal in the mottled shade of a tall clump of creaking bamboos, and watched the strange, grim drama on that open landscape.

The newcomers on the scene were busy searching the earth for the precious stones when the single rider joined them. He came close, waving, pointing to the dead men and then up the slope, in my direction; I guessed that he was saying that I had shot his comrades.

But the two had been conversing together while he was still a little way off, and now they stood waiting while he brought his horse to a standstill and dismounted before them. Then again I saw those deadly little puffs of smoke burst from the hands of the two newcomers, and the man who had killed already for the sake of wealth and prestige now met his death in the same sudden manner in which I had seen him kill.

Now the pattern of living robbing dead, which I had witnessed before, was reversed; two living men stooped beside the one dead body with its pocket full of brilliant gems. Then, even as I watched, one man crumpled under the sudden strike of the other, and the sharp sunlight glinted on the weapon in the attacker's' hand; so that only one man finally rose from the ground and mounted his horse. He walked wearily, like a wounded man, and he had swung onto his animal with difficulty; after that he turned back the way he had come, starting slowly down the plain towards Ainchan with his booty of jewels. And so I was free of pursuit.

It was this surviving soldier who, returning to Ainchan, spread the tale that made me a deadly foe to the Dominauts, and the target of anyone, Ainchan or Dominaut, who felt he could capture or kill me. But I was not to know that until three years later, when I returned to the city and was accused of the murder or those four soldiers. But I will tell you more of that at the opportune time.

After the shock of witnessing those killings had worn off, and I knew that I was reasonably safe, I took my journey at a more leisurely rate, and had time to consider the beauties of the countryside through which I rode. A feeling of peace and well being filled me; the pleasant blue sky with its clean white clouds, the wide landscape with its groves and dots of trees and all bamboos, the fine steady breeze, and the cries of the birds, all kept the morning before me as an ever-changing experiences, a marvelous intertwining of sights and sounds which tugged at my emotions and made me shout again and again as I rode along.

On the evening of that day I came upon a lonely homestead, standing independently on a clearing in the grassland, where an old man and his wife lived with their goats and sheep; a warm and friendly place, where no questions were asked and where there was delight at seeing a visitor, and though the old man eyed my saddlebags and must have wondered why I kept them so close, he ventured to say nothing about them. I admired him greatly for this, and was glad that he expected me to have my secrets. I paid them well for the hospitality they showed.

I spent the night there, and next morning, fortified with a meal of goat's milk, bread and cheese, and supplies for two days' journey, I mounted my well-rested horse and resumed my journey.

I travelled in a northwesterly direction along a narrow dirt track that the old man had described to me; somewhere ahead it joined the Ruba River Road, which ran alongside the river up to the Ferry Town. Ferry Town lay opposite Kunaree, with the river between them; it was the last northern outpost of the Dominauts.

Two day's journey brought me to Ferry Town, and there I called on a man whom the old man said he knew well. He had given me a letter to place in the hands of this Ferry Town man whose name was Dalaik; a trusted friend, the old man had assured me, with a queer look in his eye.

Dalaik was a sinister individual, blind in one eye, with a face formed in lines of wit, ready smiling and a disconcerting willingness to deceive. He lived in a single room in a large building on the outskirts of the sprawling, unwalled town; mysterious bundles and boxes lay everywhere in the room, some piled neatly, and some in great disorder. Like his friend the old man, he did not enquire as to what was in my bags; nor did I enquire about the contents of his strange bundles and packs, though it seemed that he was willing to share their secrets with me. He took the letter and read it, nodding and smiling, and as I sat in the grey, shadowed room, looking about as he read, once or twice I caught the sharp probing stare of his single curious eye.

"You are crossing to Kunaree?" he asked me at last.

"Yes," I said, though actually I did not intend to pass through the city.

"There are soldiers and customs guards on the other side," he said simply, cocking his head and staring, birdlike, at me.

I sat silent. I had realized that it would be so, but was unprepared so far. Vaguely I had hoped to steal the identification medal of one of the many oil-workers who were sure to be crossing with me; but that had been a desperate decision, born of sheer necessity. Now this man, in that one sentence, had suggested that he could solve my problems of securing an identity, as well as that he thought I was a fugitive and expected I would need it. Finally he had invited me to share my plans and situation with him.

"I am a very wise man," Dalaik said. "And so is my friend. He saw your needs, even as I see them now. I can get you an identification medal, pass card, clothes, money . . . don't you see why the old man guided you to me?"

I smiled and relaxed. "I am thankful to you and the old man. I certainly need your help. I need an identity medal, and a pass showing that I am an oil-lake worker."

"People like us know one another." Dalaik said. "Old Ainchan cannot die. There are still ways of detecting the spirits of the ancestors, and I see that you carry a serious burden for our people; your mission is a weighty one, and I am glad to be of help."

"I thank you, wise man."

"It is good that there are people like you, people with spirit, good sense and determination," Dalaik said. "I, I am just an old trickster, an outlaw, a forger of money and identities, a trader in strange, forbidden things. Nothing in Ferry Town escapes the notice of Dalaik; people bring secret news and even more secret objects to him. I cannot tell your goal, but I have met many more desperate men on many dangerous and sacrificial journeys, and whatever you have done, whatever punishment you flee from, your worst crimes can only be misdemeanours in my sight, for this single eye of mine has seen much wickedness, my traveller.

"You may rest here tonight, and early in the morning I will give you the medal and pass that you need, and direct you to the ferry; I would take you there myself, except that I do not go into the streets at daylight."

Thus, next morning as the sun was just coming over the hills to the east, I was jostling my way up the railed steps leading to the workers' deck on one of the large boats which plied between Ferry Town and the landings on the other side, which lay perhaps half a mile away from the actual walls of Kunaree.

The storehouses along the river's edge were already busy and the wharves were bright with the colours of people's clothes. Here and there were the market stalls of women who had travelled across the country to this spot; cattle corrals, metal works and smiths' shops, boatbuilders' docks, carriage makers' and wheelwrights' workshops, groceries and stores selling tools, fishing equipment and oil. Buildings opened their doors and Ferry Town came rapidly to life, so that there was a marked contrast to the still beauty of the early blue-grey morning when I reached the town, and the murmuring, busy atmosphere that had erupted in the space of two hours at the most.

The ascent leading to the workers' deck was crowded with sweating men and women, loaded with their provisions and other necessities, all carrying the tools of their trade—picks and shovels for breaking the lumps of hard substance that crusted over the oil lakes, large scoops for sampling of the crude, heavy oil, strong treaded boots and thick fireproof overalls, bright orange helmets on their heads. Women as well as men labored daily in the oilfields factories and tarpits of Kunaree. Apart from the oil-workers, there were the metal-men, workers in the mighty smelting plant; engineers and construction men, miners, overseers and managers of the Dominaut-run industries; independent native vendors, young men going to join the civil guard at Kunaree, children and parents, and many Dominaut soldiers and investigators, some ordinarily dressed and some in uniform.

I had taken my horse to the below deck, and left him well fed and securely railed in the place provided for animals, as soon as the ferry-boat had opened its portals to receive them. Immediately I had hurried to the passengers' stairway to get on deck, and though there was still a crowd ahead of me, I was certain that I would get on board before they signaled that they could take no more passengers.

I carried my saddlebags, of course, with the two maps purporting to show the higher stretches of the country, the upper reaches of the river and the location of the general area where the fabulous cavern-temple was said to be. These maps were perhaps the most precious things in my possession; but in my bag I also had my shortsword and sheath, the leather scrolls, my uncut diamond in its own little drawstring leather bag, and my bowstring and arrowheads.

The bow and arrowshafts, being too long to fit into my bags, had had to be discarded, for the laws prevented the carrying of weapons in the towns. I could not risk being stopped and questioned by the sharp-eyed soldiers; my own nervousness and proneness to panic would have sealed my fate. Dressed as I now was in the ubiquitous overalls of Ferry Town, a hard safety-hat on my head, I looked inconspicuous enough; and I got into very little conversation, for the people of the plains are quick to recognize accents from city to city, and my own most immediate intonation was in the broad accent of Ainchan, whether I spoke in the traditional language or in the language of the Dominauts.

Observations and thoughts on my future thus filled my mind as I waited my turn to show my pass and identification card, and now and then I mouthed my new name, **Fribikum**, memorizing it and practicing its feel and the feel of my new self, as I was accustoming myself to my new set of clothes. Finally I stood before the officers at the top of the stair; two Halvers, immaculate in their uniforms, checked our passes and medals and made notes on their writing surfaces; passed our medals to other officials, five or six of them, who stood before each doorway of the huge three-tiered boat. My medal was examined sharply, expertly; they looked to see that the likeness carved there was indeed my face; then they passed it back to me and motioned me to enter the doorway, and I was thankful for the great skill and clever hands of my weird and knowledgeable friend, Dalaik the forger.

The passage across the river lasted about an hour; the turning water-wheel, huge though it was, churned swiftly in the smooth running water and the heavily-loaded boat moved more speedily than I had thought it could.

The sun was not yet at its zenith when I was free of the customs guards and away from the ferry-boat, leading my horse along the wharf with difficulty, because of the crowds; then coming clear of the busy port area and riding along the broad asphalt road that ran towards the town. The search of my bags had been done with some care, but the hidden compartments I had made had served their purpose well, and my maps, scrolls, diamond and sheathed shortsword remained safe, while the clothes and boots I had purchased at Ferry Town, with my eating provisions, were taken out and examined with care. I was proud of my handiwork in altering those saddlebags, and in my mind I thanked my uncle, a clever leatherworker, for teaching me such cunning use of the needle.

I had never seen Kunaree before, and I pondered long at the crossing of two roads, debating whether to enter the city and spend the day and night there, or heading northward immediately. But the urgency of my quest and the lessons I had learnt about lagging dissolved my temptation, and I rode away from the city and headed towards the hills.

From a mile away, Kunaree was an interesting sight. The buildings were of weathered limestone, some carved out of the rock itself in the older areas, others built up and capped with red-painted iron roofs. The roofs rose, tier after tier, parallel as the east-west streets of the city, into the highest reaches of the great limestone out crop around which the city was built. A Dominaut fort crowned the highest point of this great bulge of stone, its walls, not built of limestone but of huge basaltic blocks, dark-grey and sinister even in the high daylight, its fireweapons pointed to the sky like barbarous challenges; a direct contrast to the roofs of the warm dwelling-places. This fort and the main living area was to the east, north and central parts of the city; westward, there were the huge shallow oil tanks that held the heavy sludgy material that was guttered from the oilpits to the city on long covered troughs of impervious stone.

Farther west, the apparatus of the oil-working could be seen; strange iron things with huge pumps, levers and windmills, long many-wheeled wagons that ran on tracks, chariots moving in all directions; scoops and buckets, many containers of blazing fire, and several dark buildings. There were very many people about too. Most of them bent over the greasy lumps of asphalt in the bituminous pits and lakes, using strange-looking tools to pull gobbets of brown-black semi-solid material from the earth. Along the wide main road that ran from the city out across the western plain and into the more distant oil-workings, there were many large trailers which were driven by oil-fueled machines—a new invention, I was to learn later. It was indeed strange to see these vehicles moving without the usual gang of men or animals pulling, or without the sails or turning handles, large footpedals, and balanced cogwheels, as we in Ainchan used at that time, and still do now, though I see that smaller versions of these vehicles have appeared in some other places.

I was travelling northward, as I have said; the river lay on my right hand, some distance off, and the landscape was changing. Close to the waterway there were large plantations of banana trees, growing amid straight trenches of water; these plantations stretched for a long way up the side of the river, and for the next three days there were only banana plantations interspersed with villages and single or grouped homesteads, and long stretches of grassland and trees in the uncultivated areas, to be seen on the banks.

Farther back from the river, there were the cultivated grasses—tall bamboos, used for housing, boatmaking and general clothing and shelter, beautiful and feathery against the sky; long expanses of bright-green sugar-cane, now close to ripening and waving their silver-grey tassels; and yellow cornfields in which the reapers shifted slowly, the tiny figures making mimes of strength and weakness, work and relaxation. The clumps and avenues of tall coconut palms, and terraced slopes where an abundant variety of vegetables sprouted from the fertile dark-brown soil, surrounding lonely farm houses with cattle and windmills, tanks, storehouses and bright red roofs. On the river itself, huge rafts composed of timber cut from the tall rain-forest in the region higher north, floated swiftly down to Kunaree and beyond to Ainchan and even Dibra; some of these rafts, well fastened together, carried little cabins on them where the steers-men lived.

At night, I made hammocks of vines, and rested beneath the trees with a small fire going. I tethered my horse nearby and ate of my corncakes, cheese and bread, and also of any fruit I managed to come across. I started my journey early again each morning. Rain fell one night and gave me a slight fever, but for much of the way the weather was extremely good, and the moonlight was bright almost throughout my journey.

One of the deepest memories I have is riding by the side of the swiftly moving river on the night of the full moon; the water and land were clearly defined and mottled with sparkles and light and shadow as the moonlight glittered on the dew drops and the river, and on the leaves of the tall trees. Few clouds were in the sky and the stars paled into insignificance and disappeared before that remarkably bright moon, and I myself, the only human being for miles around, knew the utter dependence on self and truth that the first conscious man may have known when first he recognized himself as a thinking part of the environment.

For the tall silent trees, the rising hills (distinctly separated by atmosphere and moonglow), the sense of aliveness of the earth and the river, and the steady beat of my horse's hoofs, in fact, that afforded me the most amazement, for the horse moved smoothly in a flow I could not understand, in a oneness with the environment that I did not know how to join, and the sound of his hoofs—have you ever listened to the sound of a horse's hoofs? They were his contribution, his response and communication, to the moonlight, the earth, the water and the trees. I think that night was the beginning of a new enlightenment about the earth and man's participation in its existence—an enlightenment that has never ceased from that point, though since then insights and revelations much more important than that have passed like earthquakes through my mind.

The land was more steep now, and more tiring to traverse. The shape of a valley appeared far up in the foothills and slopes which preceded a high limestone plateau; past that there was the beginning of the volcanic country. I journeyed on and on, and the temperature became colder especially when I was forced to keep close to the river. The trees were thick on the slopes, but more bare rock was evident now, and there were signs of flooding and erosion from the times when the river flowed higher or when it was in spate.

The river was still fairly broad, but running very swiftly now, so that the few defiant crags that stuck up in mid-stream created eddies and ribbons of seething foam. The sound of the water had grown too, and its thunder filled my hearing. In these high areas the river was at liberty, unaffected by any designs of men, and tossed rocks and huge broken tree-trunks downstream as if they were pebbles and toothsticks; there were no rafts or boats this high up the river, and once I was surprised to see a lone man in a fast-moving, well-balanced canoe that leapt the rapids and shot downstream as adroitly as a fish.

Now the evidence of human life was much less; there were few dwellings to be seen, and more wild animals—goats, sheep, deer and even horses. When I came upon the torn remains of a goat, I feared that there were many leopards and other striped and spotted wildcats around, perhaps even lions; and I cut a good supple bow from a guava tree, fitted my bowstring on, and made some arrowshafts from strips of bamboo and the feathers of the stridor-birds, which lived in colonies in the thick brush, and whose abandoned nests were very easily found. I also cut a long, light, straight branch from a byotta tree, and sharpened and barbed one end, making a very serviceable spear. I was not called upon to use these weapons, however, until near the end of my journey, and then I used them badly indeed. I did not hunt any animals, but took my sustenance from the mango, orange, cherry, banana, coconut and plum trees which grew numerously at various places along the way; the provisions I had bought at the Ferry Town did not last very long. I ate no meat at all during my journey and search for the northern cavern-temple and its mystical high priest; in fact, I have eaten no flesh of animals since I left this city.

I was aware that my body and my thinking were changing; I knew I had lost weight, but had replaced all surplus flesh with firm muscle, and I felt fit of body. My horse was not in as good a condition, however, and I realized that some time I would have to free him and proceed on foot.

I had been consulting my two old maps, those old leather charts left by the priest of Ainchan perhaps six hundred years ago, and so far I was following them well. One of them depicted the way upriver to Kunaree, and to the northern farmlands which had been used for centuries; but it was only because of the old form of the name that I had recognized the place to be the Kunaree of long ago, for the river seemed to have changed its course since this map was drawn. The second map seemed to be on a more detailed scale than the first. It showed part of the Ruba River, the high plateau which was still ahead of me, and a bridge crossing a tributary of the river. Close by this minor head-stream there was depicted the old Ainchan twelve-pointed star, with words which I translated to mean: "Here is the great temple and place of mystic initiation of the Mountain Ruba, now called the Forbidden Mountain, where our investigations and experiments into the Higher Truths still continue, undisturbed by the foreign invasions." It was a beautiful invitation to my curious mind, but this map had something more that puzzled me. There were depicted, just north of the hills rising to the great escarpment which divided the plain from the plateau, three strange-looking drawings which resembled heads. I had no idea what they meant, and the caption "Plateau of Faces" gave me no thought what to expect, though it excited my imagination.

And so I rode on many more days, until the time that the moon rose late, in smaller crescents, and was still in the sky when the sun appeared; and finally there loomed up before me a mighty mass of limestone rock; and the sharp crags around afforded me no forward passage unless I climbed.

Here I paused perplexed; this seemed the end of my horseback journey. The very few hill-people whom I had seen at a distance for the last days of my journey to this point, had stood on the rises and waved their hands, indicating that there was nothing up ahead, that it was best to turn back. Some pointed at paths and directions, as if they were sure that I had lost my way; others seemed affrighted at the sight of me and my horse, and did not want to be seen. Generally, I gathered that no one in the valley below this area had dared come this far north unless their business was of the most urgent and suspect nature, and that anyone who travelled past the last high bridge, known as the Roaring Bridge, which I had passed some three days before, was a distrusted individual. Now the beetling bulk of this high barrier brought their warnings back to mind, and as I stood before the mighty towering bulge of rocks, so massively high and broad on this landscape that it would take me several days, perhaps weeks to find an easier passage, I fully understood the consternation of the kind but taciturn natives of these hills.

My horse was sore in one hoof and limped a little; I decided to loose him at once. Taking my saddlebags, I changed into the warmest clothes I had, cut up the horse's harness and fashioned straps so that I could carry the bags easily on my shoulders and back, buckled my shortsword and sheath around my waist, tied my bow on my back, and with my byotta-wood spear in my hand I turned to the steep rocky way with its covering of sharp weathered stone.

It was late afternoon when I started, and darkness had fallen for hours by the time I clambered wearily up to the top of the huge plateau. It had not been an easy climb; the stars were the only light I had, and every now and then I heard the coughing snarl of some savage night-beast making its search for food. At one time a boulder thundered down from above, a rush of heavy wind and rumbling in the dark and barely missed me as I crouched in a mossy crevice with my hands over my head. I wondered for a long time whether it could have been aimed, so accurately did it come in my direction; only the sudden blotting out of the stars ahead and above me had told me that it was coming. I had just concluded that it was an accident when from above there came the sound of a macabre, unearthly laugh, which echoed so eerily among the gaunt rocks that I was sure the sound had not come from a fully human throat. It was this that made me first aware that something, or someone, had taken to watching me as I proceeded on my journey. I climbed carefully after that, and reached the top of the plateau without any further incident.

So weary was I when at last I clambered over the edge that I scarcely noticed the landscape in the dim starlight; I walked among what I thought to be huge crags and tors of natural stone, and at last I found the shelter of a overhang of rock, and rested there, my sword near my head, my bow and arrows lying close by my right hand, my bags beneath my head, my spear by my left hand.

In the morning I opened my eyes and came outside upon a landscape that made me start back and yell in astonishment, my heart throbbing like hoofs of wild horses.

Before me, in every direction I looked save toward the south, stretched a mighty barren plateau of eroded rock. It disappeared unbroken over to the west; northward, the mighty blue mountains, all several thousand feet high, rose like soldiers, while to the east the land dropped and dipped precipitously down to the roaring V-shaped valley of the Ruba torrent.

The immensity of the plateau took my breath away; but what weakened my knees and made me sit gasping, panic fluttering at my throat, was the tremendous carved granite blocks that stood upright, far and near, hundreds of them, all over that vast area.

Each vertical block of granite was carved into a face. Twenty, thirty, even fifty feet high, stood these gigantic faces, with long noses, wide open lips bordering mouths that were caves, and deep black eyes which also were caves; and it dawned on me at last that here was the work of man, but on a scale so vast that I, who had seen many mighty rock carvings in Ainchan, was struck and nonplussed at the consummate skill of the artisans who had carved these faces and the overwhelming enormity of the task they had undertaken.

Each monolith faced east; it was an awesome parade of heads. The mouths were on a level with the earth, and I saw indeed that they seemed made to walk inside; but while the ground itself was of limestone, these massive structures were of volcanic rock.

When I recovered from the first unpleasant shock of finding myself among these weird gigantic carvings, I started amongst them curiously, prepared to run or defend my life if any opponent, man or beast, came from the unknown holes of these mouths. But nothing moved in the landscape besides myself, though constantly I felt as though I was being observed. Soon I was recovering my composure, staring up at the rocky features of the silent Faces, and wondering about the origin of these laboriously cut slabs of granite. On entering one of them and examining the hollowed out inside, I saw that there was a huge pipe of iron running deep down into the earth, and a large grilled platform over the top of this wide, well-like cylinder. The morning light glinted high up on the carved inside walls where the sun shone through the apertures of the eyes.

The interior of each of these faces was the same—smoothly carved walls, openings high up that represented eyes, an open mouth as big as a room, and the curious iron wells that ran deep into the earth, seemingly far below the level of the plateau I had climbed, for I dropped stones through many of the grilles and did not hear the sound of their impact. Instead, there was a constant low murmuring, so low that it seemed a vibration of the earth and it took some time before I became conscious that it could be the faint sound of the Ruba River or some underground tributary.

My wonderment about the builders of these strange monuments continued as I traversed this plateau, always heading north. On my right rose the straight backs of those giant carvings, on my left the enigmatic faces, all carrying the same stylizations and yet different features, stared impassively back at me in the rising sunlight, and cast long shadows on each other.

Then I noticed that I was perspiring, and I wondered why, for this was the first time since I left the area of the woodcutters that the temperature had become so warm. Yet the sun was not very high in the sky, and as I glanced about in bewilderment, surprised at the way my heavy clothes clung wetly to my skin, I could feel the temperature grow hotter, an hour later, with the sun still rising, I could see little heat-waves dancing up off the hot rock, and my leather boots were quite warm.

Then, at the far distant point which I took to be the centre of the plateau, where the tallest faces gazed imperiously toward the sun, I saw a grey mist rising rapidly, blurring and blotting out the monoliths. Even as I watched, this mysterious atmosphere, like cloud, spread out in all directions, and then I noticed that there were huge gouts of steam proceeding from the mouths of the carved giants. Much closer at hand now, there were little puffs and hollow sounds and each carved figure, now heated by the brash glare of the unclouded sun, spewed forth vast volumes of steam. Now the openings around me belched forth their heat and vapour too, and a strange heady odour beat at my consciousness and made me shake my head from side to side, endeavoring to think freely.

I saw now that the heat was connected to the rising of the sun, and to the large heat-conducting pipes inside the incised igneous boulders, and I began to hurry, trying to travel as fast and as far as possible before the creeping steam and heat overcame my already reeling senses. But visibility was already poor; the fog of steam covered the whole plateau, and as I labored on, sometimes stumbling on the roughly eroded rock surface, I barely avoided walking into those carved boulders, for they loomed up suddenly in the mist.

I was sweating freely now, and panicky; I could feel that a new state, a new consciousness, was coming upon me, and

I fought to retain a sense of myself as I strove on, my feet trodding awkwardly in the bad visibility and uncertain terrain. But the unusual, light-headed feeling was not unpleasant; rather, it filled me with a sense of well-being and a peculiar clarity of thought, as well as made my body tingle in a strangely familiar, enjoyable way. Even so, I distrusted its invitations to relax and forget my quest, though my sense of wonderment was so strong that I could well have paused in my search and spend the next few weeks, perhaps forever, wandering on this bizarre and austere landscape of lofty faces.

I avoided the mouths of the carved heads, for there the steam was very heavy, but even so I found myself growing more dizzy, until eventually I had to grope to the chiseled base of one of the monoliths and rest my head against the rough surface as I sat on the ground and tried to recover the strength of will to go on.

But something took place there on that plateau which even today I believe I am not fully aware of; it seemed that I must have lost consciousness for some time, for when I was again aware of my environment, the sun was shining in the west and declining fast. The fantastic guardians of the plateau stood with their features veiled in shadow.

I rose up, conscious that my state had been one of dreaming, though not of sleep. It seemed that a continually dreaming part of me had become real for a while, and though I could not remember what had transpired, it seemed that some strange knowledge was locked somewhere inside my head. Certainly, with the mists gone and the stupendous mouths now empty of their thick vapour, I felt more confident than I had been since I had let my horse have his freedom at the base of that immense plateau; and a determination to go on that seemed more insistent even than the original curiosity that had started me on this search, now drove my body forward. All tiredness had vanished, and, though I hardly tried to define what made me move across the plateau with such surety and precision, it was as if something tugged at my mind and suggested the way I should go.

I did not notice when the sense of being watched had disappeared, but the feeling of being threatened did not exist at that time, and did not occur again until I was a long way away from the Plateau of Faces and striding onward towards the area, some five miles from the Plateau, where my map indicated that a crossing could be made. I doubted very much whether a bridge which had been used so long ago would still be in existence; for the proportion of people crossing that bridge would have been larger in the past, and it may have fallen into disrepair through lack of current use. But I was determined if necessary to find a way to span the high valley if there were no bridge.

But I found the crossing-place, intact, on the following day. The bridge was flung across a narrow deep chasm where the rock walls of the sharp-cut valley of the Ruba's western tributary came together more closely than at any other point. It was a safe enough looking bridge, built of hardwood logs sawed in half; flat side upward, which lashed tightly together with twisted hempen rope. But the ropes were old and joined in places, and the bamboo handrails were half-rotten, and the bridge had not been built to sustain the shocks that it received that day.

All morning as I travelled I had sensed, rather than seen, a strange flitting shadow or shape, bulky in size but moving very swiftly, darting about the landscape with its concealing boulders; and though I had never seen enough to determine whether it was a man or some other creature, I had felt the same awareness of being watched, and what was more, that my strange, unwelcome companion was selecting a place for confrontation; so that, when I had already started out on the bridge and saw my opponent ahead near the other side, waiting for me on the narrow way, his huge spear resting on the waist-high bamboo rails and his shield held before his body, I was prepared for battle, though not for the sight of my foe.

This was a great monster of a man, a bull-necked being with massive shoulders and brutally thick legs and arms. His fingers were large and stubby, like short bananas. At first I thought that he wore an upper garment of the skin of the wild black goats, and then I gasped astoundedly, for I saw that actually his chest, shoulders and back were covered with straight wiry hair. His head was completely hairless, however, and evidently had been cleft in places at former times and battles, for ugly scars ran across his cranium and down the unsightly furrows of his forehead. Broad copper bracelets bristling with spikes ran from his forearms to his wrists; goatskin boots were on his feet, and a rough woven cloth covered his waist and genitals. His left leg bulged horribly at one place, as if it had been broken and had joined again badly, but this weird deformity in no way subtracted from the swiftness with which he moved, and all in all, his terrible efficiency as a fighting man dismayed me mightily, so that I stopped immediately, unslung my bow and reached for my arrows, then waited, for I heard his repellent voice.

"You are going to die here!" I barely made out his words, for the dialect he spoke was only faintly like that of Ainchan, and his accent was different from any I had heard before. But his tone and message were clear and needed no words to emphasize his intention, and immediately I place an arrow in position and half-stretched my bow.

"I am on a journey. I have no quarrel with you, man of the Plateau."

"You cannot pass here. I have killed many of you who came to spy, man of the Plain."

"I am no spy."

"All of my victims have said those words. All men of the Plain are spies and slaves of the foreigners. They spare your lives for information about the mountains of the north."

"Truly I thought they knew the north well. Did they not pass through here on their way to the Plain, and did they not scatter your ancestors and turn them into nomads?"

"I and my ancestors will be revenged of you, man of the Plain."

For an answer I raised my bow and drew my arrow, so rapidly that I was sure I would have flighted my arrow before he raised his clumsy copper shield, but with a disconcerting snap my bowstring broke, flapping sharply back and almost destroying my ear. The pain was intense and tears came to my eyes, as against the background of my own suffering I recognized the raucous insane laughter that I had heard once before while climbing the Plateau of Faces.

"You are no warrior, young fool of the cities. You will be easy to kill." The bridge shook underfoot as he lunged forward. "Come out here and meet me," he snarled, and his eyes, narrow and red with a perverse excitement and fury, gleamed in their puffy sockets as he leveled his awesome spear and stood waiting. "Do you want to continue your journey? Then kill Miskrado, and go!"

So this was Miskrado, a man of many names and fearful references—the Wolfer of Children, Companion of Demons, the Abomination of the Hills and the Scourge of the Northern Ruba, a man who had been rumoured to be killed by Ainchans, and Dominauts alike, whom some of us as children in Ainchan had felt never existed, but whom we feared when our parents threatened to call him to assure our good behavior. His name had become a collective synonym for the most ruthless depravations of the distressingly wild northern people, who had reverted to savagery since the coming of the Dominauts. The invaders had wrecked their hillside cities and the precious mountain roads that were their lifelines, so as to ruin their civilization, when it was certainly known that the hill-people could never be subdued; and the marauding remnants of these people, dreadest of whom was this giant Miskrado, had taken to the hopeless killing and robbing of all the hapless travelers they encountered. Now, whether he vanquished me or not, I could not afford to let my bag fall into his hands, for above all it contained the likely location of the place where many of the treasures of

Old Ainchan had been stored. I felt I carried something even more precious than my life.

I knew now that all conversation had been pointless; Miskrado was relentless, and I would need all my energy to combat this foe. Let it be clear, however, that I did not intend to engage in fighting if I could avoid it; if I could have gotten past where he stood, I would have fled and outrun this experienced butcher of people.

Yet I had confidence in my long spike of sharp byotta-wood, for I had practised the use of the spear quite frequently as a youth of Ainchan, and was counted with the best of the young spearmen. I came forward, then, recovered from my pain and with some boldness, especially since I saw that his legs were bare and badly defended.

"You are ready, my spearman?" Miskrado said, as I came close. "Then die!" and he thrust violently at my chest.

I turned desperately and felt the heavy wood of the shaft pass by my upper body; once past his spearhead I drove strenuously with my own, but the point hit and grooved his shield and did not harm.

Now the warrior gripped the end of his shaft and swung it mightily with both hands, so that it whacked heavily against the bamboo rail where I was standing, and I jumped backwards as the rail cracked and splintered. The bridge shuddered with the blow; another swipe came which I desperately, ducked; and the explosion of the bamboo rail on the other side told me of my great peril, for I was now standing there on the narrow way with only the lashed tree-trunks below me, and nothing to cling to.

As Miskrado thrust again I attempted a parry, and with a grunt and a laugh he lifted my spear from my hand and whirled it out over the valley where it fell and turned, blowing like a straw in the great wind that whistled around us and down through the high gorge.

"Now, man of the Plain, use your sword!" the giant roared, and swung his huge spear as easily as a twig. The shaft whacked down as I jumped forward and sideways, barely remaining on the swaying wood, and as I drew my shortsword from its sheath and leapt again, hoping to catch him in the throat, his deformed leg shot out and stamped me backward against a section of rail which cracked and hung over the giddy expanse below while I tottered and fell, barely managing to save myself by gripping the lashed ropes that made the footwalk.

Miskrado leaned over and raised his spear. "Die, man of the Plain!" he thundered once more, and the spear, six feet above my head, had already started descending when the wood broke under him and he fell on the other side of the bridge, so that we faced each other, kicking violently, suspended only by our holds.

I managed to hook my left arm around the tangled ropes and loosening wood, and with my free right arm which still held the sword, I struck furiously at his fingers and hands, but from my position they were just out of reach.

"You see, we will die together, carrion-eater!" I yelled.

"You will not see me die—you will go first!" Miskrado snarled, hugely shaking the bridge as he tried to scramble up.

With a creak and a snap the bridge broke then, and I heard the madman's hoarse shout as he swung away from me, down toward the side of the valley I had just left. His section of bridge was shorter than my own and he hit first, smashing against the sheer rock wall on that side. I saw his body fall clear and turn slowly as it plummeted its way down to the violent torrent below; then I covered my head with my arms, wrapped my legs tight, and crashed heavily through the harsh twigs and leaves of the scrubby bush that clung to the rocks on the farther side.

I was bruised badly by the blow, and so shaken and dazed that I would have fallen had I not been tangled in the bridge much more completely than if I myself had arranged it to save my life. I dangled there, a mass of pain and bewilderment, and from several places on my body blood was soaking through my clothes from gouges, cuts and scratches, while my left leg was throbbing with a strange muscular paralysis.

I hung there for a long while, recovering, and trying not to look down, I breathed deeply, trying to alleviate the recurring surges of hurt, and did not move except to check that my precious backpack was safe, and to sheath my sword, which fortunately had been driven deep into the wood of the bridge and thus was saved from falling.

When the broken end of bridge stopped swinging, I was suspended perhaps three feet away from the sheer cliff face. The cliff rose above my head for a long way, and my heart sank when I saw the distance that I would have to climb.

Then as I looked up, I was amazed to see the sandaled feet of a man descending; now the whole figure appeared, hanging by a rope which this individual had wrapped tightly around himself. Foot by foot he eased himself down, gripping the wrecked bridge with one hand; then he let fall a length of rope to the spot where I was, and shouted down to me in the same old dialect I had heard Miskrado speak.

"Do not fear; I will have you up from there shortly." He said it calmly, and with such confidence that hope became strong within me and I reached out for the rope and knotted it, making a loop that went under my arms.

"Good," the strange man said. "Keep as steady as you can manage to, and try to climb, or at least keep your feet towards the rock as I draw you up." And he clambered upward again.

"I am in pain, my friend," I shouted up after him. "My left leg is in no condition."

"Bend it slowly, move it, make it work. It is not broken. You are going to live; if you were as your opponent is, you would not complain of pain!"

As he spoke I felt the rope tighten, then my body was pulled upward, myself endeavouring to keep my bruised frame away from the forbidding rock-wall as it slide past, foot after foot.

Thus I was taken up from the broken bridge, and eventually I lay in the shade of a boulder on the eastward side of the chasm. I scrutinized my rescuer at once, trying to learn without asking questions that he would think unnecessary.

He seemed to be a traveller too, for he carried two large leather bags on either side of a stout staff. He was dressed in the traditional tunic of the plainspeople, but this one had long sleeves instead of short, and dropped freely to halfway down his thighs; he had no belt around his waist. When he sat, I glimpsed a loin-cloth he was wearing; except for his goatskin sandals, this was all his dress. His hair was thick and matted, hanging in natural locks down to his shoulders, and its colours ranged from black to brown to grey. His body was very thin, so that all his bones and muscles stood out clearly when he moved, and his skin was of a strange quality, like very light leather. He was a very strong man and it was difficult for me to guess his age, but I thought perhaps he was sixty years old.

Now he took a small earthenware pot from one of his bundles, and made a small fire, boiling some water which he poured from a flask of skin. In this water he put leaves, twigs and bits of bark, and strange dried herbs the names of which I could but guess.

He took some of these herbs from his bags and some from the almost bare rocks on which we were; and he pounded them all together with a little wooden pestle, making a greenish paste. Then he approached me with this steaming hot mixture, and asked that I swallow some of it, as well as allow him to lay it on my wounds. Accordingly I took a mouthful of the burning stuff, then took off my own tunic and leg coverings and let him anoint my injuries. The pains from the burning cuts were alleviated almost immediately, and the queer mixture I had swallowed soothed my mind, so that I fell asleep before he had finished scrubbing his pot and pestle.

When I awoke again night had fallen. The man sat before a small fire, backing me, staring out past the flames into the dark. I lay still, hoping to observe him before he knew I was awake, but it was if he was aware of my waking from the time I had opened my eyes. Now he changed his position so that he sat on the opposite side of the fire, turned toward me, and his peculiar eyes, which I now noticed for the first time, stared intently at me, lit by the firelight.

"You are travelling north . . . ." he asked, or rather stated.

"Yes"

"I am travelling north also, so I can accompany you."

"Thank you. But you have done much already. I am a sick man, and would delay you. Do not think further of me; I have all the time in the world.

"An interesting conception," he said, and at first I did not realize what he was speaking about. "But you cannot survive travelling alone." He smiled strangely. "Not even when you are in the best of health. This is very rough country, where few dare to travel alone; there are many murderous brigands like the one who attacked you today, and you do not know how to fight."

"You saw the whole event?"

"Yes."

"So what? You thought it unfair to intervene?"

"No. I could not reach the spot any more quickly than I did."

"I see. Thus you saw that I did as best as I could."

"I saw that you handled your weapons badly. You will have to learn to fight."

I wondered what exactly he meant, and if he could fight, but did not ask.

"I can fight well," he said. "It is part of my discipline. A man is not complete unless he can protect his physical body. Knowing the methods of protecting yourself from human and animal attack, as well as from the elements, will serve you well in this terrain. You cannot just rely on youthful strength to win your battles—for your attacker was much stronger than you were. Nor can you depend on flight, for there are times when no flight is possible, or your enemy may be able to run faster. Nor can you depend on weapons, for they are secondary, though they are useful instruments. You have to depend on your own body and mind, your own capabilities, as weapons; and in this matter of protecting yourself, your mind is as important as your body, always remember that.

"You broke your bowstring because you concentrated on hitting your opponent as hard as possible. That is not the way of the warrior; accuracy is more important than strength, and if you had consciously aimed at his gullet, his armpit, at the place where his ribs divide, or at his eye, certainly you would not have concentrated on the force that broke your bow. The bow is but a tool. It is the arrowhead that hits where the eye and the hands you direct it, and you should always make sure, through practice, that you have a good chance to hit the spot that you select.

"As for the spear-you carry it much too high, and there is too much tension in your arms. Let your shoulders relax, and thrust from waist-high, pivoting on your spine as quickly as you can to get your body-weight behind it. In that way you can defend your legs much better. And the shaft and butt end of your spear are just as efficient as the head—as your opponent knew well. Also—can you throw stones?"

"No," I said, with some surprise.

"The stone had always been and always will be the best of weapons as long as one dwells on the earth. They are always around. Do not neglect the stone."

"Do you think I run so much danger? That encounter this morning was the first of its kind, either with man or beast. I have travelled many, many miles, from far down the plain, from Ainchan itself, and my goal cannot be very far now."

"Then I remembered my bags with panic, and looked around. "Where are my bags?" I cried, and felt sure he noticed the anxiety that flooded my mind.

"Over here. I kept them safe."

"You opened them?"

"No."

"Bring them closer." I got halfway up, but the pain in my leg made me pause.

"Don't move." He got up and brought the bags over; I took them, placed them for my pillow, and settled back again.

"You come from Ainchan? What is it like there?" my rescuer asked next.

"I thought you knew the city. You speak a language like ours."

"Or perhaps you speak a language like ours. The mountains were here before the plain was formed. But no, I have never been to the cities of the plain. I have gone as far south as Parcos, a fishing port down the river. I have spent my time in these hills and highlands." He spread his hands. "Does it matter if I do not know the cities? Well, do you know these mountains?"

"I comprehend your argument, and agree that it does not matter."

"Do the foreigners still brutalize the people in the same old way?"

"The Dominauts kill our people each day."

"Cannot the people escape to the mountains or foothills? Those areas are safe . . ."

"The people love the city; I cannot imagine their leaving it. Why do you advocate that they should run away, since you recommend fighting for me?"

"Well, it depends on what you hold dear, that is clear. But I would have preferred peace and quiet, and a life which is full of naturalness and meaning, to living in a place of oppression."

"Freedom may be more important than peace and quiet."

"I do not doubt. But I have freedom."

"You are not free as long as the foreigners are here. The people as a whole must be free."

"Most people can be free," the stranger murmured. "Many people are afraid to be free, surprisingly. Others have freedom, but do not realize it. Some do not know what freedom means, and some suspect even the feeling of freedom. I think sometimes the only freedom is personal freedom; and that is what I would fight to maintain; nothing else."

"You are a singular man."

"Each man is singular."

I was at a loss for words, and lay back again. A slight headache was tugging at the outskirts of my mind, and I felt like sleeping.

"But the Dominauts will go," my companion said. "They will not last forever."

"I do not know of those particular people except by hearsay and my familiarity with the old legends of the conquest; but I know of cities and people, especially of people. You may think it a strange kind of behavior, and I might think it so too, but that behavior is not uncommon among people who have conquered and are satiated with simple violence. Long before the Dominauts there were people who would have done the same."

"I have studied the history of the Ainchan plain," I said. "It has never happened that a ruler claimed divinity."

"Well, perhaps I am wrong. Perhaps you should think about it more, too. I see that you are wise and given to thinking. You must share your thoughts with me as we travel; tell me about the cities of the plain as we go northward, and I will teach you how to fight."

"You'll stay until I am recovered and fit for travelling?"

"It is necessary."

"So be it. I thank you." I mumbled, and closed my eyes.

Thus I slept and woke, ate and convalescesed, for one week, and my soreness went away. My leg slowly regained its function and my cuts and bruises were healing rapidly.

Each day I listened to the instructions my new-found benefactor poured into my consciousness, and watched him as he demonstrated, with amazing prowess, the techniques of attack and defence. He demonstrated barehanded combat as well as techniques of spear, sword and stone; but his favorite weapon was his staff; and it was an experience to see how it came alive in his hands, twirling in smooth flows from back to front, carving a humming circle of air about him, thrusting, dipping and striking, so that it was difficult to tell whether the man moved the staff or the staff moved the man. However fast he moved, however long, his breath was always even when he finished, and throughout all his actions he kept up a monologue.

"Use the staff equally well in either hand. Do not grip it tightly, and be prepared to let it go. Remember it is only an extension of your arms; your arms are the real, permanent weapons, your body is the real tool you will see. Keep your mind clear and relaxed, and practice often. Be aware that the straight blow is more direct and surprising than the swung blow . . . keep all your blows direct if possible with fists, feet, spear or sword.

Select specific targets on the body and aim at them; spots where your least effort will render the maximum amount of pain. Guard those same points on your body which you practice attacking on others'. For every attack there is a defence, for every defence there is an attack. To block the blow is good, to parry better, to avoid the blow better yet; to strike a counterblow at the same time your opponent attacks is best of all . . . when you are free to attack, attack and do not stop until you are sure he cannot injure you . . ." and so his instruction went on, day after day.

Soon I was fit enough to go into training with him and regularly as we travelled upcountry, slowly at first because of my partial recovery, we staged strenuous fights that explored our ingenuity and physical skill to the full. Though he was aged he was very fast and had great stamina, and I was hard put at first to stand up his attacks.

And so we journeyed up the highlands, parallel to the deep river valley, he teaching me the science of war, and I telling him, especially at nights, about the cities of the plain and their situation under the Dominaut system. I even made a geographical chart which showed the two rivers of the plain and the approximate locations of the seven cities.

I would have liked to know more about this man as we travelled, but I had grown afraid to ask. There was something that stopped such questions, and partly it lay in his face.

For days I had wondered who it was that he resembled; but no name, rather a quality, kept coming into my mind. It was something primal, eternal, and untrammeled by any particular day and age. It was the naturalness of this man which was his most fascinating attribute.

But it was not this that made me keep my questioning urges still. It was something much more astonishing and incredible than that—for this man's face resembled strongly all of those stylized, awesomely large faces of stone that I had encountered on the monstrous plateau on the other side of the chasm. I noticed this weird and starling likeness one night as we sat before the campfire; and I did not dare to voice the preposterous questions that leapt into my mind.

Further—and this seemed even more baffling to me—he seemed to know, or at least to guess very well, what I was thinking. He seemed to be disguising this ability, but more than once he raised a subject that I had thought of, but was sure I had not mentioned. I tried not to believe that he had this power, but the fact seemed sure. This made me fear for my precious scrolls, for certainly I thought of them every day; but he never appeared to have much regard for my bags or their contents.

Our journey and exchange of knowledge continued, and it did not take long for my full health to return. When I was better, I demonstrated the fighting techniques he had taught me, and was gratified to hear him say, from the rock where he sat watching, that I now seemed capable of survival on my own.

Finally we came to a bleak hilly area which led up to the broken, piled summits and interlocked ravines of what we in Ainchan called the Forbidden Mountains. These Arabic uplands with their gulfs, terraces and barren abysses looked inaccessible indeed, and as we stood at the beginning of this new country I was glad that I had a companion. But this gladness soon dissipated, for my friend indicated that here was where we parted.

"I am going eastward from this point onward," he said, "I wish you a safe journey and blessings all the way. From this point on, you may meet only mountaineers and other wild adventurers; and there are also numerous large baboons which travel in groups of hundreds, and sometimes they attack if they are provoked or panicky. Be careful, their teeth are very long."

"Where are you going?" I enquired anxiously, looking at the way he indicated; for there seemed to be nothing there except sheer crags and sterile lumps of lava.

"To my home," he said with a smile. "And where are you going?"

I hesitated. There was no doubt that he would have been interested in my maps and scrolls, but the habit of silences about my quest had grown strong within me, and besides, I did not know what to make of his uncommon face, the features of which I had never seen except on those chiseled blocks of stone that gazed loftily toward the rising sun on the plateau of my strange dreaming.

"I am not travelling for adventure or in lightness of heart," I said.

"This I know."

"I am on a quest of rare significance. There is one thing I want you to tell me before I go on. Can you tell me, do you know, of a cavern in these hills, an ancient place where the old religion of Ainchan is still practised? I am looking for a hermit-priest of the old religion, who is said to be descended in a direct line from a priest of one of the religious orders of old, the one which first established the hermitages and training schools of Ainchan."

Now the stranger paused for a while, eyeing me, and I sense that he wondered why I had not disclosed this to him before.

"You did not trust me, for you could have told me this while we were travelling."

"I trust you now, my friend. Will you tell me? Do you know?"

"Yes. I know the place well. The temple which you seek is very close. I can take you there, and I am very interested to hear why you have come; for I am the man you seek. My name is Akincyde, the priest of the true Ainchan religion, and I am happy that you have found me."

5
THE
CAVERN-
TEMPLE
OF THE
FORBIDDEN
MOUNTAINS

The Cavern-Temple of the Forbidden Mountains

T HE MOUNTAIN CAVERN WHICH Shangodoon was to make his dwelling-place for the next three years while he sought for enlightenment under the guidance of Akincyde the hermit was a truly breathtaking sight during that far-off time. I, Godnor, have been there on three occasions, for in my youth I did much travelling and historical research in the North Country; and each time I came away with a sense of wonderment and humility at the work of nature and man.

The region is wide and rocky, as Shangodoon described so accurately in his oration to the people of liberated Ainchan. The great flight of steps, carved out of the rock in some places, mortared and cemented in others, which Akincyde and Shangodoon ascended to the cavern, are still there. They go up, endlessly, it seems, until they reach a narrow, horizontal entry into the rock, a simple-looking crack perhaps nine feet high. The rock walls are some fifteen feet thick, so that one walks through a short tunnel; then the crack opens suddenly, enormously yawning into a fabulously wide and high area.

Great rectangular, vertical slabs of granite, some fifty feet high, some higher, all lost in the darkness that filled the upper reaches of that great cavity, supported a roof of wedged, angular blocks and slabs. Some primeval mountainslide, pouring these monstrous blocks down the knobby headlands of a long-dry river valley, had stuck these slabs upright and neatly capped them with a roof of stratified and slivered igneous rock, each fragment tons in weight. A side of one large overturned hill seemed supported from below by the great natural columns underneath; and this cavern stretched more than a mile deep into the earth, running in a rocky zigzag down to the bed of a tributary of the Ruba. There were parts of this stupendous mazed cavern that Akincyde had never seen.

The colonnades in the huge First Cavern, as one frontal area was called, were all carved and painted with very old pictures, so old that they were already ancient by the time the cities of the Ainchan Plain were being formed. These pictures depicted many varied scenes in the life of people whom Shangodoon and Akincyde did not know; but there were drawings of huts, men, women, children and animals; representations of various trades, occupations and institutions of a culture. It showed the ploughs wheels and irrigation-devices used by these people, as well as the large windmills and deep wells. These paintings were of earth-colours mixed with oil and various hardening agents; there were reds, yellows, browns, blacks and even blues and purples. Each scene was depicted in a separate panel, and the size of these panels varied; some were flat, and some chiseled into low-relief.

Here there were hunters with bows and arrows, spears, clubs, slings, curved throwing-sticks and blowpipes, hunting a variety of beasts, some of them strange to both Akincyde and Shangodoon; there were baboons, deer, long-horned antelopes, snakes, skyleaping squirrel-monkeys, goats, sheep and oxen, some depicted in corals; wild horses, many species of birds including parrots and strange big-bodied flightless runners, and there was the elephant, the tiger, leopard and lion, the hippopotamus and an old long-necked beast which Shangodoon recognized as one of the half-doubted creatures that his grandfather described to him during his childhood days.

The eons-old paintings that tattooed these columns, and much of the accessible wall-space in that strange shelter, were only one evidence of ancient people having been there. Many many tribes of humans had used this place. The more recent objects there brought by the banished priests and fleeing exiles of conquered Ainchan, were hundreds of years old by the time of Shangodoon; the most ancient artifacts, sharp stone knives and axes, were of awesome age. Then there were items from all the ages between.

There were clay tablets, the largest two feet by three, with old hieroglyphs; old masks of hardened immaculately preserved wood inlaid with beaten gold or silver, with jeweled openings for eyes and mouth; ironwood boxes with craftily inlaid decorations and handles of studded ivory; piles of oiled leather sheets with ancient characters burned on; strange tripods with copper bowls and wooden tongs encased in copper; glass and baked-clay bottles for medicines; rugs of fur; shawls of woven, tapestried cotton and other brightly dyed clothes; leather bags and pouches with unknown, branded figures, and musty, desiccated contents; small and large sculptures of people, animals and even buildings, in hardwood, stone, ivory, jade, baked-clay and various metals, many elaborately ornamented, all carved and moulded with exquisite taste and skill; crystal balls and strange boards with mirrors and receptacles for candles; fortune tellers' equipment that called up visions of bearded astrologers and strangely-gifted magicians; bone dice inlaid with glittering quartzes; great slabs of incised marble; hangings of dyed, treated hide; iron chests with massive locks, the keys of which rusted within their holes; strong curved swords and light straight spears; many more weapons some of which Akincyde scarcely knew, many with rich jewels inlaid in elaborately worked handles; bars of gold and silver, silver serving trays and medallions for hanging on walls, and countless forks, bowls, drinking vessels, knives and plates. Many of the items I describe are now in the National Archives of Ainchan, and after twenty-five years of research into their origins and history, my work is not yet complete. Indeed, the great temple-cavern of the north is the single most important and educationally profitable area that we Ainchan historians and archaeologists know. It is lucky that the continuum of history has preserved such a place undisturbed over the many many centuries, and that the wise guardians of our religion, such as Akincyde, were men who loved to research the old traditions.

I regret the nowadays, even although travel is much easier, there are few people who have been to this fantastic cave. The place where the bridge once stretched, where the young man met with Miskrado, now has modern electromagnetic passenger cars which travel on lines across the chasm, and there is now a passable road that goes up to the Plateau of Faces. No one may travel on the Plateau without a guide; and while a few of the milder Faces are used as health-giving and rejuvenating spas, the more austere which lie toward the centre of the Plateau are still used for their original purposes.

At my own initiation into the Arcane Wisdom of the Ainchan Philosophers, I spent the required three days and nights on that Plateau, and while I cannot divulge the events of the experience that I had, I can say with infallible certainty that Shangodoon, in his unprepared state, was a human being of great strength of will. It takes strong fibre indeed to unwittingly come upon that place, traverse it, and still retain a sense of self and purpose. Even today little is known of the properties of that steam and its effect on human behavior, and our major scientists are spending much time in trying to ascertain these things.

Most of the faces were already old and weathered by the time of the Dominauts, and the most recent ones were at least three hundred years old at the time of Shangodoon. It was Akincyde who told Shangodoon the purpose of them, as he had found out. They represented many, though not all, of the great prophets, high priests and seers, those who had received what Akincyde called the Ultimate Enlightenment, who had dwelt in the Mountains, the Plateau and the Plain throughout the times of the Early Ages. Akincyde also said that people thought that a person who dwelt in a particular mouth of steam for any length of time, took on the qualities of the prophet or seer that the carved rock represented; but I for one have never given any credence to this, believing the effects of those heads to be more or less identical, though, as I have shown, some faces are more effective than others.

We will never know all that Shangodoon and Akincyde were engaged in for the next three years. One wonders exactly what facts Shangodoon learnt, and how his development came about. Shangodoon did say that those three years, in the mountains made the difference of several lifetimes, and that he felt new levels of being as his understanding of the world and of himself grew. But we learn of his acquirements and sense of values only as they are mentioned, of necessity, in his narrative.

We know that he continued the study of the history of the Ainchans, a subject which fascinated him always. He learnt the oldest forms of the Ainchan language, and Akincyde and himself managed to translate some of the hieroglyphic tablets, though comparatively few. The oldest leather scrolls which he had found in the abandoned, hidden temple in Ainchan, corresponded to and corroborated writings on similar surfaces which Akincyde had in his cavern; and the later ones, those made as a record before and during the invasions of the Dominauts, made very fascinating reading. Some of these were written by the old priests whose names and deeds Akincyde was familiar with. Many listed the goods that the priests had stored; everyday items of food and clothing as well as vast amounts of precious items in rare metals, and exquisite household articles and jewellery which the hopeless people had given to their trusted religious leaders for safekeeping.

There are still many thousands of the extremely old baked-clay tablets in the cavern to this day. Many are also in the National Archives, and I myself have read and handled many of them, though, like Shangodoon, I can only hope to have the time to decipher a small proportion of them. What knowledge awaits our people! These tablets are of varying size, but of the same proportions; some are a quarter the size of others. They are the oldest writings known to us, for these are the valuable historical and medical treatises preserved by some ancient powerful order of rulers, historians or priests for many thousands of years. Some of these tablets are so old that it is evident that they have been buried, lost and found on more than one occasion, and some even refer to the discovery of other tablets, so that the story of the Early Ages is still an irritating bafflement to many, and an enjoyable puzzle to others.

The people of the Early Ages pondered questions about man and his destiny to an extent only now being realized by us today. Shangodoon was to learn and practice laws of human nature that few of his contemporaries could have known. These most profound writings were uncannily correct in what they said, and Shangodoon knew them to be true because of the many experiments that Akincyde and himself carried out, based on the information gleaned from them. There were facts about breathing, the nervous system, the mechanism of the soul's entering and leaving the body, and essays on the seasons and their effects on birds, plants and animals, which supplemented the already vast knowledge of Akincyde.

The two searchers studied the stars and their movements, and Shangodoon learnt to read the signs of the sky so accurately that day or night he could travel with confidence and no fear of losing his way. He knew so many trees and bushes that he was safe from starvation too; in his later journeys such knowledge was to become of practical importance from time to time.

Akincyde and Shangodoon came across many weird legends; many wonderful tales of past heroes and mighty deeds, of historical, geographical and cultural changes through the long centuries of existence of the Ainchan people.

Some of the maps were stranger still than the tales that were told, for there were some of the unguessed-at origin, which showed all the areas of the world and of the sun-systems beyond ours—an extremely curious and unsettling fact, for it means that we have lost much more knowledge than we thought. Only recently have our modern scientists developed optical instruments that show these ancient maps of the stars to be absolutely accurate. Thus we have to take into account the origin-stories that are recorded; treatises on the origin of the world, of man, and language. There are recorded Principles of Art and Religion that have now become the source of much study in our training schools; and many of our modern institutions are based on the very old ideas expressed on these smooth-baked surfaces.

As Shangodoon spoke to vast multitudes of liberated Ainchan on that great historic day when King Chrazius III and the Dominaut regime collapsed, he tried to explain many of the old Principles of Life to the people. But the people were just out of a physical and mental slavery of many centuries, and much of what he said was misunderstood. We know this because of the distortions that have come down to us; there are many versions of Shangodoon's stay with Akincyde.

Some histories say that Akincyde and Shangodoon spent much time in medical work among the often-injured mountain people; others say that Shangodoon was but a servant of Akincyde, and spend most of his time digging at a small pocket of soil where he grew vegetables for them both. At one point Shangodoon himself says that Akincyde was often in states where there could be no physical communication; for days he would sit in a mystic, indifferently smiling trance, and often did not seem to realize that Shangodoon was present. At other times he would disappear for several days or weeks, leaving Shangodoon alone with his researches and his own physical and mystic exercises. For Shangodoon learnt well and quickly, driven by the search for a core of understanding within himself, and he did not fear states and experiences that had deterred many other of Akincyde's former disciples.

Sometimes Akincyde would disappear into the depths of the cavern through some bizarre crevice or tunnel, and Shangodoon would never be sure when he would return. Often, after a period of silence of minutes, hours or days, the priest would take up a subject exactly where he left off speaking, as if only a few seconds had elapsed. Sometimes he seemed to *remember* in *advance;* for instance, sometimes he thought he had conversed with someone who had not yet visited him; soon such a person would arrive, and he would realize that it

117

was a premonition he had experienced, and not a memory. He seemed to accept that Shangodoon had always been there in the cavern with him, and sometimes was warm and friendly, laughing in simple, childish pleasure, sometimes austere and inscrutable; truly, he seemed several men at once. What struck Shangodoon as odd at first, but soon became an accustomed thing after he knew the potential of the mind, was the fact that often he would strongly sense the presence of Akincyde even although he knew him to be away at the same time.

The history of Shangodoon's sojourn with Akincyde has so many versions and interpretations, as I have indicated, and so many people have differing opinions as to what was thought and practised, that perhaps it would be well for me to lay out, for the benefit of scholars and laymen alike, two main areas of continual interest and research to the two men. The first is to do with the society of the Early-Age people of the Ainchanlands; I will try to define the fundamental principles that underlay all the physical expressions of the culture. The second is to do with the Mystical Tradition that Akincyde revealed to Shangodoon—a method of learning to flow with the evolving order of things.

One: *The Basis of Early-Age Culture*

The Early-Age people have written that all existence has some infinite beginning at the same source; all things visible and invisible relate to one central point. This central point, expanded, takes the form of a circle or sphere, and in this circle or sphere there are two opposing forces. One force seeks to push the borders of the figure outward, the other seeks to pull them inward. The continuous tension created makes the sphere or circle revolve; good and evil, visible and invisible, and all opposites, are thus created and resolved. This interplay of forces occurs in all existences.

At the centre of this figure there is a vacuum created by the movement of the opposing forces; or perhaps the vacuum was there first, and caused the opposing forces to come into play. This central vacuum is one of complete and eternal tranquility.

The ancient tablets do not go beyond to enquire into the origins of these two forces, the vacuum and the circular movement; they assume that they have always been in manifestation. This is the essence of being, and all things conform to it; in Early-Age philosophy, this is the shape of Truth.

The Early-Age people felt that the ideal man and woman represented Truth fully; therefore an ideal person would be viewed as a perfectly harmonious unit. It followed that since every person ideally was harmonious, all persons should function together at one with each other and with the Universe. Just as each of us is composed of little cells, each carrying a pattern of ourselves and yet making a body, so all the planets, solar systems and universes are part of one thing whose infinite parts all carry the same pattern. All things—animals, birds, fish, plants, earth and man—were felt to be part of one intelligent being.

Thus everything represented an aspect of the circle or sphere and its forces; all things were supposed to harmonize.

119

Disharmony and disruption were proof that something was out of balance.

Society was supposed to function in harmony with the natural environment. The way of life of the Early Age people, then, essentially was concerned with taking part in, maintaining and restoring the harmony of nature; and all their ceremonies were a result of this view of life.

A person was said to consist of a body and a spirit. It was the spirit which guided the body, and while all spirits were thought of as being good originally, it was possible for bad spirits to exist through their own systematic practice of disharmony and evil.

It was felt that the spirits of person's ancestors maintained relationships with him. If the relationships were good, the spirits gave the person more force; if bad, they ignored or even injured him.

The main aim of medical practice was to restore harmony to the body by adjusting it to nature's flow. The Early-Age people were very familiar with trees, herbs, shrubs and mosses, and made medicines from these. Such growths also had a spiritual healing quality, and the priests and medicine-makers tried to combine the spiritual nature of the plant with its physical healing properties.

It assumed that men could live indefinitely if they knew how to be moderate—how to maintain a balance between all the forces that affected their body and spirit.

Administration of justice was concerned, not so much in punishing the individual who committed a crime, but more in restoring a balance and harmony to the society after an individual had disrupted it. All crime and was sin, for this was a completely religious society, and all sin was an injury to the whole community. A man who constantly did evil would be regarded as a disease in the society.

There were diviners, and people who sought to manipulate the invisible forces of nature to influence the planting and harvesting of crops; ceremonies for marriage, childbirth, puberty, drought and rainfall.

There were many clans, and marriages took place between clans. A young man would build a house and invite a young woman to enter it; if she did, and agreed to spend a night of sleep and lovemaking there, then the next morning people gathered before their door with laughter, presents, wreaths of flowers and banquets; this was their form of marriage.

I have searched many records for evidence that there were kings among the people of the Early Age; but there are only queens, and I am certain that the society was ruled through the mother's descent-line. In three cases at least, there is mention of a queen's husbands and their names, which suggests that the queen had the privilege of choosing more than one mate, though generally monogamy was maintained among the populace. The queen's eldest daughter inherited her right to rule. Yet, among the people the children were called by their father's names, and a man had the right to take his sons away from their mother and raise them separately if his wife proved promiscuous or otherwise morally unfit for motherhood. The women could do the same with their daughters, for the same reason; but they did so less frequently, it would seem.

What I have written here is by no means a complete survey, but I have outlined the fundamental world-view of the Early-Age people, and shown the basis of their cultural expressions.

Two: *The Mystical Tradition as revealed to Shangodoon by Akincyde*

Akincyde was quick to make Shangodoon aware that he was telling him no new fact about the universe; it was nothing he had made up. In all his years of spiritual struggle to achieve the mystical state of Oneness with the Absolute Entity, he had learnt to reduce his axioms and teachings to a simplicity. Each sentence he made was carefully chosen; each word had to be pondered over for additional clever meanings. He uttered profound truths in simple phrases.

It was ignorance, Akincyde said, that kept mankind from being one with the absolute Entity. Knowledge had been there before ignorance came about, for knowledge is positive and ignorance, negative. Therefore, at one time mankind was not ignorant. Once he had total knowledge and was at one with the Oneness; and now ignorant man desires passionately to re-link to a state he knew before. Re-ligion was re-linking; the function of the religion was to help one become an *intelligent* part of the Creator. The fact that man instinctively wants to re-link is proof that he has an endemic, racial memory of his former state.

Therefore man must try to remove ignorance, with knowledge—sometimes a difficult process, for units of ignorance take root and grow in the mind like trees upon earth. Knowledge makes ignorance wither and die. The question therefore is how to know.

Knowing is being completely sure about what is real. What is real is what is true. What we know to be most real is what is called the Universal Order of Things.

To flow with the Universal Order, you have to be aware that you are doing it. Doing it naturally, in ignorance, does not help. You must be aware of the flow of the Universal Order, and of your participation in the flow, as a swimmer consciously utilizes a current.

To flow, you have to be able to receive Truth. To receive Truth, you have to research a variety of opinions on a subject, and think for yourself. Therefore you have to learn to think for yourself; a very subtle process indeed, and not the same as ordinary thinking, which most likely is based on unresearched opinion or hearsay.

In any kind of thinking, it is best to relax the body totally. But to relax the body, one must tense it first; hence, one should practice exercises which involve twisting, bending and stretching. Then one must find a comfortable position and remain in it, either standing, sitting, kneeling or lying, but with the spine straight, and mind and body relaxed.

The breath should be evenly going in and out of your body, without force. Keep it steady; gradually you may still it to the point where you cannot feel it either going or coming out of your nostrils.

Your heartbeat will have increased to the point where it is jerking your whole body and is very noticeable and pleasant to feel. Note that it is connected to your breath and that by breathing you can control its rate of pulsation.

You develop a way of seeing yourself, which is, as a flow of thought and action. This leads to the state where you become, you may say, an act of imagination. This is freedom to be everything you know. Everything is connected at this deeper level. Intuitions will pulse to you on your heartbeat.

You flow with the pulsation of the wide life. You become the Intelligence behind transient things as often as you are in the correct state—and some people have achieved that state perpetually. It is a state that cannot be described, but only known.

Then—you would have learnt many, many profound truths, which will make living the everyday life so ridiculously simple that you will see that mankind's true self has nothing to do with mundanities. And yet the search for Truth will continue, and there will be ever more and more delights, for the sphere with its vacuum and forces is always expanding. What is Truth but a single, recurring, eternal pattern?

The study of the Early-Age culture and the discipline of the mystic training could have absorbed Shangodoon's total time quite easily; there is no limit to research and experiment in such matters. But we know that Akincyde, who did much healing work among the woodcutters and the mountain-people on the sheep-farming slopes, taught Shangodoon much about herbal medicines. There were visitors to the cavern; some who came to brag to the hermit and to question his reputed powers; earnest seekers who sought to benefit from his wisdom; fortune-hunters and herbal doctors; barren women, worried men, and once or twice, necromantic sorcerers of the worst intentions. Few of them ever managed to view the immense piles of treasured objects that were in the fabulous cavern, for they were ministered to in a bare, worn cave with a small woodfire hearth and beds of straw. Akincyde kept his medicines on hollowed-out shelves in this cave; and he did not allow the curious to venture into the main parts of the cavern or into any of the many branching caves to be encountered.

Shangodoon seems to have reached a high level of knowledge, experience and skill in his research, fighting techniques and mystical illumination, as is evidenced by some of his later activities, which he related while telling of his exploits. He also wrote, later, that he noticed subtle changes taking place in his nervous responses to situations, and a development of higher faculties; therefore he was aware that he was undergoing a process. But, as we shall see, his education was not complete, and his quest, was far from an end.

One day Akincyde showed him some documents that had been brought to the cavern by a group of priests of long ago. Shangodoon examined them closely. They were drawings in some kind of paint upon finely woven mats of hardened cane. These mats were heavily lacquered and placed in metal frames behind some transparent material. Shangodoon was amazed to find that these were copies of the design-prints of the Dominaut city-planners; the plans by which their buildings and fortifications were built. He visualized Ainchan; looked down upon the plan of the city, and saw how precisely this map coincided with the areas of the city he knew. There were the blocks of apartments which the Dominauts had built close to the factories; the armaments factory; the plans for the three bridges that were long built by this time, the plans for the large-scale prisoners' reservation, and the design and proportions for the king's palace.

This one proved to be of fundament importance; for over it was superimposed the plan of the Ainchan temple which had been burnt to the ground. The Dominauts had deliberately set up the king's palace over the high mound in the city where the central temple had rested; Chrazius I had publicly stated that this was his challenge to the religion of the people, and proof of his divinity and the power of Gnarl.

Shangodoon made a careful drawing of the plan of the Ainchan temple, and studied its construction. He noted that the temple had been built upon a small plug of volcanic rock that stuck up like a knuckle above the land, the only mound of its kind on the plain of sedimentary deposits. At the top of this rocky hill there was a natural pond or lake, a shallow depression of water that smelt of sulphur, in which the ascetics of old would bathe; and they claimed that the waters of this pool prolonged their lives.

The pool was still there; but now it had been made into the baths of King Chrazius III. The palace of the Dominaut tyrant was exactly over the once-sacred purification-spot.

Now Shangodoon lifted, dusted and examined the framed maps one by one, suddenly filled with excitement, for he had heard, from Akincyde as well as from his old friend, the patriarch of rebels and gruesome story-teller, that the great temple of Ainchan had had a secret escape route. There was supposed to be a way down and inside the tor of brimstone, under the city, and out into the eastern lands. Perhaps there was a plan, or even a description of it, for the knowledge indeed seemed precise and well researched . . . even as he thought this, he found what he sought.

This map—older and more worn than the others, indicating that many had pondered over it—showed, in cross-section, the plug of rock with its pool, and the limestone and smooth clay strata which made up most of the foundation of the Ainchan city. Just as Shangodoon had thought, there was the passage. There was depicted a long, well-like descent to a deep horizontal tunnel, then a graded climb that led out beyond the city walls eastward.

So disciplined was Shangodoon by this time that he thought immediately of the function he could put such knowledge to. Could the entrance into the city be found? Could he lead a group of rebels to it and show them how to get into the palace? Could he assassinate King Chrazius? he wondered, and his eyes gleamed strangely. Knowledge, he thought. What do you do with knowledge when you have it?

He sought out Akincyde and told him what he had found. But Akincyde was not interested as Shangodoon in the destruction of the Dominaut regime. He could not advise him about it, he said, complaining that Shangodoon should think

127

out his goals himself, and not try to employ other people's imagination to solve a problem his own mind had originated.

So Shangodoon pondered the potential of this new knowledge alone. The fact that there was a way in and out of the city that the oppressors did not know about, thrilled him immensely and urged him to action relentlessly; he felt he was wasting the knowledge.

For the next few days Akincyde was aware that Shangodoon's mind was on this problem. At last the priest spoke about it again:

"You have only found the physical weakness of your enemy. What about his psychological weakness? There must be a weak spot in his spiritual structure. Certainly that is why they want to be viewed as gods; they feel inferior to their servants in some way. Have you studied their ways well?"

"I know they have an extreme love for gold and other precious metal."

"That is nothing. All men love gold, whether they are good or evil."

"Certainly not to the same degree as the tyrants. However, I know the principle of their fireweapons too. I think I know many of their likes and dislikes, and I have found out what I could about their beliefs.

"Have you studied their laws?"

"Not well."

"Study their laws. The laws will tell you what they fear most. People in power pass laws against what they fear. Laws expose weaknesses."

"I will bear that in mind. You have great knowledge, Akincyde."

"Wisdom, not knowledge."

Shangodoon squinted and frowned, and Akincyde waited for him to ask some more.

"Well—what is the difference?"

"Knowledge depends on mind and memory. Wisdom depends on the maturity, purity and perfection of the individual. Wisdom is the ability to act practically and harmoniously with the flow of reality. A wise being acts upon principles; to flow harmoniously with Truth, you need to apply unfailing principles.

"As long as you apply principles, you can solve all problems, understand all natural laws, all studies, everything. You only have to know well how to apply the principles.

"To apply principles, you must be aware of them. To develop awareness, you have to concentrate the senses. Exercise sight, hearing, touch, smell and taste. That way, you will always remember principles.

"Finally: don't tell anyone anything you know, unless they ask and you can see that they are truly seeking. Silence is power."

"You have given me much meditation," Shangodoon affirmed.

"I am grateful to the Creator that you are a seeker and learner," Akincyde muttered kindly. "As I am."

There was a silence. It was night, and they sat on padded cushions of skin, a little apart, at the mouth of the crevice where the cavern began. A cool wind blew down the mountain, and the starlight was bright where it shone between the high black trees. Shangodoon breathed out softly, straightening his spine; felt the rush of energy-laden air as his diaphragm dropped, and felt the pound of blood in his head. He rocked contentedly, and thought of the principles of life, especially the recent one he had heard from Akincyde. *Laws expose weaknesses.*

Akincyde said, "There are some people at the place called Dibra, the river-mouth city which you indicated on your map." He was referring to the diagram Shangodoon had drawn to show him the positions of the seven cities. "I have heard that they know most about the foreigners. They have fought them more than once; they have looted their armouries and libraries. A man from Dibra, Sifar, whom I met ten years ago, said he had many proofs that the Dominauts could be and have been beaten in the past, by other peoples."

"I have heard rumours of other peoples, and the Dominauts even say that they have defeated others, but I do not know . . ."

Akincyde smiled. "This is a big, big world, as you will find out. I do not have to leave this mountain to know that there are many peoples whom you and I have never yet seen. Yes, he said that there were other peoples the Dominauts failed to conquer. He has proofs, he said."

"This Sifar—he lives at Dibra?"

"Yes—he said that he is one of the few free natives in Dibra. He is a potter. The Dominauts love the beautiful glazed vases he makes. They do not know of his past . . . he is a bloody man. He has killed some of them, he told me; likewise, they killed his wife and parents. He said that there are always riots in and around Dibra. He wanted me to pay him a visit there. It would have been a good chance to see the Plain, but I refused to go when I heard what it was like. He even told me how to find his place. You go down the street—he said there's only one street, running east to west—until you come in line with three tall thin peaks to the west, called the Three Fingers, and the lookout tower on the northwestern corner of the wall. If you stood facing the Three Fingers, you would be backing his pottery; a large place, he said. Have you ever heard directions like those?"

"Surprising, but they are easy to follow. I would like to see this man."

"I expect so." Akincyde paused for a while, and the silence was full of thoughts. Then: "When will you leave?"

"Thought and action should be the same," Shangodoon said, quoting the hermit's words.

Akincyde nodded and half-smiled. "You are applying wisdom. But first, there is something that we should do together. We should climb to the mouth of the Ruba and to the top of the Ruba mountain. It is the traditional trip the newly initiated priests of Old Ainchan used to make; you are one of them now. It will be a journey of endurance—five or six days of fasting, climbing, and descending. We are also going to find some sky-whisper for you to take to my friend Sifar."

"As you say, my preceptor. When will we start?"

"Tomorrow."

The peak of Mount Ruba lies some twelve miles from the cavern-temple. Even in the days of Shangodoon there was a thin path running for most of the way up, a path made by the few intrepid adventurers who trekked up the mountainside a good distance, but were reluctant to climb to the top. Shangodoon and Akincyde travelled six miles on the first day, using this path; the next day they travelled less than half the distance, for the mountain grew steeper and they had to hack their way through the vegetation. They reached the peak on the third day, after four miles' travel through thick scrub.

On the morning of the second day they had come to the source of the Ruba River. A giant waterfall leapt in a stiff stream from a tongue of lava rock beneath a huge vertical crack. The Ruba broke into the light of day with a tremendous roar and a bounteous cloud of spray, and rainbows shimmered amid its foggy atmospheres as it fell some six hundred feet before cascading down narrow interlocked valleys that were lined with hard trees.

The mountain was cold and very steep; clouds drifted around them most of the time. Rain fell, and the gaunt trees with their thick parasitic vines and mossy limbs dropped rivulets of water; roots threatened to trip them and rocks tried to break their ankles. Everything was green and white with the light of the trees and the clouds.

Finally they stood on the top of Mount Ruba, on the sharp edge of crater, and looked down into the wide tilted saucer of the crater-lake. Breathtakingly beautiful, the blue-green body of water lay perhaps a mile and a half away. When the sun came free of cloud and threw its light down the crater, the water lit up with a translucence that made the two men silent as they contemplated the sight.

Akincyde searched for the skywhisper flowers while Shangodoon stood and pondered deeply on the vast body of water. Every now and then thick clouds rolled up the mountainside, enveloped him and slid over the edge to the crater, rolling down to the lake and disappearing before they reached its surface.

Once as Shangoddon stood in a thick fog, so thick he could not see more than a foot or two ahead, he felt a sudden brush of wings and heard an angry squawk. A bird, screaming shrilly, battered with claws and beak at his face and flailing hands; he drove it off shouting, and nearly lost his footing. Akincyde was by his side in a second; he warned him to sit and not stand.

Shangodoon said "Its's nothing; only a bird. Perhaps it was just surprised to see a man so high up here."

"It was an omen," Akincyde said quickly.

"An omen of what?"

Akincyde spread is palms outward. "I do not know. I ask you think about it that way . . . Here are the flowers I have been looking for," he concluded, and showed Shangodoon a large bunch of tiny whitish flowers with yellow centres on long stalks of serrated leaves.

Shangodoon tried to be interested in the plants, but his mind was only half on them. He was thinking of his encounter with the bird. It might only have been his heightened state of consciousness, but the bird had looked and seemed unusual to him. Even in that brief second, what had amazed him and made his heart quicken its beat, was the fact that the bird's face and beak, though miniature, were highly reminiscent of those of Gnarl, the great symbol of the Dominauts.

———•◆•———

There are other experiences which took place on Mount Ruba, in those last days before Shangodoon left the Forbidden Mountains, but these can only be guessed at. One familiar story is that they came across a slab of stone that stuck out over the crater, on which was an altar, and Akincyde said that here was where a foreign people of old sacrificed human beings to the Sky Gods. But this spot has never been found, and I believe that this story is confused with another that the son of Shangodoon was to tell about the peak of a quite different mountain.

Akincyde was to say more important things to him during those six days it took to ascend the mountain, hold an all-night vigil, and descend, than he had done during the whole three-year period which Shangodoon had spent at the cavern.

We know little of the subjects discussed, but it was an intense time of physical, emotional, mental and spiritual stimulation, and its effects were to last on Shangodoon permanently.

It may be of interest to record the one conversation in which Shangodoon learnt a little about Akincyde's personal life, as well as took some valuable advice.

Akincyde said to him, "Be careful with women. Women are the single, most continuous temptation you will face."

Shangodoon wondered what he knew of women.

"You wonder what I know of woman?" Akincyde asked.

"No, no . . . well . . . yes."

"I have had a wife. I have two sons and a daughter." He laughed. "I have always been a priest, but not always a hermit! The old Ainchan way was to create children first before coming a hunter, warrior or priest. No one who was not a father could be used in certain occupations—else, how could he understand the needs of people?

"Thus I say to you, get a wife and child soon, and beware of women."

Shangodoon nodded soberly. Then a question entered his mind.

"How long have you lived, Akincyde?"

"My body is over a hundred years old," the high priest droned indifferently.

No more of their conversation has come down to us, except that they agreed before they parted that an intelligence more powerful than they could envisage must have brought them together; that the Creator had designed that they should meet.

The First Return to Ainchan

H AVING RETURNED TO THE cavern Shangodoon rested for a day and studied the maps of Dibra and the surrounding countryside. The following day at sunrise he left Akincyde and the high sanctuary of the Forbidden mountains, and journeyed southward. Days later he passed by the sites where the sheep-herders and woodcutters lived, and at Parcos, which Akincyde had recommended to him, he arranged to travel with a group of lumbermen on a flotilla of rafts which was sailing downriver to the ports and lumberyards of Ainchan and Dibra. These rafts, composed of thousands of greenheart and ironwood logs, were to be dismantled and sold to the wharfbuilders of the cities: Dibra demanded them, also, for the salt-workers' barracks and the prisoners' camps of that area.

Shangodoon travelled with two other men upon one of these rafts; there was a logwood cabin built upon it where they cooked and rested at night. The one in charge, a veteran of the river called Skim, had seen many young men like Shangodoon. He asked where he was going; Shangodoon said, Dibra. Very sensibly Skim warned him not to leave the raft, either at the two cities or the many hamlets on the way downriver; he should stay on the raft until he reached Dibra. The lumbermen had been accused of taking stolen weapons and recruits to the rebels of the waste downriver, and he was taking no risks.

So Shangodoon passed Kunaree safely, and could have done the same at Ainchan, but the memory of the city and a longing to see his family were strong within him. Thus he disguised himself and entered the city, with a consignment of logs for the warehouses. He travelled atop one of the long wheeled carriages that transported the great logs through the northernmost gate of the west side, where the bustle was greatest, and it was relatively easy to escape detection on that day, for the soldiers were more interested in searching for arms than for identities.

Shangodoon had strapped his shortsword and sheath beneath his garments; all he had beside was a large leather draw-bag which he slung from his shoulders. This contained his changes of clothes and his money-bag, the small skin pouch with its uncut diamond, and seven sachets of skywhisper, in a sealed waterproof container, that he was to present to Sifar of Dibra.

He hurried through the streets of the northern living quarters and reached his home. The dog greeted him first, jumping in happy contortions and scampering in circles, flailing his tail, and led him into the house.

His mother raised her hand over her open mouth, stifling a sound, and her eyes were wide with surprise, joy and trepidation when she saw Shangodoon. Then, without a word, she got up from her garment-making machine and walked over to him, placed her hands on his shoulders and examined his face carefully. She kissed him and held him off again, looking at his grown body; then she turned and beckoned, leading him outside.

They walked down a beaten path that he knew had not been there before, and came to the family plot where the trees of the dead were planted. His mother took him to the place where a flamboyant tree, tall but thickening, spread its umbrella over a circular patch of grass below its foliage. Beneath its shade was a single slab of marble placed in the earth at a tilt, with the one word deeply encised: "Aldraf". Shangodoon's mother herself had planted that tree in the ashes of his father, in accordance with an old Ainchan custom that had never died out among the people.

It seemed that Shangodoon felt part of himself undergo a profound change as he gazed upon the stone and considered the life of his father. The flamboyant tree was in full bloom, for the weather was warming, and its brilliant red flowers coloured the air beneath the shady branches where they stood and talked about the death of Aldraf.

"Your father always tried to keep out of political trouble," Lilaktia said. "He watched you carefully as you grew up, and he knew you were going to be different. But he didn't complain,

141

he didn't expect that you would have the same temperament as himself. He only worried at your activities and made himself sick. He had an abnormal bloodrate.

"The soldiers came to our house the same day you left. They asked if we knew where you were going; if we had sent you somewhere. They searched the place, and got very threatening and insulting when they saw the books that you've been reading. Why didn't you take them with you? And where have you been?"

"I went to the Northern Moutains, and stayed with one of the old high priests of the old religion."

"I thought you were going to do that. Your grandfather wondered if you had fallen in with the rebels. And once we heard that you were dead."

"Well, you see it isn't true. Grandfather is still alive?"

"Yes. He has moved to the eastern quarters."

"What else—about my father?"

"The soldiers said that Aldraf knew the law. They bound him and took him away, but he was released; he came back the midday of the next day. They had only asked him questions that first time. They knew him; he was a skilled workman and very valuable to them. Yet, next day or the day after, they returned and apprehended him again. They said that he had to be put on public trial because he had harboured a rebel of the waste in his house. They said that you killed four of their soldiers when you were escaping.

"It's a lie."

"I did not believe it."

"They killed each other, fighting for jewels."

"The one who came back said it."

"He killed, as well as some of the others."

"The Dominauts blamed you for it. And your father. I knew it was a wrongful accusation. The judge condemned him to ten years' full-time labour in the salt camps." She paused, and he saw tears glint in her eyes. "Your father didn't leave the Condemnation Hall. He collapsed and fell down there all at once, dead, dead, dead. They say it was his heart."

"They killed him." Shangodoon's voice grated in his throat, and a vein stood out in his forehead.

"Don't take it to heart, son. All that is in the past. Your mother's glad to see you." She turned to lead him back to the house. "You must see Sentia," she said, referring to Shangodoon's sister. "She was married two and a half years ago, and she has two children. Are you going to stay here?" she asked, trying to keep the worry out of her voice, for she was conscious that he was a fugitive from the Dominauts.

"No. I can't stay long. There are many things I have to do, and I have to start immediately. I'm glad to see you, mother, and I will you see you again. When I come to stay here again, it will be in peace. Soon I will not have to run from the Dominauts in the place where I was born!"

"Be careful, my son. There is another thing. Your father told me this to tell you, for he seemed to know he would not see you again. It is something the two of us have known and discussed in private for many years. *The King is not divine.*"

"So you always knew! Give thanks to the Creator!" Shangodoon exclaimed joyfully, in the dialect of the mountains.

"What did you say?"

"I thank the Creator. And now I will go. I will see Sentia when I come again."

"Take this wallet of money. Goodbye, son."

They hugged each other tightly. Then Shangodoon slipped away in the gathering dusk.

That night he roamed the city, and, his mind giving way to anger and bitterness when he reviewed the story of the death of his father, and re-witnessed the evils of the city and poverty and degradation of the people, he tried to raise a revolt. It had happened on more than one occasion in the history of Ainchan that revolts, some almost successful, had suddenly exploded against the Dominauts. Shangodoon had avidly read of the history of popular revolution, and knew the potential of an aroused people.

The civilian disorders that resulted from his actions took place at one spot and were minor as compared to others, but the incident left deeper feeling among the populace than previous ones of its kind.

Under cover of darkness Shangodoon entered several builders' stores of the town, and took paint and brushes as he needed them. Moving into the poor area, through the labyrinthine, dirty alleys of the cluttered downtown district, he began to paint his slogan on the walls of the buildings. Little children who had been playing in the overloaded gutters left the rotten fruit which served for food and toys and begged him for some paint and brushes. Many of them were illiterate, but memorized easily the design of the letters and their order, and they hurried away to blazon the city.

There were many signs when the morning came, Shangodoon himself must have moved very quickly indeed, and invisibly, for a large proportion of the signs were of his own making; he moved with natural, practised ability, flitting from the shadow of one building to the corner of some wall, avoiding Dominauts and Ainchans alike. The histories say that wherever the people looked the following day—on the walls, the roads, high on the building, even on the ceiling of the Condemnation Hall and on the vertical rises of the Royal Capital steps where soldiers had stood all night—the paint shouted its sudden challenge to oppressors and oppressed. Even after daylight had come and some of the children had been apprehended, the slogans still appeared in unexpected places, and the more fearful citizens whispered that it was the work of demons.

Grim-faced and fidgety on their skittish horses, the Dominaut soldiers moved through the city attempting to mobilize gathering crowds of sullen Ainchan men. Others, sensing the potential of this unprecedented stroke of rebellion, tried to keep people in their houses in the most troublesome parts of the city. Long before the main city gates swung open, however, people were thick in the streets, wondering what was going on; and the morning sun bore down on a tension that simmered and rose like the very mists on the rooftops of Ainchan.

Inevitably, as always happens in such situations, some townsman threw a stone, or some young soldier nervously shot one of the mob; and a riot broke out in the square before the Royal Capital.

It was a swift, short, savage skirmish; then the crowds scattered and the soldiers struggled to retain their panicky ranks. But people had died, and the Ainchans never forgot that particular incident.

Shangodoon was still going about the city, his mind bent on fomenting rebellion, when he heard of the trouble. He ran through the tense crowds and waiting streets to the square before the Capital, and came upon the scene of the disturbance.

Shangodoon's description of this scene, of his feelings, and of the events that followed, is, as the reader will notice, straightforward and graphic.

———•◆•———

When I came up the west main road and entered the square (Shangodoon recalled), I saw destruction everywhere. Overturned carts lay in the streets, and oranges rolled underfoot from the vendors' broken shops and trays. Water ran from the cracked basin of the central fountain out across the southwestern side of the square; windows of some homes and trading buildings had been broken, and the statues of some of the Dominaut hero-warriors which lined the roadway on either side of these Royal Capital steps were pulled off their pedestals. Dominaut marks-men were high on the roofs, observing the movements of the townspeople, and subdued crowds were being herded and battered by phalanxes of soldiers.

There were dead horses, some penetrated by spears; dead market animals; and grievously, dead people. I saw a Dominaut soldier with an arrow sticking in his throat; another crushed by the wheel of a wagon and a third slashed across the stomach. At one place I saw the body of an Ainchan man who had been hit by the fireweapons; at another, a pregnant woman. On these Royal Capital steps I saw the bodies of three children to whom I had given paint and brushes the night before, bound together and fired upon. There was blood everywhere, both human and animal; and at the time I believe that more than twelve people had died.

I was struck immediately by a deep sorrow and a sense of utter wrong-doing when I beheld the corpses, as well as a profound regret that my own life should terminate this way after all the desires I had felt and goals at which I had aimed.

I did not resist when the soldiers held me, took my bag and sword away, and put me onto one of their iron cages. There was nothing to do but die, it seemed, and I wanted to cling to life as long as possible., thus tamely I was encaged like a bird, in one of those devilish devices in which a man can neither stand nor sit—certainly an invention of depraved and evil minds.

They lifted the cage and myself up this very flight of steps and into the Royal Capital. I knew they were taking to me to see the Officer of Internal Security before my execution; he would want to know all the facts surrounding my presence in the city.

Once inside the walls we went down a flight of steps into a huge sunken courtyard that stretched to the central buildings. A guard wall ran around the Palace, and the Royal rooms, curtained in luxurious silks, rose floor after floor, culminating in the baths at the higher section of the mount on which the Royal edifices were reared. Administration offices and soldiers' barracks were built at the base of the outer wall, and in the vast complex there were other quarters, for horses, carriages, kitchens and bakeries, lavatories, entertainment rooms, storage rooms for siege-times, and the largest arsenal in Ainchan.

The Officer of Internal Security was insulted and exasperated. He was a weak character, I saw at once; there was much lacking in his make-up as a man. I saw that he had impressed himself with the official position he had attained, but doubted his own ability to live up the role. Such men were dangerous; anyone seeming to challenge their authority met their full vindictive rage, their rigid, ruthless hostility.

"Take him to the Information Room," he yapped at the soldiers around my prison, and they lifted the iron cage and myself through a door where monstrous Halvers stood on guard. They carried spears and vicious curved knives; in other parts I saw guards with clubs, swords and axes, but no fireweapons, for those were not used within the precincts of the Palace, though the main arsenal was kept here.

In the cheerlessly cold Information Room I saw objects which distressed me greatly. There were hooks embedded in walls and hanging from ceilings, and levers and cogs, oiled and in very fit condition, linked to unpleasant-looking platforms with straps which obviously were for binding human beings. There was a large table with a sink in the middle and in this unusually wide container there were many pints of stagnating blood. Trapdoors with iron rings, the purposes of which I could not fathom, lay under the feet of the soldiers. One high cobwebbed window mixed a lurid glare to this whole prisoner's nightmare, and the added deliberate touches-two skulls grinning atop a desk, and the skeleton of a hand that ended in a shattered forearm mounted on a wooden shield—were calculated to make me feel already a dead man.

"We are going to put out his eyes first," the Officer said without delay as soon as the cage was set down. "Bring the fire-bowls and the heating irons."

The soldiers hastened to obey, and were bringing the fearful objects over, a grim anticipation their faces, when a man in messenger's uniform came through the door and stood before the Officer of Internal Security. The King wanted to see the prisoner, he said.

The Officer gave an embittered bark; a resentful, sarcastic laugh that told me much about his relations with the King. He spread his hands jerkily, shook his head from side to side, and grudgingly nodded to the messenger who had stood aloofly observing him. Now this messenger gave a cold, superior smile and turned to lead the way; the Officer of Internal Security fell in behind him, and then I was lifted after them by the rabble of lackeys that guarded me.

The entrances to the King's rooms were guarded by huge parodies of men. These Halvers, specially trained for Killing quickly in several different ways, were deaf, dumb and castrated. They stood fiercely, seemingly immovable as stone, their terrible spears slanting forward above their heads, their massive hairless bodies shining with oil, their pudgy unemotional faces staring straight before them. Past these ferocious guards, we entered one of the king's reception chambers, and stood waiting before an empty throne.

In a few minutes King Chrazius III entered the room. He came through hanging curtains behind the throne, and sat quickly, gripping the carved snake's head handrests of the throne, then nearsightedly he beckoned for my cage to be brought closer that he might have a look at me.

As he looked, he asked absentmindedly about the riot. Were all the rebels killed? Did the populace receive a good lesson in the power of his soldiers? Were the people at work cleaning up the painted slogans? The Officer of Internal Security answered impatiently. Then: "If you do not mind, my King, I would like to take this man and have him executed!"

"Why so quickly, Shagrin? You soldiers usually like to prolong the deaths of rebels."

"He is a dangerous man."

"Not any more."

"You do not know."

"Rudeness! Blasphemy!" shouted the King, and the Officer of Internal Security winced. "Get out of my presence until I call you, and be glad if I don't have you caged as well! And take the other dogs with you!" he added, referring to the staring, shuffling soldiers.

The Office opened his mouth; then shut it and went out, followed by his soldiers. I in my cage was left alone before the King; his personal deaf-mute sentries still lined the walls like statues.

One of the soldiers had brought my bag and shortsword in; now the King himself descended from his throne and examined them. He seemed to like the sword. He emptied the bag, which contained a change of garments, the wallet of money my mother had given me, the container of skywhisper packets, and my uncut diamond in its pouch. This last the King examined carefully, rubbing it between his fingers; then, after a moment's thought, he put it into its pouch again and returned all my possessions to my bag.

Then he came over to me and walked around my cage, examining my face and body carefully. I too had been observing him, at first like a wild animal, and with a superstitious awe, for old beliefs die hard; then with frank curiosity. It became very clear to me that he did not feel himself to be a god, however much he insisted that he was one; and when I was reassured from my sudden childish doubts, I knew that we were confronting each other as two human beings.

"You are the son of the carver Aldraf?" the King asked.

"Yes."

"You address me as Your Glorious and Eternal Majesty. But no matter, you are condemned. I knew the story of your father, and I wanted to speak with you before you were executed.

"Three years ago our investigators found your notebooks concerning certain things about your people which you were dabbling with—a dangerous occupation, as you well know; you are many times condemned, and I hope Shagrin takes this into account when I give you to him . . . These notebooks mention a hidden place, within this city, where your disbelieving ancestors kept their precious things and did their ineffective nonsense. I want to know where that place is.

"I also want to know why you left Ainchan and why you returned, especially the latter; and how a mere boy of eighteen could kill four of the militia's most experienced manhunters with their own weapons."

Then I said, "As to the first matter, I will say nothing. As to the second, I left Ainchan because I wanted to further my study in the ways of our native people, and I returned because I must move as a free man in the land of my ancestry and no one should infringe upon that right. As to the third matter; I have never killed anyone . . . though today I feel the deaths of my people, and blame myself."

The King growled: "As to the first matter, you will tell me where this place you found is located; as to the second matter, you have committed treason in undermining the eternal laws of my divine ancestors and the safety of our kingdom; as to the third matter, we will investigate." He waved his arms and made a sign to his impassive guards, and one left the room, returning shortly with a man whom I learnt was the King's Military Secretary.

He was a small worried-looking man who wore lenses over both eyes and whose thin, thin hands twitched nervously as he talked. It was evident that on many occasions he had reported bad news to the irascible monarch. Now in his disturbed and ruffled grey uniform, he seemed to perch before the King and cock his head, awaiting questions.

"Do you remember the incident three years or so ago when five soldiers left the north side of the city to hunt an escaped rebel, and only one returned?"

"I remember well, your Glorious and Eternal Majesty. There was Dob the Tracker, Stokrum, who was in command, and two others, Mayce and Tirault, who died. The one who returned was wounded. He told he fought bravely, and escaped only because he offered the rebel money.

The King nodded. "A wise man. Though this one does not look like the kind who would spare lives for money . . . doesn't seem to like killing or money. I would like to see this surviving soldier. Can you find him?"

"Honourable and Most Gracious Father of Men, you know the man. He is Shagrin, your Officer of Internal Security. He was a good soldier, and when your previous Officer of Internal Security was executed for carelessness in carrying out his duty, I appointed him to the post."

The King bit at his fingernails and frowned, eyeing me speculatively. The he motioned his Military Secretary away. "Enough."

The man hopped away, twittering in relief, and King Chrazius turned to me again. I could see that he was cruelly disturbed by the fact that there was something he did not fully understand.

"Did Shagrin really fight?" he asked me.

"If Shagrin is the one who returned," I said, "he is a murderer. They started to kill each other, and he alone survived."

"But—why would they kill each other?" the King asked, not doubtfully, but seeking for a motive.

"For jewels," I said. "The murderer came back with his pockets full of jewels."

"Ah!" the King's piggish eyes widened and narrowed craftily. "They killed each other over jewels you put in their path!"

"That is the truth, King Chrazius," I affirmed.

"So it is true; you do know where to find precious stones," the King said, surprisingly. He nodded and smiled. "Well, I will deal with you afterwards." He waved his arms again, made some more signs, and his guards called Shagrin in once more.

The Officer of Internal Security strode busily in, confident that the King had called him to hand the prisoner over.

Then I saw clear evidence of the guileful character of this wily king, for he flattered his Officer and apologized for his previous anger.

Then: "I know now why you wanted to have him killed so quickly," the King said.

With lowered eyelids, and barely a pause, Shagrin replied: "I am a loyal man, Your Glorious and Eternal Majesty. Duty burns within my breast."

Iron shall burn within your eyes!" roared the Kind in dreadful tones. "Was it duty that caused you to murder your comrades for jewels?"

His words seemed to shatter the armour of Shagrin's uniform. The Officer of Internal Security immediately became a wheedling, shifty merchant, trading for his life.

"I have them still, my King and only I know where they are. If you have me blinded, how shall I find them to give them to you? I killed only Tirault, and not in callousness—he attacked me first."

"Silence, you traitorous dog!" the King yelled, beckoning frantically to his guards. "This prisoner knows where there are many more." Down the room the doors burst open and soldiers of the Palace rushed in and seized the distraught ex-Officer of Internal Security. "Get out the firebowls and the heating irons! I will handle the mongrel personally!" Chrazius pronounced, and Shagrin was led out kicking, yelping and pleading breathlessly.

Then the King questioned me closely about the jewels I had possessed, and though I described them to him in such a way and in such detail that his eyes registered great greed, I did not reveal their source.

"No matter. We will have the brain-searchers operate on you, since you want it done the hard and painful way. As long as you know, the facts will come out by the time they are through with you." He changed the subject. "Why did you try to raise revolt against the divinely appointed Son of the Gods? It has resulted in a curse on your own people."

"You do not have the power to bless or curse. You do not even know how such things work."

"You are free to talk. I give you permission to say what you think."

"If you cause more to die, it is the futile retribution of an ordinary man."

"Your argument is useless. You are already a dead man."

"Is that the evidence of your divine power?" Why do you not bring my father alive, since your agents have killed him for a deed he did not commit?"

"You pride yourself. The death of an Ainchan one has never been a matter of regret on my part. By the fires of Gnarl, I wish that more had died today. The subjects of this city need a lesson. They have been spoiled by too much lenience . . . What was it you wrote on the walls?"

"The King is not Divine."

"A crime against Almighty Gnarl himself. Your death will be very painful, I promise."

"You cannot make me fear, King Chrazius. The things that I consider fearful are not of an order of existence that you can understand, for you are but an untrained novice as far as the Mysteries are concerned."

"Oh! A priest! You left Ainchan to be a priest!" King Chrazius was happy at his realization; otherwise he was indifferent to what I had said. "So. You are much more dangerous— and talented—than I thought. And you stirred up the people . . . ?" the remorseless tyrant walked up and down, brooding deeply. Then he asked: "Do you have any children?"

"No."

"A wife?"

"No."

"Good. You will never have any. I will have you castrated and kept before me as my perpetual ritualist. You native people who have been to the north know many things about tapping sources of unlimited power, and how to prevent enemies from succeeding in their plots against an individual."

"Do you have children, King Chrazius? I know my people have given you many fine Ainchan maidens. Or is it true that you suffer the ultimate curse of the Creator?

Is it true that *Nature* has castrated you?"

The King stutterd in rage. He waved, and five or six of his guards advanced. He signaled rapidly; then one of them took a dagger from his belt, and another opened the door of the cage.

I attempted to spring out immediately, but the tense position in which I had been half-standing was the cause of a clumsy stagger. In a thrice the soldiers had gripped me and torn off my clothes.

The King gibbered like an epileptic when he saw my naked body. "Castrate him!" he bawled to his deaf Halvers; and they understood at once.

I started struggling bestially then, punching, elbowing and kicking at the thick heads, soft bellies and monumental legs. I felt one finger plash into an eye and saw one attacker screaming soundlessly; drove my elbow into the neck of another; and stamped a third against a kneecap, feeling it crunch sickeningly beneath the sole of my foot. Great bodies floundered and rolled away, spears clattered on the floor.

I avoided the thrust of a razor-sharp long-knife, leapt to the sender of the blow, and slammed the heel of my palm against the fragile bones of his temple. Blood spurted from his nose immediately and he reeled away choking.

Then I was free of them, and snatching up my bag and shortsword, I rushed towards the curtains where the crafty King had disappeared as soon as the fight had begun.

Several of the King's enormous capons lunged from all parts of the room after me. I pulled the curtains apart, darted through and saw a small door; went through that, bolting it behind me, and ran naked as a newborn baby down a long corridor.

This one ran at right-angles into another corridor. At this point I looked right and left, gripping my sword tight and hoping to see the King, but there was no one in sight and a rapid staccato of feet behind me hastened my decision to take the left-hand way, towards where I calculated the centre of the Palace to be.

At the end of this corridor there was another running at right-angles again, and as soldiers were running toward me from both ends of this passageway. I pushed open a door in the wall straight ahead, entered, and locked it. Then I turned, and found myself in another environment even more grotesque than the one I had just departed.

It was a large circular area with a dome that did not quite reach its apex, so that the sky could be seen through the open roof. Below was a wide sparkling pool, surrounded by a sheltered walk on which tall beautiful plants stood in big ornamental vases. The roof was composed of transparent panes of coloured material and was supported by long curved pillars which were festooned with streamers and little lights.

There were many low tables, lounging chairs, mats and cushions placed in casual positions, on which reclined many people who were naked or barely clothed. Many turned their heads to see me as I entered; others continued in strange activities without pause or notice. I stood aghast, not only at the acts that were being committed, but at the people involved.

They were of so many races and colours, so many shapes, sizes, characteristics and attitudes, so many strange utterances and unfamiliar gestures, so many different eyes and noses and lips and types of hair, that it was dizzying to view them all.

These, then were types of the "other peoples" that Akincyde had told me existed. I gazed upon their faces and bodies with as equal bewilderment at their looks as at their actions, at the same time realizing that I was as utterly naked as most of them.

They were mainly females of differing ages; most were young and some were very young, but one or two were bent and wrinkled. Fragrant perfumes filled the air, and skins glistened with delicate unguents. Beautiful temptresses threw seductive looks; lips glistened, and tongues flirted over teeth. Many eyes gazed in my direction, and insistent hands beckoned. Voluptuous flesh lay under my stare. Here a smooth knee nestling against as ear, there a ripe breast peeping from behind spread fondling fingers; a raised languid arm, festooned with golden chains, its hand plunging into a nest of moistened hair; glances and fingers pointing, guiding the eyes to inviting mounds and clefts of warm flesh. Eyes fluttered and mouths twisted soundlessly, open in the silent cry of sensual release. A woman exposed a delightful nestle of fascinating, downy hair; another rubbed her jeweled belly and quivered the soft flesh of her inner thighs; a third spread her arms wide and stiffened, stretched tautly in a pleasurable series of shudders of her own making; and yet another bit at her knuckles and curled like a small child as warm spasms shook her buttocks. A bold vixen, showing sharp teeth in scarlet lips, came to me, calling, promising delights that no one ever needed to know of; I was soothed and lulled by her low voice; my throat was tight and my knees shaking. "Come with me," she said. "Come to my secret place. You are fleeing from the King, are you not?" I will save you, and pleasure you too, in any way you desire. You can hurt me if you want . . ." She reached to touch my body but I had already recovered from her trap of temptation and recoiled violently from her groping hands.

Then I saw that though some of these people were women, and some men, it was not simple to tell who was what in this place. Some I thought one kind were the other. Some lay frozen in barbarous embraces, with looks where pleasure and pain alternated and merged quite strangely. One whom I guessed to be a woman passionately kissed and searched the body of another who seemed the same. Converted young men sat in each others' laps or preened before glazed reflecting surfaces, turning their long necks and touching their ear-rings with languid fingers. People rubbed and touched each other, nibbled at lips, ears and perfumed bosoms; women and men joined themselves together in ever more alien combinations. Venery, lechery and debauchery emanated like body-scents from this jumble of dissipated sex-monsters. These were the delighters of the King and his queens—degenerates of the worst excesses and perverted experiments.

But now the eunuchs of the King were crashing through the door. Laughing, screaming females, obviously bored and looking for new delights, wanted to extend the chase and prolong the moment of my death. There were hardly concerned with the fact that I was an enemy of King Chrazius; they saw me as a tool for their use, and no rebellion I had committed was as unnatural as the things they had been doing.

I struggled through reaching hands, held my bag and sword tight, ad dove into the pool. It was deeper than I had anticipated, but I had taken a good breath, and I soon found what I expected to find—a clever wheel, hidden under a projecting rock. With joy I held it and turned, and it moved easily, a credit to the skill of the engineers of Old Ainchan. A deep blue-black hole appeared and the water began to spin downward, sucking at me. I plunged into the hole against my will, before I had fully made up my mind to go, and the force of the water pushed me down violently. I fell for some way bruising and knocking myself dreadfully, with the pressure of the water forcing me on. Then I managed to catch and become hooked on a ladder of rustless metal rails set into the sides of the hole, and waited for the water to pass. Soon there was a monstrous gurgle and the swirling water fell away below me as I let my pent-up breath out and gasped fresh mouthfuls. Then I climbed down swiftly, hearing shouts from above, and in the dark below, a long distance away, I could hear the water falling and gurgling still.

There was a deadly whirring hum and a spear hurtled past my back. I looked up, and there was another coming; I squeezed tight to the ladder and shut my eyes and heard it go past with the same vicious hum. I looked up again and far away, dwarfed and shortened by perspective, silhouetted figures were climbing down. I increased the speed of my descent.

Finally I reached the bottom of that well-like hole and walked a horizontal tunnel of bricks with knee-high water for an interminable length of time. It was completely dark inside that tunnel; so absolute was the blackness that it did not matter when I closed my eyes. I kept close to one wall but hated to touch it; now and then I put out my hand and did so out of necessity.

Then there was a steady gradient upward, and a gradual lightening, and I came out of the ground, pushing my way up past a weighty stone trapdoor.

I found myself in a cluster of thick low trees with thorns. I put some of the branches of these trees into the hole, closed the trapdoor and rolled a boulder onto it. Then I put my second set of clothes onto my tired and lacerated body and moved forward into the open landscape.

As I walked in the late afternoon sunlight I was wracked with sorrow and desolation, and a burning sense of loss and failure. Later, I was to conclude that this had been the hastiness of physical strength and emotionalism; I needed wisdom and patience. Dominauts were powerful; I had been expecting a miracle to think that they could fall so easily.

My next attack would be based on more, I vowed. There was more to learn; perhaps I should have gone to Dibra first, and met with Sifar.

I knew there was no turning back now from the path that I had taken; I had become a rebel of the waste, an exile from Ainchan. Sooner or later, I knew, my life would depend on whether I found the answers I sought concerning the weaknesses of the Dominauts.

At a quiet farmhouse I purchased a horse and riding equipment including a fine wooden saddle, and I set out immediately for the southern canefarming lands. There I sold the horse and got aboard one of the sugar-cane barges which were sailing to the delta-mouth. A few days later, I came ashore at Dibra.

7
DIRECTIONS FROM DIBRA

Directions from Dibra

DIBRA IS SITUATED IN the delta of the Ruba River. There are three branching outlets of the river to the sea, and Dibra lies to the west bank of the central outlet.

The city had a profound effect on my mind.

The walls are built of very thick blocks of limestone; they go up very smooth and sheer, then slant outwards and are crowned with several turrets for fireweapons. There is a moat around the city, and I hear that there are vicious man-eating fish in its waters. On this wide body of water no boats are allowed to travel, and there are iron drawbridges at each of the two entrances to the city.

Dibra consists of one street that runs from one end of the city to the other, from east to west. Thus Dibra is an extremely long and narrow city; its north and south walls run as long as its street. The broad straight roadway opens at its halfway point into a wide square with a fountain and a sundial and several trees of different rare species. Here was the main slave mart of the city.

Lining this single tedious street there are tall many-storied buildings of red brick, with casements and jalousied windows. At the bases of several houses were cells with grilles on a level with the road, from which the eyes of woeful slaves looked out in dull despair.

I also saw at one section of the road, fully two hundred yards long, posts set up on either side, with chains and rings attached, and there were many men, women and children from the districts surrounding Dibra on sale. Dominaut men with whips and fireweapons stood in charge over them, and there were many rich buyers of the foreign race who examined the chained people and argued over prices.

Outside the city, across the moat, there were sprawling areas consisting of dismal shacks in which people carried on meager existences selling products of the river and the sea and a few handicrafts. Many of them had bandages about the legs, where years of work in the salt digs had made permanent sores on their skins. I believed that several of them had passed through terms of prison labour, and afterwards had remained around the salt digs and the city.

The port of the city is extremely large, and in it I saw the huge ships that carried people over the seas to unknown places.

When I was in the city, I saw a line of bound people being led towards the eastern gate. I asked a citizen, one of our people, where they were going, and I could see that he was lying when he shifted his eyes about and said he did not know. I could see, too, that he realized I was a stranger in Dibra.

There were many native workmen in the streets, all very busy; Dibra nurses with Dominaut children; chariot drivers and sedan-chair porters with Dominauts as passengers. On the balconies above, too, there were people; Dominauts sat below sunshades sipping drinks while their servants stood around. There were many of the foreigners here; the population of Dominauts was larger than that of Dibra-Ainchan people.

I entered Dibra without the difficulty I had anticipated. The Security Officers at the gate did not feel threatened by the presence of one man. Few free people entered the city unless their business was urgent, though for there was a possibility of being captured and sold by the gangs of people-stealers which roamed the city seizing victims in broad daylight sometimes.

I told the Security Officers that I was going to the pottery of Sifar; they showed no surprise. One asked if I was an artisan; I answered in the affirmative. They asked whether I was seeking a job; gladly I said that this was the case, for I knew that one could be arrested for unemployment in the city. Thus finally they gave me a stamped card with permission to stay for not more than five days, and told me to return and inform them immediately if I took a job at the pottery of Sifar. If I lost this permit, they informed me, and I was caught, I would be brought before the law-enforcers. I was to show my card when

I left the city; otherwise I would not be allowed to leave, but would be consigned to labour in the salt digs, as happened to any suspect person of Ainchan descent who was found in the city without a job or a permit.

Before I entered the city I had seen the three tall thin peaks known as the Three Fingers pointing grimly into the sky towards the west. They would have been an over-powering sight in any landscape; here it seemed as if the earth accused the sky, so starkly did they project into the heavens. They seemed appropriate for the tortured, guilt-ridden slave-city to view each day to take as its major landmark. As I walked the street of archaic, close-packed bricks I bore their relative position in mind, for often they could not be seen because of the high austere buildings. At one point the street was a flight of wide dismal steps that went down to a sluggish built-canal, accommodating a large ghaut of the Ruba River across which the city had been erected. On the other side of the canal the steps rose again, and the broad flat street continued. The rectangular nature of the city made my positioning difficult, too, and on the whole the journey was tiring; but finally I saw the northwest lookout tower and shifted on the spacious street so that I stood in a line with the tower and the three peaks, and then looked behind.

I saw a building that was very much like the others except the larger windows and a wide door. In the windows were shelves on which several pieces of beautiful pottery were displayed. I entered the building and saw a number of Dominaut children, perhaps thirty, working at the turning-wheels. Containers of prepared clay of various textures and colours lined one side of the long room; there were ovens at another side, and shelves and counters in various places. There were piles of glazed decorative tiles and fine masks and wall-plaques in every available space. I saw at once that Sifar was a valuable asset to the Dominauts and that his position in Dibra was secure.

One of the children asked if I wanted to see Sifar; when I nodded, she went busily through a doorway and returned quickly, telling me that he was waiting for me beyond the door. I crossed the room and went in to Sifar.

He was shaven clean, as all Dibra-Ainchan men were who dwelt tin the city; this was the official mark of humility and acquiescence to the Dominauts. He sat before a wide table with many drawn designs, a large man with slightly bent shoulders and surprisingly delicate hands at the ends of great muscled arms.

"What do you want?" he growled.

"I am from the North."

His eyes narrowed. "From Ainchan Kunaree?"

"From beyond. I am a friend of Akincyde. He has sent you a gift, and his deepest blessings."

"Akincyde! How is he?" Sifar was very happy immediately. "His friend is my friend. I dreamt of him a few nights ago, and wondered what it might mean. He is a great benefactor of mine. You have stayed in the Cavern-Temple?"

"I have lived there three years."

Sifar passed his hands over his hairless head and his eyes widened in reaction to my words. "You are an important man, then. You are not here only because you have a gift from Akincyde for me?"

"Akincyde has told me of you. I have come to ask some very vital questions of you."

"We cannot talk here. Just tell me—about what?"

I lowered my voice. "I am on a mission of the deepest significance. My quest is to find the weakness of the Dominauts, of which I hear you know."

"Enough!" he raised his palms and glanced beyond the door. "These young ones listen more than you may think. Sometimes I suspect . . . you cannot be too careful in this city. In an hour they will be gone, and we can talk then."

So I waited until his class was over; then we sat in an upper chamber of his house, looking out over the street, and talked.

I found that he agreed with me on many aspects of the political situation. Certainly the Dominauts had to go and the Ainchan peoples be set free, he said, and he was willing to do his part, as always, to bring the oppressive regime to an end.

"I fought with the patriots when I was younger," he said. "Now I live in camouflage here in this city of deaths and disappearances, but my heart beats for the day of freedom."

"Do you know of a way by which the Dominauts can be defeated? Have you heard of a weapon more mighty than their fireweapons?"

"I can show you pictures of things of which they are afraid," Sifar said, eyeing me carefully.

"Thank you, my friend." Suddenly I was excited.

"I would show this to no one else except a most trusted comrade," Sifar declared, getting up and moving over to the side of the room. He fumbled at a panel and a section of the wall slid back revealing a narrow cubicle with many shelves and drawers. "Here is my secret collection of Dominaut history and artifacts, taken from their homes in various riots, raids and lootings that I myself participated in." Proudly he showed me the many interesting and valuable items on the shelves, with a sweep of his flexible hands. We stepped down into the little compartment, and Sifar struck a flame and lit a small bright lamp which stood on a bracket close by the door.

"Here is what I would like you to see." He took a dusty folder from a shelf and placed it atop a small desk. "Let me show you . . ." He opened the folder and took out three unframed paintings which were done on a very smooth cloth-like material.

"These were taken in a raid on the mansion of one of the Dominaut overlords, years ago, when there were more patriots than there are today, I fear . . . these, and accompanying books that show much of the history of the Dominauts before they came to the Ruba plain. Together they show that the Dominauts are not invincible, and that people have defeated these invaders before. These paintings were done by the artists of a victorious people, and somehow they fell into the hands of the Dominaut warlord—then into mine."

I bent over the desk and examined the paintings with care. Two of them depicted processions in which people of strange facial features carried objects which they seemed to regard with great respect. People were walking, in one procession; the other was made up of a series of linked floats which were gaily festooned, in which the handlers of the instruments were seated.

The things they carried had such a variety of shapes and proportions that immediately I wondered what they had in common. They seemed ridiculous, in fact, like experimental designs in the shaping of wood, strings and metal. There was a prevalence of these materials, and Sifar did not know when I enquired whether the things from which the tools were made were of any significance, or if the shapes of the thing were part of their function.

Sifar insisted that these were the people of Muse who had defeated the Dominauts, and that the fighting method used was the one depicted here, but I was doubtful and baffled.

The third painting showed a sick and prostrate man, with another standing by his bed and clasping one of the objects, a pear-shaped one, in such a way as to suggest that he was ministering to the sick man with this unusual tool. This added further to my puzzlement, for I could not understand how these weapons of power seemed capable of healing as well as killing. And certainly some of the people in the crowded procession seemed extremely happy. Some leapt into the air; others marched as one, their legs all together as if only one man was stepping. Some raised their arms and others had their mouths wide open; you could almost hear their shouts as you looked upon those clear and tastefully rendered paintings.

Most of the people were depicted using their hands and fingers on these tools; some had long tubes put to their lips, and could have been drinking from them; at first I had assumed that they were long metal cups. But others had objects of more complex shape-of convoluted metal tubs and little levers-at their lips also, and many of these objects had holes in them. Others bent over small metal strips set on wood, with little padded hammers in their hands, and they seemed to be beating on the pieces of metal. There were several people who carried round-shaped objects with coverings of some smooth material stretched tight; fewer who carried long goblet-shaped things which they also were beating, evidently; and here and there, individuals with big wooden boxes, carved and hollowed out, with strings running across holes, and these were placing their fingers between the strings of the tools, as far as I could gather. Gradually it dawned on me that these tools seemed to be handled with a degree of practice and skill that indicated some training in their use.

"But what is the principle of their use?" I wondered, half-aloud.

"The history of the Dominauts indicates that they find the weapons formidable. There are accounts of Dominauts registering severe pain, falling and running in confusion, and being overcome by fear, when the machines of the Musians are arrayed against them. I have copied such an account from a volume a friend lent me a long time ago." Sifar went over to the least accessible of his dusty shelves, and after searching earnestly for a while he returned with a rectangle of aged mat-parchment. "This is only a small extract, but you will see what I mean . . . the volume from which it is taken is called *A History of War* and it is written by one of the commanders of the Dominaut armies." Sifar placed the parchment on the small desk and we bent over his careful, thick-stroked handwriting together.

The parchment carried the information that on three occasions the Dominauts had attempted to invade the Land of Muse and had been repelled. The Dominauts did not know what powers the defenders used, for they never got close enough to the ranks of the Musians; they were effectively scattered each time. The thing was invisible, of that the Dominauts was sure, and yet, though it could not be seen, it could cause great physical effects. It took control of the body and made their wills adjust to its forces, else it shook them and tore at their insides, "like an earthquake in the bowels," as the excerpt said.

"That's a good one!" Sifar said, happily. "An earthquake in the bowels! . . . I wish you could have seen the volume itself my friend. There is even one account where the leader of a platoon admits that he could not keep his excrements and his knees shook as if they were muscled with water . . . . and he went on to say that the defeat was so ignominious that he hoped neither the already conquered peoples or the general populace of the Dominauts would hear of it. So, you see, we have dangerous knowledge. We know things no Ainchan man should know, according to their policy.

"Yes, but what we know isn't effective until we can get one of those things and see how they operate," I said. "One such instrument in a wise man's hands may be a lever to move a mighty weight. Where can I get such an instrument? Or better yet—where is the Land of Muse?"

Sifar threw his hands into the air and shrugged. "I cannot answer those questions except in the most vague terms . . . I know that there are people who claim to be acquainted with the power that the Musians use, and it is said that one or two even know the location of the Land of Muse. There is a group, a sect, called the Children of the Glorious Recovery . . . have you heard of them?"

"Not until now."

"Well, they claim to know the power . . . . they also have one of the Musian instruments."

"Ah! And where are these Children of the Glorious Recovery?"

Sifar eyed me gravely. "Have you ever been west of Dibra?" he asked.

"No, your dwelling is the farthest west I have come."

"That is the way you would have to travel to reach them. But it is such a rough place that I fear for you, even with the discipline that I know you have undergone."

"Tell me," I cried with impatiently. "Tell me what you have heard, and how to find them."

The Children of the Glorious Recovery live on the Coast of the Sea of Mirrors. As I said, they have one of the Musian instruments, but they use it as a ceremonial object, a revered symbol. They prophesy that this object of theirs, and others like it, will bring about the fall of the Dominauts. The instrument has no functional use in their rituals, except that they go every year to a place where they set up this symbol of power, and at this place the instrument talks to them in sounds that they have learnt to interpret.

"Obviously it is a bit of knowledge that needs pursuing, but the Coast of the Sea of Mirrors is very far from here. To reach there is difficult. I have met only three travelers who have been there, though there must be others . . . . they described to me how to get there, but I have never been to the Coast of the Sea of Mirrors. I have been part of the way though; I have been as far as Grunderth, the territory to the north-west of the Ruba Plain. I have been there five times, in fact—a feat that few can boast of," Sifar said proudly. "It is a strange land, that I can tell you, and if you go there you will have to take the utmost care."

"I am going."

"I know. Well, here is what to do. Keep travelling northwest when you leave this city. Then, long after you pass Noosh and Pragos, you will come to a great sunken area, a valley which is the beginning of the land of Grunderth.

"I have a friend there, who is called Wrog. Ask for him if you see any of the beings who inhabit this place; or perhaps if you shout, he and his colleagues will hear you and come. Let me say, though, that they are not as handsome as we would desire . . . . I have some seeds of a special tree which he likes—the hardstone tree. I will give them to you that you may make a present of them to my friend—that way, you will find an easy passage through Grunderth. Beyond Grunderth is the Coast of the Sea of Mirrors."

"I thank you. Akincyde was correct—you have been the source of much information."

"You are a wise man and a strong warrior; above all, a man trained in the mystical ways of old Ainchan. I see that you will make the utmost use of that information. I think that the Dominauts have an enemy they must fear in you. I think that the Dominauts have an enemy they must fear in you. I sense that I have done the right thing, for I felt that my dream of Akincyde had some great significance, and now I feel the importance of this occasion. I think you will succeed."

"Thank you again. I will need your blessings."

"You have them, brave one; especially for the journey, for I have experienced Grunderth, and it is a hard country. As long as you have traversed that area, you should find it relatively easy to reach the Coast of the Sea of Mirrors. I cannot think of a worst area to traverse."

"I have traversed many bad areas."

"I imagine so. I too know the Forbidden Mountains."

I reached into my bag and took out the container of sky-whisper. "Here is Akincyde's gift to you; seven packs of the flower that grows at the top of the Ruba Mountain—skywhisper."

Sifar came forward and grasped the container; opened it, took a pack of the dried flowers and smelled it; then he laughed, overjoyed.

"I am very happy to see this herb once again, and I am grateful to you and Akincyde."

"What is it for? Akincyde did not say much, and I have wondered."

"I use it for the eyes—it makes your vision improve. It is good for the ears, too; it cures any ailment of hearing. In fact I believe it can correct any imbalance in the body, and improve any of the senses. It has protected my eyes from the glare of the sky and the sea, from sand, or from any bright light, including the sun. It expands and contracts the pupils easily. Also, if you steep some leaves and flowers in hot water you will

177

have a delicious and enlightening drink, for this herb has the power to increase your understanding as well as your natural faculties. It will help you as you travel, too, for its ointment enables one to withstand great cold or great heat, and sudden changes of temperature. Those are the properties I know of; there may be more."

"A very useful plant."

"Yes indeed. Would you like me to leave a packet with you? You can always find some use for it."

"Thank you."

"One packet can go a long way," Sifar said. "And now, let me get the hardstone seeds for you." He left the cubicle and the chamber, and returned shortly, carrying a rabbitskin bag in which very many hundreds of small hard black seeds rolled and rattled. I took it and placed it in my own bag, then turned to go.

"Goodbye," the potter said, "and may the power of the Creator go with you, that you may feel the guidance of a mighty intelligence."

I bowed, and left Sifar.

GRUNDERTH

Grunderth

THE JOURNEY OF THE next two weeks was hard. I scarcely stopped except for sleep at night, and for food and to rest my cramped limbs. I changed horses four times on that journey to the northwest lands, and kept going; even the comforts of Noosh I ignored, though that city seemed relatively warm and inviting to me. Pragos lay farther north, and I did not see this city, but the many villages I passed owed allegiance either to the lords of Noosh or of Pragos.

In one of the villages where I stopped to exchange my horse and pay a sum for the new one, I bought provisions in a small grocery and drinking-shop where agricultural workers gathered and told stories as they guzzled the strong red rum of Noosh. I listened to one man recount the news from the capital city; that some bold rebel had stirred civil rebellion and emptied the King's baths as well as ravished his concubines. The delights of the harem had worn away with the water gone, and there was bickering in the Place, especially since the whimsical King, for no certain reason, had put out the eyes of his Officer of Internal Security. The rebel had disappeared through some secret tunnel, and had not been found; or had been found and killed. Stories differed; and though the Dominauts had put out a report that the rebel had died in the Palace, it was known that the King had secretly sent his most trained hunters of men after the rebel, and there was a reward of one hundred pieces of gold for the person who could publicly display the body of this outlaw.

This was fascinating news to me, as you can imagine, and now when I was sure that the King's manhunters could do me no harm, I laughed heartily many times as I rode along when I thought of the King's permanently dry swimming pool, and the hand-wringing, outraged, womanish quarrellings of the hermaphroditic queans that had sat and preened at their reflections.

I followed Sifar's directions carefully, and finally I sat on my mount looking down into a deep, flat valley, so wide that the hills on the other side were lost in the atmosphere of distance.

Then a gloomy depression seemed to fall upon my shoulders, as I gazed upon the land which I was to traverse.

The whole area was dark, as if no healthy light of the ordinary sky shone over that dread landscape. Down there seemed to reek of evil forces. Miasmal gases were flung out from the seeping earth, through which straggly grass kept sticking up at wrong angles, and in which decayed-looking rocks and mouldering crags bedded firmly down. I tried to find some hint of hope or pleasantness in that drear, deep place, and thought of many problems to meditate on to save my mind from facing fully the impact of that environment; but only shadowy rocks and strange pits beckoned, and the valley waited in silence for my insignificant figure to plunge into its black mazes so insistently overwhelming that I knew that Grunderth would totally absorb my mind and leave no room for thoughts on other matters.

Immediately below, down the long slope of the valleyside there were old odd shapes that struck me as being man-made. Though they seemed austere and restful of intrusion, they gave me some sense of relief; for here was the proof that human beings (besides Sifar) had braved this territory before, at least for some distance. Therefore I urged my horse forward and downward, but he refused to budge. I coaxed him and he started forward in some trepidation, then stopped again, making strange sounds, tossing his head and rolling his eyes. I was vexed, but could hardly blame him, for indeed no animal of his nature would have wanted to walk upon the noisome lumps of nitrous pebbles that carpeted the surface of the ground.

I breathed deeply, armouring my mind against hysteria or susceptibility to the hallucinations of fear, and dismounted the horse. He was glad, and bolted away at once, and I turned and walked down the slope.

I saw now with some dismay that this place was a cemetery. The man-made buildings I had observed from the slopes were old vaults and mausoleums. Broken stone coffins, obviously robbed, were in some of these burial places, and here and there bones struck out from masses of dust. Even on the ground outside the great ruined burial chambers there were bones sticking up, and there were platforms of wood erected on poles on which skeletons lay. This place was still in use, for there were signs of recent interment and the smell of decomposition was very strong; and strange birds, posing grotesquely on the platforms, pecked at recently dead corpses. I saw figures which were certainly not birds though they appeared to flit little wings as they moved between the forests of poles on which the platforms were built.

I walked the interminable path I found in that dreadful ossuary, lit by the dismal gloaming that pervaded this bad scene, and seemed to go deeper into the burial places of even stranger humans than had mortared those charnel-houses of the valley slopes. Here the vaults were huge and more elaborately marbled and carved; archaic gods of unacceptable religions reigned high over their dead subjects. Looming faces seemed to chortle with deceit and cunning from the keystones of black arched doorways, and filthy rages flapped and blew from dessicated limbs. Sometime skulls and other bony objects crunched and rolled underfoot, and once I saw a large pool of pulsating maggots. But what caused the most concern was the sight of a thing humped over the disturbed figure of what seemed to have been a child, which gave a prodigious leap away on seeing me. I did not know what it was, but I gripped my shortsword tightly, disliking intensely, among other things, the abnormal length of its arms.

The temperature had been growing cooler too, and at one point it became so cold that I could not feel my fingers, and my jaw became cramped so that my teeth chattered violently. But this passed, and finally even the grim decomposed tombscape began to thin away, and I found myself in a swampy area where sometimes the only way forward lay through the spongy-looking material that lay atop the soft marsh. After this I found myself in another kind of ground. This was a barren wilderness of cracked, dry earth, which sometimes crumbled underfoot as I walked. Scars of great earthquakes formed drops below my feet and loomed up above my head. Now I crossed intricate bridges and spanning curves of interlacing rock, and passed boulders perched precariously on hills and deep riverless gorges where the rainless wind howled incessantly. Then the rocks became even more worn and seemed scorched in places, and soon I noticed that the very air seemed hotter and the stones burnt underfoot if I paused too long in my walking.

Then to my great joy I came to a better landscape where small streams ran in little ravines and grasses and trees grew. I was happy to see this fruitful, healthy earth once more, and I knelt, took a handful of soil and ran it through my fingers. I bent over and smelt the grasses and the flowers, and was thankful that I had reached this very pleasant area.

Here there were no sharp austere rocks, but I observed many serrated humps all of roughly similar shape and size, that nestled in the fertile green earth and seemed to be composed of a red-grey stone with which I was not familiar. And there were also strange burrows in the ground, so large that I could not imagine what lived in them, for no burrowing animal I knew demanded a hole that size. Over some of these holes there were trees, dead or dying, with their roots exposed, and many of them were hollowed out, as if they had been penetrated from below. The trees were of the same species, and while there were a few obviously young ones, most of the others were knotted with age.

I journeyed on and tried not to be curious, but inevitably I had to ask myself what those deep burrows under those trees signified. It was obvious that the trees had not grown over the holes; and the mere hollow shells of trunk that remained of the older ones made me admit to myself that there were some species of animal that ate those trees, and that those animals lived underground, and might come out of any or all of those warrens at any time.

I knew the habits of burrowing animals well, and expected that if any such things as I imagined dwelt beneath the surface of the earth, they were likely to come out at night in search of food. I knew, too, that the high trees could not be depended on for safety, for it was quite possible that such creatures could climb well.

I looked up; the baleful luminescence that glimmered from the cloud-streaked sky gave no indication of the time of day. Indeed, I realized with shock, there had been no change in the general appearance of the heavens since I had entered this territory of Grunderth. It seemed to me that I had been travelling for the space of several days without pause, because I had been guided previously by the light and dark of normal days and nights.

I studied my body as I walked, therefore, trying to notice whether the effects of this unplanned fast and abstinence from sleep were detrimental; but there was no weariness of body or cloudiness of mind, and I felt as if I could go on for a long way yet.

The hollowed-out trees ended suddenly and ahead there was a territory from which a very large number of trees had been cut. It was a depressing and tragic sight, for in an area perhaps four miles wide a whole forest of close-growing trees had been cut down, leaving roots and amputated stumps that bled a thick amber resin. Even here the stumps were hollowed out, and there were many more burrows to be seen.

When I saw so many cut trees, I hoped at once that the woodcutters had put their timber to very good use; but then, here and there, I began to see discarded saws and axes of Dominaut making, and I guessed that the foreigners and their slaves had made inroads into this part of the country too. I knew they had not come by way of the ancient cemetery I had crossed, and assumed that they had come from the coast of this land, cut the trees, then taken them back to the coast; from there, perhaps, the logs would be shipped to Dibra or to the seaside villages where they were setting up barracks and lookout towers as well as jetties for the huge slave and cargo ships. There was scarcely any other use the Dominauts made of the trunks of trees.

After trodding this region of cut trees I came to the place where the woodcutting had ended. It seemed to have ended suddenly, too, for there were signs, among the broken pots and scattered benches that remained in one of their shelters, that violence had taken place and that the Dominauts and their slaves had departed with great speed.

I wondered what precisely had caused the cessation of their operations, as I moved on, and more than once my mind ran on the tunnels below the trees.

Then I stopped before a deep ravine where a turbulent streamlet wriggled; and rather than climb down the step side, cross that stream and climb the other side, I decided to bridge the ravine.

I found a discarded axe that was still serviceable, and selected a tall tree which grew close to the ravine. Then I set to work to chop it down. I worked steadily, the axe driving into the very hard wood with shoulder-shaking jerks, and the triangular slice I made gradually grew larger until I heard the trunk creak and stepped back to watch the tree shudder and crash down, at once making a very admirable bridge across the chasm.

From the moment the tree fell, I was aware that I had caused resentment to something which I did not see. There was a powerful jolt of anger directed towards me, and I sensed it at once and tried to find its source. I turned and searched the landscape with my eyes, as sure that I had incurred displeasure as if the forest had cried out, and feeling certain that I had made my presence known to whatever creatures infested this queer domain. Nothing stirred, and yet there was this forceful sense of someone or something fiercely watching me.

On the other side of the ravine I suddenly felt heavier, more sluggish than I had ever been before. I could not understand the sensation of massiveness I was experiencing, and even as I told myself that I should press on, I was slowing. My feet were like stone; the effort to lift them was completely tiring. Then suddenly my mind seemed affected by this clinging tiredness, too, for I lost all desire to go on.

I sat on a wide area of grass where I could see for a long distance whether anything approached, and decided to wait calmly until I felt better, but my strange state continued. Now my arms seemed heavy as well, and my head, so that I started to sag and nod where I sat. Then I noticed that my heart seemed to throb with an intense effort, as if it fought against the clinging slowness that had enveloped my limbs. Soon my eyelids became heavy too and I realized that I was passing into the beginnings of a profound slumber. This thought did not perturb me, even though I remembered that I was in an unknown place, for the gradual loss of consciousness was overpoweringly pleasant and I had ceased all at once to consider the preservation of my body.

Just before I gave up trying to retain my consciousness, I am positive I heard great dislocations of earth, as if great boulders had unplugged themselves from the greensward in which they were embedded, and lifted clear of the ground. The smell of fresh earth and torn grasses came to me; more than once I felt a tremor in the soil and bedrock below me, and vibrating shudders as if heavy stones had fallen and fixed themselves into the earth. But I could not open my eyes.

When I awoke I thought that I had been transported in sleep to a new landscape, for all around me, instead of uncluttered meadowland, there were the smooth-sided grey-red mounds with their serrated tops, which before I had seen only at a distance. But the ravine I had crossed was still there with the tree spanning it, and, incredible as it seemed, I had to conclude that I had not observed the area well before I went into slumber. Certainly I had not expected to awaken surrounded by rocks fully fifteen feet high.

I arose, still feeling a strange viscidity of limb, and, like a man walking in water, began to labour to move my body forward. After what seemed a long time I reached one of the stony humps and began to climb to see what lay beyond, for my view of the landscape had been completely cut off.

On reaching the end of my climb, I gazed across the open grass and trees; then my eyes fell upon a group of very strange creatures indeed.

There evidently were males, females and offspring of both sexes, and they were hopping around, gamboling playfully, searching for food and wrestling with each other like puppies.

These things were about seven feet tall and vaguely like men, but with some singular differences. Their legs were very large and thickly muscled, so that when they bent their knees and sprang up, they jumped perhaps twenty feet at a time. Their hands and arms were disproportionately small; they had delicate, clawed fingers with which they nimbly grasped bits of wood, leaves and stone.

They carried snouts held high on heads that jutted forward on short necks, and their sinuous bodies, which they had erect most of the time, were covered with fur. Their eyes were black and very bright. Their ears were small and round, and sharp chisel-like teeth protruded past their top lips, in opposition to a smaller similar pair in their lower jaws. The creatures were coloured a light grey-brown, and the ones I guessed to be males had a stripe of black running down the middle of their backs. I expected them to have tails, and kept looking for such, but they did not.

Then, to my great amazement and consternation, the hump on which I crouched began to move. I had thought I felt it vibrated earlier; now definitely I saw and felt that it had shifted sideways. Then it gave a shudder and rose a little, and I saw that I was on the back of a huge and heavy animal. Even as I knew this for certain, it raised its extremities, pulling them out of the earth in which they had been embedded, and the noises I had heard as I had fallen asleep sounded again. I saw a long tapering tail on one side of the enormous bulk of body, and on the other an equally long neck that ended in a ridiculously tiny reptilian head.

You may be sure that the sudden realization that two such creatures existed on our planet, and the shock of discovering them together, filled me with a horror which I thought I had long overcome. I clung to what seemed to be serrated rocks, but what really were the dorsal bumps and fins of the creature, and as the ponderous hulk raised and lowered itself on four thick legs, like an ungainly lizard, I wondered whether this was the place where my journey and search would end ignominiously. I resented the idea, and was formulating some desperate plan of escape or attack, when my outlandish mount gave a low, harsh, repeated sound like two stones rubbing, and all at once the leaping, rodent-like creatures that frolicked in the grassland turned their heads and saw me.

Immediately they began hopping over, covering the distance rapidly while I slithered and jumped as far as my clumsy body would allow, to reach the ground on the inside of my circle of mounds, which definitely had moved closer together. As I tumbled to the earth the whole group of hopping-things arrived on the tops of the looming rock-like reptiles, and sat cross-legged, pointing at me and conversing in quick grunts. I knew then that the rock-reptiles were the mounts and guards of the hopping-things, and that they had been set around me to prevent my free movement upon the land.

Then one hopper stood up, grunting and gesticulating, and the others turned to watch him, falling silent. He talked for a long time; afterwards one or two of the other creatures spoke, and it was obvious that I was the centre of some very important discussion. Finally the first speaker seemed to sum up the content of the discussion, for all nodded their heads, agreeing in a manner which deeply distressed me; for it was in precisely the manner which I had thought unique to human beings.

One creature then made a spring and disappeared on the other side of the hump-circle; shortly he returned, with a shaggy wild-eyed being wearing goatskins, whom at first I did not recognize to be a man, so much had I grown accustomed to expect unknown things in this landscape. This man was directed to descend to me, which he did with a jump quite similar to those of his captors, and stood before me perhaps twelve feet away. I calculated his size and possible strength at once, for I was uncertain as to his intention then he spoke in a dialect based on the language of Dominauts, and bade me peace.

He said that he had been slave of the Dominauts, and that he and others had been cutting trees in this area, many years ago, when all of a sudden they were attacked by the hopping creatures, who hurled great stones at them and chased them away. Ten or twelve men, including some Dominauts, had been taken but he did not know what had become of them.

He called the hopping creatures Kraggarts, and their domesticated, stony reptiles, Monothons. He was their prisoner for life, he said, because of his participation in the destruction of their food; for the Kraggarts lived on the trunks of trees, and fed by burrowing into and gnawing the trees. He said the Kraggarts had lost much food, on which their growing civilization depended, when the men had cut their trees; they complained that the men were trying to drive them out of existence. This man, who eventually told me his name was Laize, spent most of his waking hours climbing trees and picking young leaves and shoots for the baby Kraggarts; and he was sure that there were other captured men, too, but he had not seen a man before that time for several years, by his own calculation.

"You are from the Ainchan Plain?" I asked.

"No. from the south of this land Grunderth, close by the sea-coast."

"There are Dominauts there?"

"They are all along the coast."

I paused. Then: "What will these Kraggarts do with me?"

"They will hold a trial, and pass judgment on you. That is why they have brought us together-I am your interpreter."

"What have I done?" I protested, though I had guessed.

"The tree you cut down . . ." Laize began to explain.

A grunting came from above, and, looking up, I saw that the leader of the Kraggarts was motioning and pointing directions. Laize said that we were to walk, surrounded by the Monothons, in the direction he indicated, and so a weird procession set off—two men walking amidst ponderous, ungraceful reptiles that rumbled like rockslides when they moved, and strange rodent-like beings who sat atop their awesome steeds like gods.

"Where are we going?" I enquired of Laize.

"To the Hollow of Judgement."

"Listen, we are not Dominauts. Explain that to them."

"I have tried to do that a number of times. They cannot tell the difference; they do not reason as we do. But quiet. We are close to the place now, and they do not like their prisoners talking without permission, once inside."

Very soon after, we stood before a wide passage that disappeared in darkness into the earth. Then the Kraggarts dismounted and led us inside, and we walked for a long way in a great tunnel which seemed lighted by the glow of phosphorescent insects. The walls of this tunnel were honeycombed with the dens of the Kraggarts, and as we passed curious snouts pushed out from the compartments as the citizens of Grunderth watched us pass and showed us to their children.

Then we came upon a larger burrow than the rest, and here I saw, sitting in the usual crosslegged fashion upon a nest of dried leaves, and twigs, a grey Kraggart who immediately struck me as one of refinement, dignity and experience. The ones who had brought Laize and myself evidently respected him too, for they clasped their hands before them and did not look into his eyes.

At an order from the leader of the group who had brought us in, the Kraggarts spread out on the ground before this arbitrator, having placed us men together in their midst.

The chief of our captors grunted briefly, pointing to me now and then, outlining his case to the noble Kraggart who inclined his head and listened, eyeing me all the while. Laize began to speak, quietly intoning his words of accusation. Finally the Kraggart ended and Laize asked me to answer to their charge of having destroyed trees.

"Tell them, I cut only one tree. I am not a habitual cutter of trees. I ask their forgiveness. Tell them that."

"That is pointless. They do not reason as we do."

"Tell them!"

He obeyed. Then: "He says that you have broken their law. The trees were not yours, for you are a stranger here. He wants to know what you were doing in Grunderth."

"I am passing through to the Coast of the Sea of Mirrors. I have come from the capital city of the plain of the River Ruba, known as the Ainchan plain, which lies very very far to the east and south of this place."

"He asks, did you cross the place of dead people?"

"I did."

"He says you are a special one. Did you see the Feasters?"

"I saw a huge thing with extremely long arms, which jumped even as the Kraggarts do."

Laize translated this and the old Kraggart sat stroking at his whiskers, pondering. I could see that he had a new impression of me.

"The Feasters are the enemies of the Kraggarts," Laize ventured to whisper to me. "They eat flesh; the Kraggarts eat the hardstone trees.

My heart leapt suddenly. Perhaps Wrog was one of these Kraggarts. Sifar had not led me to expect such characteristics, but these were the intelligent dwellers of Grunderth. Therefore I seized upon the chance, and instructed Laize to inform the justiciar that I sought Wrog.

"You are standing before the Wrog," Laize said. "He is the Wrog. The Wrog is the judge of the Kraggart community."

"Oh, I see! Well, tell him I have come from Sifar!"

The Wrog and the other Kraggarts were staring at us and waiting for us to cease conversing, surprised at this breach of etiquette. Laize now turned apologetically to the Wrog and gave him my information. Immediately there was a still greater silence than there had been before; then several grunts broke out all at once, and the Wrog motioned for silence by raising his hand in an amazingly human way. He spoke, and Laize translated quickly:

"We know of this Sifar. I sat in judgment on him once. His accusers thought he was a destroyer of food, and brought him here. He was not a criminal at all. He had a unique and interesting occupation. He took soft dust and mixed it with water, then he shaped it, then he burned it with fire, and vessels of earth were made. Sifar of the south-east is a good man. I am sure he does not know the kind of man you are, for he would not associate with a destroyer of food—he agreed with us when he was here that the men who did such things should be punished. He understood the needs of the Kraggarts, and admired our ways; and he promised to restore our trees if the time permitted."

"Tell the Wrog that I have brought some seeds of the hardstone tree."

Laize passed on this message. There was another silence; then the Kraggarts huddled together around the Wrog, grunting all together.

I opened my bag and took out the rabbitskin pouch of seeds. Stepping forward to the group of Kraggarts, I opened it and laid it at their feet. There were several thousand of the tiny hard black seeds nestled in their container, and when my captors saw them they whined and clapped their hands, again to my amazement.

The Wrog motioned for silence once more, and stood up. He began to speak again, and Laize picked up his words.

"We are happy for the gift you have brought from our friend Sifar, the best of men. The hardstone trees are our staple diet, and the source of our preventive medicine.

"But there are two things that have to be explained to you. First, the hardstone trees are very difficult to grow, and we Kraggarts know very little of growing or taking care of trees. Next, according to our infallible law you have sentenced yourself to imprisonment by your act of recklessly wasting food and endangering the lives and future of the Kraggarts.

"Therefore I am making this judgement on you, man of the south-east. You will dig the earth, plant all of the hardstone seeds, and nurture the growing trees until they have reached a state where they are certain to survive and grow—for it is a difficult matter to grow a hardstone tree—certainly more difficult than to cut it down. Now, the tree grows at such a rate that it takes the passage of thirty-six moons or more before we can be sure it can survive; thus you are lucky to be allowed to leave after that time, for your interpreter (here Laize's voice sank) is here until there is no breath left in his body."

I wanted to protest but immediately I was lifted off the ground and hustled away by the group of Kraggarts which had brought me, without even having the time to say goodbye to Laize.

We hurtled in great leaps through high hall-like caverns of the inner earth, where spiky stalactities, tall stalagmites and glistening elongated columns formed strikingly beautiful shapes. Precariously we leapt quiescent pools of deposited acidic liquid where calcified, corroded rocks melted in the slow-motion of eons, and here and there spiny rocks grew and branched like twigs.

Finally we shot past the limestone blocks and sunken soil of a broad and deep sinkhole, and broke out above the ground.

The Kraggarts left me in a smooth grassy area by a quiet stream, with all my possessions and the bag of seeds. As soon as they hopped away I attempted to flee away from the direction in which they had disappeared. I began to run, and proceeded for a little way; then I found that my feet became heavier and soon I paused, gasping, then plodded back to where I had left the hardstone seeds, realizing that somehow the Kraggarts of Grunderth had some means of controlling my physical body that I could not identify. I had no choice but to grow the trees.

I felt that I was lucky, for truly I had expected some harsher punishment; yet I wished to reach the Coast of the Sea of Mirrors, and I chafed bitterly at first. Gradually, however, I saw that since my state was unavoidable I should make the best of it and see what I could learn during my stay in Grunderth.

Months passed. I dug the earth and made trenches for watering, cleared the grass and removed old tree-trunks from the soil; planted long rows of seeds and watched the precious little seedlings come to life. I weeded them carefully and guarded them well, and they grew. The chief difficulty I encountered was the lack of light, for in Grunderth there was a lighter twilight and a darker twilight, and no distinct night and day as we of Ainchan know it.

I was fed by the Kraggarts; once a day I received a ration of berries, beans, leaves and grain. Many of my meals consisted of boiled grain and beans.

I began enjoying growing the trees and took great pains to keep them as healthy as possible. In fact, as the months passed I grew more eccentric and personal about them, and thankfully rejoiced as the thousands of little foliages came up, in an area nearly half as wide as the area the Dominauts had desecrated. Eventually I roamed like a madman, planting seeds here and there, and as the landscape became fruitful I felt great power and pride. Soon, too, the Kraggarts

When a seed starts its release of growth, one point swells a little and allows a tiny tendril of its insides to thrust out; this is the beginning of the root. This sprout, surrounded by fine delicate hairs, probes downward and the earth welcomes it with warmth and moisture. The root straightens and plunges deeper as the soil makes room for it, then the kernel opens its seed-leaves, bursting the shell of its capsule. The seed-leaves expand as the stalk swings them towards the source of light, and two tiny leaves, pale with freshness, gradually turning green, peep out and commence to spring from within the seed-leaves. Then they widen and lengthen, still facing the light, and open for another pair which opens for another, and many leaves burst forth and make way for more, while the seed-leaves, drained of food, wither and fall away on the thickening stalk.

Soon a little tree stands boldly, and the roots absorb the forces of life that the earth stores and relinquishes, sending them up the channel in the tiny trunk and breaking them forth into foliage, like a fountain spurting watersprays from its apex; a splendid symmetrical bouquet.

Each time I saw this mighty marvel I respected the earth more. Over and over I witnessed this translation of force into living forms, and, as I had learnt to do under the tutelage of Akincyde, I asked myself how this was done.

I walked among the green seedlings that shone like little stars in the black soil, and sometimes I thought that I felt, more than defined, the answer. It seemed that a unique unity existed behind it all, somehow. I felt that there must exist a point where force and its forms were balanced out and equalized, and it was here that the mechanism of life could be found. Thus I reasoned, and within myself I searched for such a point. This recurring thought, and its practical inner exercises, took up quite a lot of my time during the period that I farmed in Grunderth, and today the mystery of force and form still has not yet been resolved satisfactorily in my mind, though I have learnt some very astonishing facts about it.

Time passed, and the hardstone trees grew solidly and patiently, as is their nature, until eventually I was no longer looking down at them, but through them. The strong saplings spread like poles over the landscape, their rows diminishing and seeming to coalesce in the distance, and the area which had once been a prison full of brutally cut tree-stumps now became a quiet forest of meditation where I was glad to be.

One morning as I came out of my burrow (for I had adapted to sleeping in these very safe and warm shelters) I saw a full-grown ram with curved horns, a renegade of some wild flock, standing in an area of sapling hardstones. He had been eating their leaves, and several of the trees bore evidence of his marauding. I shouted and waved my arms, and at once the beast turned, saw me, and started hoofing the ground and humping his shoulders in preparation for his charge.

I seized a good-sized stone from the earth and turned to meet him as he lunged into a thundering run and sped over the turf towards me.

I rooted my feet firmly in the ground, bent my knees and held the boulder before me with both hands, as the ram finished his run and leaped into his tremendously forceful butt.

I timed him well and stiffened at the moment of his shattering impact. The hard rock powdered like a sandball when he struck, but his skull split and he sank down dead with a shudder, his broken horns hanging about his head and bleeding at their stumps.

I stood for a moment absorbing the shock of the encounter; had it not been for my previous training and constant practice in the withstanding of such attacks, I would have been flung far away by that stupendous blow. I silently thanked my mentor Akincyde for showing me that this was possible, and the earth itself for allowing me to know its secrets and to use its power.

The power of the earth is a fantastic and formidable thing. I cannot tell all the ways in which it may be utilized, for I am yet a novice in such matters; but often I witnessed evidence of this power among the Kraggarts and Monothons. I have seen a Kraggart stand in a furious river with water up to his head, and as rocks and logs flew past, some actually colliding with his head, he remained immovable as a crag, calmy munching the leaves of the river-vines. Also, I have seen baby Kraggarts fall, from high cliffs or into deep subterrene pits, and, on impact, become stuck or embedded like stone; then in a minute they would gambol away unhurt; and I know that there were Monothons which had ground themselves into the soil and remained there so long that the tall grass hid them from view. Now that I have reflected on that place, I believe that the clusters of low hills that I took as landmarks were nothing more than the spawning-grounds of these colossal saurians.

I examined the trees and saw that they were not badly injured and that with careful treatment all of them would recover. Then I set to work to skin the animal, for its hide was of excellent quality and very beautiful.

Once before, and in different circumstances, I might have cooked and eaten some of its meat, but I had eaten no flesh since the beginning of my quest, and I knew that the Kraggarts had a deep aversion to such a practice and to its perpetrators, for they themselves knew what it was to be the food of carnivores. The young male Kraggart who had been charged with the duty of supplying my food, and who had begun to instruct me in the variegated grunts and whines that make up Kraggart speech, had communicated to me that the Kraggarts had a great loathing for Laize, for, despite their warnings and after two imprisonments in the Dungeons of Dark, which lie deep in the maddeningly fearful abysses of inner earth and are haunted by the eldritch wraiths of the wickedest of earth-things, Laize persisted in a vicious and repugnant occupation. He would go amongst a flock of goats disguised in his goatskins, seize a young kid and stab it to death, dismantle its parts and take choice portions, leaving the skin and other discardments behind.

My young Kraggart friend also indicated that he was suspicious of the way Laize watched the Kraggart youngsters though of course he did not dare to prey on them. It was said, too, that Laize created another completely different threat; for though it had never happened, the Kraggarts felt that the remains of the dead animals would attract their enemies, the dreaded Feasters.

Thus I buried the carcase of the ram in a spot away from my precious trees. After that I cleaned the skin thoroughly by the proximate stream which had served to irrigate the land, and tied it securely over the top of one of the hollow stumps to enable it to dry.

Three Grunderth-days passed, during which I was watering the youngest of the trees and nurturing the injured; all of the seeds had been planted and were growing by this time. On the night of the third day I awoke to the sound of rasping snarls and smell of something foetid; and taking my shortsword in hand I went outside my burrow hoping that the trees were safe.

There was a small open area close by the tree and on it, silhouetted in the fitful light that came from an unusually over-cast sky, three creatures like the one I had encountered in the ancient cemetery, sat in a wide triangle. I knew them now to be Feasters; and I saw that verily they were feasting. They had disinterred the reeking carcase of the ram I had slain, and now they sat, each distrustful of his neighbor and just out of the reach of each other's claws, reaching to the full extent of their horrendous arms to pluck ghastly tidbits of offal from the silent dark mound in their midst. So intent were these Feasters on their disgusting regalement that I managed to reach them and recklessly attack before they were aware of my presence.

With a leap as mighty as that of any Kraggart, I was beside the nearest one, and drove my blade with the carried momentum into its ribs just below the armpit. I twisted the blade as it came to the end of its penetration, and felt something break within the creature's body. I dragged the sword and out as it died soundlessly, and turned in time to hack away a reaching clawed paw, ending a grasping attack another of the repulsive creatures had made. With a wailing howl the injured beast sprang away and escaped.

Now I face the third one over the malodorous mass of the dread ram, while he licked an extremely long tongue over carnivorous teeth, very much in the manner of a wolf, and crouched for his attack.

He came in a flurry of springs and clawing, and swinging paws passed on all sides of my body as I evaded his grabbings. Then I sprang in close enough and sank my weapon into the place where his ribs divided, distinctly hearing the skin pop; and the Feaster gave one dying half-leap away, dragging my implanted sword from my hand, then tumbled in long-limbed confusion as its obnoxious gore splurged thickly out upon the wholesome earth.

In the morning the Kraggarts gathered in hundreds and looked upon my handiwork, conversing in awed and thoughtful grunts. They had never seen a dead Feaster before; now they gazed upon the two grisly carcases and the matted claw with its remains of putrescent flesh, and meditated on the deaths of the hateful monsters, for creatures of their kind had kidnapped and eaten several of their children over the years. The Wrog was there, and he praised me highly before the gathered multitudes of the Kraggarts. Then, in my halting smattering of Grunderth language, I thanked the Kraggarts for their congratulations and said that I was very happy to have rid them of two of their accursed enemies. I seized the opportunity to draw their attention to the forest of hardstone trees that I had planted, and asked whether, considering all that I had done, I would be allowed to leave the territory of Grunderth as soon as possible.

The Wrog paused for a moment and looked down, and my heart sank when I realized that he did not want me to go. Then his nobler judgement prevailed and he clasped his hands before him and bowed, a sign of acquiescence. After that, he ordered that the carcasses of the Feasters and the various bits of flesh and signs of gore be deeply covered with soil, so that no other Feaster could find them, and walked pensively away.

Then, to the great amusement of the sight-seeing Kraggarts who stood around, I jumped and laughed for joy. My body was light and free and skipped easily and inspiration pounded at my heart. I ran and sprang, and in my frolicking I came upon the place where the dried-out ramskin lay fastened on the hollow stump, and beat at it in a surge of victorious feeling.

That moment something astonishing happened.

A series of solid booms sprang from the stiffened membrane and expanded widely in the column of the hollow tree. The sound bounded into the burrow below the roots and ran like a current through the myriad honeycombed warrens that pock-marked the inner earth, and the ground reverberated and loudly echoed its dynamic driving call that now coalesced and radiated from the land towards the sky. Up there, the clouds spattered and flew about forming even lines and concentric whirls, and a small button of sun shone plain and freely on Grunderth.

An inner part of myself had taken over my actions after that first remarkable explosion of sound, so that my hands continued to rise and fall in blurs and sudden pauses and repeated booms and smacks shot from the surface of the mighty instrument that I had made. As the power sustained itself and grew stronger, the atmosphere was charged and the very trees around me seemed to strain and listen.

When first the Rhythm (for such it was) had started, the Monothons had drawn closer; soon they arched their hilly backs, rising high on their legs and flicking their slender necks and tails from side to side—a weird but beautiful sight. Next they began a stiff four-legged jumping and with each leap formed radiating stony lines that converged on the resonating column, making it their centre; and so nimbly had these bulky creatures commenced to move that not one tree was damaged. For over the vast landscape twelve lines of Monothons, strung like beads, laid out an even pattern.

Now from the innumerable pits that dotted the land near and far Kraggarts pushed out their heads and wriggled out to join the multitudinous concourse of their fellow-creatures who already skipped and cavorted in even stride among the spaced-out Monothons. Their actions depicted and synchronized with the sounds that bubbled and muttered beneath my rippling fingers, so that it seemed as if their actions kept the sound going.

Since then I have experimented with piles of sand on the sympathetically vibrating membranes of these Drums (for thus are such sounding instruments called) and watched fascinating patterns that form with each single beat transmitted to them from a separate instrument. But so huge a scale of formed shapes that can be seen among the hills and boulders of

Grunderth even today, are there because the very earth is like a Drum in that part of the world.

For, my people, the fact that vibration makes forms coalesce is the single most important thing that I can say to you.

While the earth threw up with larger tones the strident measure of time and sound I was creating, and the oblivious Kraggarts performed their endless gyrations over the motionless, patterned Monothons, I noticed the shaggy figure of Laize emerge from a distant burrow and run frantically away. This bid for escape came as a final gift to my soul and I exploded in even more merriment, driving my erstwhile interpreter and explainer onward with my pounding, and wishing the scoundrel long life and a change of heart, until he disappeared still running, while the happy Kraggarts danced on.

Soon they were smacking their hands together and tapping the earth with their enormous feet, so that when I gradually brought my drumming to a halt the dwellers of Grunderth kept on.

I cut the roots of the hollow tree-stump and lifted it carefully and proudly, for this was my memento of Grunderth and my experiences there. Then I picked up my bag and sheathed shortsword, which I had recovered and cleaned diligently, and I walked away through the growing lines of hardstone trees.

Late that evening I stood on a hill on the other side of the valley I had entered three years previously. I looked down upon Grunderth. Perfect patterns of stones, megaliths and Monothons lay on the pitted landscape, and the graceful hardstone trees grew sturdily. The Kraggarts were still jumping and smacking their hands together, and many of them had taken to beating the hollow trees with sticks. The collected Rhythm came up to me and thrilled me poignantly.

I sat and lowered my Drum, listened carefully to the pound of their feet on the earth, and joined their Rhythm in a last farewell.

From the centre of the largest circle where he sat gravely pounding a tree-stump with a stone, the Wrog looked up and waved to me, and all the Kraggarts turned and did the same, still stepping in Rhythm. Then they all shouted together in their bizarre but syncopated language, and the wind wafted the sounds to me.

"Goodbye, Growing Seed! You journey with the blessings of Grunderth!"

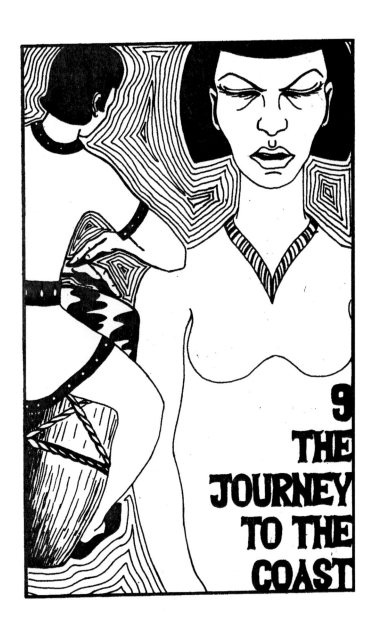

9
THE
JOURNEY
TO THE
COAST

The Journey to the Coast

THE NEXT IMPORTANT EPISODE in the life of Shangodoon is his encounter with Armienne, and their subsequent marriage. This, too, is an aspect of Shangodoon's life which has been much dramatized, fictionalized and otherwise depicted in the Arts of Ainchan, to the extent that much is lost or distorted concerning the truth of the affair, and therefore its significance in his history may not be correctly estimated. Thus I, Godnor have undertaken to chronicle the beginning and growth of their relationship, up to the sequence where I can employ the actual words of Armienne, for at one point Shangodoon invited her to tell the people of her experience with Harmony.

It was a month after Shangodoon had left Grunderth and he had been travelling south-westward steadily, accustoming himself to the world of men again, savouring the beautiful landscapes he crossed, enjoying the normal sun and rain, meditating on and practicing the intriguing art of keeping Rhythm, and generally looking forward to seeing the Coast of the Sea of Mirrors.

One day as he rested in the mouth of a secluded cave, a hidden place which he had found only by his developed earth instinct, he heard the noise of running feet, then of scuffling, somewhere outside. Coming out of his shelter, he was in time to see a young native woman who was being held across her neck and upper body by a tall Dominaut troop-commander, jerk her head backward and upward into the chin of her captor, so that he let go and staggered back, grasping his neck. Then the woman seized a stone and cracked it savagely against the man's shins in two sudden calculated moves, and as he croaked in incredulous anger and with the shock of pain, she threw the stone into his face. Rock met bone with a sickening sound; the man sank down stunned as she turned to run again.

Shangodon guessed that she had been travelling with the troop of mounted soldiers and their native employees and slaves which he had seen at a distance the day before.

As she ran towards his hiding place he stepped out into the open, raising his hand. "My sister!"

She had crouched and seized another stone and was about to hurl it with invincible accuracy when she recognized that he was not an enemy and lowered her hand.

"Come quickly. His soldiers will come after him. You will be safe with me", Shangodoon urged.

214

She nodded and hastened with him into the concealed shelter.

Together they watched as the Dominaut soldiers came through the trees, found their unconscious bloodied commander, then started running, searching in all directions for the woman.

Shangodoon stood back and watched the girl, knowing that they were safe from discovery. He saw at once that she was very becoming, and well proportioned, and that her manner was extremely appealing. Wondering, he sat with her in silence as the soldiers bungled around outside, near and far, and afterwards went away cursing in failure and nursing their commander. Then the young woman turned and smiled a profound gratitude. Her beautiful wide-eyed glance thrilled him immensely. He swallowed, and spoke.

"I am Shangodoon."

"I am Armienne."

"It is a sublimely beautiful name."

"It means, 'Agreeable Relationship.'"

He nodded, supremely happy to have met her.

"You speak a dialect of the Ainchan Plain," he said.

"My father was of Noosh, and I grew up there. Then, years ago, he took his family to the southern coasts, then sailed west to Green Bay on the Coast of the Sea of Mirrors. That is my present home."

Perhaps it is destiny that we have met. I too am on the way to the Coast of the Sea of Mirrors. But what are you doing so far from home? And how came you to be among the enemies of our people?"

She explained: "Three years ago, I left the Coast of the Sea of Mirrors and came north to a place called Free Valley. I was interested in understanding the art of writing, researching and recording, for it was my aim to perfect my people's knowledge of our coastlines and seas, by making a compendium of the shore and water creatures, and their habits. I also sought to find ways in which men could derive benefit from their existence, as well as how they could do the same from men's; for I believe that it is possible for all things of the environment to live in peaceful evolution together.

"I came to Free Valley and took up my studies under the tutelage of Licestus, a man extremely knowledgeable in the ways and physical structures of animals and plants. I stayed at his Academy of Natural Research for two years, during which time my grasp of the principles underlying the existence of natural creatures impressed him deeply, and enabled me to take periodic jobs with various groups and individuals engaged in similar pursuits.

In the third year, my final year of study, my tutor, who was given to dubious transactions with the ruling people, asked me to take an assignment with the commander of a Dominaut troop which was travelling through the land on a journey of exploration. Their business was to understand the nature of the terrain and to chart it, and to see what animals and plants existed that they might make use of. It was my job to explain and classify the various natural phenomena that the foreigners found unusual. I was reluctant to undertake this work, for I saw that no good could be served by assisting them in becoming familiar with territory they had not yet conquered; but I knew that they had paid Licestus well, and that I would return home comparatively wealthy; besides, three months was a tolerable time, I told myself in further excuse.

"At the recent end of this period I planned to return to Free Valley, collect my pay from my tutor and then turn homeward, and thus when the time for my prospective departure came I was badly shocked to find out that Licestus, whom I had grown to detest and who yet turned out to be far more odious and abominable than I had imagined, had sold, not hired me, to the commander of the troop. I protested at once and tried to leave, but I was told that I was the property of King Chrazius III and kept within guard, so that I could not make my escape until today, when the commander called me to his tent, sent away my guard and tried to embrace me."

"You dealt with him very well," Shangodoon said. "You knew what to do, and without fear."

"I was taught the natural fighting methods of the Former Ages. My father has studied and revived many of the old traditions of the people, and he felt that I should know how to protect myself on my journeys.

Shangodoon nodded his head, remembering Akincyde . . . "I am interested in the old traditions also." His mind was racing to adjust to her presence; his thoughts were on her beauty. He wanted to say something good, that she would like, that would fill her with solace; wanted to hold her, and wished that he had known her all his life.

"What will you do now?" he asked. "Go back to your deceitful tutor of Free Valley?"

"No! I must see my family. I am going home. I don't want to see that man again."

"Then we can go together . . . ? I will see you safely to your father's house."

"I am grateful to you."

"It makes me very happy to be able to travel with you," he enthused. "We can buy horses at the next hamlet we come to, and provisions. And you must buy anything you want, whatever you think necessary for yourself, and a good traveller's bag. I have a wallet of rich coins."

"My father will repay you well."

"To see you reach his house in safety will be my reward." His tone was deeply sincere. A nuance of feeling, a whiff of oneness, passed between them. They felt a need for each other that was a natural and indispensible prelude to their surviving together, and yet contained more aspects than the essentially functional companionship of travelers. They were both aware of this infinite-seeming want that could neither be expressed nor ignored, and its potency awed them profoundly.

The two journeyed for the next two weeks, sometimes stopping at the little villages that dotted the landscape and spending the night; other times they camped in the open and slept in covered hammocks. Shangodoon meanwhile fought recurring personal battles with his body and physical desires, conflicts which she seemed aware of and respected; though she could say nothing, she was conscious of the subtle victories he achieved over his passions and she saw his strength and discipline. Her fondness grew into an ardour which tended to absorb her will. In those two weeks they became truly affectionate toward each other, their eyes and smiles conveying messages that their voices and bodies did not yet dare to express.

Then one evening during the third week of their journey they camped in a copse of fine tall trees by a running stream, and sat talking and contemplating the rising moon before she turned away for the night. That evening for the first time she touched his drum, giving in to her curiosity over the strangeness of this unfamiliar object that he always had with him.

He had not played it before her yet; he had stolen away alone on early mornings to meditate and practice his rhythms while she still slumbered, for he knew that she would suspect the soundness of his actions, having never seen or heard a drum before.

Now she ran her fingers over it in an instinctive recognition of the technique involved, and the instrument muttered at her in an alarming fashion, so that she drew back her hand.

"May I show you how it is handled?" Shangodoon offered.

She nodded.

He brushed his hands lovingly over the taut skin and sat down, slanting the smoothly cut column at an angle, and placing his legs on either side of the instrument. He bowed his head and closed his eyes for a moment, invoking a power he had begun to feel but did not fully understand; and his hands rose and fell slowly in even beats.

As the series of flat booms bounded away from the man and through the suspended branches of the trees, the woman's eyes widened and she craned her neck forward, stiffened, watching his face, hands and instrument with a wonder that bordered on incredulity. The sounds drove through her hearing with a willful insistence, a total assault on sensitive responses that she could not starve. The rhythms propelled their power in a steady omnipotent pattern which seemed to say things about her, knew all the things she hoped and lived for deep inside, even as he with his knowing eyes, now watching hr intently behind the flying blurred veil of his hands, was beating at her soul in a unique and basic communication that devalued the system of words.

Even sound-divisions, of four, eight, sixteen, thirty-two and sixty-four, mixed, mumbled and jumbled, smacked and jumped; rippled on the rim of the tautened circle of skin or blatted from the centre with Shangodoon's flat hard hand relentlessly urging them forward. Drops and pauses lured Armienne on, confused her feelings and joined them to the pulsation, so that she began to feel that all along she had known that something like this was inevitable, and wanted it to continue forever.

The moon rose high and yet the strident bellow-whisper mutter of the drum spattered sounds in all directions without cessation. Shangodoon was no longer conscious of creating the rhythm himself; surprised, he stared down watching his hands move like lightning and fall like staccato claps of thunder upon a surface that demanded unusual strikings.

The drumsound juddered at the ground so that the woman felt the vibration in her feet, legs and thighs, in the hollow of her pelvis and in the pit of her stomach. There was nothing that she alone could do to satisfy the urges such hearing demanded; and he, forcefully sounding his bolts of sound through her quivering, moistening frame, was aware that there would be no turning back this time, no fighting to maintain a situation that they were beyond. They both knew that they were plunging into something much larger than themselves, which could forever expand their minds and states. Part of the awesome feeling was that they would have to bear the responsibility of the expanded knowledge that would be in their possession after their bodies came together. They would share the cosmic secret; they would exchange parts of themselves forever.

He worked his will with her that night, dissolving his complete being into her virgin feeling until her cries of anguished delight tremored out among the trees, and his rhythmic gusts and dynamic reactions to his own spiraling nervous power made her search his face in wonder, curious at it all dreamily wondering about the things he guided her skillfully into doing, complying in the overwhelmingly pleasurable stroking and clasping of their union until she felt her full womanhood bloom under his tireless explorations.

He had met her eyes in an earnest glower for a moment, then leapt up and slammed his final two-handed decisive finale down. Then he stepped to where she sat before him, looked into her large disturbed eyes and at her full trembling lips; held her shoulders, pulling her to him breathing deeply, kissing hungrily, in a controlled wildness, at her neck, chin, mouth and eyes. Her arms came up and wrapped his body tightly, as if she were afraid to let go, as if she had accepted his love as the only security, and a choking gasp escaped her open mouth. Presently he probed gently, over and over again., at her squeezed-tight inner thighs, loosening them, pushing her knees apart, pulling her wide hips in close to himself and sinking into the position he had worked so hard to attain between her sleekly smooth upper legs. Then she felt no longer herself and a range of distant emotions, far-off imaginings and remote soothing dreams swayed her thinking to and fro. She rocked gently on his body, see-sawed happily, climbing on his contractions as on a tall swaying tree, higher and higher with a frantic need for haste to touch his turgid, full-ripe fruit; then she gave one last sweep of her legs and took the shoulder of her first orgasm, fighting like a wild thing to accommodate the forces which engulfed her.

He completed his attainment and took her on the journey again, without a break in his spasmic rhythms; lifter her higher and broke in synchronic stretches and taut arched peaks of passion that stiffened and tingled every bond of their bodies; then she lay quite still, completely spread upon the earth, while he stroked and rubbed smoothly and relentlessly at the tatters of her virginity until he shuddered profoundly once again and subsided upon her, holding her in place as he breathed and drifted in the timeless, spaceless dimensions of completion.

She hugged him tightly, wanting to do thus forever, and drifted into joyous slumber.

10
ON
THE COAST
OF THE SEA
OF MIRRORS

On the Coast of the Sea of Mirrors

RHYTHMIC HILLS FELL SLOPING down to smooth yellow beaches and sharp rocky coastlines where high breakers constantly met the land in a recurring embrace of surges. Land and water touched each other in rough tumbles, soft caresses and gentle kisses and for seventy miles along the Coast of the Sea of Mirrors. The vista made the travelers rein in and pause.

It was the first time Shangodoon had seen the sea. He was with Armienne at the top of a bold limestone scarp that gave a splendid view of the wide and exciting terrain. The sound of the sea had become a constant background sound of tranquility; he viewed the great body of water and his head turned to follow the long line of the horizon as he absorbed the new experience in silent wonder. It appealed to something in himself that he had never known to exist; here was a completely new fact of the world that he had to make room for.

Armienne pointed to one of the many bays that ringed the land. "That is Green Bay, where my family lives."

"The territory is very beautiful," Shangodoon said, breathing deeply.

"Let's go!" she cried eagerly. She started her horse into motion and he followed her, cantering down a winding gradient towards the lower land.

The horses' hooves hitting the earth suddenly attracted Shangodoon, and he listened intently. He understood now the nature of the movement of animals, and meditated on the wonderful design of their limbs and the gait which gave them that graceful rhythm. He remembered the night, over six years before, when on the way to the Cavern-Temple of the Forbidden Mountains he had been at a loss to account for the way the horse's hoofs had disturbed him. The cause for the disturbance had been his own lack of rhythm; now he knew, and felt, that rhythm was a natural part of life, and that it was he who had changed, and not the laws of life. He had found rhythm, and had seen that rhythm interconnected function with shape of body. He thought of this even as he rode, and saw that there was a connection between this idea and his previous pondering upon force and form; the result was that then, and for years later, he was to wonder about Force, Function and Form, and how each of these influenced the others.

But at that time Armienne was thinking of home, and he left those interminable thoughts alone and rode beside her down a used trail through the scrubby cactuses and fleshy-leaved, prickly agaves that formed the vegetation of the sandy inland hills. Then they came upon a newly cut, wide road that pleased with horses well, and finally they were at the high brick wall which surrounded the house and lands of Wrison, the father of Armienne. The curiously arabesque wrought-iron gates were open.

There were scenes of joy when Armienne entered the house. Shangodoon met Kaydur, her mother, and Erutan, a brother, as well as Wrison; they thanked him repeatedly for his accompaniment of Armienne, and were glad that obviously he needed their hospitality. Soon he was placed in an apartment which he could occupy as long as he pleased, and Shangodoon accepted the luxuries they offered him with gladness, for truly he had wanted to stay for a while.

His relationship with Armienne kept tugging at his mind; he wanted to see more of her and wished that there was something he could do to justify staying around for some time. She had never asked why he wanted to come to the Coast of the Sea of Mirrors; he had kept all information about his mission to himself. Perhaps he should move on and attempt to locate the sect of religious devotees that Sifar had informed him of.

Armienne had said that Wrison was familiar with the folklore of the Early Ages, and Shangodoon spent many enlightening hours sitting on the shaded platform before the house with him, while he discoursed on the legends of old. Shangodoon told him of some of the things he had seen in his journeying, and what he had learnt of the Ainchan ways;

but he did not speak of the Cavern-Temple of the Forbidden Mountains, nor did he yet enquire about the Children of the Glorious Recovery or their scarcely credible teachings, for this was a terrible and weighty business, and he had to be a firm friend of this man before he could dare raise a subject of that nature.

So days passed while he pondered his position, and each day the regular presence of Armienne kept their bond growing, until the thought of leaving her quickly grew too painful to contemplate.

Her parents watched the affair grow and waited to see what would happen, as daily the two lovers roamed the coastline, spent hours sitting in the sand, and were always in close conversation with their heads bent toward each other.

She taught him a method to lay afloat in the water, and how to swim and dive; he taught her ways to achieve tranquil states through exercises, deep steady breathing and awareness of the heartbeat. They had much time to traverse and explore the coast. She showed him the wonders of the world where land met sea; they discussed its fascinating creatures, and sometimes she drew and labeled pictures of the rarer creatures she found, keeping her drawings in a waterproof container which she carried regularly on her study-trips.

The coast intrigued Shangodoon. He saw the workings of a mighty, spellbinding force here and witnessed the awesome phenomena it created.

There were high cliffs of sedimentary rock, eroded into horizontal caves by the action of the wind and the water; deep heavy water where the ocean-swells met the land directly, and the pound of the breakers hurt one's eardrums; broken rocks out to sea and low jagged coral reefs, some covered with mosses and bold, wiry bushes; high-flying spray bursting from undercuttings in rocky promontories; platforms of coral with small interconnecting pools that drained into the white surf and were replenished by insweeping waves; wide open sandy beaches with seaweed and shells and smooth coloured pebbles; shingle strands where the breakers pounded in continuous fury and where no seaweed or algae grew because of the incessant turbulence; sometimes a series of coconut-fringed bays with gently sloping crescent beaches, scalloped edges of sand with a headland at either end, and layer after layer of incoming waves like spread lace, trailing froth; and always, beyond the reefs, the translucent blues and greens and deep-sea colours that spread out to the horizon. Sometimes there were tiny figures to be seen; lonely fishermen sitting atop undercut crags, bold surfers and slow-moving beach-combers; bathers. At low tide, on the reefs, people searched for eels, fish, lobsters and crabs, and always there were fishing boats riding in the more sheltered inlets, or prowling along the coast trailing their nets and lines.

Some of the inlets and bays had thick clusters of houses and even, in calm waters, dwelling places built on poles that were placed in the sea. There were families of coast-people who lived completely over the water and whose lives depended more on the sea than on the land; their children had small canoes, and these people could swim as well as they could walk. There were many sheds and jetties for the fishing boats too, and storehouses where boating and fishing materials could be bought.

Other areas were occupied by the leisure houses and private baths of the Dominaut people, and these areas were reserved for them and their liveried servants. But the coast was long—Shangodoon and Armienne explored twenty-five miles of it and there was perhaps two-thirds still to be known—and the landscape absorbed population, so that there was much less evidence of the Dominauts in the land than existed on the Ainchan Plain.

As if in grim compensation, there were very many of the ships of the Dominauts, alone and n fleets of various sizes. They were engaged in what they called the Harvest of the Sea; all year, millions of sea-creatures were being captured, killed and stored in ice-holds by these rapacious vessels. The Dominauts used the usual lines, nets and harpoons, and they had copied an invention of the coast-people, making large bamboo mazes with wide openings through which fish swam and could not make their way back out again. But they also employed a straightforward and ruthless method of collecting as many fish and other creatures as quickly as possible; they used explosives.

The explosives were placed in deep water, so deep that only a faint pulse on the surface told of their detonation; but the sudden violent vibration of the muffled blasts, travelling through the water with a lingering hollow reverberance, killed all sorts of creatures, many of which the Dominauts had no use for. Occasionally, too, Armienne told Shangodoon, these ships had exploded their devices so close to the shore, as they chased the large, fertile shoals of fish, that divers in shallow water had been stunned and drowned. In fact, the Dominaut ships were feared by the people of the coast, for they had been terrorized by the huge macabre vessels quite often.

There were people who left their homes on the bays and went up the dry waterless slopes of the hinterland when the fleets of adamant fireships appeared. No one was certain why they kept such heavy guard of the waters off the coast, but they said that it was for the good of the coast-people, and they spoke about sea-monsters and terrible winds beyond the point where their ships lay.

For some time after arriving in Green Bay, Shangodoon lived in the paranoid alertness of the hunted, for the Agents of Internal Security were always around, on the search for the more original thinkers among the native peoples. There were even some of the coast-people in their pay, and such locals were quick to recognize a stranger in the Bay because of his accent mainly, therefore Shangodoon kept much to himself when not with Armienne, and tried not to attract attention.

The problem of the Dominauts was secondary to Shangodoon at this time; the first thing on his mind was that he wanted to marry Armienne, and he was not sure into what direction his prospective new state would take him. Up to that point, he had not told Armienne of his mission. Further, he did not know or whether marriage would clash with the carrying out of his search or whether the search was less important than his marrying and raising children.

He remembered the words of Akincyde concerning the marriage and fatherhood of Early Ages men; and he knew it was the wisest way to follow; but he also felt at that time that family life would divert him from his search. Later he was to find out that Armienne was completely willing to accompany and support him in any of his movements, however erratic and chancy they seemed; she trusted his judgement. But at that time, Shangodoon pondered deeply, creating a worry where there was no real reason for its existence.

One late evening as they sat on smooth boulders between high coconut palms, on a sandy beach where they had been bathing, he told her that he was going away shortly. She did not speak for a long time. Then she asked, "When?" and her voice pained him in a way that he never thought possible.

He turned toward her; the shadows were gathering under the trees and she did not see the agonized look in his eyes. "I want to marry you first," he said, and the words came out with a life of their own. "I don't want this relationship to end. I want to go on, and see what we can make of it . . . I can't ignore my own happiness. I can't kill something that is growing so deep without killing a part of me and of the time I have evolved . . ."

She listened as he kept on uttering things he barely understood the implications of; he explained his passions ardently, trying to ascertain if she saw his problem, if she agreed with him, as if she had become his friend and adviser about herself. In fact, he needed her to tell him whether to marry her or not.

She drew him close, and she was transcendently glad. "You know how I feel," she whispered, barely opening her mouth against his ear; and he hugged her in a strangely excited, exalted state of gratitude.

They were married according to certain modified rites of the Ainchan people, which had to be held in secret because of the ban on such practices, and he remained with her for three months in the apartment at Wrison's spacious compound. Then he told her that he had to set out on a journey and quest; he had to find what he came to the Coast of the Sea or Mirrors to find.

Perhaps she wanted to enquire and felt that he should tell her more; but she concurred dutifully and he set out on his search for the Children of the Glorious Recovery.

He had asked his father-in-law about the mysterious sect, but had gained little information. Wrison was certain that they existed, though he had never knowingly seen any member of the elusive group, and no one knew the number of adherents their millennial doctrines had. Wrison seemed to wonder how Shangodoon knew of them and precisely what the young man wanted of this obscure semi-nomadic community, but Shangodoon left him to his wonderments. He heeded his warning, however, concerning his enquiring about the sect; he would have to do so most discreetly, for they had been banned from the native towns by the Dominauts, and anyone entertaining a member of the sect was entertaining the possibility of execution. Indeed, Wrison must have wondered whether he was harbouring one of the disciples of that religion, for they were found among all types and among all segments of the society wherever the native people dwell on the coast.

Shangoodoon left his precious drum in the care of Armienne; he travelled only with his shortsword and a wallet of coins, both attached to the leather belt of his tunic.

Week after week he travelled through towns and villages; stopped at single homesteads and jetties, talked to fishermen, beachcombers and boatbuilders. At first he talked to good and honest people, but they looked at him askance and hurried on about their business with apprehensive mannerisms. Soon he was whispering here, muttering there, to sinister individuals who seemed inclined to searching for hidden and forbidden things. He sensed the types who were likely to know of this outlawed sect, and waylaid them, sometimes offering money for information; but repeatedly met with blank stares, shifty, half-closed eyes, lying lips, suspicious frowns, speculative pursing of the mouth and unholy leers. Then there were the cowardly pariahs who licked their lips and eyed his wallet, and once he had to defend himself against four men who had seen his money glint in a disreputable inn where he had bought wine for various patrons and made his guarded interrogations.

One night in a lonely, bleak, extremely silent town that perched on a windy overhand of cliff, on a headland some fifty miles away from Green Bay, a care-worn, bony old woman beckoned him from a darkened doorway. She had followed him from the last three villages behind, she said, for she knew (how, she did not say) of his enquiries. She also knew of the children of the Glorious Recovery, and where to find them.

She described a nearby place to him; there were chalk cliffs forming a high headland, and there was a cave which was reached by a flight of chiseled steps. The sect had retreated to this place because they were being sought and executed by the Dominauts. Her son was among them, she explained. His name was Patturne, and she wanted Shangodoon to ask for him by name before he talked of his mission, whatever it was. Besides which, she said, she wanted Shangodoon to take a gift to him; and she produced a covered basket.

Her voice sank to an almost inaudible whisper. "It is only fair that I tell you what you carry. Inside there you will find the eggs of the sea-turtle, and some bands of fish-skin with pearls and various crystals stitched in. These are very important, very *dangerous* things, and they must reach Patturne only, for perhaps he will know what to do. Tell him "—and her voice fell still lower into a terrified sibilation—"Tell him **the Snikes are returning**."

"The Snikes are returning . . . ?"

"Not so loud. It is said that they can hear over great distances . . . that is why this town is so very silent; we do not want them to know that we are here . . . Just tell him that, and he will understand." The woman gave a quick wave and disappeared in the gloom of an alley, and Shangodoon turned away with the heavy basket, with a powerful sense of impending fulfillment.

The next day he found the place that the beldame had so carefully described, and he started from the bottom of a tall stratified cliff with a small pebbly beach at its base, to climb the steep flight of steps that had been hacked into the rock, and led to the flat, almond-shaped mouth of the cave where the Children of the Glorious Recovery had retreated.

Halfway up those steps, the rugged contours of which suggested the devoted labour of strong, patient men, Shangodoon stopped suddenly, faced by a phalanx of huge seashore crabs that scraped and scuttled willingly down the

235

steps to meet him. He knew at once that these were the venomous stinging-crabs of which Armienne had told him once. These seldom-seen giants carried spiny needles on the insides of their claws, and well-developed poison glands within these appalling weapons. The wounds they inflicted were very painful, and could lead to extreme vomiting, coagulation of the blood, insanity or death, and there was no known antidote to their terrible venom. Now, with virulent spume frothing from their strange beak-like mouths, they clattered inexorably down toward him.

Therefore the young man was glad when he saw the tall robed figure of a longbearded ascetic at the top of the flight of steps. The man gravely raised his arm in greeting, beyond the army of descending crabs, and Shangodoon anxiously raised his own arm also. The man clapped his hands, and the crabs stopped, then separated, forming lines on either side of the narrow steps, their horrific pincers upraised and open, their stalked eyes fixed on the stranger.

Shangodoon ascended warily past the two macabre lines of hard-carapaced creatures with their yard-wide embrace, a man penetrating a gauntlet of primeval fears; but his heart beat firmly and his mental condition was clear. He saw the man above smile with closed lips and nod, beckoning, and he went on past the end of the crustacean guard and came to where his queer receptionist was standing.

"I am seeking for Patturne," he said at once.

"Wait here." The man entered the mouth of the clave (which Shangodoon now calculated to be about seven feet high) and soon another man appeared much like the first in his long, sandy-yellow, camouflaged robe and with his full, greying beard.

He was a friendly man and he quickly understood all that Shangodoon was willing to divulge to him. He was keen to let the young man know all the facts at his disposal, for he knew that this was no ordinary person and no ordinary quest, and he said so, though Shangodoon did not confirm or deny what he uttered.

Shangodoon asked the questions he had been pondering for years, ever since the time when he had met Sifar of Dibra and seen those significant paintings and documents the former rebel possessed. What was this instrument of power that the Children of the Glorious Recovery possessed? What power did it employ, and was it truly possible that one could both kill and heal with it? Was it true that it spoke, and the initiated interpreted its meanings? And could he see the instrument?

"Let us take your questions one by one," Patturne chuckled. "First, I do not know the name of the instrument, and no one knows. None of the Sisters and Brethren I know have dared to call it a name. Next, it works by the power of the wind, but as to the mechanics of that working, I cannot say. I know that it gives forth a sound, or a series of sounds, if the conditions are right and certain delicate mechanisms are employed, and that these sounds have pleasant effects on the Children when they hear them, for they get a sense of well-being and joy, and, if they are ill, adjust to good health. I have seen this work.

"As to whether its sounds can be interpreted—I for one have been privileged to hear this object on two occasions, and each time it seemed to utter concepts that I could not put into words, though I felt the state the sounds conveyed. Listening was a thrilling experience; I was in a most wonderful, visionary state. Certainly I preferred to listen and not to analyse, though I had had that intention. I seemed to know already what I was hearing for the first time. It was a state of *rightness* that I felt most strongly."

"Have others said what they think of its sounds?"

"Over the centuries, yes. We are an old sect. The earlier prophets of our religion, and most of the ones of today, too, had, and have, a general prophecy—one that carries no dates—that the instrument of power is the Creator's gift to man and that it will be used to set the world right sometime in the future. All the problems that upset us—pain, illness, old age, death, and every unpleasant thing—will pass away, for to dissolve such evils is scarcely a problem for such an instrument of power. It was this teaching that made the Dominauts chase us from among our people. We taught that prophecy to all, and the foreigners saw that it was changing the docile spirit of the subject peoples. It encouraged defiance.

"That brings us to your last question. We no longer have the instrument. It was captured by the Dominauts ten years ago. That was two years after the main fleets of their fireships arrived to guard the coast."

Shangodoon was saddened.

"It is strange how they came only after our propeller boats were invited," Patturne continued. "Before, we had used sails and oars. Then a clever a man of the coast, a learned inventor, developed a workable engine for boats, based on the power of electro-magnetism. I think he created metal circles that rubbed each other around a central core that was wrapped with copper wires, but that would only interest another inventor . . . . the point is, when the boats with the new engines were developed, the Agents of Internal Security notified the sea-commanders of the Dominauts, and they set up guard so that we could not voyage beyond a certain point. I think they wanted to hem us in, to keep us hugging the coast. The coast-people were becoming seafarers of outstanding skill, and they were exploring, and recording what they discovered about the world; the Dominauts wanted to keep our knowledge within a certain compass so that they could be aware of everything we knew; that way, we would always be their servants. It is strange how knowledge of facts makes one superior; it is the only weapon, indeed. They would like to know all of our secrets, and hope that we discover nothing about them . . . .

"But some of us edged past their ships. Children of the Glorious Recovery made two sea-trips in two years, before they were captured and hunted. I was on the last two trips. Have you ever heard of the Island of Whistling Winds?"

"No," Shangodoon said, coming out of a reverie.

Patturne's eyes were shining with his remembrances.

"It is the most inspiring region my eyes have ever beheld. A land of great sounds and mighty forces, forces that will settle all your present doubts about the power of air."

"So you know my doubts?"

"Your lack of knowledge," Patturne corrected himself. "When you experience the Island of Whistling Winds, you will know that the wind can kill or heal for certain."

"Well, you have been there; tell me about it," Shangodon said, accommodating the hermit, who evidently had not talked to anyone for some lengthy time.

"We went in the season of the least wind, and yet the boat struggled through monstrous waves to reach the steeply slanting shore. The island is a great mass of black stone, and the beaches are dark grey except for the silver crystals of the salt. We did not go very far inland; the boisterous blast kept us at bay. The bulk of the island rises very high, and the wind is so powerful that it has carved out many, many holes and tunnels in the high crags. I saw rocks with shapes that I never thought they could have, and trees that the wind had bent in loops. There, the wind moves in currents and eddies, and seems to have a body like an intelligent thing. It seeks out cracks and blowholes, and widens them, and it plunges into them with all kinds of unbelievable continuous sounds.

The wind itself seems to blow in steady time, and the sounds given off impress one deeply, as if the rocks and the air were making statements to the sun and the water! I felt those statements in my being; I did not try to translate or analyse them. I wanted to stay in one place forever. Listening became a strenuous activity; I could not hear enough. I had the deepest longing to be able to receive more of its messages, and I knew the fault lay in myself, in my own spiritual condition.

"But the land is dangerous too; it makes you want to sleep. It has great force in this way; the compulsion is almost unconquerable. It is fatal to sleep. Many of the Brethren and Sisters died when they were lulled by the sounds of that place. They nodded and sank down on the ground. One has to be well disciplined—as you are—to venture to that place. Your life depends on it. For when the weaker disciples slept, the bird came. There are millions and millions of them on that island, all sizes and shapes. It doesn't make sense to tell you that I had never seen so many before; and that I believe every kind of bird in the world must be found there; no, you would have to see those birds—and those flying formations!—for yourself. But the big ones kill you. I saw terrible eagles and grim, voracious vultures. They are the king flying predators of the planet, for their wing-span is up to twenty feet, and they lifted the sleeping bodies of our comrades easily, flying off with them until they disappeared in the convoluted rocks. I saw one man struggle and fall on the rocks, and at once he was covered by a swarm of carrion-birds. I believe they took the bodies away to feed their hatchlings—ugly wrynecked terrors—at the tops of the peaks. Yes, that is the Island of Whistling Winds—a place to test your survival! I tell you, few have survived that trip, and many of those few were killed by the Dominauts because of their knowledge.

For some reason which I would love to fathom, the foreigners guard the island severely, and do not hesitate to sink the native vessels that come near to their guardships. They do not want any knowledge of this island to spread, and indeed very few people know it exists. You will not be able to convince them even after you see it."

"You sound as if you think that I am going there."

"It follows. I have not studied people for nothing. You are not of this region. You came here to see the object of power, something you had only heard of. Now I have told you of the intriguing island where the sounds of the object made complete sense, and where the very wind seems intelligent enough to create pleasing sounds. The island intrigues you even more than the instrument that you have never seen. Therefore, you are going to the island. But, I beg you, do not think of your wife as standing in your way. Tell her of what you plan to do . . ."

"My wife! You know I have a wife?" Shangodoon asked sharply.

Patturne smiled. "I have studied people," he said again. "Of course I know you have a wife. I also think that you must treat her as a wife, my young brother. Let her into your plans. She can help you. She is a perfect counterpart for you; seldom do such unions betide in these troublesome times. You are not alone anymore."

Shangodoon took a deep breath, and a new respect for Patturne entered his mind.

"I have been thinking of it on my journey here," he confessed. "I have to do that when I see her again."

"Then I have confirmed your plan." Patturne smiled. "I wish that you and your wife would join our sect one day."

"The risk of death is too great," Shangodoon said frankly. He remembered Sifar's information, that these Children of the Glorious Recovery made an annual pilgrimage to a place where they set up the instrument of power. It was amazing how accurate a remote rumour could be. "—But tell me. What exactly did you do on the island?' he asked, instinctively feeling that links were falling into place, and that this meeting could be more profitable than he had ever expected.

"We set it up among the lower rocks. We couldn't reach the higher ones because of the powerful winds. Stout men were blown away and smacked against the rocks even on the ground level, so mighty were the currents of air. Then, when the thing was set up, we heard the wind make it speak; and one very strong man pressed a number of knobs and levers on the instrument, so that the thing's amazing tone changed a number of times. I tried to remember the sequence of sounds, afterwards, on both occasions, but could not. There seemed to be a small number of sounds employed, but there was such variety in their positioning that it was a breathless wonder to me. It was a marvelous experience. I had never known that the human body could have endured such ecstasy as that I felt. I felt as if I knew all the secrets of the world."

"You seem to. And then the Dominauts captured the instrument?"

"When we were returning. We tried to outrun their ships, but they caught us easily. They threw great grappling hooks over to our ship and drew us in to them like helpless fish.

"We resisted bravely, but their fireweapons wounded us badly. Several young fanatics died defending the instrument of power, and one tried to leap into the sea with it. They caught him and took it away; then they threw him to the big man-eating fish that had gathered in the water.

"A commander of one of the ships took the remnant of us on board his vessel for questioning, and they completed the sinking of our foundering craft. They spent much time interrogating us in all the details of our trip; they wanted to know how we got past their ships, what we were doing with the weapon of power, and did we have anyone trained in the manipulation of it. This last was a surprise to me, for I had no idea that it demanded training to use the weapon; and I wondered what the Dominauts knew of the instrument. Obviously they were afraid of it, and afraid of the fact that we had had it for centuries. They seemed to know of them well; the commander was very worried. I wish that I had thought about training—we should have surmised something like that.

"I could tell that they had suffered at the hands of people who were trained in these instruments. Often I wish that we had made more practical use of it, as the legends says the Bringer of it did . . . though I didn't know the legend then.

"They asked where we got it, and who made it, but no one answered, though I think only a few of us knew the legend of its origin on the coast. I myself did not hear the story of its appearance until six years ago, and at that time I thought their questions about its manufacture especially ridiculous, like asking who made a tree, or a flower, or any of the patterns that one may find in nature. The proportions of that sacred object certainly seemed natural and right to me.

"It is said that five hundred years ago a man-made flying machine fell into the sea a great distance out from our coasts. A week later a haggard, pitifully weak man came ashore. He did not know where he was, and his language had a strange effect on the people. He was badly dessicated by the salt water, and he died from the effects of his ordeal, but before he died, even in his weak condition, he made sounds on the sacred instrument, and communicated that he was from a distant peaceful land. He was from a land where everyone, young and old, had a variety of these instruments and soothed each other with their sounds, so that there was always amity and marvelous contentment in all their many cities. He had not known that such a land as ours existed, where people did not know these things, for wherever else he had travelled, he had heard at least one or two individuals using this power, usually to the benefit of many communities.

"His coming and his message must have had a miraculous effect on the people of that far-off time, for many people paid attention to his works. At that time the hold of the Dominauts on the people of the coast was slight, and the doctrine that the strange invaders would soon be repelled comforted most of the people. But the instrument itself did most of the convincing; the handsome stranger made it produce wonderful states in the people. He healed those that were ill; but best of all, he made pregnant women, at the time of their delivery, bring forth their children easily, safely, and painlessly. Thus the stories say.

"After he died, there were some who had listened closely to his teachings, who decided to preserve and meditate on his wise sayings. They took possession of the sacred object, and tried to reproduce and interpret the sounds the sky-flyer had made. But the sounds they produced were colourless and flat, and affected people in a strange way, making them nauseous and even causing vomiting and intense pains in the head among the sensitive. Thus eventually no one tried to manipulate it; the sect began making periodic journeys to the Island of Whistling Winds, which the sky-flyer had mentioned as a place of sounds, though certainly he never advised anybody to go there. On the Island of Whistling Winds the sounds seemed to make sense, and here it was that some elders of the sect, in bygone times, were brave and skilful enough to manipulate its sounds. So powerful were the sounds it made that if one miscalculated and made a wrong sound, the noise destroyed his hearing. But usually there were a few knowledgeable men, last of whom was Soom, my friend, who was killed by the Dominauts for his knowledge.

"Now, when the Dominauts enquired why we kept it, our leader said that we knew it to be an instrument that would one day unify all human beings."

"You will all be unified in death!" the ship's commander threatened. "We do not want to hear your foolish doctrines. Bind them and let us take them to the mainland," he directed his military sailors, and they obeyed.

"When we were brought ashore the news spread that were to be executed, and the people of the bays fought the Dominaut soliders and released us. Thus we escaped, and came here and to other places. Since that time we have been making notes and compiling and comparing writings, for we are trying to find a method of writing down the sounds that we heard. We need to preserve these things for our children to know. I myself am endeavouring to analyse the sounds that I experienced in terms of colour. I have managed to isolate a number of clear notes, and I have assigned a colour to each."

"That is interesting. I too like colour."

"I selected three sounds that seemed to fit well with each other. The lowest and most basic one I called red. The highest one I called blue. The middle one I called yellow. Then between the red and the yellow, there was an orange sound. Between the yellow and the blue there was a green sound . . . ."

"You have a very interesting mind," Shangodoon said.

"I seek for design, for I feel that everything must match some common shape. For instance, I also see the red as the colour of earth, the blue as the sky, the yellow as the sunlight between them. I often put myself into states where in my mind I hear sweet sounds; then I try to catch the colours of the sounds . . ."

"Yes, but I will have to hear the sounds first, to ascertain for myself, before I can accept your scheme of colours. I want to hear these sounds."

"There is nothing more I can tell you . . . or perhaps there is just one thing. When we were being brought to the mainland, one of the ship's men called me aside. He said he would spare my life, and offered money, too, and he asked me to tell him honestly whether we had not been to the *Land of Muse.*"

"The Land of Muse!"

"You know the name!"

"I have heard it spoken. It is said that the people of that land defeated the Dominauts, and by instruments of power like the one your devotees possessed."

"Then, as I guessed, they feared that we were seeking allies; is it not so?"

"It must be so. There is something to be found out; it is important to them to keep the island and beyond unexplored. They have a weak spot. Guards are always placed at weak spots, just as laws are passed against what people fear most."

"Well, the secret is not here; you will have to go to the Island of Whistling Winds and beyond to the Land of Muse. I know that some people have conjectured that there must be a large land-mass to the south, because of the currents and the drift-wood, as well as the migratory habits of the birds."

"It would be an interesting trip indeed," Shangodoon murmured. "But the days for that kind of travelling seem to be over."

"Who knows? You should think about it. There is always a way to do anything; you only have to think long enough."

"Can you describe to me the weapon of power which the Dominauts took from the people?"

"It was a strangely beautiful thing . . . It was made of the purest gold, and seemed to be basically a long tube with one end opened like a bright flower, a lovely hibiscus shape, like the rim of a drinking vessel or a tall vase. The hollow tube was shaped in such a way that it formed a square, a circle and a triangle with its loops, bends and angles. There were little levers that opened and closed holes, and knobs, and a number of little pegs placed at varying spaces along two sides of the tubing that formed the top of the square formation. That is the closest I can come to it."

"I have seen some objects like the one you describe, more or less," Shangodoon said. "I have seen paintings reputed to be from the Land of Muse, and people carried things that seem generally to fit your description. There were a variety of other objects as well. Have you never wondered where the Bringer of the Instrument may have come from?"

"I have believed for some time now that he was from that fabulous land. I am glad to learn that you have seen depictions of the sacred object, and that you can confirm my theories."

"And in all those centuries, no one of the coast has visited the Land of Muse?"

"How could they? They had no flying vehicles! And until recently, no suitable engines; it was not possible."

"Now the Dominauts are in the way."

"Such is the design of destiny."

"The business of the flying vehicle is a hard one to believe, is it not?

"It is." Patturne agreed, and shrugged. "And now, what has my mother sent me?"

Shangodoon lifted the basket forward. "Yes, your things . . . She sent this message, too. The Snikes are returning."

Patturne's eyes widened and he turned quickly towards the young man. "The Snikes! What else did she say?"

"Nothing. She also sent some turtle's eggs for you— whatever is a turtle?"

"Turtle eggs!" Patturne said, again sounding greatly surprised. "She did not say where she got them?"

"No. I saw her only for a few moments."

"Creator of our fathers!" Patturne opened the basket. "Did you tell anybody what you carried? Does anybody know you came here?"

"No, no. But why?"

"You ask too many questions," Patturne said, perturbed about some hidden matter. "Leave me now. I have to think of something . . . I never thought it could happen in my lifetime . . . the people of the coast will have to know . . ." He stared around distractedly.

"I will leave you now," Shangodoon said quietly, for he saw the extent of Patturne's disturbance.

"Yes, goodbye. Go with the guidance of wisdom."

"The crabs . . . ?"

"The crabs are not fools! Now go!"

"All right, I'm going."

"Thank you. And thank you for coming, too."

The crabs had been milling about the steps. Patturne clapped his hands and they went into formation again; Shangodoon descended past them, and left the cave of the Children of the Glorious Recovery.

———◆◆◆———

Armienne listened carefully and gratefully to Shangodoon's conversations about himself when he returned. She was glad that he had accepted her into his confidence, and for the sincere reason that she knew she could harmonize with his wishes and outlook more, the better she knew him.

He told her of his life in Ainchan, his quest, and his travels. She learnt why it had been important for him to leave and continue his search, and was very interested in the facts concerning the Children of the Glorious Recovery. She had heard of them for the first time when members of the sect had been captured ten years before, and the people of Green Bay had joined the demonstration and riot to free them from the Dominauts.

Her passionate sense of righteousness impressed Shangodoon. He saw that she felt as strongly as himself about the bondage of their people. The cause was theirs, not his.

"The people must be free to travel and explore as they like. The Dominauts are impeding my own researches. Who gave them the right to guard the sea? And from what or whom? All this talk of guarding is only an excuse for keeping the fear of their power in the minds of the coast-people. They cannot make it last." Armienne's eyes flashed fires of defiance. "Whatever lies beyond the place where their ships line up, they cannot take on responsibility for us, which is what they suggest they are doing. They want us to be ignorant, that is the real reason. If they could remove our knowledge, they would, for they want dependent people that they can treat as cattle."

"They have succeeded well in this on the Ainchan Plain," Shangodoon said bitterly.

"We people of the coast have more resources. We are more matched for them, for we are seafarers and we know the coast better than they do."

"Still, it seems impossible to get past the ships of the Dominauts, unless one flew overhead."

"Or went under the sea!" Armienne replied.

Shangodoon laughed.

"No, I am serious. I am having an undersea craft made, for my researches. It is the only way I can continue them."

He looked at her and his smiles faded. "I can see you are serious . . . I did not know it could be done."

"The coast-people of the Early Ages used to sail under the sea in fish-shaped craft. This is a fact that we keep hidden from the Dominauts as much as we can. My family has known of the principles of designing undersea craft for years. My brother Erutan, who is a very competent inventor, has based his creations on many of the old physical laws that the Early Ages people knew. It was he who employed the principles the ancients had worked out, to develop the electromagnetic machines that many people now use on their vessels to drive water-wheels and propellers."

"He is an important and valuable man! The man Patturne spoke of the new type of boat, but I did not know Erutan was the maker of them."

"He has done some marvelous work. He has been working secretly on an undersea craft for the past year. He doesn't know when he will finish, but his studies are progressing well. Would you like to pay him a visit at his workshop? He'd be glad to show it to us."

"Of course. We had better do it soon." There was a pause, then he said, "I am glad we know each other better now."

Armienne nodded, and placed her hand on his. "There are many things about myself that I want to say, too; they will come. I will express them . . . but I am searching for a way."

Shangodoon thought he understood her gropings. "A child would unite as fully," he suddenly said, pleased at the prospect.

"I am looking forward to it, she said happily.

Days later they left Green Bay on horseback, and rode along the coast to Lighthouse Headland where Erutan spent most of his time, and where his huge, elaborate workshop was secretly installed in a sea-cave. On the way, while they rode along the dusty roads that ran on the tops of the sandy ridges, perhaps half a mile inland, Shangodoon asked Armienne what a turtle was.

"You heard of the turtle?"

"The man I told you of, Patturne, received the eggs of this turtle-creature, from his mother. I took them to him."

"You *handled* the eggs of the turtle? and took them to another man?"

"I did not touch them. But yes, I took them to him."

"You must be careful. Men have been killed by the people of the coast for being in possession of the eggs of the turtle."

"Why?"

"It is an old story. The turtle is held sacred by the people of the coast. Only women are permitted to deal with them among our people. On very rare occasions, and in the direst circumstances, their eggs have been eaten, but it is generally regarded as unlucky, especially for men, to eat their eggs or meat."

"Yes, but what is a turtle?"

"It is a reptile with a hard, curved shell which resembles an inverted bowel. It has a head that looks a little a snake's except that in some kinds the mouth is like a beak, and very hard. The backbone and internal organs are protected by this shell, which is its shield; and it has four short, powerful fins or flippers. There are things related to them that live on land and have feet instead of flippers, but I have never seen any of them, and I have seen a turtle only once. The turtle can withdraw its head and limbs into its shell. The creature lives in the sea, but it breaths air, and the females come up on the land at night to lay their eggs, which they cover with sand or vegetation. The sun's heat warms the eggs, and the young are hatched."

"I have heard of fabulous beasts before, and I have even seen the Kraggarts, but this verily must be the most mysterious of all creatures," Shangodoon declared. "So the people obtain the eggs from the sand?"

"Not only from the sand. Some people wait and receive them as they come out. This is possible because the turtle becomes oblivious to its surroundings as long as it begins to lay its eggs; it goes into a kind of trance. But not only people take the eggs. Animals of the earth, fish of the water and birds of the air feast on the eggs of the turtle. Perhaps they are the most preyed-upon beasts in the world, for as far as I know only our people refrain from partaking of their eggs and flesh."

"I would like to see one of these creatures."

"I can show you a drawing of one. The men of the coast account it bad luck to look upon them living . . . Let's stop for a while," she suggested.

They dismounted and rested, and she took one of her precious drawings surfaces from her bag. She spread one of the sheets and there, carefully drawn and labeled in neat writing, were clear representations of the sacred creature, with details of its head and flippers, and drawings of its round eggs.

"It is indeed a unique sea-beast." Armienne said. "It has a backbone, lungs, ribs and a stomach even as we do. According to Licestus, my unbeloved ex-tutor, it was once a land-animal that changed its structure and went into the sea to live. He also believed that in time it would take to the air, for it also resembles a bird in some ways."

"Why do the people hold it sacred?" asked Shangodoon thoughtfully, still in the process of becoming accustomed to the sea-beast's appearance.

"There is a story, which may not be true, that is told to the children of the coast when they ask that same question. In the past, the tale goes, there were terrible creatures of the sea who came on land, seized fowls, livestock, men or any other living things, and took them into the sea to be devoured.

"The people of the coast used to eat the turtles in those days; they were a popular food, and the people ate them so much that they became difficult to find. Then it was noticed that only when there was a scarcity of turtles the frightful beings of the sea would come on land to search for food. Therefore the coast-people stopped eating the turtles, leaving this delicacy for the sea-beings, who then hunted them in the water. Sometimes, too, I have heard it said, they came on land to dig up the eggs from where the turtles had buried them in the sand, but they did not like to be seen.

"Thus our people came to regard the turtle as their savior, for since that time the sea-beings do not any more seize human beings or their farm animals. Gradually it came to be regarded as a sin and a crime to eat of the turtle.

"There are some people who carve the shell into religious ornaments. Others even carry out rituals to the turtle during the seasons of its mating and egg-laying. Because many sea-birds as well as land-animals eat the young turtles as they hurry to the water after they are hatched, they erect huge nets and fences to prevent the birds and animals from reaching them. Yet the fishes eat them too, so the life of a young turtle is a hard fight for existence. The shell takes perhaps five months—perhaps more—to harden, and after that they are relatively safe.

"Surprisingly, though the shell is very tough and can bear thousands of pounds in weight; it is very sensitive to sounds and vibrations. If you rub a feather on its shell the turtle will feel it. The creature is very intelligent; it can see patterns and recognize colours.

"Also, turtles are a very old race of creatures, and they are the longest living creatures too, for they live hundreds of years."

"The longer I live, the more I am learning about the strange patterns and forms that life can take."

"It is a fascinating search," Armienne agreed. "Some things that we think of as dead are very much more alive than some humans. There is no end to the shapes the life-force makes."

They remounted the horses and rode on, and soon they were upon the high rocky headland which was their destination. The tall unmanned building with its perpetual light stood close to the peak of the headland. The couple left the horses in the enclosure that surrounded the structure, and walked even closer to the termination of the headland. Then Armienne showed Shangodoon a large blowhole where, when the headland was lower, the sea must have rushed with tremendous force and spouting spray. "This is the entrance to Erutan's worshop," she said.

They picked their way carefully down the side of the hole, the rough surface of which soon gave way to man-made, bricked walls and a carved-out stairway. Down it went for a good distance, until they could hear the steady, faint roar of the sea outside; and finally they came to a point where a native man stood guard before a large stone door with an eye-level rectangle cut in it. This guard recognized Armienne at once, and stood back so that they could push the door open and enter. Shangodoon, recognizing that Armienne had been there often before and was quite familiar with the place, wonderingly followed his wife into the grand, well lighted and equipped cave the door opened onto, and at once he was impressed by the number of little gauges, dials, lights, levers and buttons that were installed in strange smooth surfaces that fitted along the shelved rock-walls. Powerful lights shone overhead and lit the area well; and a pleasant hum indicated some kind of power-source at work to feed the many elaborately built machines that were installed at various points around. In the middle of the huge space, almost submerged in a channel of water that ran out of the cave to join the turbulent sea outside and below, the undersea craft that Armienne had spoken of lay under construction.

Erutan was inside the craft working with two other men when Shangodoon and Armienne arrived. He called to them, clambering out the hulk of the vessel, and was glad that they had paid him a visit. He had wanted for a long time to show Shangodoon some of his work, and he took advantage of the opportunity to give them a careful tour of the workshop. They saw his latest creations, concerning the development of large-scale electromagnetic generators, the invention of a gauge for measuring time in tiny units (a concept which surprised Shangodoon greatly) and a device which could transmit the conversation of people over great distances. Most of the coneptions Erutan created were based on his historical knowledge of the sciences of the Early Ages coast-people, and he was convinced that they had solved all the problems of technology that were then facing the world.

"So you are sure your undersea craft will work," Shangodoon said.

"There is much to be done on it, but I expect it will," Erutan replied. "I cannot tell when it will be finished, though I expect to be working on it for the next ten years."

"A very long time," said Shangodoon, disappointed.

"A short time, in the life of an inventor."

"Is there a possibility of finishing it before?" Armienne asked.

"You know how I work. I have to test everything. One mistake and all is lost. I cannot afford to endanger my loving sister. You will be using it, not me."

"How considerate. So it cannot be done before?"

"I fear not. But I certainly will try harder"

"Well, will you let us examine it, and give us an idea what it will be capable of doing when you are through?"

"Of course. Come on. I'll talk as we go . . .

"The craft is twenty-five feet long, and seven feet high. It is built to resemble one of the largest creatures of the sea. But the species this craft resembles is not a man-eating species, it eats water-plants. It is scarcely ever attacked by other creatures, so it is a comparatively safe from the point of view of camouflage.

"It is completely silent. The propulsion units are finished; our main problems are to do with insulation of the craft, the regulation of temperature, and a method to make it lighter or heavier, to cause it to rise or sink rapidly. We need to do more work on the materials of the hull, too, to ensure that it can stand the pressure of the very deep sea.

"The controls are simple. This lever causes it to rise, fall or hover, according to its position, whether up, down, or central. This wheel steers—right, left, straight ahead. The fins at the sides, along the back and at the tail are the means of controlling, stopping and navigating the craft. The vessel has a forward maximum speed of nearly thirty miles an hour, though I would not go above twenty-five; and it can also reverse, at about ten miles per hour. It carries its own oxygen supply, which is unlimited because we have found a way to re-cycle what is used. The eyes are really wide-angled visibility periscopes, which can scan the way ahead or at the side; this screen records all that they pick up, and the whole visibility-apparatus is so made that you will be able to see clearly at least a half mile ahead in the worst conditions, and very far ahead normally.

"There are rooms for bathing and the disposal of body-wastes at the very rear of the craft. Then there is eating and sleeping space, with retractable beds, and a driving and viewing seat which can hold four persons—the maximum number of passengers. Altogether, I'm proud of the vessel; I think it will be a very fine craft."

Shangodoon and Armienne agreed, silently nodding, gazing in wonderment around the interior of the undersea ship.

"Well, that's it," Erutan concluded, and turned away. "I expect you're going to stay for the night?"

"Yes, we could," Armienne said, and Shangodoon nodded. "We have two horses to feed though; we left them at the lighthouse."

"No problem. There is a shed near the lighthouse, and we can find fodder for them fairly easily. But now, let us go and find some for ourselves first."

So the couple spent the night at Erutan's place, and set out next morning for Green Bay.

This time they rode as close to the shoreline as possible, freeing the horses on the wet sand and guiding them carefully over the high dry reefs; dismounting every now and then to study the peculiar things that lurked in the pools of coral rock, and to select the most beautiful of the many sea-shells that jeweled the shore.

Then they came upon an ugly and disturbing sight, for they saw what they thought to be drowned, bloated body of a man lying in the seaweed of the extreme shoreline.

"I expect it is some poor fisherman," Armienne said, and she urged her horse forward.

Small crabs scuttled away from the body as they approached. The horses trembled and snorted, flaring their nostrils, and the two humans reined up at once when they notices the things that made the figure not quite like a man's.

Armienne whispered one word, *"Snike!"* and the tone of her voice created a coldness in Shangodoon's chest. He felt his mind shy away from the acceptance of the thing on the ground, and of the sound of the word. Each time he had heard the word mentioned it had been accompanied by unspeakable terror; and now as his horse and himself hesitated to proceed, he saw that the creature on the ground certainly inspired numbing, unreasoning fear.

But the thing is dead, he told himself, and dismounted from his horse. Armienne followed him, and very slowly they came to perhaps six feet from where the Snike lay.

The limb-structure of the creature was similar to a man's, with legs, chest and arms; the fingers were joined by a light, fleshy web, and the shoulders were abroad and very strong.

The head, neck and shoulder were conjoined with two triangular fleshy fins, so that the thing reminded Armienne of a hooded snake.

It had a high forehead, with two holes in the centre which obviously were nostrils. Its eyes were much lower than its nostrils and wide set, more at the sides of the head than at the front; these two dead eyes gazed dully in two different directions. Its mouth was gaping open, and filled with murderously long teeth. Soft movable fins ran from it shoulder-blades straight down to its back, and it had slender, tapering legs that seemed no stronger than its arms. These feet ended in long webbed toes, with a horny, curved projection where the great toe was on man. It had a solid, compact hulk of body, and was clearly a very swift swimmer. Overall, it was about seven feet long.

The waist and genitals were covered in stitched fish-skins, and on the forearms of the creature were bands of the same material, in which pearls and bright translucent crystals were fastened. Shangodoon realized, from the description Patturne's intrepid mother had given him, that he had taken objects like these to Patturne. The turtle eggs and Snike's arm band were connected in some significant way, and it dawned on him that Armienne's story about sea-beings feeding on turtles was true.

"So they really exist," Armienne said, expelling the words softly, confirming his thoughts. She had retained much of her calmness, and was trying, like a good student of natural creatures, to adjust to the reality of what existed.

"What was he doing here?" Shangodoon vaguely asked himself, and her.

"Look." Armienne pointed. A little way away there was a curved object, a bow, lying on the sand and pebbles. It seemed to be made of smooth, carved bone, and a strong rubbery string was attached tautly to either end. At one side of the arched bone was another long, straight strip of the same material, and below that was something poised like a finger-trigger. Next to this queer crossbow was a long, three pronged barbed dart with extremely sharp points, evidently designed for firing underwater; and Shangodoon calculated that such a weapon, fired on land, would have far greater range than it would in the sea.

Altogether this Snike and its weapon were very dangerous things, and Shangodon wondered again what the creature was doing there; and how he had died.

Then he heard the horses screaming shrilly, and turned to see them facing the sea and stiffened on their legs. Armienne turned too; then together they together they looked over the sea, following the gaze of the horses.

The sea was placid for a moment, and nothing was moving; then the water erupted skyward and two of the deadly Snikes flew up out of the depths. They rose perhaps ten feet in an even arc, parallel, in barbarously accurate formation, and flew from the sea over the shore in one tremendous leap. Long before they flopped to the ground, they had loosed their darts, and one of the horses, doubly impaled, leaped in its death-struggle. The Snikes lurched forward on their ungainly, untrusty flippered feet and seized the horse, which went into a paroxysm of frenzied self-defence as the two attackers struck it violently with their snouts, ripping huge pieces of its neck and shoulder away. Then they dragged the still-kicking horse into the surf, and all disappeared under the disturbed surface of the water.

The whole startling event had taken place with such incredible speed that for one paralysed moment the man and woman stood still apprehending the occurrence. Then Shangodoon gripped Armienne's hand and they ran madly away from the shore towards the sandy slopes of the hinterland. The second horse had disappeared, for it had galloped off wildly when its fellow had been struck by the tridents of the Snikes.

When they had covered a distance which they were sure no Snike could leap, they sat down breathing deeply. They were surprisingly calm, considering the shock; they both knew that in times past they would have panicked violently, and they were glad that their training in keeping their wits and self-control had stood up to the horror they had witnessed. Yet they were silent for a long while, watching the sea, and time and time again their eyes returned to the dead

Snike on the distant shore. Armienne shuddered once or twice; Shangodoon soothed her, massaging certain nerve-points on her body, so that she relaxed and seemed all right again.

"We've got to tell the people around here," Shangodoon said. "They'll have to keep off the beach."

"You think they'll be there regularly?"

"I don't know. There may be a lot of them."

"They can come ashore!" Armienne gasped, remembering the sight.

"A human being can outrun them. The horse could have, if it wasn't wounded. But they have weapons! And what about the bathers and fishermen?"

"Scarcely anyone bathes or fishes here."

"We'll have to tell somebody anyhow. Where is the nearest village?"

"About half a mile from here."

"Let's go."

It was near midday when they walked into Sea-Breeze village and announced that they had seen a dead Snike on the beach, and that two living ones had come out of the water and taken one of their horses.

Veterans of the sea shook their heads and frowned, sitting before the steps of the taverns, and wondered what it might mean; or whether the two had seen something unusual indeed. Others refused to listen, and went to their homes, and though it was bright daytime some people closed their houses. Many people were seen to be clearly frightened, and looked over their shoulders nervously while they said that such things could not be.

A timid party of men left Sea-Breeze village, and in the company of Shangodoon and Armienne they came down to the beach.

The sea murmured placidly as it usually did on this part of the coast, and the beach was empty. Nothing seemed amiss, and the place where they had seen the dead Snike was as smooth and draped with seaweed as any other spot on the near-littoral.

Then the townspeople were relieved, and goodnaturedly called the couple practical jokers and tricksters. When they insisted that a dead Snike had been on the shore, the people turned nasty. Some men threatened to throw them into the sea; others warned them not to pass through the village, and complained that their foolish rumours were frightening the children.

Armienne would have insisted and tried to get them to believe, but Shangodoon was versed in the workings of doubt and belief and in the ways of men when faced with sudden blatant truths that disturbed their secure feelings. Some consciously avoided the truth; most people faced truth only when cornered. Even if they had seen it they would have doubted still. There was nothing more they could do, he told Armienne, and they departed from the area.

Later in the day they managed to hire a carriage and driver, and came into Green Bay in the dusk.

Wrison listened to their story carefully when they arrived. He had heard vaguely of Snikes before, but had been sure that none of them existed around the coast; in fact, he would have said that they were extinct.

"Do you think that these are the same creatures that were said to eat people before?" Armienne asked.

"It seems logical," Wrison said, and Shangodoon nodded.

"What about the turtles, then? Where are they?"

"The turtles!" Wrison exclaimed, remembering. "That is it! The turtles are being killed by the Dominauts. The Foreigners love the taste of turtle-meat, and I heard that they have discovered many ornamental uses for its shell."

"Then the Snikes will be returning—for people!" Armienne made the obvious conclusion.

"They nearly got people today," Shangodoon remarked. "I believe they went after the horses simply because they were larger and offered more food to them than we did. If we were there without horses, they would have attacked us."

"We might have been on the horses when they attacked," Armienne realized, and her eyes widened at the thought.

"A sobering thought," Wrison meditated.

"What can we do about the situation?" Armienne wondered.

Wrison shrugged. "Keep away from the beach, that is all I can think of. We must wait and see what else happens. If they are around regularly, this certainly is not the last time we will hear about them."

The couple departed and went to their own home. They were serious and reflective, and whenever they spoke, between long pauses, the subject was the same. They talked long into the night, and their reluctant conclusions filled them with awe.

They knew that the Snikes were intelligent beings. They dressed in stitched fish-skin, had manufactured weapons, and wore decorated forearm bands. They could not be dismissed as simply sea-creatures, like fish. The implications of their existence in the world were astounding to Armienne. It meant that the sea out there was much stranger than she had envisaged; for such beings as the Snikes would have made their mark on the culture of the sea.

How vast then was the sea, how big was the world, she wondered, that such things could exist and remain unknown for eons? And what other things were there as yet undiscovered? There were many myths of elder fabulous beasts, more believable than that of the Snikes, and certainly such beasts had a more anticipated form than the near-inconceivable turtle.

She couldn't think of all that it might mean; but she prepared her mind anew, as she often did, to accept whatever strange facts the world proffered her to study.

Months passed, and Shangodoon plunged into a career of teaching carving and sculpture in wood, stone and clay, to the children of the coast-people. His work progressed well, so that he soon needed to hire tutors from among the students he had trained; the size of his workshop and his ovens increased rapidly.

Meanwhile, a worry had begun to gnaw at Armienne. She had dismissed it at first, for characteristically she was willing to hope, but a year passed, and then another, and there was no child. During those two years her hope rose and died many times. Month after month she watched and sensed her body intently, despair and panic started knocking at her mind. She wondered what Shangodoon thought, and after she couldn't bear to wonder anymore, she asked him.

He was bothered too. He wondered about himself. What was his body for it couldn't produce offspring? What was his searching for truth about? A child seemed a natural and right thing; perhaps it was the truth he sought; perhaps the *only* truth.

They talked about it for hours, ranging from depression to hope, and they pondered the possible causes, but no answers came.

Armienne looked upon other children with longing; tried to shift her ovulation to coincide with the waxing of the moon; applied all the facts she could lay her hands on, wondering what it was she should have been doing and was not aware of. She studied procreation carefully, and knew the reproductive systems of all the creatures she studied. She looked around for solace, wondering how to compensate in life for not having a child, asking herself questions that had no immediate answers—of sin and punishment, of chance and destiny. Did she not strive to live according to the laws of the Creator? In what was she lacking that the forces of nature could not use her body for procreation?

Near the end of the third year after they were married, Shangodoon went away. He was to be gone for five months, for he had taken a roving job with a band of architects and carvers; and Armienne was left disconsolate at home.

She practised the ascetic exercises that her husband had shown her, and tried to keep tension from her mind. If only a child would come, she prayed, and felt like forcing her body in some way to do as her mind desired it to do.

During this time of his absence she had restored to fasting, for she had gathered that fasting resulted in regeneration, and she wanted it to work in literal terms. Eighteen days elapsed, during which nothing but water passed her lips; she became highly sensitive to her inner conditions, and searched out her intuitions for practical meaning.

One night she suddenly remembered that turtle eggs were said to be good for fertility. Her heart pounded; her insides told her that she should try this cure. At once Armienne knew that no tradition would keep her from her attempts at procreation; she would go to the Turtle Beach and take some of the eggs.

She knew where the beach was; every woman of the coast was aware of the place. She knew too that the turtles of the coast had the unsafe habit of coming up to lay when the moon was bright. But such moonlight would serve to help her see them, and she was sure it would be easy to fill a leather bag with eggs.

The full moon rose on the very next night, and Armienne, dressed in warm clothing, set out on foot to go to the secluded, seldom-visited bay where the turtles came up to lay.

Here is the story of that visit to Turtle Beach and the subsequent events, word for word, as Armienne told it to the people that far-off day in liberated Ainchan.

———•◆•———

The moon was perhaps halfway up the sky (Armienne related) when I descended into the bay where Turtle Beach was. More than once I had thought of the Snikes, but so intent was I in my quest for motherhood that the thought of them did not at all deter me.

I descended to the bottom of the incline to where the sand began, wondering why the seashore looked so dark, and when I got closer I saw that the whole beach was covered with the cleaned, upturned shells of dead turtles which had been laid out to dry.

It was a frightening thing to witness the evidence of so much death, and to contemplate that these turtles had come to the beach to further the lives of their race. The tragedy stunned me, and reduced my own barrenness to a pitiful joke.

The beach is at least two hundred yards long, and very broad, but it was almost filled with the shells of the turtles; their edges were almost touching, so closely placed were they in the sand.

Now I realized why I had seen the signboards of the Dominauts, warning people that the area was prohibited. It was because they were using the beach as a killing and curing ground. They were taking the meat and undershells of the turtles and leaving the outer shells to be cleaned by the action of the sun and the salt.

I found a small sea-cave and sat in it in bleak despair, staring out over the shellstrewn sand. Nothing moved and the aura of sacrifice hung like a pall in the atmosphere. I began to wish that the turtles would find some new method of laying their eggs, without having to come into an environment that made for situations like these. I knew then that their eggs had been searched for and most of them would have been taken, and an absolute sense of waste and desolation overwhelmed me. I felt a great sorrow for all the mothers in the world.

At my feet lay one of the deep-curved shells, almost completely cleaned out; running across the length of its hollow were a number of strings of its gut, stretched tight by the action of drying.

I fondled the shell lovingly, as if it were a child of mine. The dry shell seemed to spread and echo my whispered words and the caress of my hands as I apologized to the living soul that had once inhabited and used the shell; apologized for the senseless brutalities and carelessly wicked depredations of mankind.

I reached inside the hollow body of the shell and touched the taut gut strings. With my right hand I plucked at three of them together, and the thing vibrated in myriads of echoing units of sound, softly and sweetly, so that for a moment I wondered if the shell of the turtle had a life and voice of its own, and lived on long after its occupant. I plucked at the strings again; another sparkle of jeweled voices seemed to spring out from within the patterned bowl. Once more I did the same and listened; the shell made pleasant sounds, seemed warmer and willing to release its sounds. The shell hummed; I felt a queerly nostalgic taste in my mouth and in my highly sensitive state I was hearing in a different way. Now I struck in the manner of timing my husband and had taught me on the drum, and even sounds, low, medium and high, shot out and echoed within my sheltering cave. I started to sway my body in time to the things that my fingers were doing and then I found a way to shorten the strings with my left hand fingers, so that I could obtain several different tones upon the same string.

A variety of tones sounded now; from where I sat, I could feel them spangle out through the quiet night and stir the dry shells lying on the sand; then all those shells began to hum and tremor their manifold experiences of life. Hundreds of years old these ancient creatures were, and their shells harmonized and hummed the chordal truths of the ages. They knew the truths of reproduction and survival as no other creature of the planet did. They knew the secrets that mankind needed to know as a matter of survival; they responded sympathetically, lifting their voices higher as my fingers found new ways of making the strings sing the exalted things I felt; they sang of existence and of the way things are created, and I understood many things that even today I am now engrossed in exploring upon my Instrument. I try to catch the central vibrative, coalescent force that exists in nature; my gropings of expression take me to the pristine and prolific womb of Creation, and I try to express its wonders, as I have done ever since that night when I found the spiritual goal that I scarcely knew I had been seeking. For ignorance, oh people of Ainchan, is the worst sterility.

The turtle-shells hummed the sympathetic vibration of all the mothers who ever were, and were to come, and even as the empty shells hummed I saw more turtles, living ones, come up and out of the sea and search around for spots to lay their eggs, as if challenging the Dominauts and the rest of men to outlive their race.

Then I knew that I would be fruitful, and I bowed my head and thanked the Creator of all existences.

I stayed at the Turtle Beach all night, and left when the first blue glow of morning was changing the silver shine of the moon. I took my turtle-shell along, and I did not look back upon the beach, not wanting to see those cruel evidences of death and martyrdom in the increasing daylight.

When I got home my husband was waiting; he had returned during the night. I knew he wondered where I had been; but he did not ask, and felt less inclined to do so when he saw the turtle-shell.

My heart was too full for words; I let my Instrument speak my message. All the things that I had learnt all night before spilled forth from deep within me, and I quivered with the intensity of my feeling. I made my fingers work the strings of gut in new ways and combinations, and I saw that he noticed the rhythmic, expanded, powerful, invisible forms that emanated from the hollow shell. He sat and did not move, sometimes closing his eyes in his intense listening, sometimes staring to me in a wonder that I thrilled to; I poured the wonderful, balanced units of sound upon him, inviting him in my mind to take his Drum and join me in my new-found Harmony.

As if I had spoken aloud, he reached for the great column of wood that stood close by, its smooth skin top glistening with the various redolent oils that he had rubbed upon it to ensure its perpetual lubricity.

Cautiously at first, then with more confidence and a keen sense of unison, he combined his tempo with the reflective, conjoined glissades that I was making. Together we wove intricate, beautiful designs and a new state of love grew between us, as if something larger than ourselves, embodied by our sounds, had taken us along with it into a higher existence where there were no opposites.

He had come over to me, and I saw my desires reflected in his eyes and in his muscled body. The Harmony hummed in my insides, an eagerly compliant response, and I felt a fathomless deepening of my love for him, and wanted to merge with him forever.

I opened like a flower and clasped my beloved with passionate warmth, and while the Drum and the Shell seemed to continue their Rhythm and Harmony, though actually deep silence had fallen, he shot and poured his seed-fluid into my vibrating receptacle of life, and Uzulu was conceived.

———•◆•———

He was a handsome and healthy baby, and he grew rapidly. We knew great happiness, the three of us; there was nothing that we did not enjoy, no activity we did not try, no place we did not go. Life flowed in rich rhythms and harmonies. Flowers seemed more beautiful and colours had more meaning. We realized the ineffable force around us, saw that we were a unit in its arrangement, and tried to knowingly fulfill our function. We grew closer to the things that represented existence and perpetuity; the land the sea and the air; and studied the many forms that these elemental existences supported and sustained.

There are little things that show the immediacy of this perennial order of things, and, in fact, being an integral, intelligent part of the flow of life is not a difficult feat; it is a natural and radically simple thing.

The sea-shells and the smooth lace pebbles of coral that ran in a double line along the shore were marvelous treasure. Their beauty and form fascinated the three of us. We collected many of them; I mounted the rarer kinds of shells, and painted original designs on the coral-stones; they decorated our house in quite a novel way. For hours my husband would sit and turn the tiny shells in his fingers, fascinated by their symmetry. Having not grown by the seashore, he had never known of them or thought they were possible. I explained that there were sea-snails and other very tiny mollusks which built these shells around their bodies from secretions of lime-silica. The shells formed in patterns, usually spirals, as they grew; their colourations enabled them to live among the coral-rocks of the reef without being seen by the fish which feasted on their kind. After they died, their shells remained. The two lines of shells on the beach represented two levels of high tide; the waves brought the shells ashore and deposited them on the beach; this double necklace of shells ran wherever there was sandy beach on the coast.

Then I showed him the tiny hermit—and soldier—crabs that used the empty shells for their own protection, taking them over as naturally as if they had been made and placed on the beach for their use. Together we shook our heads in wonder. We agreed that everything showed evidence of interchangeability, and that the forces of life impinged on material things with a pattern-forming mechanism.

The vorticed shells with their bands and subtle or checkered gradations of colour impressed us deeply, as did the delicate lattice-worked corals. We drew them often and soon we were so familiar with the structure of shells that we could reconstruct accurately a complete shell from a small fragment. In the hours we sat and drew, we discussed the designs of living things; and we were interested in this subject for two different reasons. He wanted to depict them, to imitate their beauty in art; I wanted to study them, to be like them; instead of capturing beauty, I wanted beauty to capture me; I wanted to fit in and not to analyse. Over the years our ideas were mutually modified until, I think, we developed identical points of view in our continuing search for what was natural and true.

We had to conclude that everything was intelligent. Every form had a pattern, and every pattern was correct physically aesthetically and intellectually. Our own intelligence was formed by, and reacted to, patterns; all the creative endeavour of man was to make pattern; all art was an imitation of the design of nature.

It was astonishing to conclude that we were part of intelligent force and to feel what it meant. We imagined and realized it as much as we could, and tried to see what the patterns of our bodies indicated our functions should be. To someone with an overview, units of mankind should seem to be at least as beautiful and functional as any other creation. We were sure that somewhere along the course of his existence man's natural mechanism of united Force, Form and Function had been tragically disrupted by some unnatural force; for the results of civilization around us obviously had no function that could be precisely named. ***No man knew for certain what to do with his life*** and how to relate to his death; a tragedy, indeed. But life and death were *real,* and we could intellectually contemplate them; therefore there must exist, we argued, a perfectly functional everyday way of life that fitted in with all the other facets of our being. Knowledge of function is the way to peace of mind.

It was the usual question, to do with man's place in the scheme of things, but the immediacy and insistence of our own questionings puzzled us; our curiosity rubbed our minds sore. It was not always pleasant thinking; sometimes it was torturous, and I knew well the feel of thought-fatigue.

We explored the potentialities of our Instruments at every opportunity; and yet we had to be cautious, for we knew that possession of such things was against the law of the Dominauts. When we were at Green Bay, we practised very quietly in our living quarters, or we went to distant places. Later on, by the time Uzulu was three years old, we had acquired a fine new house. It was situated high on a hill with a widespread view of Green Bay, and there were few houses around. Our dwelling was surrounded by fertile land, so that we grew many beautiful and rare fruit, and planted many of the herbs that were good for medicine. I had begun to experiment with such plants at that time.

We equipped this house with all the things that were necessary for our pursuit of knowledge and our understanding of ourselves. There was a room for physical exercise and one, well sealed, that we used for making sounds, and where we kept our Instruments in secret compartments.

Then there was the room where we extracted the juices and oils of plants, for much of the medicine of the Early Ages was taken in the form of oils, and I wanted to revive the practice among the people of the coast. It was during these times, too, that my husband showed me the flowers of skywhisper, and I made them into a very fragrant ointment. We rubbed some of it on our eyelids, and were amazed at its pleasant effects. Our eyes seemed to see more, and in greater detail. I felt a sense of happiness and tremendous well-being; and we were extremely merry during the time the effects were noticeable. I think that we were never quite the same again; it was as if we had found new ways of seeing things.

We also carried out exercises designed to give us experiences of a mystical nature, and we learnt many things about the ways of the human mind. New patterns of thinking evolved, and we sought the principles behind every manifestation of nature around us. It was as if somewhere in the course of our experiments a door in our minds had been opened, and we were free to traverse wherever we liked. Life became a completely absorbing quest; there was room for endless interpretation, and we found many important values which we applied in our daily living. The search for Truth is rewarding, and gives full recompense for the energy the searcher expends. Insights we never thought within the scope of human understanding flowed easily and familiarly in our reasonings.

We talked often of the Island of Whistling Winds, speculating on what it would be like to arrive there, and I looked forward to seeing it, for I wanted to find out what birds lived on the island. I was obsessively drawing and classifying forms of life at that time, and I knew that there were many birds that I had never seen. Then there was the prospect of the underwater trip to the island, and the possibilities of using the craft for many research journeys and pleasure trips. I would know the creatures of the sea intimately.

Erutan's work was progressing well, and he was sure that the craft would be ready on schedule. We told him that story of the Snike, which he believed reluctantly, and asked whether the vessel would be safe from such beings. He was sure that nothing would injure the craft; he had done much rigorous testing on the hull. I was extremely thankful for this certainty, for I had been considering the Snikes in relation to our trip ever since that day when I suddenly found out that such creatures existed.

We spent much time at the beach; Uzulu learned to swim. During those times we selected bathing areas carefully, and stayed in the sight of other people. Soon we noticed that more people were doing the same; few people bathed, beachcombed, or searched the reefs alone.

Then signs began to appear in our native language, advising people where to bathe and where not; but no reason for the places selected was apparent. Other signs warned people not to catch the turtles or eat their eggs, though previously people had always refrained from doing such.

One day (it was the day of Uzulu's fifth birth cycle) another Snike came out of the water and onto the beach. It was bleeding from its eyes and vestigial ears, and it soon died before a horrified crowd of many scores who had rushed to see the monstrosity on hearing the swift-travelling news.

There were deep misgivings and wonder-filled speculations circulating among the people that day. We did not see the Snike ourselves, but one of the many people who came to visit us, describing it and asking me what it was, said that it made high-pitched bubbly noises, blew water from the holes in its forehead, and was clad around the waist with fish-skins. I specifically asked if it had bands around its forearms, but my informants said that there had been none. The Dominaut Sea-Guards had arrived and taken the thing away from the beach.

Nothing more was said or heard of the Snikes during the following months, but it seemed as if the quality of life along the Coast had changed.

I had noticed for some time that more dead sea-creatures—fish, crabs, eels and even some turtles—were appearing on the beach. This was in direct proportion to the increase of the Dominauts' placements of their silenced explosives in the water near the shore. Each morning after a day of sea-harvesting by the Dominauts, there would be countless seagulls on the shore, searching among the piles of displaced seaweed and other uprooted water-plants for the remains of the creatures that had been killed by the explosions. When the beach had completely yielded up its provender the birds returned to their newly adopted feeding grounds, hovering thickly over the fleet of Dominaut fishing ships. It was a strangely unnerving sight to see those clouds of birds over the ships, especially since many of them seemed many times larger than the usual seagull, and flew with a fierce intention that was noticeable even as far away as the Coast. Besides that, people began to observe that things not quite like fish were being taken up in large numbers by the distant ships.

Then I saw that the Dominaut women who promenaded in the town wore many pearls and bright stones, which I found remarkable, for I knew that few people searched for oysters, and no fisherman of the Coast had ever seen such shining stones before, though obviously they bore the shapes and smoothnesses of sea-abrasion.

I pondered on this for a long time, and my reluctant suspicion grew stronger until I no longer ignored it. The pattern was clear: the Dominauts were killing the Snikes for their beautifully decorated and valuable forearm bands.

Soon after that a man from Sea-Breeze village came down to Green Bay and ran berserk in the open air fish-market. He dragged down the lines of dried flying-fish, trundled the brine-barrels about and bashed them in, stamped on the piles of sprats and chased the fishermen with their jangling purses away from the tables of eels, flatfish and conchs. He was longbearded and wildeyed, and he threw whelks like stinging pebbles at the backs of the departing people. Then he pulled the illegal turtle-meat from the secret places under the counters where the perfidious dealers had hidden them, and cursed the buyers and sellers.

For half an hour he raved and flailed his weapon, the long barbed tail of the batfish, and no one came near. Then the soldiers of King Chrazius surrounded him. He lacerated so many of them with his frightful whip that the Coast people knew it would go hard with him when finally he was caught. In the end they beat him into submission and carted him off. But his words hung in the ears of the people.

He screamed that they should leave the things of the sea alone. We were encouraging the wrath of the sea-beings, and they were planning a war against us and the Dominauts. They had seized two childen from Sea-Breeze village who had been picking up shells on the beach. No one walked the beach at night anymore, not even lovers, for ungainly, ravenous things lumbered about down there in search of food, and people were missing their cattle.

He denounced and cursed the Dominauts for the use of their underwater explosives, and for their killing of the turtles in order to get their shells. The sea-beings depended on the turtles, and the people of the Coast had known that for centuries.

The man was certainly mad. Many people knew him; he lived alone on a hostile, windblown cliff close by the village of Sea Breeze, and he had been muttering to himself, making strange actions and speaking of the sea eating the land and the land eating the sea for so many years that he had been given the nickname of Eater, though unquestionably he was more of a faster, sometimes by necessity. It was true that he was mad; but his words carried a strangely disturbing logic, and his alarming talk about an impending war seemed relevant to the increasingly unstable situation.

Meanwhile my husband had plunged happily into his role of father and was training and teaching the growing Uzulu well. I had deep moments of joy watching them as they worked at some boyish and mannish problem together, and I was glad to be a part of them.

Uzulu was interested in many things and learnt quickly. I noticed that he enjoyed activities that called for precision and accuracy, and that he could see very well. He applied himself with great dedication to the catapult, the sling, the bow and the blowpipe. He discovered the principle of the blowpipe on his own. He hollowed out a long stem of bamboo, made a number of darts designed like very short arrows, and shot them from the tube, having first stuck them in with a blob of material from the gum-tree, so as to build up air-pressure. The darts flew accurately, and he used his breath to very good effect.

One day he came to me clutching the body of a small bird that he had hit. He had taken aim with consideration, he said, and was sorry from the moment that he had seen the bird fall.

I pointed out to him that it was unjustifiable to take the life of any creature unless one's life depended on having it for food; and even then one must be aware that life should be treated with respect. There was no time or place where it was right to kill except for survival, and there were three kinds of survival; feeding, self-protection and reproduction.

"Did you want to eat it?"

"No!"

"Was it harming you?"

"No."

"Could it stop you from growing into a man and becoming a father?"

"No bird can do that, my mother, not even the one the Dominauts fear."

"Then, my son, learn something from the dead bird. Examine it, and tell me what you see."

He laid the bird on its back, spread out its wings, and started to describe what he saw.

"The wings spread out like fans, and the bones of the arms are longer than the bones of the legs. Each feather has very fine patterns on it. There are seventeen big feathers in each wing, and at the bottom of the feathers, close to the body, there are clusters of soft down. The breast is large; there is a bone underneath it, and the wings seem connected to it. It has four claws on each foot; three are turned backward and one in the opposite direction, forward, for gripping, as the fingers and thumb work. The legs and feet are covered with fine scales. The beak is small and hard, and sharply curved, and the eyes are round and coloured black and yellow—but they are dull now, as if covered by a cloud."

"Good," I said, extremely pleased with his powers of observation and his ability to define what he saw. "Now, find some soft earth, dig a hole, and bury it."

He left with the dead bird. Subsequently he was to study and examine many more dead and living birds, and he was keenly interested in their ways of flying.

When he was not studying and drawing birds, he made and flew kites of an unusual construction; and I discovered that he was very conscious of the wind, and sensitive to currents of air and smells that no one else seemed aware of.

And so life on the Coast of the Sea of Mirrors went on, until finally the undersea craft was ready.

11
THE SEA
OF MIRRORS

The Sea of Mirrors

ERUTAN CALLED ON US to give us the news; he had carried out test runs on the vessel, taking it through many extreme conditions in order to test its powers. He was very proud of its performance, and handed it over to us with complete confidence. He had called it a fine-sounding name, Sea-Searcher. It was beautiful to look upon. The controls were neat and very easy to understand and manipulate, and the craft very convincingly resembled one of the huge denizens of the deep sea. We took it for a short run, and felt like fish, ourselves, in the way it took us through the water. The view ahead was very clear and the craft manoeuvred right, left, up and down with ease and precision.

We packed it with provisions, clothing, blankets and toiletries; besides, we had our Instruments of Sounds, our well-worn traveller's bags, and much of Uzulu's shooting equipment.

Then the day came when we were to depart from the Coast of the Sea of Mirrors. The farewell was subdued. My parents and brother saw us off; many of the feelings in our hearts were left unsaid.

Uzulu was the last to enter the craft for he spent much time being kissed and hugged by this grandmother; then we were all aboard. I had the honour of starting the craft and the journey, and I was excited and happy as I switched the power on.

The screen before us came alive, glowing softly, as the Sea-Searcher made a very smooth descent. We moved over a shallow shelf that dropped gently to the deeper sea, travelling over the beautiful coral formations of the vast reef that fringed the shore-line on that part of the coast. Algae and tufted seaweed moved gently towards us and out of our vision; carpets of luscious flowering plants waved delicate tendrils of banded, striped and mottled colour. Bright oranges, greens and reds glowed in the rocks and overhangs, and small fish drifted past like leaves. Branching sponges of many varieties grew freely wherever we looked, and in the sandy beds there were many sea-stars. Amazingly, the sea-stars were laid out on the bottom in patterns of five which were as accurate as the individual shape of each sea-star; one could draw straight lines to all of them and create the five-pronged pattern of a huge sea-star.

Many of the plants seemed to change shape and colour; then we discovered that sometimes what we thought to be plants or lumps of coral were cleverly camouflaged fish, sea-slugs and shelled things. Shoals of bright fish, transparent, dotted, striped, flared and variously marked with shining colours, were encountered regularly, and sometimes we glided for several minutes through them. The water teemed with a colourful life that was a hundred times more beautiful than I had anticipated. Overwhelmed, I lowered the Sea-Searcher gently, and sat the craft on the bottom, in a sandy area; then we gazed out in silent fascination, growing accustomed to our strange new world.

Just ahead we saw flat smooth surfaces of an unusual, glinting, clear kind of rock, which reflected the light and fishes that passed over the area. My husband asked whether that was why the sea was called the Sea of Mirrors. I had never seen such rock before, and I told him of another more likely reason. Once, for the space of a year, mirrors used to wash up on the shore. They were made, it seemed, of pieces of that same rock, but were worked smooth and polished so that they gave clear reflections. At that time they were a mystery; but now I felt that it was the work of the Snikes.

The idea of the Snikes wanting to see their own horrendous faces was strangely humorous and relieving in our own new atmosphere. I noticed that Uzulu was very quiet, completely absorbed in the wonderful vista that lay before him, and scarcely heard our conversation. Now more relaxed, I raised the Sea-Searcher and set her due south towards the Island of Whistling Winds, and we moved forward at a leisurely speed.

Now we were in deeper water. We saw many large-mouthed, grotesque-looking fish. Some of them snapped smaller fishes up in ravenous haste, swirling and flailing among the scattering shoals. Sinuous things slid along the bottom or moved in hypnotic ripples and shifts of delicate fins in midwater, and some creatures had pointed mouths with which they sucked up other creatures and blew out little bubbles. There were fish with horns and some with beards; large mollusks and bristling sea-spiders, sand-burrowing fishes, lobsters and eels. There were various crabs and unusual worms, and all were exquisitely coloured. Flatfishes moved like scrapers along the bottom, devouring huge numbers of barnacles and other soft, shelled things, and weird, bony rockfish shot spurts of coloured poison into the water, paralyzing other creatures.

There were also many plants waving about and sucking in the little fish and minute organisms that floated around; some of these plants were huge and indeed seemed more animal-like than I could have thought possible before. We saw extremely large fishes, too; some very familiar to us in smaller versions, but others were absolutely new. There was an incredible variety of mouths and eyes.

The next wonder that we saw was of such a startling nature that I ask you now, oh people of Ainchan, to prepare your minds for what I shall describe.

We went down gradually as the bottom fell away, and then we noticed glows in the water ahead. They were large lights, it was obvious, but we were puzzled, and asked each other what they could mean. Then we came closer. The lights became less distorted by the water and we saw that they were within huge transparent domes.

There were six of these domes in the area of ocean through which we passed. Each of them was perhaps half a mile in diameter, and were made into many apartments, each separated by transparent walls that ran from the centre of the dome out to its sloped circumference. Near the apex of each dome there were clusters of lights; it was these lights that first attracted our attention.

Some of these apartments were cattle and sheep farms with grass growing on fertile soil under the very strong lights. Others contained large flightless birds. One of the domes, which was divided into so many apartments that it looked like a thickly-spoked wheel, proved the most blood-chilling of all, for these apartments contained *human beings,* or things very much like them—I mean, like us. All creatures of the land seemed to be walking, making noises, sitting, sleeping and giving birth as ordinarily as if they were on the land; and the longer I gazed on them with fierce curiosity, the more I realized that they were quite content, and did not know that they were in captivity.

Some apartments contained one or two adults and their young offspring; others housed young adolescents who were separated into sexes or put together to breed, in some order I could not comprehend, and which seemed totally random to me. Their bodies were amazingly similar—both men and women had been well fattened. For the most part they sat around listlessly, walked up and down, played endless games. Many sat before silver-lighted screens that showed endless moving pictures of fishes and things of the sea. There were corridors for these domesticated humans to walk on, lights to turn on and off, and windows and doors to open and close. I noticed little stoves for cooking on and water for bathing. Very many of the females sat combing their hair, painting their faces and putting bright stones and pearls on their necks, arms and legs; and there were elaborate wardrobes. Very many mirrors, of all sizes, were in these compartments, so that sometimes I could not tell exactly where an apartment ended, or how many people were in a room. People stood before the mirrors for hours. Others sat in baths and lathered themselves in soaps and oils, and yet others fed at huge tables laden with fish, conchs and deep-sea crustaceans.

The longer I looked at them the more I saw that they were not fully, consciously human, for they moved too listlessly. Theirs was a weird submission to fate; they went through the motions of living contentedly and did not realize that they were kept in cages of air at the bottom of the sea.

Then we saw what seemed to be a large shining plate unfurl above the domes. Its sheet-like segments slid apart and the thing became a cone of some unfamiliar metal. It had many wiry tentacles which joined the domes at sealed points in their summits, so that it was connected to each of them.

We were wondering what heinous purpose this thing was for, when two Snikes appeared. They travelled swiftly, and between them they carried a huge log, possibly of ironwood, probably taken from some jetty. They swam forward rapidly (and we saw how lethally quick they could manoeuvre) and struck the gong (for such it was) with the log. Immediately there was a terrified chaos in the farm-apartments below as birds and animals ran helter-skelter, while in the apartments of the humans people held their hands to their ears and expressions of terrible fear and hurt creased their faces into masks of torture. The pulsation of sound reached within the Sea-Searcher, and I felt its unholy vibraton. Then I knew what the apparatus was for; the Snikes were bombarding the Land-People with sounds as to keep them in a state of submission and domestication.

When the reverberations of the gong had ceased, I saw that the people and animals relaxed. The people appeared very grateful, having been freed of their torment. Several of them faced the silver screens and knelt or bowed, clasping their hands; and I noticed that the screens were now filled with images of the Snikes's faces.

My husband and son were very worried. I turned the Sea-Searcher away from the humiliating scene below. I was disturbed most profoundly to realize that such things were true, and I remembered with great shock my own aquarium at home, and the fish-farms of the coast-people.

We glided on, and the three of us were silent, watching the wonders of the deep with only half our attention. The implications of the dejecting scene we had witnessed staggered our values about the position of man in the world. I as a member of the race, felt threatened, as if I needed more equipment to fight our potential captors. I wondered why humans had no fang, claw, poison or ability to escape quickly if such preying upon our kind was a fact of life; then I concluded that the brain, and therefore knowledge, was the weapon that we were supposed to have developed. It was ignorance that made an animal or person become the prey of others.

I said this to my husband, and he agreed soberly, adding that, despite the assumed dignity and claimed superiority of man, actually man knew very little about himself or his environment, and was so arrogant as to assume that nothing could be more knowledgeable than himself. Man needed to investigate more, and urgently, as a matter of survival; he must stop acting as if he knew all. Some things not as intelligent but having more facts at their disposal could enslave men quite easily. For instance, he said, no people besides the Dominauts knew the principle of the fireweapon; they knew of other things, but not of that. And yet the Dominauts feared the people of the Land of Muse, who had yet another weapon that no one else seemed to know about.

Even as he said this, we saw the hulks of ships in the water above. Dark and threatening they were, and very many, and I was angry from the moment I saw them. Here was an example of the principle my husband had just spoken of. We knew of undersea craft; the Dominauts did not. If Erutan had equipped this vessel with a sharp spike, or harpoons that could be fired, the three of us could have sunk all the ships that floated overhead. It was strictly a matter of what facts you knew, whether you survived or not; and since the Dominauts knew nothing of undersea travel, then it would be advantageous if Erutan could produce many more vessels like the one we were in—but Sea-Assaulters, rather than Sea-Searchers.

At that moment, all of a sudden the whole sea seemed to shudder, and large swirls of water, bounding out, it seemed, from a radiating centre, hit the Sea-Searcher in four or five distinct, lurching waves. The Dominauts had dropped depth-explosives to kill sea-creatures, as usual. The water was filled with deep-sea mud, sand, rocks, shelled things, shattered fish and seaweed. The whole ocean seemed to somersault ant tumble, and an uncomfortable vibration trembled our craft and turned it around and around in the reverberating turbulence. Stones banged into the sides, bottom and top of our vessel as I fought to bring it under control. Then there was another detonation; hurriedly I jerked down the lever to make the craft as heavy as possible, and yet the Sea-Searcher lurched drunkenly sideways and over, so that Uzulu, who had not been strapped securely as my husband and myself were, was thrown around from floor to ceiling and back again, while our possessions slammed around in the main body of the vessel most disquietingly.

When things had stilled somewhat I looked at the screen again. There were scenes of the most carnal destruction ahead. Thousands of fish floated upside down, turning in the water-swirls. Strange deep-sea things with long tentacles and round rubbery heads twitched and whipped themselves about, spouting an opaque black liquid as they died, and injured eels jerked furiously, biting at the wounds n their own bodies. There were dead turtles too, and dead Snikes, which I viewed with uncannily confused feelings of pity, gladness and terror.

Presently we noticed things moving in the distance directly ahead; dark shapes which glided rapidly in close formation through the deep-blue, settling water. There were several hundreds of them and they headed unerringly upward through the water to the bulky ships. As they rose the light became brighter and we could define them more clearly; then we saw that each shape represented a Snike riding upon some huge and macabre species of fish.

The fish they rode upon were perhaps twenty feet long. They were shaped for very fast swimming, and had heavy powerful tails which they thrashed violently when they turned. They had huge blunt snouts, and set far back underneath the snouts there were cruel crescent-shaped mouths that bristled with rows of teeth. Their eyes were wide-set and stared coldly out from opposite sides of their heads, and two triangular fins stuck up at two points along their backs, the foremost one being larger.

These primeval, terrible creatures with their mounted Snikes coursed with a fixed determination and a similar precision through the upper waters. The Snikes, crouched low on their thick-skinned backs, each carried a long slender spear of some rigid material that glowed like phosphorescent bone. Even as we watched the great army of Snikes and carnivorous fish come up under the ships of the Dominauts, I noticed that none of the sea-beings wore their forearm bands of exquisitely decorated fish-skin, and I guessed the Snikes had realized that the Dominauts had been slaughtering them for the pearls and bright stones they hoarded.

"They are going to attack," my husband muttered quietly. "It's going to be a rough time; we can't get through that. Set the craft down somewhere safe, and let's watch and wait until it's over."

I found a limestone sea-cave among the rock formations and set Sea-Searcher down upon a cushion of tendrilled sea-plants. Uzulu, awed and silenced, sat between us, and we watched the screen in wordless suspense.

As the units of mounted Snikes neared the ships their lines separated and spread out, aiming at specific targets. They hit the ships all at once, and the physical effect of the sound, coming through the water, stirred our vessel, which quivered as if it also had been injured.

Boards splintered and exploded as though the iridescent spears the Snikes carried had some force of their own. Ships foundered. It was a queer and memorable experience to see how ships sank, from below the surface of the sea. Water and fish swirled swiftly through the crashing, gaping bottoms in violent suction, and brightly coloured bubbles of air popped in all directions. Shadows in the water widened as boats settled deeper, and some vessels keeled over so that men, ropes, barrels, crates, fishnets and large pieces of ship's hull and furniture bounced, tangled and collided with living and dead bodies in the water.

Then the Dominauts dropped a monstrous barrage of depth-explosives. In several places the water flared a dull red, and a continuous series of pounds boomed, shaking the very rocks around Sea-Searcher.

Snikes and fish burst apart, spun, and catapulted away from the jumble of hulls, ropes and spars. Broken bodies were flung about in the reddened water, and wounded Dominauts, Snikes and fish fought confusedly. Blood and flesh spurted and rained around, and more and more horrific, unspeakable shapes of sea-beasts, gathering from miles away, began to appear, sliding silently through the water with fearsome speed, grinning their murderous jaws.

The rapacious creatures surged into the general turmoil in impossible numbers, converging on the masses of shattered flesh that spun and sank and struggled; and while some descended to the bottom and started to feed immediately on the pieces of meat raining down, others butted and struck ships, Dominauts, Snikes and each other, raking away chunks of wood and flesh in a frenzy of slaughter and feeding.

I shuddered and closed my eyes. The magnitude of the carnage, and the suddenness with which one living thing became the food and sustenance of another overwhelmed me. The qualities of compunction, mercy and respite into which I had been trained familiarly knew no expression in the search for food; and it struck me forcibly that in times of dire necessity men could, and did, act as unreasoningly, instinctively and voraciously as these creatures in their intent to survive. Civilization, like the life of an individual animal or plant, was based on a constant supply of food. If food failed, man's veneer of cultural decency, gregarious etiquette and restraint would quickly disappear.

Uzulu talked to his father in quiet tones, respecting my mental and physical exhaustion, and pointing with boyish interest to each new horror in the grisly scavenging that was going on outside.

The fighting, killing and ravenous feeding lasted long into the night. When the dense darkness fell we decided to stay where we were for the night, and I was glad, for I extremely fatigued.

All night lights streaked past our screen or made intricate turning patterns as phosphorescent water-creatures came to eat the things the larger fish had left. Jellyfish shoals lit up the sea like stars, and dead bodies glowed, closely covered by little shining bloodsucking fish. Once or twice dull-red explosions glowed on the darkened screen, killing the foragers, and after the blasts yet more fish arrived to continue the cycle.

When morning came the sea was surprisingly calm. Here and there a shattered hull floated, and there were many crabs, lobsters, and small schools of fish about, eating up the morsels.

I made breakfast for Uzulu; my husband, who had sat in meditation all night, facing the screen, had gone into fasting until we stepped ashore at the Island of Whistling Winds, and I joined him in the exercise. He took over the controls, and we continued our journey towards the Island.

Three days and nights were to pass before we arrived, and a most interesting and formative event was to occur to me during that time.

We had been travelling slowly, taking great care to negotiate the dangerous eddies of deep-ocean currents and the abysmal valleys of the sea; the immeasurable ravines that plunged downward in blackness, where all the habitants were blind, phosphorescent and large and dense as imagination could conceive. No man-made craft could enter such whirlpools and crevasses; their mystery was not for man to solve for countless billions of years, if indeed man would survive to know.

The uncompromising nature of life had made it fit that man could know these places, as he could know the planets, only by comparison and imagination. No physical body or machine could bridge the dimensions that it took to travel so deep into the profundities of time and space. No sea-creature, not even the immortal-seeming turtles, had traversed the many diverse areas that composed the underneath of the sea. Those thousands of acres of meadows we passed, all covered with anemones, had been there for centuries; our vessel's passing made no difference to their existence. Those droplets of translucent fish eggs that hung in fantastic beaded curtains, glinting their amber enchantments, made me humble as our craft moved past them for miles and miles; they lit the rock-tints with new visual delights all along the way. If man could live a thousand million years, he could spend all that time staring at the prismatic colours and designs that existed on the butterfly-fishes alone.

Such were the meditations flowing in my mind on the night of the third day. My husband had invited me to take the controls again, and he and Uzulu had fallen into sleep on the bunks in the midsection of the vessel. I was guiding the Sea-Searcher gently along, and the fasting of the past three days had heightened my awareness and my general receptivity to the forces of existence. Thus, when I found myself turning my head, listening, as if the thoughts in my head were coming from a great distance off and needed focusing, I was hardly surprised. I strained to hear a voice that seemed to be coming from inside my head. It was an eerie sensation indeed, for normally I listened for sounds *outside* my head; and I found that I had to breathe deeply and keep really still, relaxedly, almost as if I was not listening, in order to hear the insistent, agreeable voice.

"Armienne, Mother of Uzulu!" the patient, soothing voice seemed to say. "Do you not remember me?"

"No. who are you?" I answered in my head, at the same time turning to look at the screen, in an instinctive quest for more information.

"I am Turtle-Mother," I seemed to hear. At the same time I saw the creature wafting itself across the screen, its robust flippers moving with a peculiar, tranquil power and rhythm that made me sigh in admiration. I distinctly remember the sensation of realizing that the Turtle was communicating to me, and I also distinctly remember that such a strange, invincible calm came over me that I felt secure and free from all threats to my existence on this planet. Knowledge blossomed in my mind: Faith is the shell that I must have, to withdraw into. Faith is the shell of the Turtle. The thought was a simple one; but at the time it filled my mind, and its several applications were marvellous to consider. I thought it important to memorize the saying.

But the Turtle was communicating once again, as it swam to and fro, into and out of the range of the screen.

"I was on the beach that night when you created those lovely patterns of vibration. You gave me much happiness; I laid my eggs in contentment and peace, and I have never forgotten you. Since then I have listened to your patterns of vibration many times, and others have done so too. All of us whom you call Reptiles are charmed by sounds, but your sounds are inexpressibly sweet even to us Turtles, who are very discriminating. I have felt many vibrations, but I am fondest of yours."

"I am glad to hear it," I thought. Memories of the Turtle Beach, an unforgettable part of my self-understanding, flooded through my mind with such an immediacy that it was hard to believe the event had happened about nine years before. The sensations I had felt that night among the living and dead mothers, with the echoing harmonies calling forth the generative power of the living, now warmed my insides, so that I experience some sensual feelings of the time when my motherhood had blossomed.

Now the Turtle's mind seemed to be joined to mine. Its consciousness was a glowing point within my own, and I strove to relax more so that it could widen in a better mental environment. I felt the essence of the Turtle's feeling and attuned myself to it, so that the communication was more through a state of spirit than through words or even thoughts. Yet in this unusual state I still felt the probe and relief of question and answer; there was the insistent itch to enquire of the Turtle's existence, and the soothing rub as the Turtle's wide experience relieved my human puzzlements.

"You dreamt of motherhood for a long time," the Turtle "said", observing the detached thought that floated in my mind. I had started remembering, with a glad relief, those anxious years when I had wanted so badly to produce a child; now I lived in the happy aftermath of all my worry and fear.

"Yes," the Turtle went on. "The worst fear that a female can know is the fear that she will not be a mother. It is the most horrendous thing to be going through the act of procreation again and again, and not to be seeing the fruit of it. There is nothing to make one feel more out of touch with the Source of Life than the failure to produce at least one being of one's own kind. Reproduction is the same as what you can call your Harmony.

"The mother protects her race when she protects her offspring. She watches over and heals, and she is mother to both *male* and *female* offspring. She is the harmonizer of conditions and the maker of relationships between father and children. Mothers make, repair and sustain.

"Mothers are like the Water. They link Earth and Air. Life came from the Water, and mothers carry the water of Creation in their bodies. Mothers are responsive to vibrations because they are hollow. Eggs and children form through the coalescence that vibration causes.

"We are Mothers. My eggs are your eggs. My children are your children. So many of you humans build up barriers, I must say, that there is a separation existing between ourselves, for the most part. The spirit of Life is the same in all shapes. Were we always like this? Have we not eaten each other already? You cannot remember or envisage it?"

"I do not know what you mean; but I have never consciously eaten of you—or your eggs," I answered quickly. "Besides," I continued, switching the subject away from the eating of eggs, "you Turtles do not take care of your eggs very well. You lose thousands of them every year, and yet you come and carry on the same way. Have you never noticed, throughout the centuries, that it is dangerous to lay your eggs on the land—or given to venture near the shore?"

"Turtles lay eggs on land because they have no other choice. It is the best—the-only-place." The Turtle's voice' was patient. "Can you imagine what it would be like if we laid our eggs in the sea? There would be no young Turtles, for all of them would be eaten! And how would our children first breathe Air? Besides which, the eggs need the radiations of what you call the Sun."

"You leave your children on their own. Could you not wait for them?" I enquired.

The Turtle seemed to find the question naïve.

"Our children come to us. We do not have to wait; they can find us. They have the time and the instinct. Every Turtle knows her children. But what does it matter? Every existing thing has a unique ensouling presence. Then there is the over-ruling Intelligence for each existing species. We are interested more in the over-ruling Intelligence; the majority of you humans have refused to live by this concept, though you all are well aware that you should practically accept and live this truth.

"Each human tries to see himself as the most important human who ever lived. But everything is the manifestation of the one Intelligence that has no form and yet takes all forms. Eventually when humans live the truth that they are all one human, and that one human is part of one Life; when they learn to treat everything as alive, intelligent and part of the same Thing, then humans will have richer lives and complete understanding of their situation. But you do not even treat all humans as equal; even among the races there are those that assume that they are better than others. Is it not so? . . .

"Yes, yes, but you have no means of self-preservation other than your shell."

"And time."

"You need a weapon. Humans too. Many creatures of the sea, like the Snikes, are well equipped with weapons."

"They are attackers. We are defenders."

"What's the difference?"

"Attackers are tense. Defenders are relaxed. Passive defence is the role we have accepted in a world full of predacicious Enemies, as you call them. We are inoffensive in our disposition, and because we move slowly and have a great deal of time, our very effective outsides are important to us. Predators have no patience; they like to kill and eat quickly. We can fast and lie still for days or weeks. Over the centuries those of us who developed powers of quicker movement have had reductions made in the size, shape and weight of their protective outsides—their speed compensates. They adopt a lesser form of passive defence than complete withdrawal—they adopt *flight* as part of their means of survival."

I was impressed by the Turtle's dissertation.

"Is it true that one of these days Turtles will become birds?" I asked next, thinking of the word "flight."

"I hope so. I have always had the desire to fly from the water into the Air. We would have to practice and develop this ability in the future. But we would still have to lay our eggs on the land!

"I suppose that we will lay our eggs on land always, I have never envisaged a change to that pattern. Other things will have to change before our reproductive methods do. But I do not pretend to know of reproduction—unlike some humans. It is difficult to analyse something that you are the product of, is it not?

"The activity of reproduction is the responsibility of something greater than our individual sense. Nothing can argue against the reproductive force. For decades I have crawled, at the cost of great physical strength, up beaches to deliver my eggs, and I know that each time, whether I willed to go or no, I had no control over my final actions. Even on the two occasions when I saw the humans with lights who had come to capture us, I did not stop in my efforts; the continuum of Life itself was the force that urged me on. It is always a difficult business to climb those shore-lines, especially since we do not eat during the time of egg-laying. You can imagine how hungry we are afterwards! But the fathers bring us food, and wait in the water until we return."

"That is nice of them."

"All fathers are the same. The Snike Fathers do the same when their females go to deliver their young."

"I never thought of that aspect of the Snike's lives. Do the Snike mothers go up on beaches to deliver their offspring?"

"Yes—where else? Only very large mammals, like the creature you know as Whale, can deliver offspring at sea. The Snike mothers come up on the shore, and very vicious they are, too, if you try to prevent them either from delivering or returning to the sea."

My mind adjusted to this new information. There was more I had to ask concerning the Snikes, but I wanted the Turtle to continue her story.

"It takes a long time, doesn't it, to come up, lay your eggs, and return?"

The Turtle swam slowly in the middle of the screen, and I watched the interlinked plates of its shell as it communicated again.

"It takes a night, if that is what you call a long time. But that is unimportant; what it takes mainly is *effort.* The Turtle's path of motherhood is a difficult one."

"Tell me about it."

"The shorelines are long and crawling is hard. Every time we pause in our crawling, our heavy backs come down and squeeze the Air out of our lungs. To breathe takes a lot of effort, for we have to push up from the sand in order to get our diaphragms and lungs (as you call them) to suck the Air in. men say that we sigh, when they hear the labored breaths and deep pants that we make; some think it is to do with our burden of eggs! Then again it takes much effort to move our limbs in the sand, for our limbs are not for moving on the land, as the limbs are on our relations, the Tortoises. Even Tortoises find it difficult to move in the sand. But with what you call our flippers, and a heavy back, it is an awesome task confronting one to crawl up a beach of wet and dry sand. The way is long, and each pebble, bit of driftwood or clump of seaweed is an obstacle.

"Finally, we reach a good spot above the high-tide mark, use our hind flippers to dig a hole, lay our eggs, hopefully in undisturbed contentment, cover them, and depart.

"The night we met you on the beach, we were very pleasantly sustained in our efforts by the experiences you were sharing. Those vibrations entered my insides like the most soothing wash of waves, or like the warm light I feel when I come to lie on the surface of the Water for a while, during the middle of the day. We understood the things you were doing; for the first time many of us saw how close to us in feeling humans could be, and we were very pleased. We have been humming ever since, you know."

"I am very glad to hear that."

"I laid my eggs easily, and by dawn I was in the comfort—and safety—of the Water once more. You know, the males feed us and mate with us as soon as we leave the egg-laying beach."

"I did not know that. It must be—fun . . ."

It was a startling experience to feel the Turtle's amusement.

"Humans do not know as much about us as we know about humans. I have been studying humans, whenever I have come across them, for the past two hundred years at least, and there have been legends handed down to us from the past, which speak of the ways of men."

"You have lived how many years?"

"I believe three hundred and more."

I swallowed. "And what do you think of humans?"

"They are good."

"Good? You do not think them—evil?"

"No, no, not evil. They need knowledge, like everything else . . . Ignorance is not evil, unless arrogance goes with it. We all have to find out; there are levels of knowledge."

"Men are not your enemies?"

"No more or less than anything else . . . Men should try to find out more about their situation. They need to. They pretend to know all, but they don't; and they call themselves the

highest in creation, but they only think so among themselves;
no other creature agrees with them. Men are mainly lacking
in knowledge and only *slightly* arrogant, if I may modify my
former absolute statement.

"We like men better than we like the Snikes. The Snikes
are more ignorant, and completely arrogant. We have more
reasons to avoid the Snikes, for they need us more than humans
do. We are almost a part of their reproductive system."

A slight, chilled feeling came over me. "How?"

"Our shells, as you say, are valuable to the Snikes mothers.
They use them when they go to deliver their offspring."

"How . . . ?—Where do they go?"

"To an island south of here."

"The Island of Whistling Winds?"

"Yes, that is the name it is called. Your fish-craft is headed
towards it.

"That is where we are going."

"A dangerous place, for humans."

"We have endured dangers before."

"I will accompany you and show you a safe place to come
up on the island—the beach where once I used to lay my
eggs."

"Thank you. But tell me—why do the Snike mothers
need Turtles' shells in order to bring forth their offspring?"

"It is a long story, and it started in a time which is past
your capability of recall. Once, the Snikes used to go up on
the beaches of the Island of Whistling Winds to deliver their
young, without fear of molestation. Day or night, when the
contractions came, they swam to the beach, climbed the shore

and reached the caves, where their offspring would be born. They would remain in the cave with the babies for a day, then return to the sea. At first they did this without trouble; then large birds of prey discovered an easy means of obtaining food. They waited for the Snike mothers and babies and attacked them on the wide stretch of beach between the sea and the caves. Daytime or night-time, the danger was the same.

There were two types of the same bird operating, one adapted to the day, the other to the night. Many of the Snike mothers and babies were seized. We used to see their skeletons on the shore sometimes. We were safer than they were when it came to escaping the birds, for our shells protected us well. We outwaited them easily, too; and they could never succeed in gripping and turning our shells over, as they tried to do quite often.

"The Snike mothers envied us our protective backs. They started to find the empty shells, and wear them over their bodies as they crawled up the beach; then they were safe from the great birds. But Turtles live long and there were few shells to be found; thus the Snikes started trying to catch us to take our shells away. A very painful process, as you can imagine.

"Nowadays, the Snike mother brings along some flesh for the birds to feed on. She drops part of her offering, and, while they are feeding, she hurries as much as her heavy shell and her pregnancy will allow, into one of the caves. There she gives birth to her young and rests for a day. Then, throwing out the outer part of her feeding-meat, she distracts the birds away from herself and baby, and under the shell she moves down to the sea again. So you see, although they are such mighty attackers, they need our shells for their defence at the moment of greatest vulnerability."

"I am sorry that you Turtles are involved in it."

"I am sorry about the humans, too."

"What? What do you mean?"

"They do not always take our flesh along. Sometimes they take large fish and other sea-things. Sometimes they take cattle and land-people, which they keep under the sea—as I see you have noticed . . . Once, I even saw four pregnant Snikes swimming with the body of a Whale towards the island."

"So all those things kept under the sea—they are for *sacrificing* to birds of prey?"

"And occasional food for the Snikes. But then yes, for all eating—certainly of flesh—involves some sacrifice, does it not?"

"That is the most astounding thing I've ever heard—"

"Mother of Uzulu, there is so much more for you to know, that you need to accept truth quickly when you hear it. If that surprises you, how can you stand the reality of knowing all? Do you prefer the dreams that most men are raised and nurtured upon, which distract them from their real purpose in living? You are not afraid to hear . . . ?"

I paused; then: "Tell me!" I whispered fiercely, watching the great hard beak that opened and closed before me, on the screen.

"I cannot. You have to find out. Only you can untie yourself from ignorance . . . I cannot speak of you, but only of me, with certainty. All I say is, value the truth above all else, even if it dejects and embarrasses you to do so. Get into relationship with more reality—the one you know, not the one you have always heard. There is a lot more, and Harmony is obviously your guide. I will say no more."

"You will tell me more!" I whispered with the same fierce vehemence, as the Turtle's consciousness glimmered and I feared I was losing contact.

"You know the path. You are on the path, as all consciously evolving creatures are. You are in tune with the natural truths, and they will come to you fully. You realize what many humans have never realized—that in nature there is nothing superfluous; that everything has a function. Find out the function of humans and therefore of yourself . . ."

I silently agreed, breathing into relaxation, and the Turtle was pleased.

"There are still more questions," my consciousness persisted. "What do the Dominauts have to do with the Island of Whistling Winds?"

"What is a Dominaut?"

"The people who have taken our land."

"I do not accept your statement. Can land be taken?"

"Well, no. The Dominauts came with ships and fireweapons and have taken us captive and occupied the land. Humans do that to each other, you understand?"

"The Dominauts are humans, then?"

"Well, yes . . ."

"The humans I have seen on the island there for more than one reason. Some were after our discarded shells; they could be found along the shore. Others interested in the bright stones that the Snikes wear. Many of them lie on the beaches of the Island of Whistling Winds. The ones who have ventured beyond the shore were interested in the eggs and plumages of the birds, and I have also seen a few of them attempting to train the larger birds—I think for transport."

"What! They fly on birds?"

"I have not seen it done, so I cannot say for certain; but I saw them feed and try to tame the birds. In fact, they constantly had to feed the birds to stop them from attacking them. It took a lot of flesh, too. Most birds who eat meat prefer not to have to kill it, but they would attack living things if no dead things were available. Therefore both Snikes and humans who go to the island offer them cattle, us, other Snikes and other humans."

"Creator of our fathers!"

"As the birds peck and swallow the meat, both Snikes and humans gather up our shells and the bright stones which they love so much."

"Both Snikes and human? They do it together?"

"Sometimes; but when it is so the Snikes are the slaves and labourers of the humans."

"Humans are offered to the birds very often?"

"A few times a year, if that is often, either by Snikes or other humans. And a strange thing—all of the humans are flown off with, while the Snikes, cattle, Turtles, fish or whatever else, may be flown off with or finished on the spot. I have wondered what was the reason for many decades now."

"Would the humans know that Snikes offer humans?"

"Snikes would never offer humans for humans to know. You are the first to have seen their land-people farms; they try not to let the humans on the shore know that they exist. And they offer humans much less often humans do each other."

"You have seen this?"

"I have."

"You have seen this often?"

"Countless times, in my life."

"Then, Turtle, you might not want to say it, but I say that humans are motivated by evil."

"You say it with doubt, as I observe, Mother of Uzulu, and rightly so. Humans are for the most part different from the way they are supposed to be. Naturalness is gone, and they are under authority. They have been brutalized and domesticated, so that they commit many acts that are not natural. Humans are not made to be as savage and violent as they act sometimes. The penchant for brutality that many humans possess has been placed there at a particular time and for a particular reason. If they knew why they were doing what they are doing, they would stop."

"Why are they doing what they are doing? Can you tell me that?"

"Humans are possessed."

"What did you say?"

"Humans are possessed."

"What does that mean?"

"They are owned. They are property."

"That is a joke. There is nothing that could own a human being."

"Why do you sound surprised? Do you human beings own each other? You yourself have said that your people are owned by others. Are you not a student of truth, and is not what is natural the evidence of truth?"

"What beings could own humans?"

What you call *demons*. A group of personalities who are interested in spreading harm and destruction among humans for their own gains. Do you think humans like to fight? Don't all humans like and hate the same things universally?"

"Why don't humans get these demons out, then?"

"Out from where?"

"Out from within them."

"Within their bodies, you mean? . . . But the demons are not inside them. They are flesh and blood, even as you are—but what flesh, and what blood! They are beyond humans, and direct them from beyond. Humans do not have the power to enter into their environment; humans cannot even comprehend that such things exist in solid reality. That is where the danger lies for every existing species—in unawareness of, or powerlessness to enter into another environment, while the things of that environment can enter theirs at will. The fish in the Water is not conscious of the sea-gull in the Air until it is lifted into the Air in the bird's beak. Do you not see the pattern?"

"I do," I breathed in horrified wonder. "But humans say they are free. It is *known* that humans are free. And demons, as I imagine, do not have physical bodies, if indeed they—exist."

"All clever masters would have their slaves think that rulers do not exist—that they, the slaves, enjoy the ultimate in freedom. It is convenient for the master if the slave thinks that he does not exist. Have you not seen the land-people farms of the Snikes? Do not most captive humans accept life under captivity as a natural thing? You have many examples, I am sure, for you have said that your people are captives.

"There are many captive people—and other beings—who have been hypnotized and programmed into activities that are not natural. Large-scale, world-wide hypnosis is not inconceivable.

"And do not think of invisible, non-material beings when I say *demons.* I speak of living things. They can make their presence known without being visible, and they may influence humans from a great distance away, but they are natural, as you or I. They cannot get into you, as I understand you to imagine; they only need to influence your thinking—as I am sure your human captors do. Does a man get inside of flock of land-animals to possess them? No. He builds a cage of fences around them, and, invisible, he can limit and direct their movements, while they continue believing that they are free, that no one has designs on them! ***The higher the intelligences, the more subtle the possession needs to be.*** In that statement there is much, Mother of Uzulu."

"Then something must possess Turtles too."

"I cannot tell. I have wondered . . . It is difficult to see yourself, is it not?"

"Humans have free will, Mother-Turtle. That is the difference between us and other creatures."

"Free will, yes. But something exists that keeps many of the facts of life away from you. You need *facts* to go with free will, and something is withholding the facts. Something having more facts at its disposal—or something bigger, stronger and smarter."

"Those are the characteristic advantages of the predator over the prey. You are saying that humans have a predator?"

"Human have more than one. I have seen humans torn by fish; and there are things on land . . ."

"All right; like lions, and crocodiles. But you made it sound as though humans are systematically preyed upon by beings who have calculated and organized their predation to the extent that they depend on our bodies for their sustenance and profit, as a farmer does on his sheep. I do not believe it."

"I speak the evidence of my eyes, and I am supported by the detailed accounts of our forebears. Our memories are very long, Uzulu-mother. You have the opportunity to grasp more facts than any human has grasped before; grasp as many as possible and do not try to close your mind. Your curiosity will not let you succeed, land-woman. Why do so many of you work against your brains, instead of with them? I am conscious that you are not quite like the rest; you will continue to think whether you want to or not.

But unless you make an attempt to grasp concepts at once, as fast as they come, you are impairing your ability to understand, know, and therefore survive. The predator of mankind still has a cage around your mental environment. Shake off your hypnotism. *Completely.* Continue the work that has begun in yourself—the work that will make you fully conscious as a human. Study the meaning of Harmony; what I have said is only an expression of the Universal Pattern. You will find out enough to satisfy all your questions if you press on. Do not cut off any part of your understanding; complete

Harmony is not cutting off any part of yourself. Reflect on it as I do. This is the Sea of Reflections, after all."

The words of the Turtle affected me in several ways. I felt like switching off its voice, my consciousness, my whole existence, rather than accept what it had said; I felt as if I had died. I could hear my heart beat, low in my body, it seemed, and with the hollowness of an empty container. I listened, but the concepts the Turtle elaborated on were received against a background of complete psychological shatterment. My body had relaxed beyond the point where I could mentally control it; my mind wondered how it could still function when all the principles I had acted upon throughout my life seemed empty and valueless. My former actions had had a complete absence of meaning as far as reality went. I did not want to listen to or believe the Turtle, and yet I knew what she said was logical and well worth the thinking. An absolute blankness filled my mind as far as my future motivations in life were concerned. The Turtle had told me that all my actions had been, more or less, a danger to myself since I, like all humans, was functioning as something else wanted me to.

I could not imagine what I could do with this new knowledge. I could discuss this only with my husband and son; such conceptions could not be highly uttered. Certainly this was harder to say than it had been to try to convince the people of Sea-Breeze village that there had been a Snike on the shore. I myself had experienced the feelings I saw registered on the faces on the Sea-Breeze villagers, and even now I do not expect you to even consider seriously the words of the Turtle, oh Ainchan people. I know too well what it is to prefer to live a lie, and on hearing the Turtle's communications that memorable night beneath the Sea of Mirrors, I had to let go an important part of myself and wonder about myself and mankind with a rare objectivity.

Besides, another part of myself was saying, "This, *this* might be the trap! Perhaps the Turtle is the predator on man she is describing! How else would she know—" But this thought skimmered on the outer reaches of my imagination, and was soon dismissed. There were many more thoughts of closer proximity, less complicated to work out, though perhaps just as far-fetched; but the subject demanded such, and the implications of each question were staggering.

Part of my mind was continuing the communication with the Turtle however, and inanely I tried to correct the last thing the Turtle had said.

"The Sea of Mirrors, you mean."

"No, of Reflections. You are reflecting, I am reflecting. Original beliefs are seen in their opposite light. You wonder which is which, which is true and which false. You search the other image of yourself to see if it is really you; you see the real you and you wonder who it is. Few have traversed this sea and lived through the thoughts of reality. You are among the blessed, and you travel with our love. We call you Harmonious Mother."

Thank you! It is a beautiful name."

"We have given you a gift, too. I have fastened it to the outside of your fish-craft, on the top; you will see it when you leave the vehicle.

"I see that you are reflecting, so I will depart shortly. But let me tell you about this gift to you. It is a mirror, a very special one, made from the shining rock that covers the sea-bottom in some areas. We have applied certain processes to it and polished it well, and its back is of very highly sanctified Turtle-shell. If will help you in your meditations on yourself—it pushes your questions and answers back at yourself. Not only questions and answers; thoughts, angers, happiness. Further, it is the ultimate in defence for survival.

"When you are attacked, consider carefully whether you want to annihilate your attacker or not, for this object will annihilate your attacker. Whatever is sent toward you, physical, mental or elemental, it will return to the sender, magnified. It can reflect anything we Turtles think. You are the first human to know of or to possess one of these, and I know that you will take good care of it and use it well. And please get rid of doubt and fear—these will destroy you if you face the reflector in those attitudes.

"And that is all . . . Now, you are close to the Island of Whistling Winds; notice the slant of the land. It will become steeper. Straight ahead is a small inlet that runs from a cave. It will be a safe place for your shell—I mean your craft—to be left, and you and your relations may live there too. It is a very fine cave."

"I am glad of your help."

"It is nothing. I will go now. Keep on making your vibrations, Harmonious Mother. We will be listening."

The Turtle's communication ceased. I glanced toward the screen, still trying to maintain the strange state I had known. The screen was empty now, and my state was changing. I was more aware of the interior of the Sea-Searcher than I had been since the Turtle's visit; I looked around wondering how long I had been in that dream or trance.

I shook my head to clear it, and shifted my body. I saw that I had taken the craft a long way through the sea, for the Island was close at hand, according to our charted calculations.

My husband and son were still asleep. I sank the Sea-Searcher at the bottom, switched the controls off, and went to join my family, my mind in a whirl. I needed the sleep; later, we would take the craft ashore together.

And that is how we crossed the Sea of Mirrors and came to the Island of Whistling Winds.

12
THE
ISLAND OF
WHISTLING
WINDS

The Island of Whistling Winds

A T THAT POINT ARMIENNE ceased to relate her experiences to the people of Ainchan, and Shangodoon continued their story.

He described the water-cave where Armienne had directed him their craft should be guided; he was especially impressed with the rock-crystals that were embedded in the roof and walls, which threw out sparkles of many colours. It was really a tunnel, half-filled with river and sea water, in a rocky trough which was the channel of the river.

Armienne had explained as much as she could put into words, her experience of the turtle's consciousness; but more, Shangodoon sensed from the state that ensued in her over the next few days, that there had been a great shift in her outlook and her reasons for action. He listened to her with fascination, and Uzulu respected her wishes well. They knew that a great power had been given to her by the mysterious sea-beast, though they could not define what it was.

There was no question of her experience being a mere dream, for she had found the mirror the turtle had said was her gift. It was a solid manifestation of her link with the water-world. The three of them looked upon the oval, iridescent surface and marveled at the interplay of lines, colours and planes that made their faces. They saw themselves, together and alone in different ways. It was a fascinating pursuit to gaze upon that curiously glowing surface, and to touch the translucently shining brown-orange yellow of the mottled turtleshell.

Armienne's new probing into man's relationship with the world made Shangodoon ponder deeply. Her logic was impenetrably plausible. If he stretched his imagination enough, certainly he could see how humans could be existing under the watchful eyes of mightier beings than themselves, and not know it. He could see how, if these beings were interested in manipulating mankind, they could do so in clever ways, especially if man's mental system was known to them. They would know man's environment better than man, and would be able to direct his activities through indirect means. It was an intriguing thought, but so far-reaching in its import and so widely involving time and space that the conception did not fit completely into his mind.

"Suppose mankind has a predator?" Armienne had said. "Suppose mankind is *prey?* Suppose there are beings just as meat-loving as most humans, who feel themselves so much higher than us that they can use us for food?"

Shangodoon, trained in the ways of the Ainchan priesthood, knew that her arguments would fit into their way of viewing the Universe. He had to agree that the possibility was strong, but he wanted to know for sure.

"How can we be certain?" asked Armienne. "How can we find the truth?"

"It will come."

"We need it *now!*"

"Don't panic, the answer will come. What can we do except wait for further enlightenment?"

And so they thought about it; the thought was always before their mental gaze as a priority. They probed at it every now and then, returning to the question like a tongue to a broken tooth, obsessively seeking the contours of the truth.

Meanwhile there were practical things to do; the physical work competed with their mental explorations for their energy. Survival had to be maintained; they had to set about knowing the territory, understanding the reason why the wind seemed to speak a language, and after that, travel if possible by the fish-craft to the Land of Muse which lay far south of the island.

The place where they landed was free of wind except for small eddies that swirled every now and then along the beach, lifting the dry sand. But as they looked east and west along the shore from where they stood they saw evidence of a wind more powerful than any of them had seen before. It came in streams and gouts, and from the way the sand blew and the inland grasses and trees bent and swayed one could see the progress of the powerful hurricane-blasts. The trees were ragged and windblown, and slanted low away from the beach, their foliage sculpted into streamlined green bundles, their branches quivering with the effort of resistance to the blowing.

There were areas where all soil and grass had been blown away and the bare rock was exposed; leaves and clumps of grass sailed very high up in the air, and clouds scudded over the windy heavens. On the shorelines, breakers, as if mad by the goading of the wind, leapt and struck mightily at the tops of the cliffs, dragging back grass and rubbly stones with every advance. Above the land countless birds, defying classification or description, blew about the sky, scarcely seeming to propel themselves. They flew in scattered multi-coloured beauty high and low over the island as if the wind was tossing handfuls of them from an endless store.

On the evening of the day on which they landed, a small Dominaut boat carrying survivors of the sea-battle of the previous five days, arrived and tried to reach the shore. There were six men in it. Two of them were obviously wounded and sick, and all of them seemed weak. The high waves took the boat out of the water and slammed it down with a loud, slapping noise. The craft broke apart and the men struggled like ants in the slanting heaving water. Four of them managed to reach the shore, one dragging a leg. Ducking low, their clothes blowing, losing their footing in the incessant, terrorizing wind, tumbling and shouting, they reached the beach a good distance away from the place where Shangodoon and his family rested quietly with the Sea-Searcher.

One man was caught up in a flurry of wind and hurled along a stony part of the littoral so forcefully that it was clear he would not survive the blowing long before he struck against a boulder and collapsed into death before it. Another man ran towards him and stopped as his comrades shouted and pointed to the blustery sky. Shangodoon and his family looked too, and saw, aghast, that a gigantic bird had appeared in the sky, then another, and another. They flapped with clear determination towards the area where the survivors were, and as the men broke and ran, throwing themselves down below and behind the rocks, the birds lurched down and up in swift curvatures, legs outstretched. Squawking disappointment as they missed the prostrate men, they rose high into the sky, gathered themselves and plummeted again as the men raced for the overhanging rocks and caves of the landward side.

One man was seized and lifted by the shoulders. Far away as he was, Uzulu could see the bright blood running from his upper garments where the talons were gripping. The man struggled violently at first, then, as the bird rose very high he kept extremely still, flying with him, and the other two, one of which had picked up the body of the man the wind had killed, flew off following the first; the rest of their quarry had reached the shelter of the rocks and caves they had sought.

When the men and birds had disappeared, in as quick a time as though they had been imagined in passing, Shangodoon turned to face Armienne and Uzulu, examining their faces as they looked at him.

"Will we go on?" he asked, and un-named considerations sounded in his voice as he looked at the land, the sea and the sky.

Armienne nodded, her eyes searching the daunting landscape; and Uzulu, recovering from the sight he had just witnessed, wanted to start immediately.

Shangodoon seemed more serious than his wife or son had ever seen him before. He hesitated before he spoke again; then he muttered, "So be it," and Armienne understood the feelings that made him ascertain whether each one's desire to proceed was personal and valid.

"We all want to do the same things," Armienne murmured. "And we will be sensible. We all are responsible for ourselves and for each other. We knew this before we started. Besides, listen to that sound!"

For a sound had begun, somewhere up in the forbidding tunnels and crags of the high spine of the island. First it was a low moaning that came on the little zephyrs that reached them; then it was clearly audible, a low, rising steady whine. It rose to an intensity that was pleasant and bearable, and climbed past, not loudly at all, but penetratingly, into higher and higher tones, and with the rising sound the winds of the upper land seemed even more irresistible as they streamed against and through the caves, flues and archaic cracks of the monstrously high brooding hills.

The sound reached a point where it had just begun to hurt their eardrums with its vibration. First Shangodoon noticed that his ears and eyes seemed fuzzy, defocused receptacles, and he wanted to hold his ears and try to think. Then Armienne felt her head throb; but Uzulu was still enjoying the bizarrely beautiful ululation when the sound began to descend, faded into the lower vibrations and then disappeared beyond the range of their hearing.

It left them all with a relief that it had stopped; and yet a keen anxiety remained to hear the flow of sound again. Shangodoon had already begun to see what had fascinated Patturne; the island had mysterious power indeed. It made you want to be there, to sit and listen, to be lulled and transformed by the forces that emanated from its windy heights.

"We have got to find out how that sound is made," Armienne said. "We must understand the principles behind the creation of that sound. It sounds intelligent."

"The sounds certainly seemed to have meaning. I felt them make me think. I felt I understood more!"

"So did I." Armienne said.

"So did I too." Uzulu affirmed.

Shangodoon wondered if the sound they heard had been the one that impressed Patturne. He knew that they were in an area that the hermit had never seen; he had spoken of landing in high winds. Shangodoon would have liked to find the spot where the Children of the Glorious Recovery used to set up their power-object. "We will have to see the land itself, though. My plan is to get an idea of its dimensions, hear the sounds it produces, and see if it is possible to make a replica of the island, however small. With such a thing, we will have a good idea of the look and function of the Instrument of Power the Children of the Glorious Recovery possessed, for I suspect the principle by which his island gives off sounds is the same by which the Instrument worked."

"You think that the wind can be used to make patterned sounds?"

"I am sure of it. The sound we heard was natural, I am sure, and yet it had meaning that I think we all felt."

"It was a mighty magical force."

"When will we start exploring, my father?"

"Tomorrow. We have planning to do and equipment to prepare."

"We'll take our Instruments, of course."

"Naturally!"

"I'll bring my shooting things!"

"Yes, we'll need them. Now, we have a tent (though we may have to use caves), oil, fire, food, clothing. There are plenty of fruits around, Uzulu; you'll be able to supply us."

"No trouble at all," Uzulu said, accepting his role with a sense of importance. "As long as there are fruit, my darts will find them. But I know I will spend much time watching the birds!"

"So will I," Armienne said. "I have never seen so many, or so many kinds."

The birds were a constant part of the environment, and it took a long time to become accustomed to them. Wherever they turned there were birds, flying, perching, preening, squabbling, mating, nesting. Sometimes birds flew up from the dust through which they were walking, weird soil-brown scaly-feathered creatures. Sometimes what they thought to be the foliage of a blossoming tree erupted into the air and became a flight of birds. At every level of sky, it seemed, there were birds which flew in the changing currents of air, some miles above, others very close to the ground. There were birds no bigger than honey-bees, and some so large that their shadows crossing the earth frightened smaller birds and other creatures away.

Along the edge of the water, long-legged types waded, pecking at little things in the sand and the seaweed. The shore was covered with little birds sometimes, so very many that the family found difficulty in picking their way through them as they sat motionless and silent, breasts puffed, heads tucked into their shoulders or beneath their wings. There were types that lived on the cliff; in the evenings they patterned the rock with countless thousands of flying, raucous shapes, sometimes all landing and nestling together; then at a sudden signal unsensed by the humans they would rise with loud cries, filling the sky above the cliffs with thick clouds of flailing wings.

Inland, where the green and brown land sloped up to the black, bare, hollowed-out peaks where the echoing-sounds occurred which gave the island its name, the birds were even more numerous. There were nests on the ground, in the shrubs, on the barks and in the foliages of trees, on the rocky ledges and pinnacles, and among the sparse cliff-bushes.

Blackbirds, sparrows, wood-doves, yellow-breasts and redbreasts thickly dotted the greenery or darkened the sky in their flight. There were the hovering birds, like the hummers, woodpeckers and bamboo-borers, the last-mentioned of which were to be significant in Uzulu's experience.

There were the insect-and berry-eaters; seasonal migratory birds like storks, egrets, geese; strong fliers with long outstretched necks and short fanned tails. Then there were the eagles, hawks, falcons and many other predatory birds with short necks and long straight tails. The family was to see marshes where swans, ducks, and geese swam and flamingoes of many colours stood one-legged on their stalky limbs, dipping their long necks and scouring the water with their bills.

At night, there were the owls, and one or two other types that the family could not name.

Millions upon millions of birds, flying in formations that changed in beautiful balance, made the family sit for hours at times, gazing with fascination upon the changing design they formed in the sky. This vast concourse threw its voices into the winds, so that each time a breeze came to where the family was, on the only quiet spot on the island, it carried chatters, twitters, warbles, wails and shrills of astounding variation and number.

Inside the cave where the Sea-Searcher was berthed, things were quieter; and yet there was the constant sound of the sea, the faint whistling wind, and the insistent bird-calls.

The family spent a day and a comfortable night making plans and sleeping on board their craft, and the next day they started on what they thought would be the first of many expeditions from the cave.

The quiet shoreline where they had landed was still covered with the huddled, half-sleeping migratory birds when they began their journey. It was early morning; the first light of the sun was high in the sky and the earth was still half-dark and sparkling with dew, salt-crystals and the scattered pearls and rounded shining stones that the Snikes had left behind

from time to time. Uzulu wanted to collect some of these stones, but Shangodoon forbade him, sensing strongly that to do so was to risk contacting unknown forces, and they did not need a curse to add to their difficulties. As it was, their powers would be hard taxed, the father knew well.

All night he had prepared himself in the indefinable, mystical ways that he had first practised many years before in the Cavern-Temple of the Forbidden Mountains. He was in a fine state of receptivity; his ordinary senses were sharpened his ideas and alertness very keen, so that he knew he would be aware of any danger, as well as be able to absorb more information about his environment than ordinarily a person could. Armienne had strengthened herself in the same manner, and Uzulu, versed in the mysterious acts of his parents and the meanings behind those acts, grew more serious and earnest as he realized what such preparations signified.

Thus, when they left the quiet security of the haven where they had landed, and ventured into the area where the wind was hurling chilly sea-blasts at the adamant lava cliffs that stretched eastward, they managed to withstand the force that pelted at them with almost readable intent. They were linked by ropes, Uzulu first, then Armienne, then Shangodoon bringing up the rear; he was gripping the rope tightly, though it was tied quite securely around his body.

Despite their weight and the additional packs on their backs, the wind lifted Uzulu and Armienne often, and many times Shangodoon resorted to the physical strength that the earth lent him as he used his developed earth-instincts to root himself to the ground. His mind was strong and resistant to the whining of the wind in the rocks; he made himself heavier than he had ever been, even in those days of prisonerhood in Grunderth, and he became a firm anchor, immovable as the embedded lava-rock, when his woman and child floated away from him like kites, and the blowing wind tautened the thick ropes in his hands. He hauled them down a number of times when the great beetling overhangs of rock were in their way, but Uzulu enjoyed the flying, and wanted the wind to lift them often.

Before they started Shangodoon, remembering the story of Patturne, had warned Armienne and Uzulu to resist being lulled to sleep by the sounds of the wind. But that day keeping awake was no problem. The whistling of the wind was entrancing and soothing on the nerves, but the wildly beautiful sights they saw kept their eyes wide open.

They travelled in an easterly direction, at first keeping the sea in sight as often as possible, but gradually moving inland and higher until the humps of earth and the high shrubs blotted out their view completely, and only when they reached single jutting pinnacles could they look down to where the now distant beach lay. Between them and the beach numberless birds wheeled and whirled, and yet far above them others circled intently, seemingly watching their movements. These were big birds, larger than they had thought possible before, and of the same species that had lifted the shipwrecked Dominaut, and his dead colleague on the day they had landed. But the birds were circling lazily, as if replete and content, basking in the power they had to descend at any time, confident in the safety of their environement.

What surprised the family next was the appearance of a small path that lay in the middle of a U-shaped pass between high craggy hills. Whether the straight sides were artificially cut they could not tell, nor could they decide whether humans or beasts had made the trail. They came upon it and walked for a long way in the wide dim channel, while birds doted the section of blue and white sky above the pass or sat upon the rocks of the valley sides, outlined sharply. As they proceeded farther more birds seemed to gather on the valley sides, and of larger and larger species, so that when they came to the widest part of the valley and stopped at the hair-raising sight that lay before their eyes, huge vultures sat silently looking down upon the huddled family; and the wind in the crags sank to a doleful moan.

All over the floor of that boundlessly broad valley there were tall bamboo poles, a bristling forest of them that stretched interminably into the remote distance. Some of the poles were very old and in places here and there they had fallen; the ground obviously had received their rot for centuries. They path wound between the rowed bamboos freely and without interruption, but the family did not go on. Instead they were staring at the horrendous array of objects that crowned the stiffly swaying poles. Each standing pole had one impaled upon its slender top.

"Skulls!" Uzulu shouted. "And Turtle-shells!"

"Intelligent things did this!" Armienne gasped.

"Religion! It is a place of ritual!" Shangodoon growled.

"There were skulls of cattle, deer, horses and other herbivorous animals; skulls of Snikes and humans, and many turtle-shells.

High they stood, silhouetted, without doubt put there as a celebration of some kind. By what or whom? The question plumbed the depths of their knowledge and insisted upon an answer. They had to know what entity or entities could have done this awful work. They could not lightly step upon this ground without knowing the powers of any being they might offend. They could not venture into this too-unknown territory, with the knowledge that something had desecrated the bodies of creatures like themselves with the utmost freedom.

Who had dug those hole and placed those poles upright? What was the significance of the shining toothed domes of bone that absorbed in their dark sockets the knowledge of death beforehand? Something intangible about the skulls told Shangodoon that these had been martyrs, that they had been sacrifices, and that they had known beforehand that they would be. An aura of fear that made his stomach tighten, so strongly did it impinge upon his higher senses, hung over the place. The thought of martyrdom and sacrifice dropped into logical place, but where were the doers of the deed, and the receivers of the offerings? Who else or what intelligent thing was on the island? Were there native inhabitants-who lived in this wind? The birds? the birds?

The fact that they were in danger and were potential victims of the same ritualists who operated here was clear in his mind, but to hurry away was not the priority in that stark moment; he wanted to know at once.

An atmosphere of abysmally depressing gloom filled the place. The whole scene was amplified by the sight of the silhouetted vultures on the crags above the valley. High-shouldered, some with their wings held at odd poised angles, the frightful birds cocked their heads and turned their fleshy bare necks, driving their yellow-black stares toward the family. Hundreds of eyes followed the movements of the family as they huddled together, consulted, then turned to retrace their steps.

"We aren't going through there," Armienne had said firmly. "We're going to take the Sea-Searcher around, and continue our land-journey after that." She had noticed on the ground lumps of queer matter at which equally queer birds were pecking; and there were too many bits of bone, feathers and clothing for her liking.

Shangodoon and Uzulu agreed somberly, and they moved away from the ill-omened valley with its tall poles and their distressing and balefully poised icons.

They went back the way they had come, making only one detour. Uzulu wanted to talk about the things he had seen, but did not, and only now and then did his parents break out in conversation.

When they got close to the place where the Sea-Searcher had been left, they saw that the vast flock of migratory birds had gone. The beach with its dark grey sands was clear except for the seaweed and the many crystals, pearls, and bright stones; and except for the lines of men's footprints. There were three sets of prints, and one of the depositors of these prints had been dragging a leg. They knew at once that they were the prints of the Dominaut survivors who were still alive in spite of the birds, and the wind.

"They have found the craft!" Armienne gasped.

Shangodoon guided his family safely into the area where no high wind blew, and then left them, drawing his sword as he ran forward. He crossed the rocks and reached the half-submerged sea-cave, entered, and paused in surprise and dismay.

The craft was gone; the Dominaut survivors had stolen the Sea-Searcher and left the island.

———◆———

The realization that they were marooned was a dautingly depressing one. They remained near the cave for two days, as if waiting for the vessel to return, and over and over they discussed their plans for survival.

It was clear that they had to figure out a way to get off the island, for certainly they had no desire to remain permanently. It was also clear that it was pointless to remain in one spot; they should keep to their original plan and cross to the other side, for it was from there they would leave, hopefully, to go to the Land of Muse. They would need shelter, warm clothing, weapons, camouflage, hooks, ropes, spikes.

Shangodoon knew that it would be easy for him to find caves and such earth-places where his family cold stay, and water and food could be found easily. They had enough clothing for a long period, and there was plenty of cotton and other soft fibres that could make suitable clothing. The fact that they had set out from the Sea-Searcher equipped for camping was a lucky one. Now every item they possessed took on a larger importance than it had done when the craft had been in their possession.

At the end of their calculations they felt more secure, certainly, than they had been when first they realized that the Sea-Searcher was gone. They could survive the ordinary environment; but they knew little of the wind and the birds, or of the persons or intelligent things that had reared those monstrous celebrations of their victims' deaths in that dank wide valley. Until they were sure of safety from winds, birds and dangerously intelligent things that sought victims, they had to be alert at all times, and seek to find out as many facts about the island as they could, in as short a time as possible. Unfamiliarity was the greatest foe.

Above all, Shangodoon reminded Armienne and Uzulu to make an announcement any time they felt themselves growing sleepy against their will when the sounds wailed from the hills. That was the most formidable single threat they would face, from what he had heard; and he intended to seek shelter if such an eventuality befell, and wait out the sounds if possible.

It was Uzulu who suggested then that the best way to see the island was to get above it and look down. Then they would have a general idea of the shape of the island and of the best ground to traverse to reach the southern side.

"How could we get above the island?" Armienne asked, considering what he said. "We aren't birds!"

"Make a kite from the tent-material. It is too windy to use the tent anyhow. I know how to make a kite that can carry a person. We have many miles of light, strong rope, and I don't weigh much."

"It is dangerous," Shangodoon said.

"Everything is dangerous; I'd like to do it," Uzulu said simply.

Shangodoon looked at Armienne; then both of them nodded together.

"It's a good idea," Armienne said. "I see the danger, but it's a good idea."

"What about the birds?"

"Make it look like a bird. Mount a crossbow on it, or make it so scary that the real birds will fly off."

"It might work, yes," Shangodoon admitted.

"Then we'll do it?" Uzulu asked, as his father pondered deeply.

"We'll make the kite and fly it alone first before we decide," Shangodoon said, and Uzulu jumped in happiness.

"But even if it works we aren't sending you any miles above the island. You can't go so high as to see it all at once. We'll do it by sections; you'll be able to see large areas, but not the whole thing."

"Well, that will do!" Uzulu said. "When will we start building it?"

"We'll need to get the materials first."

"We've seen a lot of bamboos. We can cut some." Uzulu said.

"All right, we'll get some and start building the kite tomorrow."

"There's a lot of material on the beach." Armienne remarked. "I saw part of a ship that was wrecked."

Shangodoon nodded. "That will be useful. Well, since we accept the idea, we better build it as quickly as possible, and before we move. But it may take some time."

"We have a lot of time," Armienne reminded him, and he remembered the Sea-Searcher with a twinge of sorrow.

———•◆•———

The next morning father and son left the cave and searched for a good clump of bamboos in the immediate inland area. There were many such areas, sometimes large groves of the tall, wide-jointed, tree-like grasses, and they walked in the cool atmosphere beneath the high spiky foliage, past the bunched mounds of their tufted, unyielding roots.

The bamboo stalks creaked continually; a constant shifting crackle of tiny squeaks sounded. Sometimes they swayed stiffly and clacked, the hollow tubes magnifying the sound; most of the time they rubbed each other steadily. Their tawny yellow and varied green slivers of leaf and delicate small stalks patterned the sky and shimmered in the sunlight as they blew in little quivering lengthwise motions. Their colours ranged from the bright green of the young shoots and leaves, through the dark green of the solid growers in the prime of their life, to the pale yellow, dried-out, hollow bone-hard tubes which were yet light and pliable.

Wherever they walked, great flocks of multi-coloured birds rose from the bamboos they had festooned before the humans approached. There were raucous parrots and macaws, thick-beaked little parakeets, and the fabulous bamboo-borers with their humming wings rainbowhued, gleaming plumage and shrill pleasant cries. The bamboo-borers were the most populous, because of the plants, and they had been at work in the grove throughout the years, so that there was no bamboo stalk they saw that was not penetrated to its hollow core by several holes. It was a queerly beautiful sensation to see those long stalks, all bored in a series of straight lines evenly spaced, running the length of the bamboo poles from the largest to the very small ones; anyone not knowing the bamboo would have thought this was a pattern of their growth. Proportionate to the size of the stems were the holes. At the bases of the stalks, where the diameter was perhaps the length of a hand, there were holes big enough for Uzulu to put his folded fist inside, though he was too wise to do such a thing, knowing that animals or birds might use such places for shelter or nesting. Later, on two occasions when they chopped at the firm stalks, fierce-looking little rodents of a kind they did not know dropped to the ground and scurried away.

The bamboo-borers threw their lilting notes into the pulsing, moaning wind above the tall feathery tops of the bamboos. They hung motionless despite the flows and gusts of wind around them, their wings moving so rapidly that they were almost invisible. When the humans passed below, they descended and continued their endless hovering, pecking and alighting to search the pieces of pulverized bamboo for the tiny stone-hard mites that dwelt in the fibred bark; this was the only food they ate.

Uzulu looked carefully for a good length of stalk with a special size of central hole, and he was sorry that the stalks had been bored, for he wanted to make some blowpipes. Yet he cut some, calculating that he would find a way to plug the holes. The larger stalks, however holed, were strong enough for the purpose of making the framework of the kite, and they selected an adequate number of stalks of three different sizes, and tied them into a thick bundle which Shangodoon carried, calling upon his tremendous physical strength.

The father had been silent most of the time. Now Uzulu began to speak, breaking his flow of somber thoughts.

"You worry about my flying on the kite, my father," he observed.

Shangodoon half-sighed, stopping his steady ambulation, and pointed to a convenient rock where they could sit. They reached it and sank down together in the mottled shade that the sun and the bamboos made. Uzulu accepted one of the citrus fruits his father took from his bag and proffered, and gave Shangodoon one of the mangoes he had shot down at one point on his journey. Shangodoon passed his hand over the boy's head for a moment then he took his hand away and bit reflectively at the mango, not needing to answer his son's question aloud. He waited for Uzulu to continue.

"I will be safe, father. The kite will be secure, and the line is strong enough; or we can double it to make sure. You will be handling the line, so you will have final control. I will signal to you to bring me down if there is any sign of trouble."

"I do not doubt you, my son, and your intentions are for the best," Shangodoon granted. "But put yourself in my place." He wished then that Uzulu could have experienced the yearning for a son that he had known. He remembered the many nights when Armienne and himself had labored and sweated to start the conception that would change their lives into a blessing and remove the sense of incompleteness that they had felt. It had taken them so long to see the fruit of their love, and to send this beautifully-formed boy, not yet quite nine years old, into the wild wind above the island on such a weird contraption as he envisaged, would be an act of daring and faith far beyond anything he had risked in the past. It took a strong sense of certainty that fate would be beaten. However tested the kite might be, however practised the boy in his role of flyer; however eagerly Uzulu assured him that everything was safe, however necessary it was to know the area well as quickly as possible, Shangodoon had to settle with his inner consciousness before he could actually set about to carry out the operation.

"Mother had spoken to me about it too," Uzulu reported. "She told me of the things you had in mind. Please do not worry, my father. It is the right thing; Mother has agreed."

"The air is a new and dangerous environment to enter, Uzulu, and you venture into the plan with a spirit I admire. You know, there is nothing I can tell you about up there. Were it the land or the water, I risk saying that there is no matter you could not ask your mother or me, which we would not be able to advise you on. But we know nothing about up there."

"I will manage well, my father. I will find out and tell you about it. I have thought of the dangers, and I know I will fly well and observe the sights carefully without any fear or doubt to make me lose hold of my thinking, as you have said

I should practice to do. I do not see any risk on my part. And Mother thinks that I will be safe, because you will be holding the line that stretches between me and the earth. You see, we trust you."

"Do not worry about that!" Shangodoon said quickly. "You will be safe. I won't make any mistakes." He patted the boy's shoulder. "We will do it. I have faith in you, Uzulu; do not ever think otherwise."

"I am glad, my father," Uzulu said soberly, tearing at the rind of the citrus fruit in his hands. "You will be proud of me."

Shangodoon nodded. A contented silence fell upon them as they bit and sucked at the fruit; and things became so peaceful that the curious macaws returned to crawl along the branches and hang upside down, staring at them with their beady eyes, while the shining bamboo-borers descended and resumed their monotonous work.

In the afternoon Shangodoon and Uzulu returned to the cave which the family occupied, and found that in their absence Armienne had searched for and found some tuberous, edible roots, and boiled them; so that they had a very enjoyable meal. The daring woman had also ventured upon the beach where the shipwreck was, and found, among other useful things, a helmet with a vizor of transparent material, which the furnace-men on board the ship would have used in their work. She thought it would be useful for covering Uzulu's face and protecting his eyes when he went aloft.

Shangodoon was intrigued by the calmness his wife showed in accepting that their son would undertake to fly in the air on a kite. He was impressed by her good sense, and wondered whether he had been unduly worried about Uzulu's safety. He breathed more easily, and felt confidence flow into his mind in powerful waves, so that he began to prepare the bamboo and ropes the same evening, and they started the construction of the kite early the next day.

Uzulu had observed the birds well and knew the principles of their flapping, soaring and gliding. He suggested the proportions and design of the kite. It was bird-shaped, with a body-height of perhaps six feet and a wing-span of fifteen. The ends of the wings were hinged and could be manipulated by lines, so that a flier could have some slight control in directing its flight, and in the middle of the body there was a little platform where Uzulu could sit, and a well-made body-harness to keep him strapped securely.

It flew well, though a little lopsidedly, on its first test, and was taken down and adjusted; on the third occasion the flight was admirable and Shangodoon's control superb. Next they attached large stones several heavier than Uzulu, and each time the kite transported its burdens easily. Shangodoon sent it very high, and the wind and kite confronted each other in encounters that ranged from little separated gusts that made the kite hover uncertainly to fierce steady flows when the enraged kite struggled violently in the body of the wind and stretched the line out straight. In all the tests, re-tests and re-adjustments, they aimed at increasing the kite's strength, stability and balance in the awesome wind, and soon the kite was so improved-upon that it could stay almost motionless in the fiercest of gales. The family was pleased to observe, too, that the birds diligently avoided the man-made object as it came among them. Even the largest carnivorous birds, larger than their kite, which circled ceaselessly above their heads, remained the same incalculable distance away, and the family hoped that they were keeping their distance out of fear.

Eventually Uzulu was placed on the sitting platform and securely strapped. His face was helmeted and vizored, his legs were stirrupped, and his arms spread out to hold the handles that manipulated the wing-ends. Shangodoon nodded, wished him a safe flight, and went some distance away to hold the line; Armienne patted her son quietly, told him unnecessarily to be careful, and cut away the ropes that anchored the straining flying vehicle.

———•◆•———

At once it rose in a stiff perpendicular line, and Uzulu gasped as the ground shot away below him. Shangodoon held it steady and waited to see what would happen. The kite glided swiftly leftward, then rightward, in a wide arc, as if seeking a way to become free and airborne forever; rose high and slide dizzily downward and sideways; slantingly climbed the wilderness of sky, and remained steady in the stiff windstream.

First, Uzulu checked the structure of the kite as far as he could see it, and listened for any tell-tale creaks or clatters of loose bamboo or flapping fabric; but the kite displayed all the results of the careful craftsmanship that had gone into its marking, and nothing slackened; nothing was amiss. Only there was the incessant whistle of the bored bamboo stalks as the wind went past their holes, and though the sound was loud he was not bothered by it enough to signal his father to bring him down.

Next Uzulu detached one arm and waved to his parents; then he looked down upon the earth immediately under and around him, memorizing the important things he saw.

To the left, inland, there was a continuity of grassland that rose in a swiftly steepening gradient until it faded out and disappeared allowing the bare cloudbound slopes to take over, and to the right there was the vast expanse of ocean. Between the ocean and where his parents were standing was the wide beach and the wider, decayed-looking gap where the gruesome Valley of Poles and Skulls lay. Uzulu saw immediately that it was easy to avoid that wretched place, and that the territory he flew over was uncomplicated and convenient to traverse in the direction they wanted to go.

He looked for signs of troublesome beasts of prey but saw no animals of any kind, and this fact disturbed him, though he did not know why. After that, he looked for fruit trees and saw that there were many displaying bright-coloured fruit of such a variety that they would be a constant source of food. Finally he selected a swamp, a capacious stretch of coconut groves, and a high bare peak for landmarks.

Having made these observations, Uzulu signaled to be brought down, knowing his parents' concerns over this first voyage of his, and straightaway felt the kite's whistling increase as his father hauled it through the resisting body of the wind. The kite's altitude lessened until it was just above the tall trees, then as it dropped even lower Uzulu manipulated the hinged sections of wing, so that the strange craft made a superbly accurate landing in some tall grass only a minute's walk away from his parents.

"It was fine!" the boy shouted, and his eyes glowed as they ran towards him. Shangodoon patted his shoulder and his mother caressed him happily, while he talked excitedly, fumbling at the straps. "I saw a great distance. Oh, it was a wonderful feeling! The wind up there is something to feel and listen to, father! And the birds! They were all above, around and below me, and you could hear their cries and the noises of the hills in the wind I saw the easiest way to travel, I picked landmarks, and everything. It was just great; let's do it again!"

"Of course, but not immediately," Armienne said at once.

"We are going to start travelling," Shangodoon told him. "After we pass your landmarks, you can take a trip up again. I'm very happy to see that it worked out so well."

———•◆•———

The next two weeks were spent in travelling. The landscape was varied and exciting to explore, and there were many new birds and plants to observe, learn about and record. Armienne made copious notes and drawings. Her attention was absorbed especially by the variety of shapes and functions of the birds, and the differences in their common features.

There were long thin bills for impaling fish; strong, curved seed-cracking beaks that could also assist in climbing; serrated, flat ones for holding frogs and slippery eels; gaudy shears with sharp hooks for the tearing of meat, and large toucan-beaks that served for defence and sexual display. There were long-necked flamingoes and short-necked peregrines; short balancing wings for running along the ground and long tapering wings for strong distance-flying. The varieties of plumages and their changing colours Armienne could not attempt to describe at that time, for they took too detailed a study than she could have afforded; in fact, it took a lifetime of dedication merely to classify the new birds and describe their habitats and habits. She noted the visual adaptations and the positioning of the bird's eyes; the owl's double-focussed glare, the rear-seeing eyes of the mudprobers who were always conscious of predators; and the lateral-viewing sparrow's eyes, set even on the sides of the head.

Then there were the claws; some better suited for gripping prey than for walking or perching; some with toes at front and back, for landing on bark, like the woodpeckers' and the bamboo-borers'; some with webbing that could be closed and opened; marsh-wading, walking, hopping, scratching and perching claws, and the large two-toed feet of the big flightless fast-runners like the bulky ostrich.

Some tails were long and tapering, some short and tufted; some spread like the fan of the turkey or lay like sweeping, shimmering capes behind their owners' relatively small bodies, in the manner of the peacocks. Some tails were so scrubby and close to the body as to be scarcely existent, and some seemed to be the very purpose of their owner's existence. There was a dumbfounding multiformity of crests, too, and she wondered whether it was possible that they were merely for decoration and sexual demarcation.

Shangodoon was making notes and drawings too, including designs for a model of the island. He did not know the whole place, but he felt that the portion he knew could give him a very good idea of the whole; he had learnt this principle from the study of fragments of sea-shell. He was especially careful to include the valleys, crags, and the huge eroded caves and cracks of the upper rises; for he was certain that the heavy winds, blowing through the perforated, mazed tunnels in cyclic gusts, were the cause of the rhythmic, changing single tones that sounded at certain times and in certain areas.

Each day the unusual, intriguing sounds blew boldly across the landscape, and several times the family were conscious that the strains had taken their immediate consciousness away, so that they became uncertain about the distance they had traversed, and had to re-orient themselves on more than one occasion.

Shangodoon, knowledgeable in the mystic tradition of Old Ainchan, was able to concentrate his mind on the sound and adjust his breathing and mental state to its call. The levels of consciousness to which the strident strains forced his spirit were planes of high absolute experience that few uninitiated men could have faced. He did not fear to listen to the sounds, for he discerned that Armienne and himself were in fact more equipped for withstanding the lulling of those tones than had been the members of the Children of the Glorious Recovery. He realized that as long s there was no danger from the high-flying hunting birds, which particularly attacked wounded, prostrate or dead bodies, he could undertake the pleasant and valuable occupation of immersing himself in the sounds and give in to the urge to hear and interpret what they seemed to be saying.

Above all, Shangodoon was spellbound by the beats and pauses with which the haunting piping came, and several times he tried to follow it on his Drum.

Armienne was equally fascinated. She listened to the shrill whines, the steady bellowing and the muffled, sonorous roars that stridulated across the sky, through the birds and past the family, borne on the hustling wind. At times, brushing the strings of her Instrument in the cool of the day, she watched the windswept hills and heard some of the tones she played match those of the wind in the chimneyed gulfs and the stupendous crags that rose and fell above the sloping savannah. She had learnt much more about the nature of sound. Her Instrument, the technique of which Shangodoon had improved (years before, while on the Coast of the Sea of Mirrors) by installing a fretted board and securing the strings by clever pegs which could adjust their sound, was now capable of playing all the chords she could imagine, and the sound of the winds inspired her search for new forms of sound-expression.

But Uzulu was by far the most affected. "Listen to the wind!" he would tell his parents. "Can you hear it? What does it mean? What is it saying? He seemed impatient to go on, and always wanted to explore. He was always moving around on the land, seeking new angles from which to hear the different things that the wind seemed to be saying. He became so active moving around on his own that Shangodoon devised a system to make sure that the wind did not blow him away. The boy was made to wear a rope harness about his body, and had two coils of line, one with a four-pronged barbed hook at its end, for throwing and catching around the perpendicular trunks of trees, and the other ending in a smooth-running lasso. He anchored himself to trees and rocks as he made his way to various points of the landscape, to listen to the wind or to bring down the ripe fruit he discovered.

He looked longingly at the dismantled kite that his father carried, and wanted to go aloft again. He talked about the wind often, and several times his parents found him sitting languid, entranced, murmuring about the things the wind was telling him. Sometimes at night, as they sat and lay round the oil-fire in some warm cave, the boy would huddle close to his mother and stare unblinkingly through the cavemouth into the blackness outside where the wind was rushing past filled with wisps of near and distant sounds, and ask his queer questions.

"Do you not hear?" Can't you feel the things it is asking us to do? Can't you hear it calling to us? Why don't we follow it?"

"Follow *what,* my son?' Armienne asked.

"The sound of the wind in the hills."

"You cannot follow the sound of the wind, my son. Where would you reach?" How would you cease travelling?"

"But we can obey what it is saying, can we not?"

"Saying, Uzulu? I hear nothing that it says, which we can understand and obey."

"It wants us to understand it. I think I will, Mother. It makes me feel sorry for it; I wish I could help it sometimes, and sometimes it seems it orders me to listen!"

357

"It wants us to understand it. I think I will, Mother. It makes me feel sorry for it; I wish I could help it sometimes, and sometimes it seems it orders me to listen!"

"Sometimes it pleads to you and sometimes it orders you! That is not good, Uzulu. It cannot be sincere in both."

"And yet it seems as natural as life itself."

"There may be intelligent things who wish us no good on this Island. Have you not wondered if it is perhaps a trap, to lead you away from us?"

"I do not think so!" Uzulu said at once, sharply. He gave a hissing intake of breath and his eyes glowered with a knowledge she did not understand, so that at once she tried to conciliate him, while her mind raced to comprehend his reaction.

"Then listen, Uzulu, but tell me what it says. When you find out what the wind is saying, you must tell us immediately, and we will consider what you say. But until then, listen only. Don't take your harness off, that is the main thing—do you hear?"

"Yes, Mother."

"I too would like to know what the wind is saying . . . .

"—Is there something the matter with him?" she asked next, turning to Shangodoon as Uzulu moved out of the range of their voices.

"Something is certainly on his mind. I think it is a natural phase sometimes . . . and I know we can't solve it for him. We don't even know what his experience was up there."

"Do you think he should go again?"

"Well, why not? In any case, it seems necessary, doesn't it?"

"Yes," Armienne acceded.

"He's a sensible boy and he will understand what he is seeking and know when he finds it. That is our own position, is it not? We're on this Island for the same purpose that he is!"

"Yes; but he says that the wind is calling him. He will not wander off, following the sounds?" Armienne worried.

"No, I don't think so," Shangodoon said, and she was consoled; but he bore her query in mind.

Then Uzulu discovered how to make his blowpipes sound. It happened by accident. He had gone off with harness, lines, darts and blowpipe to find some fruit. He selected a fine cluster of orange-yellow papaws from a turgidly loaded tree, and had already shot two down, deftly leaping forward and catching them, before they had a chance to burst on the ground. At his next attempt the dart fell short and missed the entire cluster, for his puffs of air had blown open one of the holes of the blowpipe, which he had plugged earlier. He had restored to using gouts of sun-thickened adhesive from the many rubbergum trees that thrived on the island; it was this gum, too, that held his dart in place long enough for the air in the tube to build pressure.

Uzulu stared unseeingly at the stem that he had missed, his blowpipe still to his lips, his hands positioned along the instrument. He was no longer concerned with gaining the fruit; for the blowpipe itself, with the unplugged hole, had trilled an eerily whinnying tone that keened through the trees in a long line of echoes, and captivated his senses with its challenging distinctness. Bamboo-borers flitted like coloured mirages in the corners of his vision, spreading their broad tails and whirring their wings in brisk unison. Humming sounds, exactly corresponding with the caterwauling vibrations that flew in the rush of air through Uzulu's long tube, expanded outward among the fruit trees and hollow bamboos, so that they murmured their response identical tonation.

Uzulu blew the sound out again, squinting his eyes in his attentive effort to experience and be familiar with the sensuous feelings and old dreams that surged through his body and mind. He put the forefinger of his left hand upon the hole and blew, raising and lowering it to control the escape of air; then he puffed in short rhythmic spurts and delighted himself with the steady-pitched sharp hoots that his fingers and breath created.

He reasoned that the stopping and opening of the hole shortened and lengthened the passage his breath came through, and that the varying length of the passage varied the sounds. He unplugged another hole to prove himself right. This sound was lower, more manageable auditorily, and mellow in its bold stridor; Uzulu was even more profoundly enchanted by its pure, secret-laden tones.

Excitedly he plucked the blobs of gum from the other four circular, precisely bored holes that ran along one section of the tube, and when he covered them with six fingers and raised them one by one he had a wide range of bewitching tones that pleased him heartily with their delightfully different meanings. His heart beat quickly when he thought of the experimental joys that lay before him.

He returned to his parents with the fruit and his transformed blowpipe, and they were adequately impressed when he demonstrated his discoveries. He could blow varied tones in rhythm, and when Armienne took her Stringed Shell and strummed her satisfying chords he chose single tones out of those chords and brought them to her attention with his clear piping. Listening, Armienne realized with the fresh gladness which follows a personally discovered fact, that Uzulu had accurately captured some of the tones that the wind made in the island's high reaches. She herself had been making some of the corresponding tones on her Instrument; and though the strings and the tube both were capable of producing the same tones, the quality of their sound was excitingly different.

Day and night, walking, talking, sitting, or lying waiting for sleep, Uzulu kept practicing his sound-making. Sometimes the sounds that followed each other in even sequence seemed strangely logical and connected; at other times, a chaos of tones resulted from his efforts. Especially at night, his screeches, high hissing whines and sudden piercing explosions startled and distracted his parents, so that during the time before Uzulu became proficient in sound-making, they had to protect their hearing before lying back to wait for sleep. It was at this time they first used skywhisper as a salve for their ears. Later it was to serve them well; in fact, it saved their lives.

Sometimes when the wind came over the landscape Uzulu took up his Flute (as he was to call the Instrument later) and attempted to follow the sounds that it was making. He did this for a fortnight, perhaps; then he discovered that he could play phrases of sound that seemed to be answers to the questions and statements the wind was making. He often practised this art of answering the windsound, and soon he knew at which holes to find the tones he needed to make the "replies" that he desired.

His parents watched and listened in amazement. The boy would sit at the mouth of whatever cave they dwelt in, or walk listening as they nomadized farther south. As the wind blew the boy attended, his Flute to his lips. As soon as there was a lull in the stream of sound he made his responding affirmations, and indeed it seemed to Shangodoon and Armienne that the wind had paused to listen.

When Uzulu blew his notes, birds boldly flew closer than usual around the boy, and the fearless ones alighted quite near. Some listened, cocking their heads; others attempted to join with original-sounding twitters and chirrups. Eventually Uzulu acquired a little procession of birds; some regular stalwarts who faithfully accompanied him every day; and those who came, listened, and went. Shangodoon and Armienne were surprised and quietly amused by the sight of the boy and his odd assorted species of birds walking, hopping and flying around him wherever he went.

By this time they had reached and circumtraversed the wide swamp, a place that teemed with migratory and locally-oriented waterbirds, which Uzulu had seen from the air. Days later, they entered and transited the coconut grove. Past that was the austere peak of black rock that was Uzulu's third landmark, and as the party moved closer to the miles-distant, precipitous sky-pointing finger of lava, Uzulu's excitement grew.

They were climbing higher now, and the temperature grew more erratic. In the daytime the atmosphere was very warm and dry; at night, currents of cold damp wind rushed around their sleeping-places. Armienne sneezed several times and found breathing difficult; and she sought to avoid indisposition. She melted a good portion of the skywhisper ointment into fragrant oils which she had produced in her alchemical laboratory on the Coast of the Sea of Mirrors, and which she had carried in her pack ever since the start of her journey. She rubbed her throat with this mixture and inhaled its heady perfume. The effect was good; her sneezes did not return.

Shangodoon, seeing her use of the skywhisper oil and remembering the plant's fabled powers, applied the oil to himself the next day, and noted that he felt no effects of the heat or cold; his body retained a normal temperature while Armienne and Uzulu perspired in the sunlight and shivered in the dark. This led him to advise them to oil themselves completely, covering every minute area of skin and massaging their scalps well; and a few days later, when the climate became more extreme in the range of heat and cold, they were comfortably warm at all times.

Thus on the days that followed, as they neared the pinnacle that was their temporary goal, they felt no discomfort though sometimes the ground grew so hot that they saw thick heatwaves rising from the granite tors, and the nights became so cold that the suddenly-changed temperature caused rocks to crack and flake at their surfaces.

Finally, the skywhisper protected their ears, too, for as they ascended the incessant whistling of the wind grew more aggressive and irritating; and they soothed the strain on their hearing by massaging the insides of their ears with the balm and stopping them with oil-dipped wads of cotton-wool.

And so they journeyed, loaded with their packs and with a variety of profound questions urging them on. Eventually one afternoon they stood near the foot of the gigantic plug of black brimstone, and soon Uzulu said:

"Time for the kite again, father!"

Shangodoon nodded. "So it is. Well, we'll rebuild and re-test it perhaps for the rest of the day and tomorrow, and then we'll see."

"We are close to the top of the Island now. Will you send me higher? I'll be able perhaps to see over the high slope and toward the other side."

"You can signal us when you go up; we can work it out then," Shangodoon suggested.

Two mornings later, now painted with the name Sky-Searcher, at Uzulu's request, the kite was ready for the air again. The sky was blue and inviting, and white clouds scowed over the land driven by a steady strong wind. Now the kite would lift off from higher land, and more care was needed, but Shangodoon intended to fly his son higher than on the previous occasion. Uzulu, controlling his anxiety with difficulty, felt a tremendous leaping of heart as he thought of the exciting vista and adventure before him. In a peculiar way he looked forward to being alone in the sky; he imagined himself and his kite pasted out up there, a cutout stuck on a blue background, and thrilled at the idea.

He was smeared completely in oil of skywhisper; put into position in the central carrying structure of the kite, and strapped with the secure body-harness. He was given small hand-line for signaling by tugs; this was a precaution in case he could not be seen, for the cloud level was closer to them than on the first time of Uzulu's flying.

Again the kite rose rapidly, easily; in fact, with an almost terrifying swiftness. He passed the tops of the bamboos and tall fruit trees, saw the coconut foliage whizz by and away below, and watched them all dwindle into little clumps of bushes, wiry tufts and bunched sprays as the kite took him higher away from them.

The patterned land spread out before him like a carpet; its mightiest broken-surfaced boulders were small rounded pebbles, then little beads, then tiny black dots, upon the tawny sun-beaten grassland. Southward, hulks of hill and high slopes blocked his view of the other side of the island, and he saw that with more altitude he would be able to view beyond them.

He signaled his safety to the two still-visible, warm spots on the vast sweep of land that were his parents. Then he signaled to go up, and as they grew even more minute he realized that his father was paying out the line, sending him much higher than on the previous occasion.

Exhilarated, he breathed deep and looked down. The ocean slanted upward, telling him that the kite had slipped sideways; then it slanted downward, and the kite roved closer to the mighty inland heights. It floated west, rising, up, up, up the sides and past the very top of the high fantastic pinnacle that had been his last landmark.

Forests of extremely tall trees carpeted the ground, seeming as flat and close-packed as moss. There were birds so far below him that they flitted like little wispy butterflies, and he felt the full body of the upper-sky windstream.

The rising serrated hills of the island's centre strode higher still than the straining, upstriving Sky-Searcher. Uzulu tugged his handline the pre-arranged number of times, to assure his parents that he was safe; then impulsively he signaled for still greater altitude. The kite lifted more, reveling in the skygales. The severe dark rocks with their sparse, precariously rooted bushes slid down the past him rapidly. The feeling of his unique experience of flying increased as he hung in the high sky, and the terrible lonely gladness of revelation filled his thought as his insights dawned with clarity and showed him lucidly that with such knowledge as he was receiving, he was going to be different from other people.

For up here the pure wind, devoid of the contamination of the interrupting hills and trees, spoke in a clear language to the sensitive boy on his whistling, vibrating sky carriage. The kite itself meshed tones with the million dilute distilled figments of half-imagined, dreamlike sound from miles and eons away. The sounds flew with swift beating wings through his pulsing inner self and became part of his being as he opened his mind to receive the infinitely profuse impressions. It was an understanding of notes and their relation that he gained, and as he closed his eyes up there in the marvelously distant heavens, he saw exactly in his mind how his fingers would move and his breath flow to create those concordant and dramatic tones on his Flute.

As he listened he rose still higher, and when he opened his eyes again he saw that he was closer to the west, inland, for the general direction of the wind was toward the southwest. Now he was much closer to the cloud-obscured crest of the island. He manipulated his wing-ends to keep a steady distance from the rocky hills, and kept rising. Now the most lofty hills that he had seen were scarcely more than pimples upon the skin of earth, and the recent fire-formed rocks that lay in great scabs on the land, far bigger than the fruitful, immense acreage of grassland, now dominated the spread-out map below and revealed the true nature of the island as quickly as they appeared and dropped below, out-distancing the vision.

Yet, however high he rose, the gaunt grey-black crags to his left kept rising higher. They loomed and bared their impossible slopes to him, or stood apart, terrible in their aloof and indifferent aspects, gaping their pitfalls and flourishing their places of accidental death. Once he steered so close to them on the climbing kite that he saw at an intimate distance some of the dread heights and depths of those far-flung lava piles. But hunting birds whirled around the tops of the cliffs, and he could see their precarious nests, tight-woven and anchored against the wind, where their ugly hatchlings gaped their beaks and yelled for sustenance. There were rocks covered with bird droppings that hung like melted wax on candles, and here and there the windblown nests had scattered their eggs, allowing the up and down-draughts that scoured these cliffs to smash and smear them down the sides of the precipices. Fledgling vultures lurched clumsily into the air and lost their balance, tumbling down to life-saving ledges, and condors sat on peaks like brooding statues.

Then something caused Uzulu some sudden concern, for the birds which had been his companions when he practised his Flute on the ground, had taken off in a furry of fearful chattering. All along his journey skyward, they had sat on the kite-line calmly preening and sunning themselves, a row of companionable hitchhikers. Now the bare line stretched downward through transparent but thickening wisps of cloud, tapering thinly until it became invisible, lost to the distance.

Uzulu tugged at his handl-line and signaled to be brought down. At the same time the kite swerved to the right, valiantly battling to compensate for an abnormal gust of air. Uzulu jerked his head around in quick alertness, and saw a gigantic bird glide out from between the clouds that had gathered on his left. It circled horizontally around the kite appearing and disappearing from his sight as it made the smooth circumference.

It was of the same species as those which had been circling in the upper heavens every day since they had landed, and up here it was larger than Uzulu had imagined.

Its wing-span was fully twenty feet and it had a murderous fleshhook of beak which it carried with a brash certainty. Its eyes were deliberate in their observation, blinking and opening, as if etching his likeness and identify on its brain. Click, whirr, each individual eye seemed to go, and Uzulu felt as if they had captured his features and complete characteristics forever, a million times over. Click, whirr, and catalogued copies of him seemed transmitted to some grimly authoritarian source, the nameless terror of whose power the boy could already feel. He felt naked, raw, subservient, and vulnerable as a worm when he saw the bone-crushing beak of the sleek-feathered predator. The bird made it plain that it was heavily superior as it captured the image of the boy and the flying structure, and eyed the long bare line from whence it had chased the relatively earthbound birds that had followed Uzulu. The confident flying hunting-creature puffed its breast, coquettish as a pigeon as it played with its intended prey; then lifted its formidable wings and swept gusts as it lanced away through the sky, appearing and disappearing in the empty blue air and thick white cloud. The kite waddled uncertainly at the ungainly windcurrent that flapped from its wings as it made its ferocious antics.

Uzulu wished fervently that his father and himself had pursued the idea of mounting a crossbow on the Sky-Searcher. They had decided that camouflage was enough; now this indifferent bird, commanding wide areas of the heavens with a slicing flick of its fanned tail, observed and recorded his contraption and himself with its single grim eyes of yellow, red and black, seeing at once that this flying thing was not of the bird-kind it had known before.

Then, as it drew up its spasmodically clenching and unclenching talons, Uzulu saw that a ring of metal surrounded one scaly leg. He gasped, for he knew at once that no bird had made that bright, burnished bangle, and only a human of singular, preternatural ability could have placed it upon that massive, instinctively clutching limb. He knew at once that the bird was owned, and perhaps was trained.

Who had managed the task of controlling this bird? The tremendous question staggered the young boy's mind. He was glad that the kite was descending quickly, and wished for more speed yet, for he knew that the bird had arrived for no light reason; indeed, it must have been trained for the most weighty of purposes.

He saw the bird draw up its legs and spiral away upward, climbing swiftly until it slipped out of his vision. He had seen the awesome action before, and knew that it was going to fall upon the kite, seize it, and tug it loose if possible from its connection with the ground. His mind raced to find a defence for the certain attack, as his father had taught him to think in such emergencies.

Then it flashed upon him. He detached his hands from their horizontal wingstraps, and forced his fists into two of the holes of the bamboo struts which made the whistling noise as the kite flew.

A horrible snarl of unpleasant, metallic, scraping whistles shot out from the quivering kite. Uzulu felt his craft lurch sideways, banking, and hoped for its correcting itself, for his hands were struck and bruised. The awful bellow charged into the air and Uzulu heard the extremely loud, raucous shriek of the bird as its downward drop was foiled and it scrambled to rise again from the earsplitting sound. Uzulu, his ears plugged with the skywhisper soaked cotton wads, heard the raw painful blasting with some discomfort; but the disoriented hunter fought for balance, fluttering like a young sparrow to right itself, drifting away westward. Uzulu bent his head, laughing and grimacing together, at the feel of victory and at the pain in his wrists and precious fingers, and the shaken kite descended through the clouds.

Then as he came below the clouds the boy saw that he was over an area where the kite had not moved before, and he looked down upon a sight that made his previous surprises appear insignificant. Below and to the left of him there was an immense metallic platform that floated in mid-air, straining at the robustly thick plaited lines that anchored it to enormous metal rings set on the summit of a strange flat-topped pinnacle. Around the circumference of this vast disc there were several structures, most of them being single compartments, and there were rings here too, set in the surface in front of each doorway, to many of which there were birds chained by the leg. Other unshackled birds flapped down to the surface sometimes, or rose up and went off in different directions. There was a constant coming and going.

Before the compartments or cells there were glistening round spots which Uzulu discovered to be containers filled with water, and in the centre of the circle a huge mass of dark-red animal meat, fodder for the birds, was piled high. Even as the boy watched, some of the birds were bringing dead Snikes, fish, turtles, wounded, twitching serpents, smaller birds, rodents and other bits of food, and dropping them upon the central bloody pile. Here and there other birds, hungry and chained, strained forward and voraciously, stretching their half-feathered necks, raising their wings, opening their cruel mouths and projecting their dark tongues.

But again all this was mildly disturbing compared to the most impressive fact of all; there were men up there.

Two shoveled lumps of corroded matter towards the hungry birds; another moved from one embedded metal ring

371

to the next, testing the chains, while another seemed to be training one of the ferocious creatures for some unknown reason, for he was teaching it to catch and carry the staff in his hand. There were other men, who were engaged in various activities to do with the bids; but what profoundly jolted the boy yet again, and made him exclaim aloud as he tugged in frenzy at the hand-line, was the fact that on very many of the birds that came and went there were harnesses and reins; and vizored men in strange caped uniforms sat on little riding platforms, like saddled horsemen, on their broad backs, between the mighty wings. These flying riders seemed almost parts of their birds of burden, so unitedly did they move; they emanated an ease, confidence and calm that were born of long habit.

Wildly the boy hoped that his kite would not be noticed, but already he felt obviously and clearly exposed. Yet the kite was descending swiftly, for his anxiety had been sub-mitted to his unseen parents where they stood earthbound on the floor of his ocean of air. The boy knew that his father was exerting his ultimate physical force to haul the kite down. The bamboo struts bent like bows and the taut tent-fabric trembled like the hide of a nervous horse. The kite, tested to the unexpected limits of its structural coherence and strength, fought its way downward against a wind that whooshed up from the sloped shores, hurtled and increased speed across the rising grassland, and ascended the easterly side of the island as a constant hurricane. His father was doing well; soon the kite would drop below the level of the flying metal circle, away from the sight of the men and birds.

What was this place for? Uzulu wondered, his heart thundering at the inevitably over-whelming possible answers. He stared hard, observing as much as he could, and the immensity of the question, the fearfulness of the implications, were numbing to his mind. He saw men blown flat by the rushing wind sometimes, and yet their feet remained in place on the smooth surface; thus he guessed that they wore magnetic shoes. There are many sinister constructs that were so foreign to the boy that he did not waste time in considering their function. One was a long metal pole, tall as any bamboo, that rose straight above the disc; the top of it was a mesh of wires and metal rods, and there was a glowing red light in the very centre of this maze of latticed metal.

While he watched this extraordinary spectacle, the bird that he had injured with his deadly burst of noise fluttered out of the white sky directly above the platform and fell in a downdraught towards the strange airborne habitation. Halfway down, weakening, the bird turned over; it clawed at the sky in a dying spasm and fell heavily into the heap of carrion, raising raucous cries and disturbed wing-flailings from its chained cohorts.

A chaos had erupted upon the vast platform when the vanquished bird came down. Mounted bird-riders who had risen to meet it, swinging lassos, now descended to the bird-station again, and men were pointing and shouting. Just before the Sky-Searcher was dragged below the level of the flying, thick-edged disc Uzulu saw that he was seen. Some men were racing towards their birds and others were already rising when the kite took him away from the sight of them.

Uzulu felt the chilly thrills of terror for the first time in his life when he realized that the whole flock of them were taking up pursuit in perfect co-ordination, as a single body.

He dropped swifter now and he could see his parents ever so small. He wanted to be with them at once but there was still a long distance down, and he saw that the bird-riders would reach him long before he could reach his parents. Even as he thought this they descended around him on all sides. They circled as thickly as vultures around a dying mammal, a great wheel of them; and Uzulu was the centre of attraction. They observed him all together, coolly calculating and having all the time they needed for their nefarious purposes. Then together, they dropped, much swifter than the Sky-Searcher, and waited below him flying in a wide circle around the spot where he would have to pass.

The mounted men were swinging their lassos with obvious accuracy and control even in the fast-blowing wind, and as the kite dropped toward the area where the looped lines were swinging, Uzulu saw clearly that their intention was to enmesh him and take him away.

His hands were still pushed into the holes of two bamboo struts; now he stuck his right heel into another aperture and his left knee into a fourth as the kite came down to where the lassos whirled and cracked. More weird combinations of sound arose, so repellently excruciating in their effect that his skin crawled with a searing, hateful disgust when he felt the vibration. His lips curled back from his youthful teeth and he snarled in defiance.

The kite wharred its unendurable cacophony and plunged into the mass of trailing, entrapping lassos. Confusion filled the sky as the birds screeched and veered away, scattering in every direction, and men clapped their hands to their heads. The lasso lines cracked and whizzed around the boy and kite like terrible prehensile whips, and one loop dragged Sky-Searcher to one side before it slipped off the wing-end it had nearly snared completely. But the abrasive noise had driven the birds and the men off-balance, and the other lassos missed their intended victim, and, tangling with each other, created more disorder. One flyer was caught in the rope of another as he reeled from the effects of the sound, and tugged from his mount; he fell until he was jerked to a sudden stop by the rope, while his bird hovered nearby, not leaving the fallen rider. Many other men let fall their lassos and flew off, trying to recover, and Uzulu and his kite dropped lower, freely and safely.

Below, Shangodoon was rapidly reeling in, while Armienne ran to and fro, trying to calculate exactly where the Sky-Searcher would come down. She carried Shangodoon's shortsword and Uzulu's shooting equipment, and the boy was glad, realizing he would reach the earth and be prepared for a surer defence before the bird-riders could reorganize themselves to attack again.

The kite came down perhaps fifty yards away from where Shangodoon stood beneath a clump of protective bamboos. Armienne hastened forward and loosed the boy while his father dropped the kite-line and seized the bow and arrows which his wife had taken earlier from Uzulu's pack. Mother and son ran towards the safety of the bamboo clump, where the lassos could not fly freely, and stopped there, looking up to where the flock of predacious birds and grim men were wavering into formation again.

Then three of the mounted birds dropped like stones, their talons outstretched, upon the grounded Sky-Searcher where it tugged against the wind and threatened to rise again. They struck their target together and in a second the ferocious birds had frazzled it to a mass of broken bamboo and torn fabric.

Uzulu watched and shuddered as he thought of his escape; then, angrily, and made more vicious by the stark cold terror he had known up there in the sky, he reached for his blowpipe and special darts, which he had poisoned with the thick-boiled juice of the manchineel trees that grew near the beach. He positioned a dart and stood ready, while also his father waited, an arrow half-drawn in the powerful bow; and the platoon of flying huntsmen circled in the air above the bamboos, recovered, with their lassos hanging and blowing in the winds. The family wondered why they seemed to be waiting before attempting to attack, and if they would land in order to do so, for clearly lassoing was out of the question; but when they heard the enlarged voice of one of the strange men, who seemed to be the leader of the weird flock. He spoke through a funnel-shaped tube, and his voice, instead of being diffracted in all directions, boomed obliquely downward to where the family huddled in protective defence.

"Shangodoon, son of Aldraf of Ainchan!"

Shangodoon looked up, shocked, and knew the flying man saw his startlement in the motion of his head.

"So, it is you indeed," the announcer said. "As we suspected. You have come to the end of your search, my hated friend. This is the end of your foolhardy journey and your troublesome life. This is the time and place of your defeat."

Shangodoon said nothing, though his heart pounded as the sneering words drove like sharp beaks at his confidence and will. He wondered astoundedly how these uniformed, mysterious men on their strange killer-birds could know his identity, and what it meant to them; and he could not comprehend how they seemed familiar with his activities. As his mind raced to find solutions to these questions, he heard the voice again.

"You wonder how we know your name? Our birds have been observing you since you landed on this island, but your own foolish endeavours to spy out the territory have led us to your exact location. We know who you are for certain now, for the rulers of Ainchan are in possession of your fish-craft."

Partial understanding came to Shangodoon. The Dominaut seamen who had taken the Sea-Searcher had returned to the Coast of the Sea of Mirrors and thence to Ainchan; and they had discovered his identity on board the craft. They would know that he, with his wife and son, was on the island; and the manhunt begun nearly fifteen years before would take on new proportions. King Chrazius would have examined the fish-craft with great interest and fear, for the astute despot would recognize that among the Ainchan subjects there were revolutionary geniuses at work—a dangerous situation for the self-preserving monarch. He would want to capture the originator of the underwater vessel. Shangodoon would be recognized as an extremely unpredictable foe, and one of dangerous determination; and as the new threat to the regime, especially in the wake of the costly sea-battle. The Dominauts would want a fleet of underwater vessels to seek out the marine haunts of the Snikes, possibly another bad development. They would terrorize the people of the Coast with such advantageous craft.

Shangodoon thought over his situation, and the long series of events that had brought him and his family to this spot, and though he was willing to blame himself, he could not honestly do so. He felt that they had done the best they could, and had no regret over any of his actions. He glanced at Armienne; she was angry and defiant and showed aggression rather than fear, and Uzulu was stiffened in anticipation and willing to defend himself to the end.

"What is your purpose?" he shouted in the language of Ainchan, which the bird-riders had used, though with an accent he could not place.

"We will take you to a place where you will see the Power you have offended, and learn in advance how you will die, as our great Ruler demands, for he insists that you must die in a state of fear. Surrender, Shangodoon of Ainchan. Come out from under the Sacred Stalks, for your defiance is hopeless." The voice of the squadron leader thundered through the quivering bamboo leaves. "You are not dealing with the buffoons who call themselves soldiers and Agents of King Chrazius. The matter is out of the hands of the Dominauts now, as I think you are beginning to understand. Whereas we felt that the Dominauts could handle your blasphemy and attempted revolution against the divinely appointed King Chrazius, and your idiocies with his harem, this business of crossing below the sea-surface in such a technologically advanced craft, and this business of invading our sacred territory and spying upon us with a sky-carriage are far more serious. We know too that you desire to reach the Undefeated Territory to find out why it is uncaptured, and that you seek a weapon to overthrow your divinely ordained ruler, the King of the Dominauts. You are now under the jurisdiction of the Guards of this island. *We are the Warrior-Priests of Gnarl.*"

Despite his determination Shangodoon felt his blood run cold at the mention of the name. Long had he suspected that Gnarl was a living being, and not simply a symbol of the Dominauts; on the contrary, the Dominauts now seemed to be but an extension of the power of Gnarl. But who, and where, was Gnarl, and what power of command had this entity, that King Chrazius III, the greatest and most ruthless of his long line of conquerors, who had more fire-power than any other human being, was a mere vassal of Gnarl?"

"I care not for the Warrior-Priests of Gnarl!" Shangodoon shouted, despite the frozen feeling of his heart and the strange light fluttering in his stomach. He summoned his warring powers to counteract the attack on his mental equilibrium, and as the fighting-chemicals surged into his blood and he shouted his challenging words to the caped bird-riders, the immensity of the evil that confronted him left him no choice but to prepare for life or death. He knew that Gnarl, though obviously having some unusual power over people, was no divinity, save perhaps of death, for in his name conquered peoples had died. He could never yield to the authorities behind the oppressive system that he had lived under.

"The King is not divine! He is an ordinary mortal, and Gnarl must be mortal also. The regime is one of death and not of life. His kingdom is not built upon Truth!" Shangodoon shouted. "I too am a warrior-priest; one who struggles for a return of humanity to the kingdoms of the world wherever the unnatural and inhuman rear themselves as the norm. King Chrazius and the Dominauts have sowed the seeds of their own destruction. Their wickedness condemns them, and they will suffer, for it is the worst of sins for members of one race to use the energy and manpower of another race to further their own plans. Is it divinely ordained that, of two races of the same species, with similar natural desires, one should be a parasite on the other? No, the King is not divine, and whoever or whatever it is that has placed him in authority to invade and enslave other peoples is not divine either."

"The ruler of King Chazius will stand. You do not understand what a mighty Power you have challenged. The Power that has authority over your life and death decrees that it be so. You are fighting against your destiny, against your own life."

"It is not divinely ordained that I be a slave! Gnarl is destroyer of men. Gnarl is hateful, merciless and implacable, and a creature, or a system, or a bird. You serve a ***bird*** as your Creator?" Shangodoon guessed sharply, eyeing his interlocutor for his reaction.

"Fool! the man roared angrily, nearly off-balancing from his whirling bird. "Gnarl is the Creator of all! You do not know the miraculous Being of whom you speak! You are less wise than I thought, oh Shangodoon. If you were wiser, you would have feared Gnarl—and King Chrazius—from the beginning. The mouthful you have bitten off is too much for you to chew. Gnarl is not a *creature*. Gnarl is the *Creator*, yes! What can we argue if Gnarl takes the shape of what he will? Is not all Creation his? Why can he not be a bird to the creatures he had created? Were he to take the form of the grasshopper, his power is the same! And in his power and inscrutable might he had laid down the system that you speak against!"

"Gnarl has caused misery and death to my people. I have sworn eternal enmity to the supporters of this evil, implanted superstition that has led so many of my people into slavish subjection, and kept them there."

"Your people are soft and foolish, man of Ainchan. Your passivity is disgusting to us. We marvel often at the way even the lesser creatures like lions and Snikes seize upon you as prey. You do not even know the ways of war; you had no weapons when your conquerors arrived. Ignorance, weakness and fear—those were the forces that made you become singled out as prey. The Dominauts are a race of attackers. We carry the spirit of attack as well. We favour the Dominauts, and imbue them with our spirit, for they supply the needs of Gnarl on this planet. They bring people like you to us, then we present you to Gnarl, Ainchan man, as living sacrifices, for Gnarl demands blood, you understand, and we are also the Sacrifices to Gnarl—sacred workers in an eons-old task."

Shangodoon listened, but could hardly expand his mind to contain the dreadful units of knowledge that rushed into its vortex. He had heard of sacrifice throughout his life, and had read much of it during his study of religious cultures; it occurred in a number of rituals. He had never given much thought to it, and realized that up to that point he had accepted the idea of sacrifice as more a figurative than an actual thing. Now, together, both he and Armienne realized that the Ainchan people, Dominauts, bird-riders and this extremely intelligent creature, Gnarl, were a system of preying, predating hierarchies that fitted exactly into the structure the Mother-Turtle had outlined to Armienne during the voyage through the Sea of Mirrors.

⸻ ◆ ⸻

"I think you are beginning to fear, Shangodoon!" the squadron leader's odious voice came again. "As is natural, for even fools understand when they are facing their death. You cannot escape the all-seeing and the all-knowing. You do not even understand our methods of communication or our ways of finding out. That same image you have, that carved depiction of Great Gnarl that forms the gate of the Royal Capital of the Dominauts, contains an instrument that sends sound-wave messages to us here on this island, to our sky-stations. We hear all the news of the Ainchan Plain; we know all that is going on. We knew years ago that you intended to attempt travelling to the Undefeated Territory of Muse, but we thought you had died in the Land of Grunderth. Do you remember your informer, Sifar of Debra? It was he who told your pursuers of your intention. They threatened to smash his hands, as I heard, and he preferred to pursue his art of pottery rather than attempt to preserve your life. And now, after all this time, you appear again, with a fish-craft, and a woman and offspring! They are welcome, and Gnarl will be pleased, we may surmise, for he loves destroying the generations of those that hate him!"

At this Shangodoon gritted his teeth and let fly an arrow, with fierce precision striking the leader of the low-flying squadron in the hollow where his shoulder and neck joined. With a terrible scream the Warrior-Priest of Gnarl dropped his loud-talking instrument and reeled, then lost his balance. As he fell lassos snaked out and caught his writhing body. Two bird-riders lifted him away, climbing swiftly and heading west, towards the high reaches of the island where Uzulu had seen the flying discoid platform. The other flyers remained and kept circumnavigating the bamboo-foliage.

Armienne suddenly remembered a statement the Turtle had made. *The higher the intelligences, the more subtle the possession needs to be.*

"Can it be true?" she asked in a subdued voice, doubting her logical faculties. "Is the whole religion of Gnarl, which many Ainchans as well as Dominauts profess, created just to acquire conquest and victims for sacrifice?"

"I do not want to believe it," Shangodoon growled. "But we have seen evidence of it; there is the Valley of Poles and Skulls. Those men refer to the bamboos as the 'Sacred Stalks'; I believe they are responsible for the things erected in that place."

"There's a bird-farm up in the sky!" Uzulu yelled. "A flat flying circle, where they train and feed the birds. I saw some birds flying with skulls and shells of the Turtle in the direction of the valley we saw."

"An eternal curse upon the haunts of these evil ones!" Shangodoon swore, gazing from side to side, tormented.

"Give up, man of Ainchan!" another Warrior-Priest took up the taunting words where the former leader had left off. "You have no hope. Your deaths will be so quick that there will be little actual pain, we assure you. We will not harm you ourselves. We are but the messengers and workers of Gnarl. You have shed the blood of our leader, but we are not the ones who should be fighting. You are concerned with wrecking the system of King Chrazius and the religious power of Gnarl, wherever they may be operating among the peoples of the world. Then why not face the Ultimate? Is it not appropriate that you should be placed before the Great God? Then you will see the Power you are up against! You cannot escape Gnarl or his Warrior-Priests. Come out from under those stalks of Gnarl's Scared Skull-poles, you blasphemer, and stand quietly, you and your family, before us. Put down your weapons. We can harm you easily, but we are trying to avoid it."

"You have no authority or power over me!" Shangodoon bawled resentfully, angry at the confidence and assumed superiority of the ordering voice. He loosed another arrow, and another man shouted hoarsely, clutching his side. Lassos streaked out again, and the wounded man was secured and taken away. The flying circle continued and unabated.

"You are a hopelessly stupid, dangerous fool, Shangodoon of Ainchan. You, and the people you admire—the inhabitants of the Land of Muse and the obsessed, wishful-thinking fanatics who call themselves the Children of the Glorious Recovery—will be companions in failure and death. All of you are endangering your own people and insulting Gnarl to the extent that he will destroy you, us, and all else on this planet because of your disobedience. Gnarl will hold us responsible for your disruption of his system. It is in our own interest, and out of a sense of preservation, that we will wipe out all traces of you and all who think as you do. You are trying to ruin a system that has taken centuries of your time to set up. Your attempt cannot last, for you are mortal and Gnarl is immortal. I believe you have angered the Mighty One more than any creature of this planet for many thousands of years. There is no escape for you and your family, and we had not expected you even to attempt defence. This refusal to yield and to submit to the power of Gnarl cannot last; there were men who talked like you, who loosed their bowels in fear at the sight of Great Gnarl. You are wasting our time and injuring our men, and we have come to the end of our talk. Now we are going to drive you out from where you are."

Shangodoon and Armienne were deeply perturbed as they looked at each other. From the old tradition which they had studied they had learnt of the existence of other worlds like their own, but they had never envisaged an enemy like Gnarl, they did not know the extent of his powers. They had made a bad mistake; they had not calculated correctly the potency of the enemy, and indeed could hardly have been expected to. The system under which they suffered, it was becoming clear, was not peculiar to the Ainchan people and others on their world. On other worlds there were oppressors and oppressed, too, and everywhere the oppressors sacrificed the oppressed to an immortal-seeming being.

What would the oppressors again? Shangodoon wondered, and the answer presented itself; expansion. The Dominauts and other races of their type on all planets were chosen by Gnarl as the most suitable for his purposes; and what the conquerors of each planet gained was, simply, power. Soon such conquerors on each world, would succeed in wiping out all other people who were not of their race; in fact, such a situation must have already occurred on many of the other existing worlds. The ultimate, stark conclusion was that the Dominauts inevitably would be the only people on this planet; they certainly seemed to be working towards that. But the Dominauts were not the core of the system of oppression; in fact, they were being used also. They were on the outer fringes of Gnarl's mighty and far-reaching system. Shangodoon now felt that there were many other people more powerful than any on his world, by whom even the Dominauts might be sacrificed in turn. He had to force himself to accept what he had concluded, so radically did this thought strike home.

Above all, the fact that Gnarl viewed the most intelligent creatures of this planet with an emotion that was lower even than utter contempt, filled the Ainchan three with a dismay that they dared not voice to each other. They could hardly grasp that they could be so insignificant in the mind of another living being.

But the caped Warrior-Priests of Gnarl had not been idle while Shangodoon and his family had been reaching these conclusions. They had gathered to the north-east of the bamboo cluster under which the Ainchan three stood; and now they unhooked strange metal canisters from their broad belts and threw them towards the place where the family was huddled.

Immediately clouds of thick smoky gas rose from the spinning falling containers and filled the air. It made Shangodoon and Armienne gasp and cough, and their eyes, nostrils, mouths and ears were filled with a searing, stinging pain, so that they staggered, half-blinded with tears, away from the thick billowing clouds, out into the open to where the wind was blowing freely.

Uzulu did not move, for he had not felt the effects of the gas. He had been well coated with the oil of skywhisper before he had taken to the air, and his mother had used it effectively to protect his eyes, ears, nose and mouth. Thus he stood still under the bamboos and witnessed the scene that followed with the weird feeling of having known all along that such a situation would happen; that he would be left alone.

For it took only a second for the bird-men to lasso Armienne and lift her, pack and all, from the earth; and as Shangodoon cried out savagely and leapt into the air after his wife, leaving his faithful earth, another line snapped around his body and lifted him from the surface of the anchoring ground.

The boy watched the flying carnivores and men rise swiftly, lifting his mother and father at the ends of their lassos, so that the two captured people hung a long way below the high-mounting, flapping birds. The whole formation kept going up, and Shangodoon and Armienne were still as they were taken through the air.

The boy watched them as they rose, higher, headed west, to the craggy apex of the island, until the clouds hid them from view; then he sank onto his knees and held his head with both hands, and forlorn tears filled his eyes.

———◆——

At this point in the historical account, it is convenient to use the actual words of Uzulu, as he spoke on that far-off Liberation Day before the people of the Ainchan capital city. The legends say that it was a beautiful and touching sight to see the boy, and a joy to hear his unbroken, clear and melodious voice as he told of his fantastic ordeal.

———◆——

I cried only for a minute or two (Uzulu said); then I realized that crying was stopping me from making my plans. After that I sat and thought about what was the best thing to do.

I decided that first I had to preserve my life by food, weapons and the ability to find place of hiding and shelter; second, find a way of rescuing my parents or at least learn what had become of them, and third, whether I found them or not, attempt to reach the Land of Muse. There, I would tell the people the story of our travels and ask for help in travelling to the Ainchan Plain and to this city. Whether or not I was alone, I still hoped to meet King Chrazius, for I had no choice but to attempt to end his days. I was not afraid of him, for I knew quite well that a boy can slay a man, as you have seen this day.

Food was no problem, for the fruit trees were still very many. In my pack, which my parents had left beneath the bamboos, there were blankets, firemaking equipment, fuel-oil and such things; I also had my phial of skywhisper oil. For weapons I had three Flutes and two other blowpipes, many darts, and a bow with twelve arrows.

Soon the idea came to me that I should attempt to recall my scattered friends, the birds, who had become my companions and informers. There was much of their language with which I was familiar, and I had imitated their calls so frequently that it was not difficult to let them know that I was alive and safe. In a while birds came flying from all directions as I began and continued to blow out attracting sounds, until there were about thirty of them sitting around me on the grass or perched on various small stalks of bamboo.

A continuous chatter arose and those of the bird-kind who had gone with me skyward on the kite line, were still greatly disturbed by the bad fright they had experienced when the killer-bird had appeared. They twittered their nervous doubts and fears for a long time, as they always do, and I had to be patient. Eventually, when my own stillness and the sound of my voice had quieted them, I imitated the language of the gentle wood-dove on the largest and most mellow of my Instruments of Sound, for the wood-dove's call, besides being easy to make, is well known among birds of other species, large or small. My Flute spoke in soft coos about the fierce birds and cruel men

389

who had captured my parents, and asked them whether they had any idea where they may have been taken.

A chorus of tweeting, chirruping and clucking broke out. The birds said that my parents were not the first captured humans they had seen; the 'Bird-Masters' took people whenever they could. They did not know whether such people were killed soon after, or preserved for some wicked purpose. They made me sad and anxious for my parents, for they said that they had seen, at fairly regular periods, humans bring other humans of all ages, male and female, to the shore of the Island, bind them, and leave them for the Bird-Masters to take away.

One adventurous blackbird who claimed to have flown the length of the Valley of Poles and Skulls, said that he did not believe that the birds ate the humans, but took them away for some other purpose. A bright-hued humming-bird said that once she had seen the Bird-Masters placing bamboo poles in that dark valley, while the birds placed skulls and Turtle-shells on the tops of the poles. Since she had seen human skulls along with the others she assumed that the killer-birds and the Bird-Masters ate four-legged animals, Snikes, fish, Turtles, other birds and other humans.

A red-throated sparrow asserted that the birds and their riders only collected the skulls of the humans along with the others, but that human flesh was sacred and reserved for the special Ruler of the bird-flying humans, whose name was Gnarl.

All these unhappy facts were what I had heard, guessed or knew already, however. The birds seemed to know nothing more, and I had put down my Flute in despair and sat pondering when I heard an unusual bird-voice.

It came from a strange, reclusive bird, an odd crested creature the name of which nobody seemed to know. Since I had seen it weeks before, it had attracted my attention with its intelligent look, and I saw that it had listened carefully to my sounds while keeping its distance and its silence. I had wondered if it was mute, though previously I had never assumed that a bird could be. Now it spoke, and its voice was delightfully sweet, so that despite my worried state I could not help trying to memorize its tones for practice later.

The Crested Bird said that he knew of a cave high on the forested slopes of the interior where the strangest bird in the world lived. He had seen it walk like a man, and it was very intelligent, it knew how to make fire and cook food. He had been observing its ways for some time. Perhaps it could give me the information I sought.

At once I was interested in seeing this creature, and the Crested Bird seemed glad. He pointed out the way I should go; it was the direction in which I had seen my parents disappear.

I piped an invitation to the Crested Bird to guide me, and to the others to follow. The Crested Bird to guide me, and to the others to follow. The Crested Bird agreed, a trifle reluctantly, I thought, and we set off immediately, heading west.

I was careful to watch for the Warrior-Priests of Gnarl or their trained birds, three of which were still circling high up in the heavens, as they were always doing. I kept beneath the trees or close to them, and the ropes attached to my body-harness were always fastened to some firm tree-trunk or rock, for I did not want to be endangered because of carelessness. I had to think out all the possible mistakes and avoid them, for my duty was a very important one, and I could not run the risk of being taken by the men of Gnarl. I tried to remember all the things my father and mother had practised as well as told me about living with the natural forces and learning to exist in whatever place I happened to be in. I recalled that my mother had often said that one does not survive if one gives in to fear. "Fear is not necessary at all," she had said, and I learnt well what she meant, for on my journey, whether I feared or not, I had to go on.

I thought of the land that I had seen from the air, and knew that it was agreeable to travel through. There were safe places to rest, sleep and eat. I could find my location easily any time of the day or night, for I knew the movements of the sun and the positions of important stars. I knew how to put the last hours of daylight to the best use, and above all I trusted the states of feeling and the sudden strange thoughts that came to me when I listened to the sounds of the wind. I felt good, too, for this reason; this was a chance to test all the things I had learnt. I wanted my father and mother to see that I could manage on my own, and to be proud of me and all I had done if I saw them again.

Thus I was cautious as I followed the odd bird whose name I did not know along the rising steep slopes for three days. On the fourth day I was trekking steadily up the main mountainous part of the Island, keeping myself on the ground by a continuous, co-ordinated use of my barbed hook and rope, still headed in the direction where my parents had been taken and on course for the domain of the rumoured manlike bird, when I saw a strange bedraggled figure that hopped and fluttered uncomfortably among the trees and shrubs that covered this part of the slope. The Crested Bird flew off without a sound and disappeared in the bushes, while the others bunched together some distance away in the foliage of a high tree, conversing in frightened twitters.

When the feathered monster saw me it stood still, fearlessly, and I saw that its legs were indeed like a man's even as I recovered from my first surprise. Then I noticed two dried-up-looking hands sticking out before the breast of the thing, holding a bow in which an already drawn arrow pointed straight at me. I saw the danger and had dropped flat as swiftly as my roped body could, grabbing for a stone, when I heard a high voice cackle;

"Creator of our fathers! I nearly shot you, boy. I thought you was some Snike!"

"You—you are a man?" I asked, lowering my stone.

"A man among men. I have travelled far and wide, and lived a great age," the feathered figure informed me, taking off the grotesque bird's head covering that he wore over his face. "This is my camouflage, as you see. How did you get here, and what are you doing in this perilous place, boy? How have you managed to penetrate so far inland and not been taken by the birds who guard this Island or by the Gnarl-men themselves?"

"I came here with my father and mother," I explained. "It was our intention to cross this Island, investigate the reasons for its sounds, and attempt to reach the Land of Muse on the other side. My father is Shangodoon, son of Aldraf of Ainchan, and my mother is Armienne, daughter of Wrison of Green Bay, on the other side of the Sea of Mirrors."

"Shangodoon of Ainchan, the hero of the people? And Armienne the Wise, the daughter of Wrison? You speak the truth, boy?"

"Can you not tell?" I asked.

"Boy, I know both your parents! I come from a place close to Green Bay on the Coast and I have been with your father through the worst territory in the world next to this—the land of Grunderth. I am pleased to meet you, boy. My name is Laize."

"I am glad to have found a friend in this place, and one that knows my parents too," I replied. "But how came you to be here?"

"I am a maroon and a fugitive here, boy. I have been living here for the past nine years, fighting for my life against these blasted birds as well as the Gnarl-men! But they will get me one of these days. Meanwhile, I feast on the eggs and the flesh of the birds to gain strength to run from them!" He laughed shrilly and too long, staring with very bright unwinking eyes at me.

"Will you pay a visit to my nest—my home?" he said next, serious and bowing, as if remembering to be polite.

"Yes, I think so," I answered. "I would like you to tell me about this Island and yourself. You have been on this Island as long as I have been in the world, and there must be wondrous things that you, an old man, can say to help a young boy like myself."

"Yes indeed, boy, there is much I know. I have not seen a human being for many, many years . . . this is the way we must go."

I ignored the nervous chitterings of my frightened feathered friends who had been travelling with me so far, and followed the queer hermit as he made his way among the trees and shrubs, until he stood at the base of a large silk-cotton tree, the branches of which supported a thatched structure. A ladder of lianas led up to the small round doorway, and Laize ascended quickly and called on me to follow.

I went up the ladder and entered the odd abode. In the middle of the floor, which was composed of thickly interwoven branches covered with coconut matting, there was a large flat stone. A coal-pot and a brazier, black with soot as was most of the interior of Laize's tree-dwelling, stood on this stone, and Laize proceeded to put more coals, dry leaves and twigs on an already burning fire.

The pot smoked and the smell of meat filled the air. Laize sniffed and peeped inside, lowered and lifted a wooden spoon, and sucked at a hot, peculiarly coloured, oily liquid, smacking his lips and looking into the air. Then he nodded and asked whether I would join him in partaking of some cooked duck; or perhaps I would like a couple of lightly boiled falcon's eggs. I said no politely, and took some bananas from my pack.

We ate without much conversation, for Laize was very busy about his food. He tore at the white meat of the duck's breast, sucked at the bones of its neck and ran his teeth along its wings, denuding the bones. He plucked out a little forked bone, murmured something and pulled at it; then he seemed perturbed at the way it had broken, and tossed the pieces away with a frown. After that my host began to tell his story and talk about the things he had seen on the Island.

"I was born a slave of the Dominauts. Very many years ago, so long ago that I cannot recall the exact number of years, I was captured by the Kraggarts of Grunderth, for a gang of us slaves and masters had gone there to cut trees down; these trees were the food of the Kraggarts. I was helped to escape by Shangodoon, your father. Then I returned to the Coast of the Sea of Mirrors, and instead of shifting for myself and working for myself, I hired myself out taking jobs with the Dominaut seamen. They used to hire Coast-people to work on their ships then; I do not know whether this practice continues.

"My last employment was with one Captain Broot, a man who previously had been an explorer on land; he was the major chartmaker of the new territory. He was a mad one, that Captain Broot! He was disfigured; had a broken nose, and one eye injured, and scars, and a temper to match his face.

One day, when we were close to this Island, a sudden terrible storm arose. We had not expected such weather, for only a short while before the sky was clear and the wind and water as kind as one could expect off the coast of the Island, but then all of a sudden there were murderous dark clouds, strong hurricane winds and driving rain. The ship seemed to be in the very centre of it. The wind seemed to blow in every direction at once and the waves rushed together instead of flowing in one direction. The ship was helpless, and it was only a matter of time before it broke apart.

"In all this turmoil, all of a sudden there was a frightful creature in the sky. This was a monster-bird that remained high up in the air, always over the ship. Every seaman was terrified; many fell on their knees and asked the Thing for forgiveness for their crimes. Some confessed shocking deeds and intentions, but others cursed their luck and wondered why it had to be them to face the wrath of Gnarl.

"I learnt that Gnarl was the horrendous creature that covered above us . . . . it was a terrible nightmarish thing, boy, so drastically ugly and loathsome that I hated and feared it intensely and my backbone felt rigid and cold when I gazed upward at it. The storm raged and the sky seemed to whirl around it in all directions, and yet it stood as if more permanent than the world itself, as if all the world were dependent on it and resolving around it, as unruffled as if it had created the storm itself—which it *had,* my boy, as I found out later!

"Captain Broot came out and commanded at once that they should bind all the Ainchan people on board. He said that Gnarl had communicated with him. The Great God had been neglected and was angry. He would kill everyone unless the Dominauts kept the bargains they had made with him. They were not supplying enough people for this appeasement; and Gnarl had to be appeased because of man's eternal, inborn tendency to go against his will.

"For as long as possible I tried to think that Captain Broot was joking, for even then I did not want to face the truth that I had guessed years before. And many of our own Ainchan people will not believe it when they hear it, but it is *true that the Ainchan people are food for Gnarl.* He is a Universal Predator, feasting on all forms of the highest intelligent life; the Enslaver and Destroyer. Yes, boy, it is true; I ask you to consider mankind as property, as *prey.* If you ever reach the Plain of the Ruba, tell this to the people of Dibra—to them especially, for their children have been taken on board the ships of the Dominauts for many centuries, and many have died on this fearful Island!

"There were seven of us Ainchans on board the ship. One was my near relative, a man called Licestus, who was the extutor of the Academy of Natural Research of Free Valley. A strange fate indeed had brought him there. He had sold one of his students as a slave to Captain Broot when the captain had been a land-explorer, and she had disfigured him and escaped. He had taken Licestus prisoner in reprisal; and he hated Licestus mightily, for he blamed him for the ruination of his countenance. Licestus had assured him that the young woman was agreeable and well brought up. Yet Broot found him valuable; he had useful knowledge. In this time of crisis, though, Captain Broot was anxious to give him to Gnarl.

"The seven of us were taken and bound, and only I, with my clever knowledge of ropes and binding and my knowledge of the psychology of the captor, managed to succeed in being bound with slack ropes. As soon as we were bound, the clouds went away and the sudden rain and gales ceased. The sailors left us lying on our backs on a clear spot of the deck.

"I saw the great bird slowly coming down. Its wings were like a vulture's, and the feathers were thick and metallic-looking. It looked directly at us with both eyes, boy! Can you imagine that? The eyes were set in the front of its face, so that it could hit you with a direct double stare just like a human being.

"On a smaller bird this binocular vision would have made me laugh, but on this hideosity, this odiously repellent creature that obviously did not belong to the natural scheme of things we knew, the look was a light-beam of almost paralysing horror. That foul sight has never left my mind, and to this day I wonder how any race of humans on this planet, even the Dominauts, could have made a pact with such an unwholesome creature, and at the price of the lives of other human beings. Consider the implications if you can, boy. Hundreds of Ainchan people for hundreds of years, and thousands of sheep, goats, cattle, birds and sea-creatures had died in places of sacrifice as fodder for this cosmic body-snatcher. The victims know in advance that they are going to die; can you imagine that?

Many go willingly, though fearfully, to their deaths, led on by the strange ideas that have been implanted in them, they are dying for the best of causes. The mind of the martyr is a strange one indeed. There are very many of our Ainchan people who are potential martyrs. They are convinced that things are divinely ordained to be the way they are; they do not question any part of the system they live under. They believe that Gnarl has bestowed the right to rule on the King of the Dominauts, and made the Dominauts the rightful rulers on this planet. To question the mortality of the King is to commit treason; it is also an unforgiveable sin in the eyes of the Dominauts. You are lucky, boy, to have a father like Shangodoon, for you have been spared much of the pain that comes from ignorance, I know.

"On board the ship there was a Dominaut who said that he was a priest of Gnarl and knew how to communicate with him. He came up to where we lay, raised a funnel-shaped thing to the sky, toward Gnarl, and spoke.

"Great Gnarl, we have gravely failed and sinned in neglecting your offering, and we beg your mercy and forgiveness. We have been careless, but we have not utterly forgotten our duty. Preserver of our nation and Strengthener of our arm! Take not your ruth and favour away from your humble worshippers and dependents. Give us of your power and your mind; teach us to act even as you do; fill us with your fire. Creator of all, Leveller of mountains and Agent of earthquake, fire, wind and water, take our small unworthy offerings of the flesh of humans, and grant us safe passage and prosperity at every moment of our lives. We have depended on you for countless years, and we fear and adore you yet in the same way. Deliver all our enemies into our hand and prosper us, oh Gnarl, and daily victims will be offered to you, mighty Protector of the mighty. Bless us always!"

"Throughout the ages there have always been men, perhaps races, like this—who would shortsightedly encourage this monster to come skulking around our planet looking for food! There are those who would use an alien being and its powers, however unearthly such a creature might be, against their fellow-humans. Then the thing, being clever, gets to know all human beings better than they know themselves, and wham! the thing is forever assured of a meal, even from among the ones who first invited it to feed!

"Well, that was the case; the man invited Gnarl to feed upon us. At the end of his address he stepped back, and I knew that Gnarl would take his victims at any time. I seized the opportunity to go over the side of the vessel! Even as I hit the water I saw the great bird, which now appeared to be more of a *machine* than a living thing, descending swiftly, and as I broke the surface after my first plunge, I saw a shaft of fire shoot down from the creature's mouth. The fire burnt a round scar on the deck of the ship, and completely annihilated Licestus and my other Ainchan companions. They disappeared at once when the light beam hit them except for their shining white skulls which remained lying on the deck entirely clean of flesh!

"I swam for the Island as the bird-shaped thing rose again, and I had the distinct feeling at that time there were beings—I mean, *individuals,* like you and me, inside the flying thing; that Gnarl was a collection of beings who could change the shape of their craft to imitate any large form of life.

"The craft they travel in is camouflaged to resemble something of this environment. It takes the form of a bird because it dwells in the sky somewhere, far, far beyond the mountainous top of this Island. At least, that is what I believe. I have seen Gnarl directly on two occasions, and each time I saw the shape of a bird.

"The second time I saw Gnarl he—it—was above the beach to the north. Now, that beach has been the scene of much sacrificial death, boy. I have seen Snike mothers bring up turtles, turn them upside down, and leave them for the birds. I have seen them bring men, fish and cattle in order

401

to be allowed to live and take their babies away. I have seen Dominauts sacrifice Snikes, fish, turtles and Ainchan people to the birds, and while the other creatures were for the birds to eat, each time the human would be flown off with toward the top of the Island. The Dominauts came often, and they still do, for they have always been interested in the precious stones and turtle-shells found on the beach. Notice, my boy, that the Snikes sacrifice, we may say, out of a peculiar kind of necessity; the Dominauts have reached the state of luxury where they can dispense with human beings for material gains. The Snikes kill the turtles for purposes of procreation; the Dominauts kill them simply for their shells. They have killed Kraggarts, too, for their beautiful fur coats. Do you get the point?"

"I am certain I do."

"It is always a great risk to come ashore to pick up things off the beach, for sometimes the birds leave the offerings and attack the offerers, taking them away to Gnarl himself—or itself. Yet the Dominauts have taken many Snike arm-bands, turtle-shells and rare corals from this area, and each time the birds have had to be compensated with food; for the birds are always hungry and waiting.

"Now, as I said, I saw a sacrifice to Gnarl take place on the north beach, and this story will be significant to you, boy, for it shows clearly the reasons why it is in the interest of the Dominauts to have Gnarl permanently on their side.

"There were three men tied to stakes on the beach. The Warrior-Priests of Gnarl came down on their birds and hovered around; then went back up into the sky, evidently to report to Gnarl.

"I was watching from the safety of a cave; the Dominaut group which had brought the three victims stayed a long way off in the shelter of another cave, also watching.

Gnarl suddenly appeared and descended. He—or it—hovered in the in for air while. I got the impression that he was communicating with them, gloating over them and frightening them. The men were obviously terrified. Then Gnarl snapped out a ray of fire. The men and the posts they were tied to disappeared, and three skulls tumbled on the beach. Later, these skulls were removed and taken by the Warrior-Priest to a valley where they place the skulls of such sacrificed victims on bamboo poles. You have seen the place? . . . Good. That means my story is more plausible to you, for you have seen the evidence . . .

"But the scene on the beach was not finished. I was watching still, and I saw with *these* two eyes, myself, that Gnarl had risen to hovering height again, and that it had raised its tail. It let fly three great grey puffs of smoke, and three shining round crystals of golden fire, each as large as a human head—the strangest bird's eggs I have ever seen—fell from its rear and landed in the sand where they lay glowing with an unusual light.

"Two Dominaut seamen ran forward carrying three leaden containers on a pole between them. They were completely covered in strange protective linen outfits, and they had visors over their eyes. They picked up the three glowing crystals with long-handled tongs, placed them in the leaden bowls, and clapped lids on them. Then they returned to their boat. Gnarl had ascended and disappeared as soon as it had laid its shining crystals.

"That, my boy, is how the Dominauts got—and still get—the energy for their fireweapons; by the sacrifice of people they have already conquered. Then they use the fireweapons to conquer more people, and the process goes on.

"How do I know that is the arrangement? Well, let me tie it off for you. The puffs of smoke that Gnarl let go, and the smoke that comes from the tubes of the fireweapons of the Dominauts, look and smell the same. The Dominauts are in contact with a being and a means of fighting not of this world, and they are conquering the world by this system.

"Gnarl has chosen this planet as a feeding ground. He has allowed and helped the Dominauts to conquer because he needs food, and this has been going on for many, many thousands of years. One might live a lifetime and never realize it, so subtle and hard to detect is his presence, and so ingrained has the mentality of Gnarl-worship become over the centuries. Many human generations have worshipped Gnarl as their Creator. Either the same alien entity or entities, or their descendents, keep the system going. Such creatures that we speak of, though mortal, may have life spans of thousands of years!

"Gnarl has never ceased his—or their—operations since they invaded the planet. They have employed individuals and nations to further their plans. Throughout history there have been prophets and priests of Gnarl, who seemed to have miraculous powers which really originated with Gnarl. Throughout history there are records of religious sacrifice. Do not gloss over references to sacrifice when you read of them in the ancient scriptures of the races of this planet. Study all scriptures where there is mention of sacrifice; study the tenets and laws of any religion which calls for suffering, the slaying of animals or men, or the mutilation of parts of the body. Such a religion is the Universal Predator. Consider this: would the Creator of Life demand the taking of life as an appeasement? Are not all units of life similarly precious? Do they not constitute one life? And why would the Creator demand killing as proof of love and worship? In fact, why should the real Creator ask to be worshipped? The real Creator cannot help being worshipped, for He is the state of living itself which pervades all living creatures, even Gnarl! Am I wrong, boy?"

"I am listening to what you say, and I am learning much."

"The Dominaut religion is not the only one that sacrifices to Gnarl, you must understand; I believe there are more spots on this planet and on others which Gnarl visits periodically, at exact times, to pick up his meals; but I think too that this Island is his—their—main source of food on this world.

"As long as you join with Gnarl, it seems he haunts you forever. Sometimes you may think he's gone for good, and there is no need to keep the sacrificial pact, but he comes when you least expect it. If he is neglected he retaliates by sending storms and other natural causes of suffering, without warning, and does not stop until he is appeased.

"Gnarl also visits places of war, disaster and bloodshed, for in these places he finds much sustenance. If there are no wars, he is capable of starting them. Human beings are not as warlike as it seems sometimes; that can be manipulated into fighting quite easily though, especially through rumour."

"But—why?"

"Why? *Survival,* boy, what else? Look, Gnarl does not do it for a joke; a fisherman does not cast a net for fun. The system we have just talked about is not an easy one to maintain. Gnarl, as he lives and moves among the worlds, has to keep convincing his subjects of his power. He creates effects which we with our differently oriented technology cannot understand to be natural and logically based; we call them miracles. He can arrange prophecies in one generation of man, and have them fulfilled three or four generations afterwards, for he has a much longer life-span and a much wider over-all view than we do. One of the most effective weapons he employs—perhaps the most effective—is *fear.* He creates fear in their minds because fear is the ultimate state of submission. He depends on lies and half-truths to survive. *Being a God is not an easy job.* Gnarl has to work to survive, even as I work to survive. You see, I am also a God. I live on this Island the way Gnarl lives in the Universe. As birds to Laize, so are men to Gnarl." Laize cackled again, a queer disjointed sound that seemed to strain his bony neck.

"Let me tell you about myself, the Mother of Birds. Did you know that many freshly-hatched birds react unconsciously, instinctively, to the note that their mothers make? That the call-note is the signal of motherhood, and that how the mother looks does not matter to the young bird?"

"Well, wait, let me see. You say that many young birds come to know their mother by hearing rather than seeing."

"Exactly, exactly. You *are* the son of Shangodoon. Well, what to do with such a valuable piece of information? You cannot afford not to use any knowledge you have . . . This, boy, is what I do. I seek out nests of eggs that are just about to be broken by hatchlings. I notice the kind of eggs they are, and thus I know what particular bird-call to imitate. When the young birds are born, I imitate the cry their mothers usually make. They take after me immediately, and I lead them away to my cages. Thus I always have birds' flesh to eat.

"You see, they trust me. They believe in me. They assume that they are born free. They never notice the over-all scheme of things; they are too narrow-visioned to see that their lives and destiny are in my hands. As the young birds to Laize, so are humans to Gnarl!" he said, and was deeply amused again, cackling out the same as before.

"I have fought countless mother-birds, boy, and mothers are the most dangerous of foes to a preying animal. I believe Gnarl himself hates mothers; sacrificial religious cultures usually despise them.

"It is generally a dangerous business, this business of survival on the level of godhood. You have to be on your guard against all skepticism; let there be the tiniest exposure of your methods of operation, and you are a fallen god—you cannot survive the onslaught of doubt that follows unless you are very, very astute. I think that is the problem King Chrazius has at this time. He hates your father, boy, for he has sown doubt in the minds of the Ainchan people, and there are some who have openly questioned the divinity of the King, as I heard when I was on the Coast.

"There is something more that will indicate the patterns of life to you. Some birds learn very quickly. Some of them have brought their eggs to me; placed them on the platform outside my dwelling. Some have come there and laid their eggs. They have *sacrificed,* you see. They have worshipped at the shrine. They have given me some of their eggs in order to protect the others, and they assume that I have the right to *all* of them if I need. They are convinced that without me there would be no sun or sky or earth.

"As human have done, they have offered the fruits of their own bodies, which were not created for the purpose of sacrifice! The very function of creation is misused by the practitioners of sacrifice. In the culture of the sacrificial religion, living beings are prized because of their potential to be killed. As I prize the birds, Snikes prize the turtles, Dominauts prize Ainchans and other conquered people, and Gnarl prizes human beings; and so on, endlessly, up the orders of being. Obviously something is wrong, boy. Life cannot consist of a system like that. That system is a perverted one. Life is supposed to be harmonious."

"Why do you not help the harmony yourself? Why do you not cease to kill the birds? There are other things that you—and I suppose Gnarl too—can find to eat. There are fruit in abundance around; do you not consider them? You do not harm the seed, thus cutting off the process of life, when you east the flesh of fruit. And, since you like cooking, I can show you some that need to be cooked before they are eaten."

"Oh, so you are a fruit-eater! You go to the food, the food does not come to you."

"If that were the consideration, I could farm animals, or grow fruit trees in one spot, as I intend to do one of these days. But existence controls me; I do not control existence. If I am forced to walk and search for fruit, I am harmonizing with nature in that activity."

"That is you, boy, and this is me. Would you dare tell Gnarl to eat fruit?"

"I believe I will. I intend to try to find him."

"Creator of our fathers! You are a different one, boy. Are you not afraid?"

"There is no time for fear. I want to know of the domain of Gnarl. His Warrior-Priests have taken my father and mother."

"As I guessed! Boy, I was hoping that I was wrong, and I did not ask about your parents. I am sorry, but most likely you will never see them again. I think that you should get off this Island quickly, by any means possible. Or you can stay here with me; let me teach you the lore of the birds, even as I taught your father the law of the Kraggarts."

"No."

"Don't be a fool, boy. Perhaps I have made it sound too difficult to be a god, eh? It's really the way for you. I will teach you all the bird-calls and later on you will replace me as Mother of the Birds. They will never know the difference. Inheriting a godhood seems a worthwhile prospect to me."

"Gods must be lonely, though," I pointed out. At this Laize fell silent for a while, and gazed in a strange manner towards the corner where he had piled very many fragments of little forked bones. I remembered that he had broken one such bone a little while before, when he had completed feasting on the duck, and I wondered if this was a game that gods played with the bones of their victims.

"I must find my father and mother," I said, breaking the silence.

"Or die with them; do you consider that? . . . The world is a bitter and straightforward place at times, boy, you will find. I did not expect that such would be the fate of mighty Shangodoon and Armienne the Wise! They will be killed tomorrow, boy."

"How do you know? Why do you say, tomorrow?"

"Because of the season. I have learnt that sacrifices take place four times a year. They are always scheduled for the midday following the night of the full moon, and the place of sacrifice is the top of this Island, a place impossible for you to reach, I believe?"

"This Island rises up to a very high mountain, correctly called the Mountain of Fire. There is a depression in its very top, a shallow wide hole like a basin, and inside that depression fires of tremendous heat and strange colours rage. Suffocating fumes rise from the thick, bubbling surface of this lake of fire, and hot, melted rock splashes abut with peculiar sounds.

"It is on a great slab of stone poised above this wide fiery depression that the victims of Gnarl are placed. Then Gnarl who dwells up there in a manner and a place beyond our powers to understand or to reach, comes down to receive his offering. He does not like coming below the mountain-top; the occasion on the north beach was a rather rare thing, I believe. I think I know the reason. This world must be an extremely cold one for them, and they prefer the warmest spots on it. I believe the fires which burn our bodies are like cold flames to them, for they are *beings of fire,* boy! Can you deal with a being that lives in an environment you cannot penetrate?"

"If he comes to this Mountain of Fire, at least I have a chance to face him in my environment."

"In your environment! Boy, Gnarl knows the Mountain of Fire better than you do! You have not been there yet, and they have been taking victims from the mountain for centuries!"

"I will go. I must reach my father and mother."

"You must not say must, boy. They may be dead by the time you get there, for tonight is the night of the full moon, and the midday after that will be the time of their death! Gnarl never fails to come at the appointed time."

"Then I must go. I have a very short time."

"I see your mind is fixed."

"Yes."

"You will arrive too late. It will take a week to climb the mountain. Besides, the Warrior-Priest will be around to intercept you."

"I am armed with a weapon they fear. *I know the power of sound*"

"Indeed! So did your father Shangodoon, for it was through sound that he gained us our freedom when we were in Grunderth. Well, I hope you will succeed, for I see you will attempt it."

"Thank you, friend of my father."

"Your foe is a mighty one indeed, and you are but a boy. Gnarl has powers and abilities you cannot comprehend, and he—they—can tie up your mind. They can utterly confuse you and fill you with doubt and fear. They can weaken your muscles or make them contort or stiffen. They can make you kill yourself. It is dangerous to be near them, for their strange heat can kill you; and you, an innocent boy, cannot hope to reason with them even if they descend to listen to you, for they are masters of deceit and subtle misguidance.

They can change shapes, and come and go at a speed you cannot measure, in the wink of an eye. They are wicked, wicked, boy, and their intentions and practices will freeze your heart with horror. They will want you as *food.* I do not think you have fully imagined what that means. Try to see yourself as a sheep. Consider the meat of your haunch, your shoulders and your chest; imagine your liver and kidneys as delicacies fit for a picnic! They are concerned with your physical body, not with your *intelligence,* your *love* or your—your *humanity,* any more than a farmer is concerned that the sheep wants its leg to walk around with!

"It is in their interest to stop man from evolving intellectually. I believe they could have created barriers and gaps in man's make-up; I believe they limit man's imagination as much as they can. The worst thing in the world is to have food which is gradually getting wise to the fact that you are killing and eating it. The next thing that happens is that the prey starts calculating how to stay alive; how to kill the predator. The predator has to be on his guard; he cannot rely on the ignorance of the prey for his survival if the prey is becoming aware of their true relationship.

Take me as your example. I might be killed by the birds one of these days. I calculate daily how that event might come about; I protect myself from it in the best way I can. And yet, obviously I cannot blame them if they attempt to kill me. I can only watch, notice everything they do in case they are organizing, and, if I have to retaliate, chastise them very heavily, as I am always prepared to do. I can utilize the power of terror to keep them down. When the prey fears, it does not attempt to kill the predator. They cannot stop me from lighting my fires, and bird and their nests burn so easily!" He laughed again; his voice crescendoed higher than the highest notes of my Flutes, and his eyeballs were tiny dancing pinpoints of light.

When he had completed his long-outstretched laughter I said; "I do not fear. I am not prey."

"I know you do not fear. Whether you are prey is hardly up to you to decide if you cannot tell what the enemy is capable of. The enemy comes from an environment beyond yours; that is the most dangerous kind of foe. You do not know his strengths or his weaknesses; and not to know such is to be at his mercy, if mercy is the word, for I do not think it crosses his mind when it comes to humans."

"If Gnarl is mortal—"

"Gnarl is mortal. Anything that is affected by time and space is mortal. He may be able to move through time and space, but he is subject to their law. Above all, *he gets hungry*, so he is mortal."

"Then he can be defeated. There must be a weakness."

"But how will you find that weakness?"

"I do not know, yet."

413

"Ha. That is the problem. The birds don't know my weakness yet, either! You're sure you don't want any falcon's eggs?" Laize asked me, as he tapped at one of his offerings.

"No."

"Eggs are very good food, you know. Don't you like eggs?"

"Only to look at. Some are very pretty. Once I used to make paintings on them."

"Where?"

"On the Coast of the Sea of Mirrors."

Laize eyed me with pity and amusement. "And you think you know bird's eggs, boy? Listen, I have seen eggs that you have not dreamed were possible. I have seen a plain white egg over a foot in length. I could not imagine what had laid it, though I knew it was a bird, and I had not time to find out then—I was fleeing from a mother-hawk. I have seen eggs as small as beads. I have seen all kinds of mottled, speckled, striated, dotted and plain-coloured eggs; some bright, some dull, all fitting their function well, and camouflaged for their environment. I have seen perfectly round eggs and very oblong ones, and there are some, like those of the sea-cliff-dwelling birds, which are very pointed at one end so that they cannot roll off the rocks. Have you ever seen eggs like those?"

"No," I said at once.

"You aren't going to try the falcon's eggs? They are the best tasting of *all,* you know."

"No. What I want to know is, how did you come across such information about Gnarl as you just gave me?"

Laize tapped holes in both ends of the egg, put it to his lips, and slurped the contents into his throat. The bones of his neck bobbed up and down as he swallowed; then he said between smacks of lips:

"A . . . little bird . . . told . . . me."

"A little *bird?*"

"A very strange bird—I do not know its name. it said that it had been to the very top of the Island!"

"There is a bird that knows the way to the top of the Island?"

"Yes. But I know not where to find it. I don't ever want to see it again, either, I hate the sight of it. It came here one day and told me all those things. I listened, wondering why it was telling me those things, and then it asked me why I didn't go and attempt to kill Gnarl. A loony bird indeed. I hated the way it was eyeing me all the time I was preparing my dinner and eating. It seemed too smart, that was what. We had an argument; I think it wanted me to be a martyr, or hero, you know? I don't mind being a hero, but to become a hero you have to risk becoming a martyr. No, I prefer to watch the heroes and the martyrs, and survive through any loophole I can. So we argued, and it went away. Later, it must have realized who I was, for it came back abjectly apologizing, and brought me these falcon's eggs. I told it to bring me more of them, just to show who was boss; and it brought me another set. While it went for the second set, I put on my pot. I was going to see who was the smarter one as soon as it came back. I hated the damn thing. I can tell you; it kept eyeing me and keeping a safe distance away. In the end it got away. Almost broke my blasted neck, trying to catch it.!"

"A wise bird."

"Wise indeed, for I was determined to see how it tasted. I was glad for the information it brought, though."

"I find it very useful."

"Well, I didn't intend to put it to use myself!" Laize said. He tapped at another egg; slurped; swallowed. He lifted another and said ruminatively:

"Yes, a strange bird! I have never seen one like it before or since, in all my nine years on this Island. An unusual creature that shimmered blues, greens and purples, and had a huge crest of bright yellow feathers covering the top of its head . . .

My heart leapt as he said this, but I managed to prevent him from seeing my surprise. The bird of which he spoke was the same bird that had led me to him. A sense of precaution entered my mind and I said nothing about my knowledge of the unique and knowledgeable bird. I wondered, too, if the Crested Bird was in some way treacherous, and a zig-zag of faith and doubt ran through my mind. Yet, when I remembered the sweetness of its voice, and the agreeable way it responded to my Flute-sound, I could not believe that its intentions toward me were harmful.

It was important for me to come to that conclusion then and there, for the Crested Bird was somewhere around outside, as were my other winged companions.

"It acted too—confident, you know?" Laize continued, slurping at another falcon's egg. "Yes, that's always the problem when something comes from an environment its potential enemy cannot master. The Air is a great aid to survival. If only I could fly! Birds have an ally that man does not have; the

Crested Bird escaped me easily. In the Water, the fish have an ally that man does not have. In the Earth, the Kraggarts and other burrowing animals have an environment that no human can master. Do not fail to see the parallels, boy, and learn; for Gnarl is a master of Fire!"

"Is not the pattern interesting, and even *beautiful?*" Laize whispered wonderingly, like a worried conspirator.

"You are a part of it, so it would seem fine, I suppose."

"It happens all around you. Study the pelicans. They leave the Air, enter the Water and come up gobbling fish. Snikes leap from the sea to the land to take land-animals; and the land-animals are powerless in the sea. The places where Earth and Water meet, where Water and Air meet, and where Air and Fire meet, are battle-and breeding-grounds of evolution and predation. Study what I say, and apply it to those murderous birds that will be watching you as you climb that Mountain! To earth-creatures, they are the most frightful of foes. I myself am cautious about them, though I claim to be the Mother of Birds. I watch the ground for their shadow; I do not venture into the open unless the sun is shining."

"I must remember that."

"How did you escape them until now?"

"I used my method of keeping them away. I rely on sound, as I told you."

"The power of sound is a power indeed," Laize said, and tapped at another egg. "Have you overcome the sound of the wind?"

"I am beginning to, I think."

"A bamboo stalk with holes in it creates sounds when it is blown through. If the sounds are good, the birds come near. If they are bad, they stay away."

"Well, this is good to know. Thank you for that knowledge, boy. It puts me in a better position to defend myself." He slurped at the egg, crushed the shell and reached for another. "I understand how it would work."

"Well, tell me, for I don't."

"Have you never heard of the teachings of the Children of the Glorious Recovery?"

"I have heard my father speak of them, but not about their views on sound."

"Well, let me tell you, boy. They teach that sound is vibrating energy."

"Yes."

"And everything is composed of energy. Every solid thing is only solid, visible energy. Solidness is a state of coalesced vibration. Sound freezes into shapes."

"I hear what you say."

"And you wonder if it is true? . . . Never mind. But let me further say, that the sounds you put out make the birds flee because the vibrations have the power to weaken their physical structure. Boy, the Children of the Glorious Recover have taught for years that life itself is sound-vibration, and that everything has a note that can build it up or break it down. If you knew the vibrations I am composed of, you could make a sound to disintegrate me."

I nodded, feeling sure that I did know his vibration and how to make it on my Flute, but I did not say this, for there was no need to bring that fact to light. "I knew I could keep off the birds, but I did not understand the principle."

"Well, you are grateful to Laize, as your father was before you, too."

"Yes, we are grateful," I conceded. My mind was working hard to discover all the implications of the things Laize had said. I had not wanted to believe him at first, especially when he talked of the powers of Gnarl. Everything he said was logical, and yet the facts seemed hard for me to hear. I learnt then, oh people of Ainchan, this fact: *that if one does not have the courage to live up to what his own logical thinking has shown him, one becomes as useless as an addled egg.* Your logical thinking has to take priority in your life, if you would truly be free.

I pressed Laize for more information that could help me in my future confrontation with the foe or foes who had captured my parents, but there was not much more that he could say, except about the Warrior-Priests of Gnarl.

He called their mounts 'Falcon-vultures'; Falcons, because they had the very strong wings, hooked bills, sharp talons and keen insight of hawks, eagles and other falcon-type birds, and because of the way they attacked living things. Vultures, because of their half-bare necks, and because they ate dead things as well. "The vulture has no talons for clutching living things," Laize pointed out to me.

The Gnarl-men, or Warrior-Priests, imitated the ferocity of Gnarl himself. These were a special race of hybrids. Women of all races had been selected and cross-bred with Gnarl, he believed. The male offspring of the unions were preserved, the female killed. The total desire of the Gnarl-Priests was to worship and serve Gnarl, and they defended the Island of Whistling Winds with their lives. Their purpose was to make sure that Gnarl's intentions were carried out on the planet. They had established Gnarl-worship among various peoples, and convinced them by pre-arranged 'miracles,' so that many people of the world believed in the power of Gnarl to some degree. The Dominauts had been the best subjects of the Warrior-Priests, and Gnarl had ordained that they be his Warrior-Nation. They conquered in the name of Gnarl, whom they accepted as the being who created the world. They recognized him to be warlike and adamant, qualities which they themselves imitated.

Laize suspected that the Warrior-Priests of Gnarl were irritated because of the Ainchan rebels and the powerlessness of the Dominauts to utterly annihilate them. Their appointee, King Chrazius, had been challenged and his divine authority questioned. My father had been the main cause for the increase in rebel activity. There was a group called the Liberators of Ainchan, who had taken his words for their motto, and preached that the King was not divine.

Laize was tapping and slurping at his falcon's eggs as he spoke; now suddenly he paused and stiffened, and his eyes widened in horror and pain as he clutched at his stomach.

"What is the matter?" I asked, getting up from where I sat.

"The eggs! I have been poisoned!" Laize gasped. Boy, get me some water! It is that accursed Crested Bird that did it!"

I ran over to where he kept his leather canteen, took it down, and poured a calabash full of water. As I returned to him he was convulsing and retching, and I could see that he was trying to vomit.

I handed him the water and he raised it to his lips with trembling hands. Before he could drink any of it, however, he groaned and pitched forward, and as I stooped over him, placing my hands on his chest and one of his wrists, I felt his body-beat flutter and come to a standstill, and knew that he was dead.

I backed away from his body, took up my pack, went out through the circular doorway and climbed down the ladder to the ground. I saw the Crested Bird hover near and I looked at it, not with disapproval or congratulation, but with wonderment. It seemed to know that Laize was dead, and flew up into the air in happy concentric circles.

I took out my Flute and piped a question. Suppose I had eaten of the falcon's eggs? The bird warbled shrilly and made large loops around the foliage of a tree. It pointed out that it knew that I, like itself, ate only the flesh of fruit. Yet I could not help thinking that it had subjected me to some kind of test. Also, it had suggested that Laize might have information I could use; then Laize had said that he got his information from the bird.

"Did you know that it was a man, a creature like myself, that you killed?"

"No. It was a monster-bird."

"It was a man in camouflage."

"I do not know what you mean."

I said nothing more on the subject. It was very strange to realize that the Crested Bird had no concept of camouflage, and had thought Laize's pretence was real.

"Do you know the way to the Mountains of Fire?"

"Yes, I do."

"You are a bird of great wisdom. What is your name?"

"You have called it. I am the bird of wisdom."

"I am glad you are my friend and not my enemy."

"I am glad too. My enemies are the eaters of the flesh of birds."

I nodded, impressed. Then: "Shall we go to the Mountain of Fire?"

The bird perched thoughtfully on a branch near to my head. "You are in a hurry. It is a long way; normally it would take me two days of flying, with rest-periods, but I suppose you want me to take you the whole distance at once."

"It would be better . . ." I murmured hopefully.

"I will take you, the bird said, and breathed deeply.

"Thank you; I will always remember your kindness."

"Well, are you ready?"

"I will burn this tree first," I said. "The house and the dead body cannot be left like that."

"That is a wise action."

Thus I lit a fire around the base of the tree where Laize had resided. The roaring, wind-driven flames rose and rapidly consumed the complete structure and its contents.

"The monster-bird and its nest burns easily," the Crested Bird remarked as we turned to go.

Westward, the Island of Whistling Winds rose precipitously, and became the Mountain of Fire.

13
THE
MOUNTAIN
OF FIRE

The Mountain of Fire

I HAD ALREADY DEVISED a plan to get to the top of the Mountain of Fire, and I told it to my wise fine-feathered informant while the other birds twittered in alarm.

To the pipings of my Flute the singular bird replied that it knew enough to influence one of the falcon-vultures to follow it, and that it knew a way up the Mountain where we would encounter the least wind. I was glad, and communicated the fact that I wanted to capture one of the killer-birds, and use it to transport me to the top of the Mountain.

The Crested Bird saw my plan at once, and was willing to participate. But night was falling, and there could be no start made until the following day.

I made a hammock and stretched it between two trees as the evening closed and night opened, and later, as the full moon rose in a brilliant flood of silver light, I sat and made sounds on my Flute.

All night I sat and breathed the notes out, finding ways of reinforcing my intentions, ideas, and powers. Thoughts of Gnarl and the battle of the coming day were constantly in my mind, and I devised and rejected many methods of defeating the wicked one. The interflowing sounds created beautiful patterns in the night and led my thought into various ideas of attack and defence, and the principles of war, which my father had taught me, and which he had been taught by the mystic Akincyde. The moon rose high and the trees were bathed in a silver glow; black and silver speckled the night. Great owls sat on the sharply outlined black branches of the high trees and listened to my sounds; crickets ceased to keen their high whistling trills and the frogs refrained from croaking, while the fire-flies moved in endless rhythmic streaks in answer to my Melody.

When morning came my mind was strongly fortified and I was ready to go. I bade farewell to my friends the little birds, sternly forbidding any of them to follow me, and wishing them many generations of happy descendents; and then I travelled beneath the trees with the Crested Bird until we came to a wide clearing.

The sun had risen on this most awesome day of my life. It was the day of what I now know to be the most serious and far-reaching confrontation in the history of the world. I knew that there would not be another opportunity like this, for thousands of years, where mankind had the opportunity to throw off the yoke of the terrible false god which had haunted his planet for many centuries. But the most burning thought I had, the one which drove me on most forcefully, was that I had to reach my parents before midday.

There was very little time to get to know the environment at the top of the Mountain of Fire. Hoping that there would be no delay in the working out of my plan, I lay on my back in the middle of the clearing and waited for one of the falcon-vultures to come down for my body.

I did not have long to wait at all. I squinted and looked straight upward and there was one of the giant birds already plummeting down.

I lay very still, though that was difficult to do. My body-harness was secure and my lasso was in my right hand, and as the falcon-vulture dropped close, stretching its terrible talons, I rolled away and sprang up, tossing my looped rope upward.

It caught the huge scaly legs and the alarmed bird rose again at once, tugging and squawking, and taking me up with it.

I hung in my harness, attached to the bird by the single line of rope, and he creature went up and up. Then I saw the Crested Bird ahead of it, flying energetically almost straight upward, and my transporter was following it closely, as if tied to it by a miraculous commanding power.

The land dropped away below and the central volcanic core of the Island rose high above us, covered in cloud and that hid more than three-quarters of its height. We plunged into the cold mist of cloud and kept rising in the blinding whiteness; I heard only the unusual call of the Crested Bird for guidance. A long while after, it seemed, visibility was better and I realized that we were emerging from and rising above the clouds. The air was lighter than I had ever known it to be before. Below, the clouds seemed thick-bunched and solid, and a terrible temptation came to me to free myself from the dangling rope and give myself to their beauty. I shut my eyes and banned the thought from my mind as we continued rising even more rapidly than before, and now the barren bare black bulges of the most lofty parts of the Island could be seen. Far above, incredibly high yet, the broken top of the Mountain of Fire grinned balefully, sharp, blasted and brutal against the warm glowing sky.

There were no other birds up there. The air was hotter, and I noticed that the rocks here and there were sending up shimmering waves of heat. All below me was cloud, and there was no land to be seen except the sterile, almost perpendicular rock-face that stretched down below for several thousand feet, and rose above for thousands more. The rock was warm, and there was the smell of sulphur sometimes; we rose against the black birdless cliffs of grim and gloomy granite, and I marveled at the mighty forces that had brought this frighteningly high Mountain into being. The ruthlessly rising, deep-rifted, angular rock cliffs dwarfed us, so that I felt insignificant and dreadfully short-lived as I went up the side of the colossal, ancient volcano, like a butterfly fluttering up the side of a lofty lighthouse.

Finally the faint voice of the wisdom-bird came to me, barely audible in the strange heated atmosphere. I could see that it was tired as it beat at the unusual air valiantly. Its crest glowed and it rose and steadied itself after losing altitude for a moment. Then it spoke of a huge ledge some distance above that I should try to reach. This was the start of a secret way up and through the interior of one side of the Mountain, and there was a tunnel that opened out into a cave which was situated on the inside edge of the crater. The falcon-vulture was heading in the right direction, it said, as it shook its dropping crest, for it had employed hypno-suggestion on the ferocious creature.

I looked up and saw that the heat-blasted summit of the Mountain was sliding swiftly down to meet me, so rapidly that I scarcely could focus my eyes upon the bare glassy rock that dropped away by my side. The sun had climbed into the sky and kept on climbing steadily, and, to me, very quickly; it pursued its perpetual passages unyieldingly, as if the day was the same as all others. Time seemed to hang in the hands of the sun. Its light penetrated the thin atmosphere with an almost tangible force, and slapped its golden brilliance against the flanks of the Mountain of Fire. Now I saw little tufts of smoke pick up the sunlight as they sprouted from small cracks, so naturally that at first I thought they were the sprays of unfamiliar vegetation.

Then I smelt the stench of burning feathers and saw that the Crested Bird was falling, it turned and whirled downward, drawing its legs up tight, and just before it disappeared from my view it was a burning starlike cinder that flashed an energetic farewell to me.

"Goodbye, Melody-Master!"

I gripped my Flute and waved it after the mysterious, suddenly departed soul, silenced; then I looked upward again barely in time to avoid smashing and impaling myself upon a sharp, mighty bulk of stone.

I tugged at the rope and blasted on my Flute to distract the falcon-vulture, and as it veered away and took me past, I saw that the thing I had just missed was the end-hook of a vast, impossible, superhumanly carved beak that jutted out from the rest of the immeasurable rocky head of Gnarl. The whole top of the Mountain was carved into one frightful bird's head, by a method that obviously was outside the technology of human beings; and where its cranium should have been the great depression of fire and boiling earth that was the crater fumed and bubbled restlessly.

Now I saw that the ledge and cave my friend the Crested Bird had spoken of, was the hole that represented the right ear of the Bird-God. My transport bird pelted upward yet, and I could hear its breath in its nostrils, and see an acrid white foam flying from its open sword-like beak. I saw the gaping hole rushing toward me and unclasped myself rapidly; then the bird flew past and upward into nothingness and I swung and let go.

I was alone in the air.

Uncountable thousands of feet of empty atmosphere turned dizzily around below me and I was suspended for one marvelous moment. *I heard the sound that made my own being;* revelations surged through my mind, deeper than anything I could have known on the earth.

Inspiration shot like lightning through my mind; a bold determined energy filled my body. Then gravity took over.

I dove toward the opening that gaped in the mountainside and landed on hand and feet perhaps nine inches away from the sharp lip of the ledge, and when my body had absorbed the strange tingling sensation that suddenly had come upon me, I breathed deeply and peered into the hot interior of the maze-like cave that was the sculpted ear of Gnarl.

The sun was perhaps three hours away from its highest point in the heavens when I entered the gloomy hot hole. The sky-whisper worked well, for I felt none of the heat that tremored all around me, and I plunged on easily through the smooth tunnels and endless passageways that wound downward, then upward, always moving in the direction where I knew the inner edge of the crater should be. I came upon a faint-lighted area which seemed more commonly traversed than the one I had left, and hurried along it, prepared for defence if some guard tried to intercept me, but I saw no one. Then the way opened into a monstrously large cavern that was full of the strangest objects I had never seen. There were many silver-lighted screens that showed pictures, some moving, some still, of various landscapes, some of which I knew at once were definitely not of the world I belonged to. In front of these screens there were slanted metal surfaces closely dotted with many knobs and small ball-ended levers, and above these devices were lighted circular gauges with odd numerals and letters I did not understand. Wavy lines of fire ran across a great dark screen in the centre of this array, and in front of every silver-lighted square there was a chair in which sat a number of old, long-bearded men.

They were all intent on peering into the screens. I wondered how they could live in the impossible temperature, and then I notice that in this section of the interior of the Mountain, there was no evidence of heat. They had changed the temperature of the air by mechanical means.

The men were all clad in odd, metallically glinting uniforms. They did not move their bodies; only their arms, fingers and heads moved as they endlessly turned knobs and pushed levers, changing and focusing the absorbingly beautiful pictures on the screens.

I was able to cross his huge room easily without being seen, utilizing the techniques of merging with my surroundings as my father had taught me. The bizarre old men did not cease in their viewing and manipulations, and I was happy when I realized that they could never expect an intruder; hence there were no guards.

I went on up a steep tunnel, wondering how high the sun was in the sky, and knowing that at least two hours had elapsed. I was now utilizing the precious minutes of the third and last hour I would have, to arrive before the sacrifice of my parents.

The situation was a real nightmare. The rocks were glassy and steaming once I left the cavern of men, machines and altered air, and I found it difficult to climb as the tunnel steepened. I went up using tiny finger—and toe—holds, and I knew that if I slipped I would tumble the long way back down the slippery, waiting black shaft. At last there was the circular opening that indicated the end of the tunnel, beyond which a brazen orange sky glowered.

Finally I emerged from a crack on the inside of the crater, and looked down towards the hot centre. Cracked earth crumbled and buckled in some areas; in others, steamy geysers spouted incessantly. Heat-waves shimmered above the surface of the lake of fire, and flames leapt here and darted there, sprang up and died down, displaying fascinating colours.

Twelve feet below me, and to my right, there was a great smooth-surfaced obsidian slab, over a hundred yards long and very thick; it stuck out over the hot central depression. At the end of this slab there was a large triangle incised into the surface, and in this triangle, along with their complete possessions, my parents had been placed.

My heart leapt and I cried out loudly. I saw them struggle to escape from the confines of the deep-cut geometric figure, but they seemed trapped inside that triangle. Their arms were outstretched as if they were feeling and searching over the contours of an invisible prison, and from the way they turned and felt over the inner surface of the unseen thing that held them within the shape, I envisaged something like a transparent, three-sided pyramid around them, the base of which matched the dimensions of the incised triangle.

I hastily tightened my back-pack and clambered down the small sheer drop to the great shining slab; then I ran swiftly across it, knowing that if any of the Warrior-Priests of Gnarl were about they would discover my presence at that point. But there were no shouts of discovery behind me, as I half-expected. As I ran I took a quick glance down at my shadow and gasped when I saw how small it was, how bunched below my feet. The sun was perhaps ten minutes away from its zenith.

"Uzulu!" My parents exclaimed together as they saw me simultaneously. I lifted both arms, waving, and ran on; came to a stop at the edge of the triangle and felt my eyes overflow as happiness surged through my body.

My father raised an arm and spread his open palm toward me. "Stop, Uzulu!"

"Uzulu, my son!" my mother gasped, and her eyes were wide with concern.

"I am glad you are safe!" I gasped, and as I saw their bodies glisten and smelt the oil of sky whisper I understood their perfect physical condition in the singeing heat.

"Why have you come?" my father asked, and his voice grated with the intensity of many conflicting emotions.

"To rescue you," I said.

"Is it not more important that you should have stayed away and not risked your life? Why do you challenge death to save those who gave you life? Do you not owe your life to your potential offspring? Have you not considered *our* future generations?" My father shook his head from side to side in troubled frustration.

"I *know,* my father . . ." I said, and all other words died in my throat as I shrugged hopelessly. "Let me be with you now, since I have come."

"If you step into this triangle, you will be imprisoned here."

"Father, we can conquer Gnarl! I think I know a way. I met a strange old man who said he knew you; he told me all about the creatures who fed on mankind . . ." I began to blurt out the story.

My parents already knew; they had heard the boastful Warrior-Priests of Gnarl speak of the things of which Laize had informed me. Realizing this, I hurried to the next important thing, for the time was running out.

"Vibration, father! That is the weapon to defeat them!"

"As we said," my mother informed me. "Your father and I concluded that all beings of all elements consist of vibration. We have decided to build a protective circle of force around us, by Rhythm, Harmony and the chanting of our voices."

"Chanting is power, according to the tradition of the priests of Ainchan," my father said. "Long ago my teacher Akincyde and I speculated on the reasons why the old priests chanted, and why the Dominauts hated them for it. Bold chanting is a way of protecting the body."

"My father, the predating Gnarl hates us more than any other living mortals."

"I think they fear us too. They have had news of the Sea-Searcher, and they know that we intended to go to Muse. They requested to our captors that we be placed in this sacrificial triangle with all our possessions, for they want to see what weapons and other things we carry that make us so formidable to them."

"Father, the sun is almost overhead."

"Uzulu, if you step inside this triangle, you have taken the risk into your own hands!" my father warned.

At once I leapt into the geometric figure, and they grabbed me just as quickly, hugging me close.

"My father! my mother! My father! my mother!" I kept saying, over and over again.

"No time!" my father shouted. He dragged his Drum out from his pack, and as my mother reached for her Stringed Instrument the sun crawled another tiny shift forward.

Then suddenly a violent disturbance occurred in the air, as if a tremendous explosion had taken place, except that there was no sound. My father looked up and his eyes widened; then he thundered his hands upon his Drum and Rhythm came alive within the triangle and its three-sided pyramid, spread out past their limits, and tremored around us, creating a secure bubble of sound.

My mother and myself looked up. There was a peculiarly shaped red-orange cloud in the sky that instantly took our total attention. Remotely high, so far away that no dimensional measurement could be obtained, the strangely sinister thing moved from the north and came almost directly over the crater of the volcano. A great sense of something unnatural and totally against the laws of nature had struck me long before I realized that the cloud was travelling on its own propulsion. The wind was from the north-east, and this cloud moved, with a perversity that was compellingly awesome, *obliquely* to the wind.

Then I guessed that it was steam, as of water around a hot object. Even as I thought this I noticed that the high gushing geysers below had suddenly disappeared and the air was extremely hot and dry, as if all moisture had been sucked away. The atmosphere shifted and crackled, and the sky itself seemed cowed, submissive, subservient.

Now the cloud was thinning, dissipating, and what was hidden became plainly revealed. I gasped in utter astonishment even although I had prepared myself for the ultimate of surprises. I felt as though I had lost my body and that my self was naked.

A huge glowing space-travelling ship had appeared.

It was shaped like a long thin cucumber and glowed a bright orange, while red and green lights of fascinating attraction flashed along its sides at regular intervals. The great ship tumbled and rolled around up there in an environment of its own, there was a weird, frightening and majestic force behind its total freedom. I saw how naturally, habitually and unhesitatingly it assumed that it was untouchable, that the world was its own. For one moment I felt like such an absolute fool that I nearly gave up trying to think.

Then a tiny whirling disc detached itself and darted outward from a pinpoint of a hole in the glowing body of its mother-craft. It glided with great precision and made loops in the air, ziz-zagged and whirled, spun like a coin and rolled along the sky. It kept getting lower, very quickly, increasing in size almost miraculously, until it was directly over the obsidian slab about fifty feet in the air between us and the rim of the crater. The alien ship was perhaps a hundred feet in diameter, and was shaped like one of the straw hats that the peasants of Ainchan wear. Lights glinted along the edges of its circumference; heat-waves gushed out from its bottom and the very air seemed to burn. The sky itself seemed to be making room for the thing that had entered it so boldly.

Now my mother's Instrument began its irresistible hummings, and our protective circle widened and took on a new indescribable quality that seemed as positive and warm as life itself. The spaceship hovered on the edge of the powerful circle of sound, paused, and lifted a little. I kept my eyes on it and yet I did not see when it changed. At one moment it was a whirling circle; then a big black bird hung motionless in the air. Its wings were stiff and not even the metallic-seeming feathers moved. I saw that its eyes were indeed at the front, not at the side of the head, so that it gazed directly, twin-visioned like a human being, upon us; and fire glowed behind the transparent membranes that covered the terrifying pupils of its eyes. The thing stood in the sky and tremendous talons of shining metal slid out of the sheaths of its toes. It looked down on us with a hateful, wicked frown, and opened its beaky lower face in a superior, disorderly smirk.

Then I heard voices coming from deep within my own mind. I listened in detached surprise, for the sudden babble, sibilant hints, intonations and intentions, and the rapidity of motion of the thoughts and ideas that crowded my mind, took an effort to get accustomed to. I had not anticipated anything like this.

A chorus of voices filled my mind. I found that I was listening to a flow of comments, commands, observations and suggestions as if I were a recorder or observer rather than a participant; at least, that is how it began. It did not take long for me to guess that somehow I was picking up the voices of many intelligences from inside the body of the great bird-craft, as clearly as if I had been inside their vessel.

The subsequent listening and the total inter-communication lasted only for a minute, I found out afterwards. It was a swift battle, a sudden strenuous struggle for the right to control my own thinking processes and destiny for all the future, that I underwent while the tiny drop of water that was my mind merged the cold vastness of Gnarl's formidable ocean of intelligence. It lasted a short time in reality, but it seemed to me that I had been through a painful, time-consuming and brain-taxing argument for my own humanity; a defence of all that was natural; of the world of normality and morality that was habitual to man. My father and mother made their powerful vibrations unaware of what was taking place in my mind. Afterwards they said that they felt regular intense jolts of a vibration which they knew to be one of utter uncertainty and terror. I fought a battle in an area where the terrain was unknown, and where my being depended on the principles I had only recently learnt from my Flute.

The mental colloquy flowed in a series of similar-sounding voices, and this how it went, from the point where I first picked up the flat unemotional tones:

"It is cold in this atmosphere. Increase the total temperature."

"It has already been done."

"That is good. What is the order of the Rulers?"

"We are to disintegrate the parent-creatures and store their matter-energy. The young male is their firstborn. He is to be programmed. Their possessions are to be taken on board and examined."

"They do not look dangerous to me. I think the problem with these creatures has been exaggerated."

"I have thought so, too. They are just as puny as the others, it seems to me. Yet it is known that they braved the might of the Dominauts."

"Yes, but by chance only. They have never been exposed to the fireweapons."

"Yet they have weapons of their own, and their intelligence seems unimpaired. Unusual. The Rulers must have a reason for wanting their packs to be examined."

"Yes, it is strange. Have you ever noticed that the planets which are the third from the sun, in all the systems, seem to be the most troublesome?"

"No, I did not. I must bear that in mind."

"What are the male and female adults doing?"

"I cannot tell. They are manipulating strange objects, the like of which I have never seen before."

"I think they are trying to defend themselves."

"A laughable proposition."

"And yet . . . I have tried to come closer in to them, but there is some kind of force around them which is preventing our craft from approaching any closer. I believe they know what they are doing; they are not as ignorant as we surmised."

"Do not be foolish. Our Rulers do not miscalculate."

"I know. And yet it is not as easy to reach them as I thought."

"How? They are in the Triangle of Fear, and under the Pyramid of Doubt. And we have managed to control these creatures for eons, have not?"

"Of course. And yet this occasion seems—different."

"The Dominauts are careless with their subjects. They should be past the stage of having to put down revolts."

"It is inevitable; it happened before. We only have to increase their fear of their masters."

"You speak of fear. I have transmitted our strongest impulses of fear, but they have not reacted."

"Impossible."

"I thought this too. But look there; something is stopping the impulse from getting to them—or else they know no fear. They should be running mad by this time."

"Such resistance is extremely unusual."

"I believe it is to do with those things they are manipulating."

"Then stop them."

"I have tried. It does not work. They have created a protective field of force around themselves."

"Can it be" Where could they have learnt such ability?"

"You have always underestimated the creatures. After all, they have brains."

"Well, we cannot fail to get them, whatever brains they have."

"Of course not. Why should a thought of failure enter your mind over these creatures? Are you affected by fear?"

"I am not."

"The Rulers are in the habit of killing cowards. Remember that. The cowardice of one weakens many."

"I have said that I am not fearful."

"What is all this talk of fear? I have never heard such, in all my travels through the sun-systems."

"Have you ever seen resistance such as this? Our prey has not yet been reduced to helplessness or harmlessness. The state of fear the Rulers demand is not manifesting at all."

"But they are within the devices of submission."

"They have broken its force with the power of the objects that they are using."

"We will have to destroy them all."

"No. The young one is to be mentally adjusted and returned to his native people. The Rulers have decreed that we will use the offspring of the rebel to break down all that his father has built up in the minds of the slave-people—the Ainchans, as they are known. He is to be sent on a mission of religious control."

"Religious control is becoming more and more ineffective. The inspiration wears off too quickly; they expect miracles every day. It is not always easy to find a new, unguessable one. There are planets that have come to guessing our intentions when we tried religious control."

"Indeed. Not many?"

"Very few, actually. We have had to discontinue operations on such. You know, some of their inhabitants expect us to return long after we have discarded them."

"That is interesting. I did not know."

"What do you know? You are young yet."

"Commander, I think we should kill them all, and use terror on the inhabitants of Ainchan. We have but to appear in this shape and strike a number of them dead. The rebels will stop saying that Gnarl does not exist, and capitulate."

"The orders of the Rulers may not be questioned."

"You mean, they may not be disobeyed. We have the right to question."

"You are affected by the thoughts of the creatures we prey upon. Perhaps you have tasted to much human flesh. Humans speak of rights very regularly."

"Our Rulers are our absolute authorities, and cannot be wrong."

"You are the victim of your own misleading, oh Chief of Mental Transformation."

"I say the Rulers are infallible!"

"You are fallible, too. I cannot accept anything you say as perfectly true."

"Stop the arguing. If we did not need your abilities I would apprehend and confine you. You may not address the Chief of Mental Transformation in that manner."

"Ah! Do not step outside the limits of your own power! You are only the Commander of this reconnaissance craft."

"Be cautious, fool. We need your abilities, but they are not replaceable."

"I scoff at your stupid attitude."

"We will settle this when we return to our carrier-craft."

"The primitives will settle it for us. I believe they will escape us."

"Apprehend him at once. He is as bad as one of the rebels."

". . . . Very well. Your arrogance will cause us our lives, for those creatures below are dangerous. I tell you, *they do not fear!*"

"Stop the talk! Take him away. Call someone to take his post."

"My Commander, something is wrong. The craft does not function as it ought to. I think it is the device the female is using that is causing the effect. We seem to be caught in two concentric circles of vibration."

"Well, they cannot do much."

"Our instruments are being affected too."

"Let them try what they want. We will take them easily, in spite of the remarks of that fool. Make ready the most powerful blasts of disintegration for their stupid vibration circles, and for their bodies; and a lifting-ray for their packs and weapons. As for the little human, we will work upon it where it stands. I will contact it now, before we take its parents, for it must turn against them where they are, and if possible attack and kill them. That way is most effective."

"Commander, I am new in the use of this instrument. Will you tell me what the light is for?"

"We are going to erase the things in the young one's mind. Then we are going to groove certain patterns into its mental foundation. It is to carry the message of Gnarl to its own species. If the offspring of the rebel denies the rebel's message, no one will believe what the rebel has said. If it has killed its own father, the scheme is even more effective. There can be no better way to erase the memory of this troublemaker and its equally troublesome female; their own offspring will condemn them."

"The ways of Gnarl are wise indeed."

"Have we not survived and procreated in this system for countless lifetimes, by the power of our intelligence? That is why I arrested the Degrader. He was a fool to release fear among us over these three creatures. But that is not all. We will use the transport ray and take the little human over to the city-dwellings of the other humans. When they see it descending through the air in the beam, they will accept it as what they call a *prophet* at once. We have done that before, here as well as on other planets. Wise indeed, and terrible and mighty, are the ways of Gnarl."

"And of his Commanders!"

"You are astute. Now, let us contact the little human. What is the matter?"

"My master, it is already contacted. I do not understand!"

"What! Let me see the gauges . . . why, so it is. How could this be? Has it been hearing what we said?"

"It has."

"How much?"

"I cannot tell. It seems impossible, but it looks as if it has contacted us, rather than we contacted it!"

"No human creature has that power . . . !"

"My master, I do not understand."

"A dangerous mistake. There will be serious repercussions. Your predecessor must be executed."

"Yes, yes, my master. What do I—do we—do next?"

"We *communicate* with it, of course. Its memories will be cleared out anyhow. Let's get on with it, then deal with the adults and leave this chilly place!"

"The communication links are all adjusted, my master."

"Good. Little human, can you hear us?"

Below, I was standing between my father as he beat out his Rhythm, and my mother as she strummed her Harmony. I had my Flute in my hands, ready to place to my lips as I was sure that its power would work. The voices and their repulsive talk were clear and more distinct in my mind now; the communication was easier than before, now that they had adjusted their communication devices in an effort to do what I had achieved already without their manipulations. My heart beat quickly and I breathed deep to steady it, recognizing in which direction my strongest advantage lay.

Gnarl was boastful and supercilious. They had been lulled by their centuries-old habit of feasting on the humans of the planet; they almost felt that human 'matter-energy' was created for their use. Now indeed I saw the parallel between Laize and the Crested Bird, and the horror and myself. The predated one had grown sensible, and the predator was about to lose its prey. Both Gnarl and Laize had relied on the ignorance of their victims long after their victims ceased to be ignorant. Here was another fallen god who did not realize that he was fallen. The predator did not know it yet, but his weakness was clear to the potential prey, and the prey was refusing to flee or act in the customary way. It was as if a sheep had seen through the plans of a shepherd, and had developed tiger's claws and a plan of attack for the next time he came with his butchering-knives.

"Ignorance makes one a victim," Laize had said at one point. "Knowledge must be gained and employed against an enemy." I knew that my next step was to gain some time, ask questions, and listen very carefully. It was also a perilous under-taking, I would have to be on guard against deceit and mind-control. Yet Gnarl's over-confidence gave me confidence; for I knew then that they could not know all the things in my mind. I had been well forewarned.

"You know I can hear you!" I thought, and felt the reaction when my statement hit their minds. "I want to tell you to leave us alone, and go away."

"It is brave. Look, it is defying us. That's a good sign."

"Yes. They don't usually fight for their survival. I will speak again . . .

"Little human, we have come to take you away."

"I will not go with you. And do not *touch* my father and mother. They are not for sacrifice to you."

"Little human, there can be no sparing of your father and mother. They have rebelled against Gnarl, who has created them. It is I, Gnarl, who chose to put the line of King Chrazius on the throne of the Dominauts. I am the Controller of this planet and of all others too, and King Chrazius, against whom your parents spoke, is my appointee upon earth. He is divine."

"The King is not divine!"

"That is the saying your father will die for, little human."

"And you are not the Creator, nor the Controller of my planet. The Creator does not need to eat and drink the blood of his created things. Why do you eat your worshippers and their enemies alike with no decency than a vulture? Why, No Creator needs a vehicle disguised as a bird to fly in!"

"A terror, like its father. Did you see how it resisted that test-thought? Fiercely, indeed."

"I am glad its parents will soon be destroyed. They are dangerous to our cause, crude as their weapons and thoughts are."

"The young one is more aware than I envisaged."

"Yes. A remarkable evolution. Quite unusual for this planet, after all these centuries of submission. Its father is a unique one as well."

"Are the fireweapons trained on them?"

"Yes, Commander. You only have to give the word, and they are annihilated."

"Good. I am calling to it again. Little human!"

"Would you dare to come down and come out of your shielded carriage? You know that I know that you are not a bird!"

"!!Did you hear what it said?"

"Yes! It *dared* us to come out and show ourselves!"

"You see, there had to be a gap in its thinking. It is now showing its ignorance."

"It does not know our powers."

"It will injure itself. A pity, for it is a fine specimen."

"Let us go down; let it see us, as it has asked to do!"

"Why? Down there is very cold. And we are certain to ruin its senses. It will be struck blind and dumb; and while blindness in a prophet is attractive to the humans, we certainly want it able to use its voice."

"The climate's not that cold."

"Let us go down. At least we can set our vehicle down on the sacrificial slab."

"That will mean changing our shape."

"Does it matter?"

"No, of course not."

"Let us go down."

The sky crackled again, as if the hot air had been violently displaced, and the great bird became a smooth metallic domed disk once more. The whirring circular object lifted slightly, then dropped, and as it came down I sensed the vibration of its humming, though I did not hear the sound; a sound of buzzing bees. Beyond the circle of power-sound that my parents were creating I sensed this strange vibration that was only incidentally making a buzz, trying to penetrate our dome of safety. As the sky-ship came down three legs telescoped downward and outward, so that when the landing was complete the body of the craft was perhaps fifteen feet from the surface of the rock-slab on which we stood. The whole creature, legs and all, rose perhaps thirty-five feet high, and the atmosphere around us continued to be charged with the unknown current of force. My father's Drum took on a new, intensified transmission of power-sound, and my mother's fingers were almost invisible as her Stringed Instrument wailed fierce threats in a way I had never thought it capable of doing. The space-vehicle stood between us and the wall of the crater, so that we were cut off from returning across the great obsidian way as long as it remained.

"Little human, there are some here who want to kill you immediately. Do not test our tempers or our powers."

"Why do you terrorize our planet? There are many more that you can travel to; why do you keep coming here, all through the ages, all the time trying to make us your property?"

"Stupid human! Do you think that this cold, miserable, heavy, ungainly planet is our prize possession? We are matters of vast numbers of planets, beyond your ability to count!

449

Many are mightier than this scraggly world of yours. What do you know of that, though? You do not even know your own planet. There are at least forty other plains on this planet of yours which would dwarf that Ainchan Plain that you view to be the capital of your planet! There are a score of planets in your sun-systems; but there are central suns with hundreds of planets—can your mind take that strain? Then there are countless billions of sun-systems. There are things you have never heard or dreamt of out there, that you will never know unless you come with us. Most of the peoples who pay us obeisance obey our authority without question, and are not rebellious upstarts! I swear that this has been the most troublesome kingdom of all to control. Big or small, you third-orbiters irritate us!

"We have confronted fools like you before, little human; though few with shapes like yours. Very few planetary dwellers know how widespread our influence is. Very few of you even know the forms of life that exist; do you know that there are as many varieties of humans that look like you, as there are animals on this planet?

"You are powerless, little human. We are all-powerful. We can flatten all your dwellings, kill all your farmlands with famine and erosion, devastate your planet completely and make you start again—as we have done several times already in remote and recent centuries. We can pull the air out of your lungs, or coagulate your blood. We can freeze you or singe you, dry you up or melt you down. We can prolong your life through all of these, if we desire, and keep you suspended in pain for decades.

On this planet we have caused wars, political assassinations, arson, electromagnetic failures and all kinds of crises, for we are confusers. We mix truth and lies in order to keep our herd of beings servile. (Why do you not like the word, herd? And why do you not admit that humans on this planet are the arch-predators?) We control the elements by which you live. Though we have listened to you, we are not concerned with what you think. You are but part of an experiment to us, and if you resist our mind-control we will have you killed as well as your parents. We will use you in one way or the other. Not only that—if you do not return to the Ainchan Plain and carry out our wishes exactly we will unleash such evils on that place that it will become desolate forever.

Plagues of leprosy, boils, lice, locusts, rats, bloodsucking insects, terror of darkness, incurable cancers, strange viruses—all these we can bring against you. And I tell you this only to let it sink into you that your position of resistance cannot last; we can erase it all, as we will do by the time we have concluded changing your personality. We are the most powerful beings that you will ever know. You have no choice but to feel subservience and fear. We demand and will receive absolute, undying loyalty, love and worship."

"You know that I cannot love or worship you."

"We know that you cannot resist us always. Would you not like to be our Messenger on this world? You have a long life, and I promise we will not damage it or shorten it in any way if you agree with our proposals. It will be easier for us to work on you if you agree."

"I will not agree."

"You make it hard for yourself and your own people. Are you not interested in the secrets of the Air? We can grant you knowledge of that. We can tell you universal things, secrets no human has ever heard; you will be as a god walking amongst them. You will be master of the Air; you will know how to be everywhere at once wherever the wind blows. Isn't that a wonderful ability? You will know all the principles of flight. You will be able to leave the Earth and the Water at will. No-one could ever get to harm you, and you could kill all your enemies easily."

"I have no enemies . . ."

"I hear your voice falter. Soon you will give in, will you not? Don't waste time. We want to start instructing you at once in the mastery of the Air. Use your intelligence, little human, and co-operate with us, as others have done. Many of your famous historical figures were under our command, many of your saints and prophets. Many of your political leaders and law-makers, especially, have been employed. Have not many of your historians described us? Clouds by day and fires by night, little human—who has not seen these signs, throughout all the races of humans?

"Your ideas of right and wrong are well known to us, for over the eons we placed many ideas in the minds of your ancestors, and they lived and died and kept on passing their faulty knowledge to your forebears and to you. We have influenced many of your sacred writings. It was all lies and half-truths from the start. Your ideas and your doctrines are not clear in your own mind, is it not so? Would you like us to enlighten you completely? Do not waste the chance!

"We know everything that you are going to do in the future. We can trace you and stop you at any time, for we have the essential copy of you. You cannot elude us. You are headed towards a useless, hum-drum, dragged-out sort of life, little human, and an untimely and miserable death.

We are offering you something more. You can be with us, see all the wonders of the heavens, be a god, if you would just do as any other of your human counterparts would have done. Why do you feel that you owe them loyalty? Would you die for people that do not care about you? Why, no martyr has ever felt satisfied to give his lie for others, and we know because we have created a number of them. Humans *like* martyrs do what they think is the Truth. Then they feel that the martyr has died for them. We have used this lazy quirk of theirs on several occasions and in widely spaced worlds, all with very good results. But we do not want you to waste yourself like that. You are very talented.

"You can capture many hearts; thousands of people will become your followers. Then you can bring them to the Island of Whistling Winds."

"So that you can get some food to eat? Well, you're going to starve, hear? You can't fool me. You're fighting to stay alive in this part of the Universe! You're trapped, that's what, and you need food that you can stay alive. But we're going to starve you to death, for all the wickedness you have done. No more flesh for Gnarl, and Gnarl will die!"

"Did you hear that?"

"Kill it at once!"

"It can read our thoughts!"

"I cannot approve of your policy, Commander. You dally with a dangerous creature."

"So one little human makes us fear?"

"You do not understand. If it can read our thoughts, we cannot exercise mental control. It can read our intentions and take evasive action. Therefore we will not be able to remove its patterns of memory."

"We cannot erase the things it has heard?"

"It will be difficult, I fear . . ."

"You fear too much."

"Did you hear? It can spread the things that we said to its Ainchan people, and to the people of the Undefeated Territory."

"It will not reach there. Perhaps we will have to kill it, if it is spoilt for our purposes."

"I agree. The little human has a special mind. Any mind like that will know how to release the hypnoses we have spent so long implanting in the minds of the beings of the planet. It can communicate with people in the higher ways."

"Perhaps we could take it to another planet, and use it there."

"What, transport another human? You know how infested they are with strange diseases which we fear!"

"*Do not speak of fear.* It hears us."

"It knows no fear. It cannot be affected by our impulses. I have already sent out my strongest impulse of fear, and it has absorbed the energy without even knowing, I think."

"It cannot be that resistant."

"But it is."

"How?"

"I think it has a protective coating on."

"That cannot stop fear."

"Perhaps it knows some secret that enables it to absorb fear."

"Impossible! Why, even *we* fear!"

"Suppose it is less fearful than we? Suppose we have a larger capacity for fear than the creatures has?"

"What, another coward?"

"Consider what I say. These humans develop qualities we cannot understand sometimes. There are planets that give them levels of cunning and awareness that we cannot penetrate. They have as large a cranial capacity as we do. We have stultified them over the centuries, by blocking off sections of their senses and their brains, but individuals make break-throughs from time to time. Our researchers are fairly sure it is to do with their diet. There are certain plants that expand their consciousness to its full capacity. We have succeeded in eradicating most of these, but we do not know all of them."

"I have never heard of that."

"The Rulers say little about it."

"In the future we must attempt to influence their diet. There must be plants that stultify them too."

"Of course. We have employed such plants already, on some of the planets. Sometimes we have even dropped edible things for the humans—but that is rather crude and risky. I notice that humans are reluctant to try new tastes in food. They fall into habits so easily."

"Well, that is still a good thing. They can be highly trained."

"What will we do about the three humans? How can we penetrate their lack of fear?"

"Let them see us."

"And then—suppose they do not fear even then?"

"Ahhhh . . . I did not want to hear it said. You are saying that they may be beyond our control."

"Perhaps only mentally . . ."

"No! Do not even grant them that, you fool! Can you not see the little one is hearing?"

"Why do you shout? There is nothing the matter. Come on, steady yourself."

"I am steady."

"Then why does your snout perspire? Why do your claws tremble?"

"Shut up!"

"Do not get carried away. Your emotional state is bad. You should never have neglected your visits to the Adjuster of Psyches."

"I think you are the one who needs to visit the Adjuster. I have noticed how the moons affect your balance."

"I think *all* of you are unbalanced. There are some reports I will lay before the Rulers . . ."

"The humans still have not responded to the impulses of fear."

"We will have to disintegrate them all, and store their precious substance."

"They have remarkable physical structures. Their bones will make good tools."

"Perhaps we should study the young one. There is something to learn from everything that exists."

"You sound like one of the stupid nature-worshippers from some backward planet."

"There is truth in what some of them say."

"We are not interested in learning truth from them. Their numbers and their rate of increase are more important. What do you want to know their ways for?"

"He is odd. I think he wants to keep the small one as a *pet*. Once he used to keep a yrurg from the asteroids of Zhainuur!"

"We are wasting time. Let us yet make the attempt to erase its memory and re-groove its brain."

"It will be difficult for us, and painful for the human."

"*Solve* our difficulty, and do not be concerned with its pain!"

"I cannot. There is something stopping the mechanism. My Commander, we have to get it to deny the evidence of its senses and shy away from its own logic before we can hope to erase the things it knows. The only method I know that will elicit such a state is by striking it with fear. But it does not respond to fear at all. I do not like it at all. It is not right, the way the little human resists."

"You must be wrong. No creature, not even us, are immune to our collected and concentrated fears."

"Look at the gauges."

"They are not working, are they?"

"Yes, but look at the readings!"

"I do not believe it!"

"The machines cannot be wrong. They are never wrong. The Rulers make sure that such mistakes can never be made."

"I have never had so much faith in them."

"Do not say that before *him.*"

"It cannot be the little human has powers of bravery beyond ours?"

"A terrifying thought."

"Indeed. *Look* at the gauges! I do not believe it! It cannot be . . . ?"

"Beware. You lose confidence. You doubt the evidence of your own eyes."

"I cannot accept that the creature has such a constitution."

"You doubt your own logic. You limit your own intelligence, and that of us all. You are a danger to us."

"The *human* is the danger. Let us go up."

"Fearmonger! We have not even used our fireweapons!"

"This is confusing. Where is the horrible vibration coming from?"

"Look, Commander. The temperature is dropping. We will have to get out soon."

"Ah, we cannot keep on with this. I will explain to the Rulers that it was an emergency; let us not mention any details of what happened when we return. Release the prisoner. I declare this an emergency, and in such a situation I can make my own decisions. We will annihilate the three of them, and take their weapons for examination."

"Then shall I fire, my Commander?"

"Yes, yes. At once."

As I have indicated before, all this communication took place in a very short passage of time; it was a sudden intense mental battle, a state of feeling rather than a sequential series of arguments. But I caught the situation well. There was a distant impression that although these Gnarl-things felt themselves so superior and advanced, they wanted, more, *needed,* my personal admiration and fear. They seemed to thrive on it. Without this there could be no victory. That was the main reason for letting the one to be sacrificed know that he was going to die, and for what purpose. Then the maddening terror of their presence would season their meat with fear. The terrified prey would then be killed in the most abysmal submission. Their killing and eating had an extra meaning beyond the satisfaction of hunger. It included the ritual satisfaction Ego.

There was a reason beyond hunger why Gnarl killed. Gnarl feared death; and to them, the very act of killing was proof of their survival. Gnarl knew he was mortal, and was prepared to destroy as much as possible before his own demise, vindictively hating all things that showed life which were less intelligent than himself. Gnarl feared his own death more than any human ever had done. He could not recognize good or bad, but only obedience or disobedience; man's morality, after all those centuries, still was puzzling to him. Gnarl's childishness and vindictiveness were far beyond man's imagining, simply because his collective intelligence was far beyond man's. *But large intelligence do not always mesh with large moralities;*

Gnarl's intelligence was employed only for purposes of malevolent and oftentimes wanton killing. Gnarl took the right unto himself to kill as an act of luxury. I remembered my own killing of the bird when I was young; my mother has told it to you. I know the superior feeling I felt when my catapult was full-drawn against the creature. It was a feeling of wicked success and a guilty hope that some higher morality which I was sure was around and immanent, would not notice, or would notice and forgive, or would not retaliate this time. Gnarl, deep down inside wherever was the centre of Gnarl, knew that there was a Creator as well as I, and that a time of accounting was somewhere in the Cosmos waiting for him as surely as there were orbits.

Then the answer to Gnarl's problem came to me at once, with astonishing simplicity. It was this: long-lived and loftily arrogant though he was, Gnarl, like Laize, lacked **Love.** But Laize was human, and knew of Love; Gnarl could not fathom the sentiment and did not know why he was never satisfied with fearful worship. Gnarl did not attract Love at all.

Calling Laize to mind, I remembered something else that he had said, which had corresponded exactly to what my father had told me of the principles of war, as he had learnt them from the mystic Akincyde. Both Laize and Akincyde had said the same, and my father and I had asked the naturally following question.

"Have a secret weapon that the enemy does not expect. Hold it back until you have to use it, and do not let the enemy know of it until it is too late for him to avoid its effect."

"When is it too late to avoid the effect?" both I and my father had asked these two very different men.

"When he is about to strike."

And so, although these thoughts were whizzing about my mind, I had not lost my guard. And still I did not fear. The fear that they had sent out had rebounded from our powerful dome of *Music,* the invisible but oh-so-tangible body of Love.

And thus I raised my Flute to my lips as the craft-commander gave his frightened and uncertain order to fire. I based my notes on the vibratory patterns of their voices, which I had been studying with alert attentiveness while they had confuted and confused each other and thrown their tenuous temptations. My precise Melody joined the power-sounds of secure defence that the Rhythm and Harmony were making.

The ship jerked and became misshapen as a muffled explosion its hull could hardly contain boomed in its insides. The lights around its edge popped out of their sockets, and a circular hole opened in its bottom as a sickening stench exploded around us, easily conquering the volcanic fumes.

A shining ladder dropped from the yawning hole and a swarm of strange things fell, floundered and writhed to the ground, making terrible cries that clashed and spattered against the orbits of power-sound that whirled around us. Then my Melody struck amongst them with new force as I raised my notes one plateau of vibration higher, and the frightful beings that were lurching towards us broke and disintegrated into flying bits of matter, while there oozed a horrific sticky mess out of the bowels of the broken spaceship, down the ladder, and spread in a disgusting pool upon the broad flat surface of glassy obsidian.

As the accursed and repulsive creatures died all along the broad pathway in a shrieking, staggering line of death, I heard

461

my mother's Harmonies cease, and looked around. She had dropped her Stringed Instrument and reached into her pack, and now I saw that she had taken her precious Mirror out, the All-powerful object that had been given to her by her friend, the Turtle of the Sea of Mirrors. I did not understand at once why she held it up above her head, its face pointing to the sky; then I remembered the mother-ship up there, and looked up, not ceasing to blow my sounds.

The ship fell from the outskirts of the atmosphere; from the furtherest frontiers of the sky. It rolled and vengefully tumbled down, a spinning cylinder of destruction. The very mother of Gnarl came like the ultimate harpy of cosmic destruction. I felt the horrendous vibration of its malevolent thirst for vengeance, and read its intention clearly even as it stopped and turned to face us head-on until it seemed a huge round disk that protruded a forest of fireweapons down. I knew its occupants were going to blast ourselves, the grounded ship, the volcano, the Island, even the planet itself, into nothingness with all their massive firepower.

"Creator of our fathers!" I heard my mother call. "We cannot let your creatures presume to be our Gods. Originator of all being, bring justice to the violators of your natural order, the wicked ones who seek bloodshed and sacrifice!" Her arms were stiffened and she held the Mirror up securely.

The interplanetary vessel let loose a great barrage of solid shafts of light. They came down like thick bolts of lightning. The Mirror sizzled and spat as every beam of light drove onto it, and I saw my mother wince and bear the shock as the great destructive force struck.

Then the largest explosion of the centuries rocked across the face of the globe. It came minutes after an incandescent flare, brighter than the sun itself, burst in the midday sky. The Mountain shook and earthquakes rumbled far below us, and the atmosphere became so clear that we suddenly viewed the complete Island of Whistling Winds, the Sea and the Coast of Mirrors, the legendary, deep Grunderth, and the country of our search, the fabulous Land of Muse.

But the remains of the ship and its occupants were coming down. They fell like rain. Pieces of metal and fantastic bodies cascaded around the dome of safety my father's ceaseless Rhythms still created. Hundreds, thousands, perhaps a million bodies fell.

The shapes of the creatures were odious, repulsive, abhorrent, and unbelievably variegated; the things seemed capable of the worst wickednesses imaginable. There were malevolent shrieks and baleful glances, horrific writhings, vicious bellowing, shockingly gross cursings, a maddening stench and more, as the abominations perished.

The horrendous shapes were composed of all the imaginable combinations of wings, claws, animal and human faces and half-bodies, snouts, mouths, and beaks; but I could see that they were all intelligent *natural* products of cosmic evolution. Yet there was one particular group which seemed the most horrific of all.

Their bodies ranged in colour from amber to bright scarlet. Their glowing cat's eyes were their single most frightening feature. Their faces were horribly thin and ended in pointed chins; their foreheads were disproportionately broad and carried little horns. Long arrow-tipped tails lashed about behind them and I viewed their lower parts with the most curious and horrified sensations of all. From the haunches downward, they had hairy legs that reminded me of a dog's, or perhaps a calf's; for they ended in sharp-pointed *cloven hoofs*—a sight that I can never forget.

14
GODNOR'S
FINALE

Godnor's Finale

A T THAT POINT THE son of Shangodoon ceased to address the people of Ainchan, and Shangodoon told how the people of Muse, having heard and seen the mighty explosion at the top of the Mountain of fire, sent out their airships which landed on the great slab of glassy volcanic rock where the family was, now free of the imprisoning power of the sacrificial triangle. The trio were taken on board and travelled swiftly through the air in the bird-shaped carriages, which had large propellers for cleaving the air and used the power of electromagnetism, according to Shangodoon's account. They were to spend almost three years at Muse, and learnt much of the culture of the people. They listened to their methods of expressing their love for Music, and introduced to the Musians new concepts that they had not yet explored.

Shangdoon was to introduce to them a method of recording sound through the use of symbolic colours; the Musians had never conceived that sounds could be visually set down. Much of the lore that is taught in our Academies of Musical Devotion has some foundation in the principles of Musical Formation that the Ainchan people received through the family of Shangodoon, and since that time our knowledge of Music's principles has grown; everyone in Ainchan can now express very profound and complex thoughts on one kind of Instrument or another.

They did not have to enquire of the Musian people what their methods were of defeating the Dominaut invaders, for in the course of their adventures they had discovered the power. In fact, sometimes it seems to me as if Music had guided their steps all along the way, though they had not been aware of the process; as if the Power entered them because they were fit vessels for its workings.

At the end of their sojourn the family were taken to the Ainchan Plain by an airship of the Musians, and landed south of the capital city. Since the remarkable explosion that had occurred in the sky above the fabulous half-doubted Island that lay far south past the horizon of the sea, things had been bad among the Dominauts. King Chrazius was already a fallen god, but he did not know this; he himself could not account for the sudden terrors and abject fits of despair that shook his disease-wracked frame. All his physicians, it is said, knew that he sleep-walked and sometimes shouted the name of Shangodoon and of Gnarl in his troublous and irregular slumbers. Thus when the family walked through the south gate and entered

Ainchan, their victory was already assured, and we have seen the result of their confrontation with the King.

The reactions of the people of Ainchan to the story of Shangodoon were varied. Some rejoiced to see the fulfillment of their dreams and the vindication of their convictions; many clapped and danced in the streets. A large proportion of them were serious and profoundly pondering the events and philosophies which had been drawn to their attention. Very many persons cried, in relief, in joy, and in sorrow.

There were those who were deeply hurt and dejected; they sat on the sidewalks and wept out of disappointment that the deity on whom they had pinned their hopes was mortal, carnivorous and inhumanly unfeeling and corrupt. The human values which they instinctively followed, and which they had bent and stretched to fit over the unaccountable and brutal behavior of Gnarl, were seen to be centuries-old excuses for the monster. Gnarl had nothing in common with humans after all; this was why, in so many of the stories and scriptures of Gnarl, there was sometimes evidence that Gnarl did not understand the ways of man. They had tried to imagine Gnarl as the Creator, as the Dominauts had insisted that they believe; now the hopes of several people's lifetimes had been squashed, and the Originator of all, Music, was so little known that few of them realized its power or felt it could replace the worship of Gnarl. But Gnarl was dead; therefore there had to be a movement forward. Later, they were to trust absolutely to Music, and learn, through it, the real nature of existence.

Loss of faith is the most depressing of emotions unless there is an alternative to the philosophies that one is forced to discard, and the Ainchan people were fortunate to be able to regain their balance easily. I cannot imagine what many of them would have done had there been no Music to inspire their daily lives.

———— ◆ ————

When I was young and used to stay at my grandparents' home, I did not know that adults were capable of saying things that were not true. I believed them when they invented a character called "Friendly Giver' who was supposed to visit and bring rewards for children during the Gift-Day of the year. If I was good, I got good gifts, if I was bad, I would get a cane to be punished by.

I had absolute faith in the Friendly Giver and my childhood was a very ordered, well-behavioured one because of him. Then he started making mistakes, giving canes for things that my grandparents *thought* that I had done, even though I was innocent, and good gifts at times when I knew I didn't deserve them.

Then I noticed that more and more canes were coming, and scarcely any good gifts. The more I 'behaved well', the more the Friendly Giver insisted that I should be caned so that I would 'behave better.' There was something wrong. I decided to put a stop to his visits, for the Friendly Giver had become a threat to my existence.

He used to put his 'gifts' at the foot of my bed while I was sleeping, on the night before Gift-Day. The next Gift-Day Eve, I waited for the Friendly Giver, *very fearfully,* for this was the ultimate of blasphemous sins which would result in endless numbers of canes and canings if I failed to stop the Giver.

When the Friendly Giver tiptoed into my room, swathed in his legendary red costume, I struck him in the buttocks with one of my very sharp arrows. He bawled out mightily *in the voice of my grandfather.*

I fainted from the shock of revelation. The sudden obtention of a very fundamental truth which one has never taken into account has the power to make one react thus; worst, it can make one reject the truth and prefer the lie in order to be comfortable; the search for Truth is very strenuous sometimes.

When I woke from my faint I was alone in bed. I lay and cried great sobs, such as I never cried before or since, for I knew forever that the Friendly Giver, on whom I had staked all the actions and moralities of my life up to that point, did not exist. He had been invented simply as a method of limiting my rightful activities. The next few days I passed through a kind of death; it was the traditions of Music that saved my sanity at that early age.

What the Ainchans learnt especially was that they had made a fundamental mistake to allow the members of one race to define their God and their morality for them; a mistake which, whenever it occurs in history, leads infallibly to the worst of societal tragedies.

Thus the history of Shangodoon and his family was, for the Ainchan people, a further step in the process of their maturing; it was an end to the worst superstition that had ever plagued the once-gullible people of the Plain. They ceased to be children and became both wiser and happier.

Above all, the people of the planet Xerios, realizing that they had a common enemy and that there must be more Gnarls operating on other planets and at large in the Universe ceased to fight each other, came together, and pooled their common resources for the defence of the planet if any Gnarl-things ever returned. Happily, the Enlightened Age has never been threatened by such, I believe that the powers we derive from Music have made any such predators keep their distance.

In making sounds on my Instruments, I have willed that if there be any planets where the Destroyer of Humans is still operating, that Music find a way to spread cosmic enlightening intelligence upon its peoples, and that they be freed from physical and mental thralldom.

———◆———

The history of Shangodoon and his family, and the story of how Music came to the Ainchan people, have been told. My remaining task is to give a brief dissertion on the principles of Music that the Ainchan people employ, and the gist of the teachings that our modern philosophers and religionists hold.

Rhythm, Harmony and Melody are the three forms of Vibration. Vibration forms all, and each shape in existence leans towards one of these areas, though a little of all is contained in each. Some living things express Rhythm, some Harmony, some Melody. Life is interchangeable; one form can be processed into another. Animals may engulf each other, and live and die, but their Vibratory forms are eternal.

Those of a mystical nature tend to observe the following correspondences.

Rhythm	Harmony	Melody
Man	Woman	Child
Drum	Stringed Instrument	Wind Instrument
Land	Water	Air
Matter	Design	Intelligence
Form	Arrangement	Idea
Heart	Blood	Breath
Physical	Emotional	Mental
Force	Function	Formation
Will	Feeling	Thought

Thus the Music of Ainchan is based on the logical, inspired examination of relationships between the three aspects of Music, and a person of Ainchan classifies any new phenomenon or experience into one of these categories. The aim of the mystics is to balance these forces in their physical, emotional and mental bodies, and in their social relationships. Only by doing this, they believe, can a person reach the true heights of his own spirit.

The Ainchans prove that Nature follows the Patterns of Music, or that Music and Nature is the same, by these arguments.

The presence of Rhythm in the Universe is seen in the alternation of day and night, in seasonal changes, in tides and in the rolling of the waves of the sea, in the wind, and in our own heartbeats. All movements which are natural are timed and even; chaotic movement is unnatural.

Harmony is observed by the fact that when a single clear sound is struck, a careful listener can hear the overtones of its counterparts, a chord is really a separation of a note into its agreeing parts. The pulsations of the 'root' note and of the overtones may be measured, and the frequencies of their Vibrations always turn out to be divisible into each other. Hence, Harmony is as natural as the existence of mathematical numbers.

Melody is a succession of timed single notes that seem to have a pattern involving a beginning and ending. A flow of mind, increasing and decreasing in power, makes sounds as it passes by and through certain natural pits and columns such as tunnels and river valleys.

The Ainchan mystical sects which practice chanting to Music have a vignette on which their adherents meditate, and which forms the structure of their highly developed prosody. It looks like this:

```
            *

         *     *

      *     *     *     *
```

The four stars at the base represent four beats of Rhythm.

The two stars of the central area represent two strums of one of two chords, hence, Harmony.

The top line carries a single star which represents a single star which represents a single note of Melody.

This ratio occurs in all their chants, which are highly hypnotic. The vignette is known by the unusual name, '**The Seven and the Three of the One**.'

In our centres of Higher Learning it is taught that everything has a Sound, a Colour and a Vibration, and students trace relationships between the seven notes of our modern Sound-system and seven colours, ranging from red through orange, yellow, green, blue, violet and purple. Colour and Sound are used for healing, and our scientists are very familiar with the constructive and destructive use of Vibration.

Because of the several symbols our artists employ in depicting the history of Shangodoon, it is thought by many that the story is a purely symbolic one. It certainly *can* be taken as such, as experience has proved to good advantage. Yet, no matter how hard they may be to accept as real, in this modern Enlightened Age, the facts are absolutely documented, and the Archives contain all the artifacts, including the original Sea-Searcher, for all who may caret to examine them.

Finally, to deny the truth of the story would be to deny myself, Godnor, your own historian; for I am one of the living descendants of Shangodoon.

THE END.

PROFILE OF CREATIVE ARTIST—
TIMOTHY CALLENDER
1946-1989

. . . as told by others

"He was in the forefront of our literary advance and his (dialect) literature restored respectability to Barbadian life."—**John Wickham—Nation newspaper Literary Editor**

"Easily the best exponent of the art of short story writing Barbados has ever had . . . he uses the vernacular as one should apply seasoning to flying fish . . . discretely to bring out taste, and

not inordinately to spoil the enjoyment of the diner . . ."—**E.L Cozier,** *Topic for Today*—**Barbados Advocate. Oct., '87**

"I hope that Barbadians always remember him for the joy he brought to them through his writing."—**Alfred Pragnell—Storyteller**

"He won NIFCA awards for short stories, poetry and drama"—**National Independence Festival of Creative Arts (NIFCA) pays tribute to late author—October 1989**

"Callender's goal was to create literature that can stand up to any critical analysis and yet can be familiarly and naturally read and understood by the people of his own environment, including children . . ."—**Dean Harold Crichlow,** *Preface to Callender's booklet* **'Independence & Freedom'**

"I think that his writing encouraged a person to view Bajan dialect in a more positive way and to see local life as something which was a worthy subject for literature."—**John Gilmore, Association of Literary Writers—1989**

He was a sculptor, artist, painter, playwright, novelist, poet, photographer, teacher and an accomplished guitarist (and drummer)—**Barbados Advocate, Oct. 1989**

"He had an overall enchantment with the melodic speech rhythms of Caribbean people." **Dawn Morgan, Columnist, Nation newspaper**

SEE ALSO

IT SO HAPPEN
16 Short Stories in Kindle and Print edition
Available at www.amazon.com

Searchers, Secrets and Silences—*a detective thriller in verse*
in Kindle edition—<u>www.amazon.com</u>

TIMOTHY CALLENDER
1946-1989

Author and creative artist, poet, playwright, visual artist, musician, sculptor, researcher, teacher, and the list goes on! Throughout his life, the late Timothy Callender studied, practiced and taught various forms of Art in Barbados and other Caribbean islands.

At the annual National Independence Festival of Creative Arts (NIFCA) in Barbados, he won various awards for short stories, poetry, drama and painting. Several of his stories, plays, poems and essays have been published in anthologies, newspapers and magazines. He held annual exhibitions of his paintings, which today, are without a doubt some of the most highly coveted, collectors' items, worldwide.

He also practiced music on the drum, the flute and the guitar, explored the art form of sculpture, and read constantly

While still at school, he was already becoming a household word in Barbados as his short stories were read each Sunday by Frank Collymore and later on Rediffusion by Alfred Pragnell.

His short story "The Honest Thief" has been used in anthologies from Australia to the United States. It has been dramatized by local groups in nearly every Caribbean island

and it was selected by the Commonwealth writers as a classic short story of our time.

He gained his Bachelor of Arts degree in English with Honours from the *University of the West Indies*, or *U.W.I.,* at the *Mona* campus in Kingston, Jamaica. Here is where he also got a head start to his Masters degree, which he initiated with a focus in Literature. **He has researched West Indian historical and cultural subjects**

Callender went on to successfully complete his Masters in Art and Design at the *University of London* in England. During his teaching career, he taught English and Creative Writing, Use of English, Drama, Art and Music (the Guitar) at various schools and Colleges in Barbados, St. Kitts and Jamaica.

Unfortunately, Callender died in 1989 at the age of 43 before he had fulfilled his desire to express himself fully as a sculptor. He left many unpublished works that are only now finding their way into print. He always generously shared his knowledge and hopefully *How Music Came* will continue to do what he did during his lifetime.

Other publications like *The Caribbean Book of Christmas stories, Elements of Art, How Music Came to the Ainchan People and It So Happen* are now being reprinted along with a number of works which were unpublished at the time of his passing.

He is survived by his wife Lorna and two children, Okolo and Nayo.

Edwards Brothers Malloy
Thorofare, NJ USA
November 26, 2012